Dayville, CT 06241

P9-DDF-884

Sapphire

Also by ROSEMARY ROGERS

JEWEL OF MY HEART
RETURN TO ME
SURRENDER TO LOVE
AN HONORABLE MAN
WICKED LOVING LIES
A RECKLESS ENCOUNTER
SWEET SAVAGE LOVE
SAVAGE DESIRE

ROSEMARY ROGERS

Sapphire

MIRA®

ISBN 0-7394-6182-6

SAPPHIRE

Copyright © 2005 by Rosemary Rogers.

All rights reserved. Except for use in any review, the reproduction or
utilization of this work in whole or in part in any form by any electronic,
mechanical or other means, now known or hereafter invented, including
xerography, photocopying and recording, or in any information storage or
retrieval system, is forbidden without the written permission of the publisher,
MIRA Books, 225 Duncan Mill Road, Don Mills, Ontario, Canada M3B 3K9.

All characters in this book have no existence outside the imagination of the
author and have no relation whatsoever to anyone bearing the same name
or names. They are not even distantly inspired by any individual known or
unknown to the author, and all incidents are pure invention.

MIRA and the Star Colophon are trademarks used under license and registered
in Australia, New Zealand, Philippines, United States Patent and Trademark
Office and in other countries.

Printed in U.S.A.

To my patient family and my loyal readers

1

Martinique
French West Indies
April 1831

"One kiss, *ma* Sapphire *douce,* one kiss, else I will perish," the handsome, dark-haired Frenchman declared, bringing both hands to his heart where he stood chest-deep in the pool of crystal blue-green water beneath the waterfall.

Maurice wore nothing but a pair of buff doeskin breeches, soaked through and clinging to his body like a second skin, and the sight of his bare, muscular chest and dripping hair slicked back over his head made Sapphire's pulse quicken and her knees go weak. "You'll have to catch me first, Maurice." She laughed and splashed him, swaying her hips provocatively beneath the transparent shift she wore for her late-afternoon swim.

Maurice lunged forward, his hand striking out, but

she turned and dove headlong into the pool, touching the sandy bottom with outstretched fingertips before she came back up, lungs straining for air.

"Got you!" He caught her ankle and began to drag her toward him, running his hands up her bare calf.

"No!" Sapphire squealed, kicking her free leg and laughing. "Release me, kind sir."

"Not until I have my kiss, fair damsel." Stepping back, Maurice found his footing on the sandy bottom again and pulled her into his arms.

Surrendering at last, Sapphire looped her arms around his neck and tipped her head back, allowing her wet, waist-length auburn tresses to fall over her shoulders and dip into the water. Closing her eyes, pressing her hips to his, she reveled in the feel of Maurice's body against hers.

Maurice had caught her eye at a ball last autumn when he and his brother Jacques had returned from school in France to join his father on a neighboring plantation. She'd felt the magic from the first night they met. A few innocent kisses, followed by heated glances across crowded rooms and several furtive meetings, and she'd fallen madly and hopelessly in love with Maurice, and he with her. Visions of a magnificent wedding in the garden at Orchid Manor danced in her head. Her only quandary was convincing dear, sweet Papa that Maurice was the right man for her—the only man for her.

"Sapphire, we should return to the house," Angelique called from where she and Jacques were floating on their backs by the cliff that enclosed their favorite swimming pool. "If we're gone too long, Papa will come looking. Remember, we're supposed to be listening to the baroness's harpsichord recital."

Only a year older than Sapphire, Angelique was not only the sister of her heart, but her best friend. The two had been inseparable since Sapphire's parents adopted Angelique. Though ebony-haired and native born to the island, the daughter of a slave, Angelique's skin tone merely appeared sun-kissed year round and did not give evidence of her true heritage. "I don't want to go to dinner and listen to Papa's boring English guests." Sapphire pouted, turning to brush her lips against Maurice's. "I'd much prefer to stay here."

"Perhaps you should return, *ma petite*," Maurice whispered softly in her ear. "I would not want to anger Monsieur Fabergine, my future father-in-law."

He teased her earlobe with the tip of his tongue, sending little shivers through her body. Despite the warmth of the afternoon, the water was cold and she trembled as unfamiliar and exciting sensations coiled in the pit of her belly, making her nipples grow hard and ache with anticipation.

"Meet me later tonight after your dinner, in our special place, *oui?*" Maurice suggested huskily in her ear.

She grasped his strong forearms and looked into his eyes. "Yes, and then we shall go riding. I adore riding in the dark, through the jungle and along the beach with only the moon to guide me. It would be a hundred times better if we were together."

"Or, we could pursue...other diversions."

Maurice covered her mouth with his and she melted into his arms, sighing. Sapphire was not as generous with her affection as Angelique was, and, unlike the beautiful free-spirited native, she had guarded her virginity carefully. But her resolve was beginning to wane. She was fully a woman and eager to experience all there was to being one. What reason was there to wait? she wondered, light-headed as she finally tore her mouth from his, gasping for breath.

"Come sit on the bank and dry a little before you dress," Maurice murmured, wrapping his arm around her and guiding her toward the shore. He picked up a blanket and led Sapphire just off the path to a clearing among giant ferns, palm trees swaying overhead. He spread the blanket and took her hand again, easing her down onto the soft carpet of the jungle floor.

"I can only sit a minute." She smiled, inhaling deeply and savoring the scents of the jungle paradise. "Angelique is right. We should go before Papa finds us."

"Ah, papas," Maurice sighed, nuzzling her neck. "They are overprotective of their beautiful daughters, *oui?*"

She lifted her chin to gaze into his eyes and rested her palm on his broad shoulder. "*Oui*, at least this father is." Sapphire brushed her lips against Maurice's and he closed his arms around her, easing her back to the ground, deepening the kiss. When he again molded his lean body to hers, she felt the evidence of his desire, and heat rose in her cheeks.

Maurice drew his hand lightly over Sapphire's rib cage, up under her breast, and she sighed. Then he moved his hand slowly over her breast and squeezed gently, bringing a moan from deep in her throat. How could anything so forbidden feel so wonderful?

"Sapphire! *Mon dieu!* You, sir, remove yourself from my daughter at once!"

"Papa!" Sapphire had not heard the riders until they were upon the clearing beside the pond. She gave Maurice a push as she sat up and crossed her arms over her breasts.

"Bon *après-midi*, Monsieur Fabergine. How are you this fine afternoon?" Maurice had asked politely, as if nothing had happened.

"How am I?" Armand Fabergine sputtered, dismounting from his fine bay gelding, waving his white leather crop. He was dressed in a riding suit of white knee-length breeches, a white silk shirt, a pale blue coat and expensive boots. Behind him, several male guests on horseback strained their necks to get a look at Sapphire and her lover. "In truth, Mr. Dupree, I am not good," Armand said in lightly accented English as he pointed to his daughter. "*Fille,* get up. Get up at once!" His lips were pale, his eyes narrowed in anger.

As Sapphire stood, her father grabbed the blanket and wrapped it around her shoulders.

"And where is Angelique?"

Her father didn't often become truly angry with her, but he was right now—so angry, sparks seemed to fly from his gray eyes.

"Coming, Papa!" Angelique sang.

"And you," Armand snapped, looking Maurice up and down with contempt, "are fortunate that I am a civilized man. My father would have shot you down like a dog had you dared to lay a hand on one of my sisters. You had better go from here now, because I cannot promise not to lose my self-control and thrash you."

"No, Papa!" Sapphire cried.

"You shame me, daughter. Cover yourself!" He

glanced over his shoulder. "Please, gentlemen, could you give me a moment?"

The three Englishmen reluctantly backed up their mounts and disappeared behind a giant elephant ear plant.

"Angelique!" Armand called.

"Coming, Papa!"

Out of the corner of her eye, Sapphire saw Jacques duck and disappear under a clump of ferns near the shore. She turned back to look at her father. It was Angelique's way, even since childhood. She never disobeyed or argued with their parents or Aunt Lucia. She would nod, smile prettily and do what she damn well pleased.

"Papa, you don't understand," Sapphire pleaded.

"What is there to understand?" Armand bellowed. "This...this young man, who is no gentleman, has obviously attempted to take advantage of you."

"No!" Sapphire released one corner of the blanket and stepped back to loop her arm through Maurice's. "Maurice and I are in love, Papa. He has done no wrong—he would never take advantage of me."

"*Love?* What do you know of love?" Armand scoffed, taking a step closer. He had grown thin in the past year and his dark hair had turned almost entirely white, but he still had a voice of authority that made men nervous.

"I should go, *mon amour*," Maurice said as he stepped back.

"I think that is wise, Monsieur Dupree, before I forget that I am a gentleman and deliver the painful lesson that you deserve."

"I will see you later," Maurice whispered in Sapphire's ear, and then he turned and hurried back toward the shore to gather his clothing.

Angelique came up the bank already dressed, carrying her slippers. "Papa," she said sweetly, "we were just going up to the house to prepare for your dinner. I simply cannot wait to wear the new gown you brought for me all the way from London."

Sapphire took a step toward her father, defiance in her eyes. "You cannot do this to Maurice or to me, Papa. I won't have it! We're in love…we're in love and we intend to marry!"

Armand looked down at her, his jaw firm. "You will not marry Maurice Dupree," he said coldly. "He is not fit to clean your riding boots." He turned and strode toward his horse.

"Papa! You can't just walk away from me. I am not a child any longer and I will not stand to be treated like one!"

Armand put his boot into the stirrup and swung onto his horse. "I am still your father and the lord over this plantation and all who live here," he told her quietly, staring straight ahead. "You are all my responsibility, which means I will do as I see fit, with my slaves *and* my daughter. I could lock you in your room or return you to the care of the Good Sisters of the Sacred Heart if I must."

"You wouldn't dare send me back to school!" Sapphire shouted after him as he rode away.

"I will not be swayed," Sapphire insisted as she followed Angelique out of her bedchamber and into the wide, lamp-lit passageway. Orchid Manor had been built by her grandfather in the style of the great French châteaux of the Loire Valley, but he had created an airy West Indies ambience with wide doors and windows that opened from almost every room onto stone patios and lush gardens.

"I won't do it, Angel." Sapphire tossed her head as she fastened a pearl earring to her lobe. "When Mama died, he told me I was an adult now and that I would be treated as such." She lifted the hemline of her new plum-colored silk dress with its fashionable bell-like skirt and low-cut décolleté and ran to catch up. "And now, when I have found a man to love, he speaks of sending me back to the convent school. Never!"

"You mustn't run or you will ruin your hair." Angelique reached up and fussed with an auburn pin curl above Sapphire's ear. "Do not bring up Maurice at dinner this evening. Do not bring him up at all."

"Not bring him up at all?" Sapphire said sharply. "I want to marry him. We want to be married at once."

Angelique smoothed the skirt of her pale pink gown. "You should not be so free with your heart. You are young—you've much to learn about love. There will be many Maurices who—"

"Not you, too!" Sapphire flared.

"I am on your side, the same as Papa." She turned toward the music wafting from the garden where the musicians played for her father's English guests, all business associates. "Come, we don't want to be late and anger Papa any further. We will talk about this later."

"You sound just like him," Sapphire spat. "You have not heard the last of this, you or Papa!"

"Could we have any doubt?" Angelique murmured under her breath as they breezed into the large dining room elegantly furnished in white and blond Louis XIV furniture.

"Ah, my lovely nieces," Aunt Lucia declared, embracing the young women and leaning toward Sapphire. "What have you done now? I don't think I've ever seen Armand so infuriated."

"I did nothing wrong!"

Lucia, a round figure of a woman with red hair and a beautiful face for a middle-aged woman, looked to Angelique, who only lifted her brows and shrugged gracefully.

"Come, come," Aunt Lucia said gaily, brushing back her mountain of lemon-colored satin skirts and petticoats. "Everyone is here and it's time to be seated. Lady Carlisle's gown is lovely, *oui?* And look at the headpiece," she said with a French accent that always seemed to be stronger when there were guests or strangers about. "Isn't the little bird tucked in the lace *simplement divin?*"

"Simply divine," Sapphire said sweetly, forcing a smile as she walked to her chair near the head of the table. She did not care for Lady Carlisle. Only yesterday morning Sapphire had overheard the countess in the library talking to her friend Lady Morrow. "Monsieur Fabergine is quite charming, but his red-haired daughter is entirely too free-spirited for a young woman. She would do well to have her wings clipped by her father before she is lost to good society forever. I wonder," Lady Carlisle had continued, "if Armand realizes how difficult such a hoyden will be to marry off?"

"Papa," Sapphire called, smiling. "Please, everyone sit," she announced to her father's guests. "Join us—dinner is served."

Armand walked behind her chair and eased it out for her. "You look lovely, my dear," he said. "The color of your new gown becomes you."

She was still angry with him but her smile turned genuine as she sat and peered up at him over her bare shoulder. "Thank you for the gown, Papa. It *is* lovely." She smoothed the skirt as she slid her chair forward.

"A lovely gown for a lovely woman," he whispered in her ear. "Even if she is a hoyden."

She looked into his eyes and had to cover her mouth with her hand to avoid giggling aloud. Apparently he had heard about Lady Carlisle's comment concerning her behavior.

"Merci tellement," Armand said grandly to his guests, helping Aunt Lucia into her chair before taking his place at the head of the table.

One of the married male guests aided Angelique, Sapphire noticed. All men adored Angelique because she was never argumentative and there was something about her dark beauty that men seemed unable to resist.

"Please," Armand continued, taking his chair and opening his arms grandly. "Here at Manoir D'orchidée, Orchid Manor as you would say, we are quite informal."

He waved to one of the new servants, a girl from the village that Sapphire suspected had caught her father's roving eye. It was a vice of his that her mother had always overlooked; an *innate male weakness,* Mama called it. Be that as it may, when rumors circulated years ago that Angelique was actually Armand's daughter by one of the native women, Sapphire had decided that the man she would marry would not have this *innate male weakness*. She would not stand for it.

The servant girl, Tarasai, who was no older than Sapphire, approached the table, eyes downcast, carrying a large white porcelain soup tureen with gilded handles. With the serving of the tortoise soup, the two-hour-long event of dinner commenced, and as course after course was served and carried out, Sapphire found herself sinking further into her chair.

Since her father's English guests had arrived a week earlier, dinner conversations had been incredibly dull. The middle-aged men spoke of nothing but crops and their health, and as boring as that was, Sapphire found their talk of gout and the price of cane presses more interesting than the Englishwomen's tedious conversations concerning London society. Aunt Lucia was quite adept at smiling and nodding and adding a *oui* or a yes in all the right places, and Angelique occupied herself by flirting with the men in the room, servants and guests, old and young. But Sapphire simply could not feign interest.

Waiting for the next course to be served, Sapphire lifted her gaze upward with a sigh of boredom and focused on the giant crystal chandelier hanging over the dining table. Orchid Manor was quite modern in many ways; the rooms were lit by efficient oil lamps, but her father insisted on using only candlelight in the dining room.

Sapphire heard a quiet whine beneath the table and felt a cold nose push against her hand. She made sure that no one was watching, then tore a piece of bread from her plate and eased it under the table. One of her father's hounds licked it greedily from her fingers and nuzzled her hand for more.

Lady Morrow, who was the same age and temperament as the fifty-ish Lady Carlisle, was telling Aunt Lucia about a lady who had to dismiss her maid for pilfering soap from the larder. Sapphire rolled her eyes at the pettiness of the conversation and reached for another piece of bread to feed the dog.

Baroness Wells, seated beside Sapphire, met her gaze and smiled. Sapphire liked Patricia. Patricia was a newlywed and she could be quite fun, but she was Lady Carlisle's niece and, therefore, well under the wretched woman's thumb. Sapphire had tried several times to convince Patricia to go riding or swimming with her, but each time Lady Carlisle had rejected the idea on the grounds that a white woman was unsafe in the jungles of Martinique. The fact that many aristocratic French families lived quite safely in the area did not seem to be a consideration.

Sapphire offered another piece of bread to the hound, and this time he drew his nose just far enough from beneath the white linen tablecloth for Patricia to see him. Patricia spotted the black nose and lifted her napkin to her mouth to hide her amusement.

Lady Carlisle cleared her throat and Sapphire suddenly realized that the women at the table were all looking at her. Apparently someone had asked her a question, but she'd been too preoccupied with the dog to listen.

"Sapphire, dear," Aunt Lucia said smoothly, "tell Lady Carlisle about the altar cloths you and Angelique recently embroidered for Father Richmond. I was just telling the countesses how well schooled you were by the nuns."

"The truth?" Sapphire asked, knowing very well that was not what her aunt was seeking. "Angelique's cloths were quite lovely, her stitching perfect. Mine were bloodstained from continually pricking my fingers with the damn needle and had to be thrown into the rag bag."

Lady Morrow and Lady Carlisle gasped simultaneously. Sapphire smiled sweetly while Aunt Lucia tipped her wineglass, draining it in one gulp. After that, the conversation moved to the difficulties the ladies had had shopping for Patricia's trousseau in Paris before she was married last fall. Sapphire was left to feed the dog the rest of her bread, and Patricia's, as well.

At last, the final porcelain dish was cleared, and Sapphire rose hoping to slip out of the dining room unseen.

"*Dames,* would you care to take a turn in my garden?" Armand asked, pointing to the floor-to-ceiling doors left open to the stone patio. "The gentlemen and I thought we would retire to my study for a cigar and then join you for drinks, if it isn't too cool outside."

"Cool?" Sapphire groaned, dabbing at her neckline with her napkin before placing it on her plate. "Heavens, Papa. It's a warm enough night. I doubt we'll catch a chill."

He rested his hand on her elbow, smiled and leaned forward. "Please, Sapphire," he said quietly. "I understand your anger with me, but these are my guests. I do a great deal of business with these gentlemen and it will not harm you to be pleasant to their wives."

She sighed. "Yes, Papa. I understand. I'm sorry. I'll send Tarasai for wraps if anyone is chilled."

"*Merci.*" He walked away, leading the men through the dining room toward his study, leaving her with no choice but to escort the women out onto the patio.

"Please, ladies, join us for a cordial on the patio. We have some rare orchids I think you'll find quite beautiful."

"I'm sorry," Angelique said sweetly, standing behind her chair. "But I'm not feeling very well. A bit of headache. If you'll excuse me."

"Certainly. Yes, of course," the women murmured at once, full of concern for Angelique.

Sapphire groaned inwardly and called Tarasai to bring refreshments to the orchid garden.

By the time Sapphire walked outside, Aunt Lucia was showing Patricia one of Armand's hybrids, a stunning pale pink orchid with a deep black center, and the two countesses had their heads together, whispering. In no hurry to join either conversation, Sapphire walked toward a small pond stocked with bright orange goldfish. Gathering her skirts, she crouched and stared into the pool to see if she could catch a flash of orange tail illuminated by the light of the torches placed around the perimeter of the garden that separated it from the vast rain forest.

She didn't find any fish, but she saw a shiny green frog with orange speckles, and when it hopped off a rock onto the patio, she followed it. As she approached the far side of the garden, she caught part of the countesses' conversation.

"Naked?" she heard Lady Morrow whisper harshly. "No!"

"Yes," Lady Carlisle insisted. "That's what Lord Carlisle said. Well, at least practically so."

"Shocking," Lady Morrow said. "And to think poor Monsieur Fabergine has this to deal with while still in mourning."

"That and the dark-skinned girl. Can you believe she sits at the dining table as if she's one of them?"

"Dark-skinned? Whatever do you mean? I thought she was a French relation or something.…"

Dismissing the frog, Sapphire raised her chin a notch and strode over to the two women whose heads were bowed as they gossiped. "Excuse me, ladies, but I couldn't help but overhear that last of your exchange," she said, looking one directly in the eyes and then the other.

"How rude of you to listen to a conversation you were not invited to be a part of. Have you no manners whatsoever, young lady?" Lady Carlisle demanded. At least Lady Morrow had the decency to avert her gaze in embarrassment.

Sapphire took a step closer to the countess, her eyes flashing with anger. "You speak of manners? My mother always taught me that if one has nothing nice to say, one should not speak at all."

"What did she know?" Lady Carlisle hissed. "She was a common trollop!"

Stunned by the countess's comment, Sapphire stared, eyes wide. "My mother was no such thing!"

Lady Carlisle moved closer to Sapphire. "Your mother was nothing but a New Orleans whore, the same as your precious aunt. That is how your father found her!"

"How dare you!" Sapphire shouted.

"Sapphire." Aunt Lucia appeared at her side, laying her hand gently on her arm. "Please—your father's guests…"

Sapphire pulled her arm away. "No! Did you...did you hear what she just said about my mother? What she accused you of being?"

"Ask Lady Morrow," Lady Carlisle said as she drew herself up in her gray flowered gown, her hideous headdress with its bird bobbing as if it were pecking a hole in her head. "Her cousin's brother knew them in New Orleans. He and Armand were business associates."

"Edith, that will be quite enough," Aunt Lucia said sharply.

"It's not true! It's a lie! Aunt Lucia, tell them, tell them my mother was not—" But when Sapphire looked at her aunt, she realized something was amiss. Did these women know something she didn't? *"Non,"* she whispered in shock.

"Sapphire, *ma petite*..." Aunt Lucia reached for her hand.

Suddenly the whole garden seemed to spin around Sapphire, the bright torches, the heavy scent of jasmine, the sound of the countess's sour voices. "It's not true. None of it is true. It's all lies!"

"Sapphire, this is complicated," Lucia said calmly. "Let us go inside and—"

"No!" Sapphire cried, pulling away, her heart pounding in her throat. With tears filling her eyes, she rushed off the patio and ran into the jungle.

2

Sapphire ran wildly, tears streaming down her cheeks as she shoved her way through the underbrush, taking the shortcut to the stables in the humid darkness.

"It's not true," she shouted over and over again. "It's not true! My mother was not a whore!" And yet she knew in her heart of hearts that it *was* true; the look on Aunt Lucia's face spoke the truth. Her mother, her beloved Mama, her father's Sophie, had been a common woman of the streets—a prostitute. And somewhere deep inside, Sapphire realized she had always known her mother kept a terrible secret. There was a sadness Mama could never put aside, not even with the love of her daughter and devoted husband.

"But how could you do it, Mama?" Sapphire whispered as she slowed to a walk. She was panting so hard that her chest ached and her stomach turned queasy. "How could you have died not telling me the truth?" she demanded of her mother, looking up into the starlit sky, calling to her somewhere above.

But of course there was no response, neither from the heavens nor from her mother, who had been dead for nearly a year. A year…yet it seemed as though they had just buried her mother in the lovely place she and Papa had chosen. Her illness had been swift—a sudden loss of weight, blurry vision, thirst and light-headedness. A physician had been called, but he was unable to cure the strange disease he had called the sugar sickness, and she died three weeks later.… Her beloved Mama was dead and now these people were saying such awful things about her!

Sapphire immediately felt a sense of comfort as she approached her father's vast stables. The stables had always been a place of refuge when she was sad or hurt or angry. Here, alone with the horses, she found she could lose herself in grooming and caring for them, or simply standing in their presence. Riding through the pounding surf, she'd always found a sense of release and freedom that she had seemed to crave more and more in the past year.

Ahead, she saw the dim glow of a lantern in the tack room and she felt her heart flutter. Had Maurice come, hoping she could slip away from her father's dinner party for a few minutes? Her steps quickened, her heart beating in anticipation as she slipped in the door. Hearing nothing, she walked quietly down the worn cobblestone center aisle, setting her feet on the paving blocks that had been carried here from the shores of France as ballast on a merchant vessel decades ago, listening to the familiar sounds of the horses shifting in their stalls, the contented chuff and the occasional whinny.

A sliver of light came from the doorway that had been left open a crack, and her heart swelled with anticipation. Her beloved was here! "Maurice?" Sapphire whispered, walking slowly toward the light.

Then she heard a sound, a female voice, and she hesitated. "Angelique?" What on earth was her sister doing at the barn? Taking a horse to meet Jacques?

"Sapphire?" Angelique called from behind the door. "I thought you were in the garden with—"

"Oh, Angel." Sapphire rushed for the door and flung it open. "You're not going to believe—" She clasped the door tightly with her hand and stared.

Angelique pulled herself from a man's embrace.

"Maurice!" Sapphire's heart fell as her world came crashing down around her.

"S-Sapphire, *mon amour.*"

"No!" She grabbed a pitchfork from where it rested in the corner of the tack room.

"This is not how it looks, *ma chère.*" Maurice walked toward her, his arms open.

"Not how it looks?" Sapphire shouted.

"Sapphire, please," Angelique protested.

Angelique was wearing a simple A-line dress that fell to just past her knees, a dress similar to those worn by the native women. It was what she always wore when she sneaked out of the house to meet men.

"Do not get in my way!" Sapphire threatened Angelique as she took a step closer to Maurice, jabbing the tines of the pitchfork in the air. "You said you loved me! You said you wanted to marry me!" Her voice caught in her throat as a rage swept over her. "You said we would make beautiful babies together!"

"I do wish to marry you, *mon amour.* I do love you. It is only that—"

"What?" she demanded. "It is only *what?* You love me, but you kiss my sister?" Her last words came out of her mouth ragged and forlorn.

"Sapphire—" Angelique interrupted, reaching for her.

"Not now," she snapped, thrusting the pitchfork at Maurice again. "I'm going to run my true love through his black heart," she hissed, lunging toward him.

Maurice threw himself against the wall and slowly began to inch his way toward the door, his palms pressed to the wall. "Sapphire, *s'il vous plaît*, let me explain. This has nothing to do with you and me. What you and I have is true love—"

"True love!" Sapphire laughed bitterly. "Get out of here," she ordered, spitting at him.

Maurice ran out the door, and by the time Sapphire turned the corner, he was halfway through the barn.

"Never come back," she called after him. "Not ever, do you hear me?"

She stood there for a moment staring into the darkness as the barn door slammed shut, then, leaving the pitchfork outside against the wall, she turned back to the tack room.

"How could you?" she whispered, her gaze settling on Angelique. She tucked a stray tendril of damp hair behind her ear. "You knew I loved him."

"I'm sorry," Angelique said, looking at the ground.

"You're sorry? You have betrayed me and that's all you have to say to me?"

Angelique turned to her, lifting her eyes to meet Sapphire's. "You don't want to hear anything else I have to say right now."

"Yes, I do," Sapphire challenged, taking a step closer.

"I think I have a right to hear what you have to say, considering the circumstances."

"I'm sorry I let him kiss me, but he doesn't love you," she said softly.

"What do you mean?" Sapphire stared at her. "Of course Maurice loves me!"

"No he doesn't. If he did, he wouldn't have kissed me."

"Don't say that!"

"Sapphire, listen to me. Maurice loves your father's land, not you. He loves what he thinks you can do to further his situation. He has an older brother, you know. Younger sons do not inherit a father's plantation, and the family is in debt. If Maurice cannot find a rich wife, he will be forced to find a position in trade."

Sapphire tucked her hands behind her back and leaned against the wall. "It's not true. It can't be."

"Sapphire, this isn't the first time he's tried. Even the first night we met last autumn at the ball, he tried to get me to meet him in the forest after everyone had gone home."

Sapphire shook her head in disbelief, trying to think back. "But we danced every dance together that night. He said I was the most beautiful woman he had ever seen and that he had fallen in love with me the moment he laid eyes upon me."

Angelique nodded. "You probably are the most beautiful woman he ever met, but he is not a loyal man. You deserve better."

"You're confusing things! You were kissing him. What about Jacques?" Sapphire asked. "I thought you liked *him*."

"Ah, Jacques. I do like him, but he has no intention

of *marrying* me. Not that I would have him." Angelique ran her finger along the edge of a rough-hewn table scattered with brushes and combs for grooming. "Since I am half native, no respectable man will ever have me, no matter how many beautiful gowns Armand Fabergine buys for me or how many tutors he brings to teach me Latin and literature."

"That's not true," Sapphire said quietly.

"It is true and you know it. That's why Mama left her money to me when she died and not to you. It was so that I would not have to marry. She did it because she knew you would inherit Papa's land and fortune. She did it so I could take care of myself." Angelique took a step toward Sapphire. "Do you want to hear Maurice's plan?"

"What?" Sapphire whispered, tears welling in her eyes.

"He knew Papa would never agree to allow him to marry you. His plan was to seduce you, and when you became pregnant, Papa would be forced to allow you to marry him to save your honor."

Sapphire did not want to believe Angel's words. But Angelique never lied. Not even when they were children and were faced with punishment if they did not confess to some trick they had played on the servants or when they had sneaked away from their governess to swim naked in the ocean with the village children.

"You shouldn't have done this, Angel."

"I am what I am, and if you expect more, I will only break your heart over and over again." Her eyes, now filled with tears, searched Sapphire's. "Can you forgive me, my sister?"

Sapphire looked away, focusing on the pale light

glowing from an oil lamp that hung from a wrought-iron hook protruding from the wall.

They had been the best of friends—sisters—since the day they met. Sapphire had sneaked out of the house one day, abandoning her music tutor to hike in the jungle. On the beach she had encountered two big, ugly stray dogs that had trapped a small, barefoot native girl against a tree. Sapphire had driven the dogs off with a large branch and taken the little girl home with her to have Sophie bandage the girl's cut knee. They had discovered that Angelique came from a nearby village and that she was recently orphaned. Her mother had died of a fever and her father—well, she didn't know who her father was—but one had only to look at the face of the eight-year-old to tell that a Frenchman had fathered her. Perhaps Sophie had suspected it might be her husband who had sired her. That very day, Sophie Fabergine had welcomed the orphan into her home and from that time, raised her as if she were a daughter.

Sapphire looked up. "I'm still angry with you, Angel," she whispered.

Angelique threw her arms around Sapphire and hugged her. "Of course you are. I deserve it and I would expect no less of you." She walked to the far wall, stood on her tiptoes and turned down the lamp, enclosing them in darkness. "Now come on. Let's go home."

Sapphire was not entirely surprised when she entered her bedchamber to find her father and aunt waiting for her. Angelique took one look at their faces and backed up. "I'll go to my room."

"*Non*, Angelique." Armand spoke from a woven

beachwood chair under one of the open windows. If he noticed Angelique was not in her ball gown, he gave no indication, nor did he make mention of the fact that Sapphire's hair was tangled and hanging loose, her gown tattered.

"What I have to say affects you as well as Sapphire," he sighed. "Come in and close the door behind you. You two ladies have shared enough with our guests today, do you not think?"

"What is it that cannot wait?" Sapphire demanded. She knew Aunt Lucia must have told her father what the women had said in the garden about Sapphire's mother. She had a hundred questions for her father but she just wasn't ready to ask them yet. "I'm tired, Papa." She approached her chifforobe, pretending she was about to begin undressing. "It would be better if we talked tomorrow."

"*Non,*" Armand said sharply, startling all three women. "Tonight, young lady, you will not have your way! I will speak to you now, *fille,* and you, out of respect for your father, will listen. I should have had this talk with you—your mother and I should have—years ago, but we cannot change that now. Our guests have remedied that, haven't they." He hesitated. "All we can do is go on from here. Now sit down on the bed." He raised his hand in Angelique's direction. "You, as well, Angel. I warn you, I will not be handled by the three of you. Not tonight."

Astonished by her father's demeanor, Sapphire did as she was told and silently walked to the bed to sit beside Aunt Lucia. Angelique sat on the older woman's other side.

"Let me first say that I am sorry, Sapphire, that all has come about in the way that it has. I must say that I did not always agree with your mother's choices, but they were hers to make," he said. "I know you understand that Lord Carlisle came to finalize a business agreement with me, but he also came to meet you so that I might finalize my plans to send you to London—"

"London!" Sapphire jumped off the bed. "I am not going to London!"

Armand rose from his chair. "I told you to sit, *fille,* and you will sit!"

Under her father's angry gaze, she leaned against the bed but did not sit. She crossed her arms over her chest and waited stubbornly.

"In my grief over the loss of your mother, I have allowed you to run wild."

"Papa, I have not—"

"Do not interrupt me again!"

Sapphire pressed her lips together in silence, but she felt as if she could leap out of her skin. Had her father lost his mind? Go to London? What could possibly be there for her?

"I have allowed you to run too freely," Armand continued, beginning to pace in the large, airy bedchamber. "Since your mother's death, I have allowed you, against my better judgment, to cease your lessons, to run about the island, unsupervised, to meet with men in private that you should not—"

"Papa, Maurice and I—" This time, he only had to give Sapphire a look and she was silent.

"You will go to London with Lord and Lady Carlisle and Lucia has agreed to go as your chaperone."

"But what about me? What am I to do?" Angelique rose, suddenly as upset as Sapphire, obviously for a different reason. "Can't I go to London, as well?"

"Well, I suppose you may," Armand said, taken by surprise. "I wasn't certain you would want to, my dear. To leave your home village, to—"

"Of course I want to go!" Angelique clasped her hands together excitedly. "Oh, Papa, you don't know how much I've always wanted to go to London."

Sapphire glared at Angelique, unable to let go of her anger toward her yet. "I thought you wanted to go to New York. No, wait, that was last week. Where was it you wanted to go this week? Athens? Paris? Or was it Brussels?" Sapphire mused.

"I want to go to all those places," Angelique responded, nonplussed. "But most of all, right now, London. Oh, thank you, Papa!"

Sapphire turned to look at her father again. Her mother used to say that Angelique was always so easy to please, unlike Sapphire. Nothing was ever good enough for Sapphire, nothing was ever entirely agreeable—unless it was her idea. "I don't want to go to London, Papa." She looked down. It was hard for her to give in. She glanced up at him again, her arms still crossed over her chest. "If this is about Maurice—"

"This is not about that loathsome boy!" Armand said abruptly, turning on his heels to look at her. "Sapphire, you don't understand. You don't know who you are."

"Oh, we're back to that again, are we?" She moved away from the bed. "I'm still nothing but a child to you, still unable, in your eyes, to make my own decisions, unable to decide for myself what is best for me?" She took a step toward him. "Well, you're mistaken. I know precisely who I am and what I want out of life. I am Sapphire Lucia Fabergine, daughter of Sophie and Armand Fabergine, and I want nothing more than—"

"You are not my daughter," Armand said, looking her in the eye.

Sapphire's throat constricted and her knees went weak. "What?" she managed to say.

"Sapphire, come sit beside me," Lucia said calmly, trying to take her hand and lead her to the bed.

"No." Sapphire pulled her arm from her aunt. First this terrible thing about her mother—and now this? She stared at her father. "Is my entire life a lie? Has anyone ever told the truth in this house? Papa, what are you saying?"

Armand's lower lip trembled. It was obvious he was in pain, not just emotionally, but physically, as well. "Please," she said quietly, reaching out to take his arm. "Sit and tell me what you have to tell me." Surprisingly, he allowed her to lead him back to the chair.

"It is true," he said when he was seated while Sapphire sat on a footstool at his feet. "I am not your father, but you must believe me when I tell you that you are the child of my heart. You must know that, Sapphire, before I go any further."

Tears welled in her eyes as she stared out the open windows into the dark jungle. Lucia came to stand behind her and pushed a white handkerchief into her hand.

"I'm listening," Sapphire said, watching the filmy gauze drapes fluttering around her bedposts. A giant green moth had found its way into the room and now fluttered about the lamp, lured by the beauty of the dancing yellow flame, perhaps to its own death. *I am like that moth*, Sapphire thought. *I know that what I am about to hear will destroy me, but I cannot resist knowing the truth.*

"I met your mother and Lucia in New Orleans."

"He was as handsome a man as either of us had ever seen," Lucia offered, looking to Armand with a smile. "But from the first night he had eyes for no one but your mother."

"But she was a prostitute," Sapphire heard herself say, trying to keep the bitterness out of her voice. "That's how you met her. That's what Lady Carlisle was talking about, wasn't it? That's what Mama was always trying to hide from me. It was her secret."

Armand folded his hands together and was quiet for a moment. *"Oui,"* he said finally. "I met your mother in a bordello in New Orleans. We fell in love and I asked her to marry me, though she had given birth to another man's child without the benefit of a wedding ring. She agreed to marry me and came here to Orchid Manor, bringing Lucia as her companion."

"And that's it? You're telling me that I'm merely the product of some chance encounter between a stranger and a...a night-blooming flower?"

Armand studied his daughter's face and thought to himself that she had always been so strong, stronger than him or Sophie. Her eyes were red but she did not cry. It had been like that always, even when she was a child; the time she had fallen from her horse when she was seven and had broken her arm, she had not cried. Nor had she cried the hundreds of times she'd skinned her knees or elbows, either. She was strong, his Sapphire, stronger than anyone he'd ever known.

Armand sat back in the chair, crossing one leg over the other. "Listen before you make judgments. Do you not wish to know why your mother was in that place?"

"Do I?" she asked, setting her jaw.

"It doesn't matter," Angelique declared, sliding off the bed and coming to stand beside Lucia. "She is Sapphire, and she is as good as anyone on this island. Women do what they must to survive—isn't that right, Aunt Lucia?" she asked. "Tell her."

Lucia looked into Angelique's dark eyes. "It is why I found myself in Madame Dulane's in New Orleans. I was a common street whore in London and was given the opportunity to travel to America with a kind benefactor. When he grew bored with me, I took to the occupation I knew—but this time, instead of working the streets, I found a place where I would have a bed and food."

Sapphire felt her head spinning. It was all so much to digest that she didn't know which question to ask first. Aunt Lucia and her mother selling their bodies to men? Her sweet, quiet, gentle mother, a whore? It was an impossible thought, and yet the look on her father's and aunt's faces revealed the truth.

"Did you really meet my mother in New Orleans, or was she also a London whore?"

"I did meet her in New Orleans," Lucia answered calmly, "but she, too, sailed from London, though not of her own choosing."

"Not of her own choosing?"

"Sapphire, it will do you no good to be angry with your mother now. She did what she thought was best at the time," Armand said. "She thought you should not know the truth of your birth until you were older. Then she became ill so suddenly and there was no time…"

The room was silent. Angelique had returned to sit on the bed. Sapphire stared out the window for a moment and then turned back to her father. "So whose daughter am I, if not yours?"

Lucia rested her hand on Armand's arm and murmured something. He looked at her and nodded. Lucia waited until he had taken a seat in the beachwood chair again and then she spoke, opening her arms as if introducing a performance or work of art. "I have had to piece much of this story together because your mother was not easily forthcoming in her tale, but this is the best I can tell you. There was a young girl in Devonshire," she said, adapting the tone of a storyteller. "Her name was Sophie and she was a strikingly beautiful woman with auburn hair and a smile that caught the eye of every man in the county, I would suspect."

Sapphire turned to look at Lucia, unable to resist being drawn in.

"She was a farmer's daughter who could read and write and who yearned to see the world, at least the world beyond the hills of her little English village. Then one day, the summer she was seventeen, a handsome young man stopped at the local inn to eat."

"It's like one of your romance stories," Angelique said softly. "Or maybe a fairy tale."

"He was an earl's son," Lucia continued. "A viscount in his own right and his name was Edward. It was a meeting completely by chance, though some might say by fate." She walked to the window, the silk of her bright, multicolored dressing gown flowing behind her.

"Had Sophie not been leaving the tavern, having delivered her father's fresh vegetables at the very moment that his lordship entered the tavern, they would never have met."

Lucia paused, and then went on. "He fell in love with her at first sight, and she him. And even though they knew their love could never be, for they were not of the same social class, he couldn't stop himself from riding to the village regularly to see her, and she could not stop herself from sneaking away from the farm to be with him."

"And then what happened?" Sapphire asked, although she could guess.

"They married in secret the following summer," Lucia said solemnly. "And they sealed their love—"

"With a night of passionate lovemaking," Angelique injected.

"And Edward gave his new wife, Sophie, as a token of his love, one of the largest, most beautiful sapphires in all of England. A sapphire that had once belonged to the great Queen Elizabeth."

Sapphire heard her father move in his chair and turned to see him produce a small, worn wooden chest. "This is your mother's casket," he said quietly, opening it and removing a black velvet bag. "And this—" he carefully removed an object from it "—is the gift she saved for you."

Sapphire gasped in awe at the sight of the stunning sapphire that was as large as a walnut, sparkling bright in the lamplight. "For me?" she whispered as she stepped forward to take it from his hand. It was cool in her palm, yet it seemed to radiate a warmth that surprised her.

Armand closed the lid on the box. "Inside are also letters from your father to your mother. Love letters, I
would assume." He shook his head, suddenly seeming
sad. "I never read them, not even after her death. She
had never offered to allow me to read them."

"They're for me?" Sapphire asked.

He nodded.

"And then what happened?" Sapphire asked again.
"Please tell me, Aunt Lucia."

"Well, the couple spent a magical night together and
then parted, he to travel to London to tell his family of
his marriage and she to her father's cottage to inform
him of her good fortune." She turned from the window,
folding her hands together. "But Edward's father, the
Earl of Wessex, was not pleased his son had married a
country girl, a girl without title or wealth."

Sapphire hung her head. "The family would not accept the marriage."

"Indeed not. According to your mother, the Earl of
Wessex was very angry because he had already chosen
a bride for his son, a bride from a family with great af-
fluence and a proper lineage," Lucia said, lifting her
forefinger that sported a wide, spiraled gold ring. "And
so he sent a representative to Sophie to say that his son
had made a mistake and wanted to have the marriage
annulled."

"But Sophie knew it couldn't be true," Sapphire said,
almost feeling her mother's pain in her own chest.

Angelique met Sapphire's gaze, seeming to feel her
pain, as well.

"Sophie knew." Lucia nodded solemnly. "And when
the young Sophie could not be persuaded to sign the an-

nulment—not even for money—and when she to threatened to go to London herself and find her beloved Edward, Lord Wessex began to fear the country girl. So...he had her kidnapped."

"Poor Mama," Sapphire sighed. She could not imagine that such a thing happened to her soft-spoken, timid mother. "Please go on," she whispered after a moment of silence.

"So..." Lucia took a breath. "Sophie found herself in the hold of a ship for the journey across the Atlantic Ocean, abandoned on the docks of New Orleans. Lord Wessex had so feared the country girl who had stolen his son's heart that he sent her all the way to America."

"I cannot believe it," Angelique murmured.

Sapphire closed her eyes, remembering her mother before she had become ill and hollow-cheeked, and then she tried to imagine what Sophie must have looked like when she was eighteen.

"Sophie was without money or food or a place to live, and by then she knew she was carrying a child."

"Edward's baby," Sapphire said, still finding it all so hard to believe. "Me."

"She was carrying you," Lucia continued, "and though she still had possession of the sapphire Edward had given her—safely sewn in the hem of her only gown—she refused to sell it, for she knew it would mean her child's legacy. Instead, she sought employment. She was hired as a cook in a tavern in the French Quarter and slept in the attic above the kitchen, but when the evidence of her condition began to show—"

"They put her out on the street," Angelique guessed angrily. "It's always that way."

"They did, but Sophie would not be defeated, because even after all she had been through, she knew in her heart that Edward had loved her and she knew that the baby she carried would be with her always—even if she and Edward could never be together again. Determined to protect her child, Sophie sought work in the only place a pregnant woman without a husband or proper guardian could find employment. She found a kind madam and good friends there."

"You," Sapphire said.

"It's where we met and instantly became sisters, the dairy maid turned fallen woman and the dockside London whore," Lucia said proudly. "And there Sophie's daughter was born."

"I can't believe you kept this from me," Sapphire said, turning to Armand, the jewel clasped tightly in her hand.

"It was important to your mother that you be loved, that you know the love of two parents." He sat back, the casket on his lap. "As time passed, the lie seemed to become truth. After a while, I began to forget that you were not the child of my blood."

"Your mother gave birth to a beautiful girl, born with her mother's red hair and her father's eyes, one blue and one green."

Sapphire drew her hand to her mouth and inhaled sharply at this revelation. She had asked her mother many times why she had one blue eye and one green when her mother's and Armand's eyes were brown, and the response had always been simply that children took after many relatives. Now she knew the truth.

"And Sophie named her daughter Sapphire." Lucia's

eyes now shone with unshed tears in remembrance, "for the gift her father had given them. And Sophie went about her life, determined to give her daughter a better life than she had known. She dreamed that she and her daughter would some day return to England to find Edward so they would be reunited, and their little girl would be given the name and recognition she always deserved."

Sapphire sat again on the footstool, feeling more than a little light-headed. "And that's why you want me to go to London now, Papa—to find my father?"

"This is not about what I want, my dearest daughter. It cannot even be about what you want." He turned to the window. "It must be about what your mother wanted. It was her dying wish that you find your father, that you seek out your inheritance and what is rightfully yours."

"And why are you telling me this after she has been gone nearly a year?" Sapphire demanded, wiping at a tear that threatened to spill. "Why do you decide now to tell me all this? Why send me now? Why with those awful people?"

"Because I am a weak man and it has taken me this long to get up my courage to send you away from me. I am sending you with Lord and Lady Carlisle because I know you will be safe with them, because I can trust Lord Carlisle, and because I know they will help you make the proper social associations in London. You won't have to stay with them long, dear, only until your father invites you into his home."

"I still don't understand. Why are you doing this now? Why must you send me away now?" she flung at him.

"Because it is time."

Sapphire thought for a moment and then lifted her gaze to meet Armand's. "And if I don't want to meet him?" she asked, defiance in her voice. "If I refuse to go?"

3

Three weeks later

"There you are, *ma chère.* I thought you had gone to bed." Armand stood barefoot in a silk dressing robe on the edge of the garden patio outside his bedchamber, staring into the darkness. Torchlight behind him cast shadows over the stones at his feet and the end of his slender cigar glowed in the night.

"You are not supposed to be smoking or drinking—you know that." Lucia strode up to him and snatched the cigar from his lips to place it between her own, then inhaled deeply.

Armand chuckled and lifted his other hand to take a sip from his crystal tumbler. "Ah, Lucia," he murmured thoughtfully, enjoying the burn of the rum. "I will miss you."

"You certainly will." She exhaled and the smoke curled around her head and rose, dissipating in the warm night breeze. "With no one to keep you from drowning yourself in rum, you'll be dead in six months' time."

Armand grinned, continuing to stare out into the jungle beyond the house, swirling the last of the rum in the crystal glass. "Sometimes, I think, *ma chère*, I should have married you and not Sophie. You, I think I could have made happy."

"You've already had too much rum, haven't you." She inhaled on the cigar again. "And I am far too old to be anyone's *chère*, certainly yours. Besides, you had your chance with me in New Orleans years ago." She moved to stand beside him. She spoke again after a moment, softening her voice. "She was happy, you know, perhaps not in the same way you might have hoped, but she *was* happy with the life she chose with you."

"The life that was forced upon her, you mean."

"You are mistaken, Armand, if you think Sophie married you unwillingly. She would not have disrespected you or herself or Sapphire in that way."

"I loved her, you know, very deeply. And even after a year, I still miss her so much. Though she never loved me as she loved her Edward, she still made me very happy, and now that I'm without her, each day seems hollow and empty. Even the native girls I bring to my bed cannot..." He sighed. "The loneliness remains."

"She loved you, Armand. Surely you must know that." Lucia said. "And Sapphire loves you."

"Which is why she must go now," he said firmly. "I do not care what she says, she will be on that ship tomorrow when it sails."

Lucia groaned. "You know I have not been in agreement with this idea of yours from the beginning. Because she loves you, Armand, I think you need to reconsider. One year, what would one more year matter? She would be a year older, a year wiser and—"

"*Non*," he said, clasping the glass tighter in his hand. "I will not have Sapphire throw her life away to the likes of Maurice Dupree or any man like him, and I will not allow her to sit here and watch me waste away." He looked at her shrewdly. "And I will not have you tell her about my illness, either, do you understand me? If she knows I am sick, I will really have to tie her and crate her to put her aboard that ship tomorrow. *Non*, it is time my dear daughter had her wings and I will not clip them with my human frailty." He drew his hand over his abdomen. "It seems as if a fire burns in my stomach day and night, and now I am spitting up blood. I will not allow her to watch me die!" The exertion of his conviction made him cough furiously.

Lucia sighed. "Oh dear, Armand." She reached out to smooth his back with her hand, waiting for the spasm to pass. "Don't work yourself into a fit."

"I'm not," he wheezed, struggling to catch his breath, pressing his hand against his stomach. "But neither you nor my *fille* will coax me from my path this time. My wishes will be done. Sapphire will return to London as my dear wife wished, and her father will lay her rightful claim upon her."

He cleared his throat, allowing his mind to drift as he thought of the lovely young woman who was his daughter. Since he had first seen that precocious three-year-old in the New Orleans parlor, surrounded by courtesans, he had known she was destined for great things. He had fallen instantly in love with Sophie, in

part because of her sad eyes. Sapphire had been a striking beauty, even as a child. She had the lovely face and
the remarkable rich auburn hair of her mother, and the
piercing eyes—one blue, one green—that he later
learned were her father's. She had grown into an even
lovelier young woman, and was desired by many, but
conquered by few, he realized. "My only regret, *ma
chère,*" Armand mused aloud, "is that I am not able to
take Sapphire to London myself."

"I shall care for her as my own daughter, you know
that." Lucia drew the cigar away from her lips. "I promise you. I'll see that her father recognizes her or he'll
have me to contend with, and Lord Wessex doesn't
want to challenge a girl from the London docks, I promise you that."

He smiled and reached for Lucia, wrapping his arm
around her shoulder. "Come to my bed, *ma chère.* There
is no reason why two old friends cannot keep the sheets
warm for each other."

She smiled up at him. "Good try, Armand, but speak
for yourself. *I* am not old."

"Not old!" He laughed and then coughed again.
"What must you be?"

She dropped the cigar to the stone patio and ground
it out with the toe of her silk slipper. "My age is none of
your concern or anyone else's." She turned away, flipping back the skirting of her silk dressing down and lifting her head high. "This old whore intends to go to
London, and once Sapphire is properly wed and bed to
a man befitting of her station, she intends to find a rich
man to see to her needs in her declining years."

Armand tipped his gray head back and laughed. "I

have no doubt you will do exactly what you set out to do, *ma chère* Lucia. That's why I can see the end of my life now, because Sophie's dream will come to fruition. You, my dear, will see to it that our Sapphire will become Lady Sapphire Wessex, or I know you will die trying."

"Still awake?" Angelique whispered.

Sapphire lay on her back beneath the immense silk canopy of her bed, listening to the familiar night sounds of the jungle. Moonlight spilled through the floor-to-ceiling windows of the bedchamber. The bed was placed in the center of the room where it would get the most ventilation on hot summer nights. The sheer draperies fluttered in the night breeze.

"How could I possibly sleep?" Sapphire whispered back, glancing at the fine china clock on the bed table. It was after midnight.

Angelique stretched sensually beside her on the bed, raising her slender arms above her head. The bedchamber was supposed to be Sapphire's alone; Angelique had her own room of equal size and luxury a short walk down the hall, but the two girls often shared a bed. "It is exciting, isn't it? Tomorrow we set sail on the greatest adventure of our lives!"

"I'm not certain *exciting* is the word I would choose," Sapphire answered. "I cannot imagine being trapped on that ship with Lady Carlisle and Lady Morrow for three weeks. I fear I'll go mad with their incessant gossiping and ridiculing." She stared at the ceiling as she lifted arm over head to rest her wrist on her forehead. "I still can't believe Papa is sending me away." Her initial response to her father's decision to send her to London had been to refuse out of stubbornness, but in truth, she wanted to get away from Maurice. And though she had mixed feelings about finding her father, it was important to her that she do it for her mother.

"He's sending you away because he knows the world has great things in store for you. He has always known it. We all have."

"What great things? That's ridiculous!"

"The daughter of an earl?" Angelique dangled the words as if they were a sweetmeat. "I see you as a high-born lady, making your entrance into London society dressed in a lavish ball gown, the suitors clamoring to have just one dance with the Lady Sapphire."

"And why in heaven's name would I want to dance with any man?"

"You must dance so that you can meet and marry a great man, of course. You know it's always been your dream. It's why you read those silly novels and poetry all the time, isn't it? Because you fancy romantic love?"

Sapphire frowned. Marriage was the furthest things from her mind. She was in too much turmoil to even contemplate such a thing, even if it was inevitable. "I don't understand why you're so eager to go, Angel. This is our home! There's so much I'm going to miss, and not just Papa and Orchid Manor. I don't know that I can bear to leave my horses."

"Don't be silly. They have horses in London."

"This seems so easy for you and I don't understand. You were born here. Our mothers died in this place."

"I'm eager to go because there's nothing to keep me here. Our mothers aren't in those graves," Angelique said with her usual practicality as she sat up beside Sapphire, resting her back against the headboard. "And Armand isn't my father."

"You don't know that." Sapphire picked at the thin fabric of her knee-length sleeping gown. "He could be."

"So could any number of white men on this island, you know that." She looked at Sapphire in the darkness. "But that was never important to me. What's important is the journey we're about to embark upon."

"You know that when we arrive in London, things will be different, there. Everyone here loves you, but—"

"Some better than others!"

"*But* the way you give yourself so freely to men," Sapphire continued diplomatically, "might be...might be misinterpreted." It seemed to her that Angelique had always been a sexual creature, even from the time they were little girls. Certainly from the time Angelique was fourteen and had climbed through the bedchamber window after lights-out to surrender her virginity to a neighboring plantation owner's sixteen-year-old son.

"You worry too much," Angelique told her. "I am what I am, just as my mother was what she was, and I will not apologize for either of us."

Sapphire glanced at Angelique. "We could find you a husband, too, you know. You look more French than native and Armand has already said you must use his surname when we arrive in London. With Armand's name and the money Mama left you, surely—"

"Marriage is your dream, puss," Angelique said as she gave Sapphire a gentle push, "not mine, nor will it ever be." She stretched lazily, like a cat. "I want to get to know a hundred men, a thousand, and not over biscuits and tea."

"Angel, the sisters and Lady Carlisle were all correct. You're quite incorrigible."

"Quite." Angelique turned her head, a mischievous smile on her face. "What's amazing is that you're still so naive," she teased, "especially now that we know you were brought up amidst such bawdiness—your mother and Lucia's colorful past in New Orleans, Armand and his slave women, me."

Sapphire said nothing. She wasn't like Angel. She couldn't accept change so easily, especially not when she had believed one thing her whole life only to find it untrue. Three weeks had passed since Armand told her the truth about her mother and herself and she was still trying to make sense of it all. The more she thought about it, the angrier she became with her father, this Edward. Why hadn't he tried to find her mother? Had he looked for her at all or had he just gone along with the annulment and the new marriage arranged by his family? She intended to ask him just that the moment she saw him. It had been her mother's dream that Sapphire meet her father, to be drawn into the loving embrace of the family, but what Sapphire wanted was an apology—that and to be recognized as Edward's daughter, but not because she wanted any sort of relationship with the man. She wanted the recognition for her mother's sake. And for that reason, she was going to London. Not for Armand, not for herself, but for her mother.

"Now we're off to begin the journey Sophie dreamed of," Angelique murmured. "You to find your rightful legacy and a handsome, titled man to wed, and me to sample an entire new continent of men!"

"I'm not sure that is what my mother had in mind." Sapphire absently reached out to stroke the delightfully smooth silk of one of the bed draperies. "Please don't put it in quite those terms at the dinner table when Lady Carlisle asks you of your plans once we arrive in London. I overheard her talking with Aunt Lucia yesterday and she is not at all pleased that you are being included in the traveling party, though she didn't actually say that to Papa. I think her husband's business profits with Papa are far too great to deny the request to escort us, but she has managed to get her invectives in just the same. I do believe she suggested to Aunt Lucia that you might search for a good position as a lady's maid."

"I'll try to hold my tongue for your sake," Angelique replied with a laugh. "It's the least I can do, considering that Lady Carlisle has barely recovered from the incident at the falls. I understand Lord Carlisle was quite taken with us both."

Sapphire couldn't resist a smile as she slid down in the bed, thrusting a pillow under her head. "We should get some sleep," she said. "Four will come early. Papa says we're to sail at first light while the tide is favorable."

Angelique slid down beside Sapphire, drawing the light sheet over them. "I still can't believe it's happening. I can't believe I'm really leaving this island."

Sapphire smiled, and although she was not entirely eager to go, she couldn't help but wonder what awaited her so far from the familiar shores of Martinique.

* * *

Sapphire stood on the rail of the sailing schooner the *Elizabeth Mae*, holding tightly to the ribbons of her bonnet. The sun was just beginning to peek above the horizon in the eastern sky, and there was a good wind that would carry them safely from Martinique's rocky shores. She gripped the polished wood rail as she gazed down on her father and the maid, Tarasai, who had escorted him to the dock.

Sapphire knew the young native woman adored him and, in the past weeks, she had seemed to be able to cajole him into caring better for himself. Sapphire hated leaving him, but at least she knew there would be someone here for him, seeing that he didn't smoke too many cigars or drink too much rum. She managed a smile and a wave as he looked up to meet her gaze. He had dressed carefully that morning in a finely cut coat and trousers with a starched cravat around his neck, all the latest French fashion. He wore a straw boater on his head, tilted jauntily, and in his hand was an exquisitely carved cane. Monsieur Armand Fabergine had orchestrated this fine image of the man she had thought to be her father, the man who would always be her father in her heart. A lump suddenly rose in her throat and she made a little sound.

"Steady, there," Lucia, who stood behind her, whispered in her ear. "Remember, this is difficult for you, *ma chère*, but more difficult for him."

Sapphire pressed her lips together and nodded.

One of the sailors called for the gangplank to be lifted and Armand tipped his hat.

"No, wait!" Sapphire cried, running.

She heard Lucia and Angelique call to her. She heard the high-pitched voice of Lady Carlisle. "There, you see, I warned you, sir, she will be nothing but trouble..."

But Sapphire ignored them all, gripping the skirts of her new sensible cotton traveling gown and racing down the gangplank, the ribbons of her straw bonnet streaming behind her. "Papa!"

"Sapphire, no. You must go, my daughter," he chastised, but as her kidskin boots hit the wooden planks of the dock, he opened his arms to her.

She threw herself into his arms, burying her face in the lapel of his black coat, deeply breathing the scent of him. As long as she could remember, this smell, the feel of these arms around her, had always meant safety and security. She had always known that no matter what she did wrong or what trouble she found herself in, Armand Fabergine, her papa, would be there for her.

"*Mon dieu*," Armand whispered, resting his chin on the top of her head. "Please don't make a scene. Lord and Lady Carlisle have been very kind to agree to escort you to London. Please do not shame me."

She looked into his eyes that were watery with emotion. "I would never shame you, Papa." She dared a little smile. "At least, not on purpose."

He grinned and pulled her against him. "Of course you would not, my dear Sapphire. Now you must go. All wait for you."

She hugged him tightly. "But I'm afraid I'll never see you again."

"Do not be foolish, my dearest. You go only for a visit. A few months, a year, perhaps, and then you must return to Orchid Manor and tell me of all you have seen."

Sapphire nodded because she knew that was what he needed, but she knew as well as her father that if she returned in a year's time, he would no longer be here. "I love you, Papa," she whispered.

"I have loved you always. Remember that."

She lowered her chin to allow him to kiss her forehead as she took in the scent of his clothing and his fine cigars, one last time. Then she turned away and walked up the gangplank to board the ship, her head held high, as befitted the daughter of an English lord.

4

One month later

"Lord Wessex, so glad to make your acquaintance at last."

Blake turned from the open window in the law offices that looked out on the busy London street, and settled his gaze on the short, stout barrister walking toward him. "Mr. Stowe," he said sharply, ignoring the barrister's thrust out hand, "I am not accustomed to waiting."

"My apologies, my lord." Lowering his head in a cordial bow, Stowe continued. "There was a distraught widow on my doorstep this morning. I couldn't turn her out."

"We had an appointment, nine sharp." Blake brushed past Mr. Stowe and the bespectacled clerk seated uneasily behind a high mahogany desk.

"Right this way, my lord." Stowe bustled by, leading

him down a short hall into a spacious office paneled
with dark walnut wainscoting and two walls of floor-
to-ceiling bookshelves filled with leather-bound legal
volumes. "Please have a seat."

Blake glanced down at the red leather wingback chair
in front of an elegantly carved walnut desk large
enough to accommodate a small dinner party. The barrister had good taste, at least. Blake had a desk similar
to this in his own office back in Boston. "A Dresden
Partners pedestal desk," he said, nodding with approval. "Ebonized molding, very fine."

"Th-thank you, my lord." Stowe hesitated, seemingly
startled by Blake's compliment. Then he walked behind
his desk, flipping back the tails of his black serge coat,
and waited to take his seat until Blake sat first. "It was
my father's, God rest his soul."

Blake eased into the chair and caught a faint scent of
good French tobacco on the red leather, a scent as tan-
talizing as a woman's. It was a chair he wouldn't mind
adding to his own collection. He'd lived in the mansion
he'd built in the exclusive Beacon Hill area of Boston for
nearly two years, but it was still not entirely furnished.
He liked to choose his furnishings carefully, taking consideration with each and every chair, table and chest of
drawers. It was how he preferred to acquire all of his
possessions.

"Your father was obviously a prosperous man, and I
can see you have followed in his footsteps." Blake sat
back, pinched the fine pleats of his black wool trousers
and crossed one leg over the other. "But your firm did
not come recommended by my associates here in Great
Britain. No one had even heard of you when I placed in-

quiries. Have you the sense it takes a man to get out of the driving rain? I haven't the time for incompetence."

The barrister offered a hesitant smile, obviously unsure how to take measure of Blake Thixton, the new Earl of Wessex.

"I can assure you, my lord, that I am quite competent." Stowe brought his hands together, settling into his chair. "And now the estate can be settled." He picked up a pair of round-framed gold reading glasses and pushed them onto his nose before reaching for a pile of documents on his desk. "As stated in my letter, some months ago when Lord Wessex died without issue, his chattels were passed on to you, his closest heir by blood as the grandson of his uncle."

Blake's gaze drifted beyond Stowe to the shelves of books behind him. "I never knew Lord Wessex, sir, and while I was born in London, my parents immigrated to America before I was old enough to walk."

"Funny how that is, sometimes. Makes no difference to the law, though. By the laws of English entailment, you are the legal heir of the late Earl of Wessex." He skimmed the document written with great flourishes as if it was the first time he had seen it. "There is the title, of course."

Blake frowned. "Of little use in America. My business acquaintances are more interested in the volume of their merchandise I can ship than what titles I hold in *society* in London." Tenting his fingers, he settled his gaze on the barrister.

"The title stands throughout the world, my lord. Many Englishmen now living abroad—"

"What is there besides the title? I'm not impressed

with the pretenses of society on any continent. Is there land, Mr. Stowe? Land is something that lasts. Are there coal mines? Gold bullion, perhaps?"

Stowe's eyes darted upward, over the edge of the document and then quickly down again. "Land, yes." He cleared his throat. "A lovely town house on the fashionable West Side of London. Very nice. I had the pleasure of attending several balls there and more than one card game."

"I don't gamble," Blake said, unsmiling.

"And a country estate in...hmm, let me see." Stowe set a page aside and began to skim the next. "Yes, here it is. Cedar Mount, in...Surrey." He continued to study the paper in front of him but said nothing more.

Blake allowed a full minute of silence to pass, then another, thinking about the many business ventures he'd left behind in Boston to come to London and claim this inheritance. He'd have wasted six weeks' time on this trip by the time all was said and done, and now Stowe was going to tell him that the picture he had painted in his letters was not quite as rosy as he had suggested. Blake shifted his gaze back to Stowe. It was beginning to seem that the only good thing about this trip was the fact that he'd gotten away from Clarice for a few weeks.

"The money, Stowe," Blake said, making an effort to keep his temper in check.

"Two hundred fifty-two pound."

"That's it? That's all the money Wessex had when he died?"

"Of debt. He was two hundred fifty-two pounds *in debt.*"

"Repeat that last remarkable phrase one last time."

"Of debt…"

"Of debt?" Blake exploded, coming out of the chair and slamming both palms on the desktop.

Stowe blinked but did not startle. Blake had to admire him for that. There weren't many men who could look him in the eyes after one of his outbursts.

"But the properties are fine ones," Stowe offered.

Blake sat down again, this time only on the edge of the leather chair. "I don't have time to sell real estate. I told you my trip would be brief. I have a shipping business to run in Boston."

"I…I'm certain arrangements could be made…I could sell the properties for you or you could hire a land broker, but…but there is the issue of the family."

"The family? What family?"

Blake presently had no family of his own and found the entire concept bothersome in general. He knew marriage was inevitable and he did hope to have a son one day to pass the business to, but so far he had done an admirable job of sidestepping any serious relationships—including one with his closest business associate's eldest daughter, Clarice. It wasn't that he didn't like women; he adored them. He adored them elegantly dressed for the dinner table and then elegantly undressed in his bed, preferably not speaking. He also liked maids, cooks, seamstresses, and even preferred them because they never possessed any expectations beyond their own immediate pleasure. They had no delusions that a smile or a pleasant word or a tumble in bed would lead to a marriage proposal and a mansion on the bay.

"I have no family!" Blake fumed.

"The late earl's family, the Countess of Wessex and her three daughters by her late first husband—Lady Camille Stillmore, Lady Portia Stillmore and Lady Alma Stillmore."

"You apparently know the family well enough to rattle off the names without looking them up, which means the countess has been here to see you. Perhaps she was even the distraught widow on your doorstep this morning? And the late earl made no arrangements for his wife and stepdaughters, should he predecease them?" Blake asked, again barely keeping his temper balanced.

"My lord," Stowe said delicately, "rarely do men think they are going to die. Some even fear that if they do make preparations, it will hurry them on their way."

Blake smiled and looked away. It was truer than he or any man cared to admit. His own father, a cold, hard man but an astute entrepreneur, had died without leaving a will or any means to support his wife, Blake's stepmother. Had it not been for Blake, she would have been penniless and on the street, because like his English father before him, Josiah Thixton had left all he possessed to his eldest. Not that Blake begrudged his stepmother one penny of his inheritance—he saw that she continued to live in the manner in which she was accustomed until she died—but he had always wondered why his father had not guaranteed that.

Blake looked across the desk to find the barrister staring at him. He chuckled and slid back in the chair. "So there is debt, two properties and a gaggle of penniless, hysterical women—is that what you're telling me, old boy?"

Stowe hesitated, then sat back in his chair, removing

his wire-frame glasses. "I might have presented the tidings more delicately, my lord, but that is an accurate assessment indeed."

"Why do you stand here, monsieur?"

Armand turned absently from the window, where rain trickled down the glass in rivulets, to look at the native girl standing quietly behind him. He'd found Tarasai quite by accident in the village. She was lovely, bright and, most importantly, she pleased him, not only in his bed, but in conversation. She had a gentle way about her and seemed to know instinctively when to speak and when to be silent.

"They are in London by now if they have not run into trouble on the voyage across the Atlantic."

"The weather has been good, monsieur," she said in a soft, lilting voice. "And the ship that carried them across the sea was a good one. Your *chères filles* are well, I feel it in my bones."

She hugged herself and he could not help but smile. Then he coughed a dry, racking cough and she was at his side at once, one hand on his back, the other on his chest.

When the fit subsided, he stood again and reached into his pocket to take his handkerchief and wipe his mouth. "Ah, Tarasai, I am so tired, so very tired."

"You should not worry so, monsieur. It is not good for your health."

Slipping the handkerchief back into his pocket, he looked at her. "I am afraid it was wrong of me to send them away. Selfish of me. They were happy here. It should have been enough, *n'est-ce pas?*"

She slipped her small hand into his. "It was time for

your *beau papillon* to be set free, monsieur. She was too big for this island, too full of *la vie*. Her future waits for her there across the ocean, a life of adventure and happiness."

He sighed. "I hope you're right, Tarasai. I will never forgive myself if she comes to harm through my ambitions for her."

"I know that I am right," she said softly. "It is in the stars."

"Your coat and top, sir?" The butler met Jessup Stowe in the front hall of the prominent men's club.

"Yes, thank you, Calvin." Jessup gave himself a shake as he handed the servant his umbrella, then his top hat and drenched overcoat. "Still coming down pretty hard out there," he remarked as he smoothed his thinning gray hair with the palm of his hand.

"Yes, sir. Your table is ready, Mr. Stowe, and Mr. Barker already awaits your company."

"Thank you, Calvin." Jessup pulled his slightly rumpled waistcoat down over his stomach, thinking that either the striped fabric was shrinking or he was gaining weight. "And thank you for taking those wet things."

The butler nodded, backing up. "I can show you to your table, sir, if you'd just like to—"

"I've been eating at that table six nights a week for the past seven years since Mrs. Stowe died, Calvin. Surely I can find it." Jessup started to turn away and then turned back, snapping his fingers. "Calvin, one more thing."

"Sir?"

"It's possible, though not probable, that I might have a guest coming. A Lord Wessex."

The butler looked at him oddly.

"The *new* Lord Wessex, the earl's heir," Jessup explained with a wry smile.

"I see, sir."

"He's an American and doesn't know his way around London, so I think he might be a bit out of sorts tonight."

"I'll show him to your table at once, Mr. Stowe, should he appear."

Looking both ways to be sure no one was watching, Jessup slipped a coin from the small pocket of his waistcoat and handed it to the butler. "I know Mr. Porter prefers we not tip personally," Jessup said quietly, "so just between you and me. You're always so kind to me, Calvin. Kinder than any of my sons has ever been."

"Yes, sir. Thank you, sir." Calvin took one last step back, then turned, pleased and trying not to show it, and hurried down the hall.

His waistcoat reasonably straight, Jessup walked into the parlor of the prominent though slightly threadbare men's club frequented by barristers like himself. He nodded to several gentlemen at the bar and proceeded to the dining room beyond. His old friend, Clyde Barker, also a widower, was already at the table, already on his first glass of scotch.

"Jessup." The ruddy-faced man rose, his legs appearing a bit unsteady.

"Clyde, good to see you." He clasped his friend's hand and then moved closer to wrap his arm around Clyde's shoulder. "I look forward all week to Fridays, just to see your ugly face."

"And I the same." Clyde grinned, taking his seat at the table covered with white linen and set with crystal.

The waiter caught Jessup's eye as he sat down and headed for the bar when Jessup nodded.

"So how was your day, old friend? Not too tedious, I hope."

"Not at all." Jessup settled in the comfortable, high-backed brocade chair and stretched his legs out beneath the table. "I had the pleasure of meeting with the new Earl of Wessex."

"Really?" Clyde set down his glass and leaned closer, always one for a bit of gossip. "They say he's an American, a cousin of the last earl. Mrs. Barker's brother Barton knows a business associate who's dealt with him. In shipping, I think." He chuckled, which wrinkled his aged face. "Astute businessman but a real bastard, he says." His eyes crinkled. "And rumor has it that he's quite a man with the ladies...."

Jessup glanced up as the waiter set down a glass of bourbon. One a night was all Jessup allowed himself, as he had promised his beloved Emma on her deathbed. In the grave or not, he would remain true to his promises—not just because he'd loved her, but because he feared if he didn't, the old bird would punish him when he met her at the pearly gates.

"I don't know. He seemed a pleasant enough chap." Jessup shrugged.

Clyde stared shrewdly, still leaning on the table. "Really? That's not what the tone of your voice says."

Jessup took up his glass. "Well, I'll confess he is an interesting character. A very bold young man, very sure of himself."

"Like all the Thixtons." Clyde sat back with satisfaction and reached for his glass. "Well, except for Edward's father, Charles. Did you know him? Now, *there* was a bastard." He lifted his glass thoughtfully. "You know what they say about bad traits skipping a generation."

"The American is a distant cousin, not in the direct family line."

"Still, you know what they say." Clyde smiled and lifted his glass higher in a toast. "To good friends."

"Good friends," Jessup echoed.

Clyde took a long sip before setting his glass down. "I already ordered the trout and parsnips. Should be along anytime."

"Excellent."

"And what did the American have to say when he discovered that what he inherited was mostly debt?"

Jessup frowned. He had suspected everyone in London society knew the state of Lord Wessex's affairs when he passed away. They always knew. "You know very well I cannot reveal the details of the conversation I had with a client."

"That bad, was it? They say he has a temper."

Jessup folded his hands on his lap. "I saw no temper demonstrated in my office. Lord Wessex was a complete gentleman." *Not exactly a lie, Emma.*

"Does that mean he hasn't met the old biddy Countess of Wessex and her ugly ducklings yet? I hear they're staying in town."

"Oh dear," Jessup mumbled, taking the linen napkin from his lap to wipe his mouth. "I sent him to the town house to stay, thinking the countess was still in the country."

Clyde laughed and reached for his nearly empty glass. "Oh, to be a fly on that wall. Do you think she's already proposed marriage between the American and her eldest shrew, or do you think she'll lay her cap for him herself?" He winked. "She might just have it in her, you know. Some say it was the threat of scandal that made Edward marry her in the first place. Gossip she actually set in motion to ensnare him."

"Oh dear," Jessup muttered again. "Dear me, I've made a muck of this, haven't I."

"Charles." Clyde waved to the waiter. "Another round for us both. I believe Mr. Stowe may be feeling a little faint," he finished, highly amused.

Jessup laid his hand over the top of his glass. "Dear, dear me."

"Stowe."

Jessup saw the American striding toward him, looking none too pleased.

Jessup grabbed his napkin and pushed away from the table to stand up. "My lord."

The Earl of Wessex was dressed handsomely in a black overcoat and white silk neckerchief over a black evening coat and striped white waistcoat. He carried his top hat in his hand, and was brushing back a wisp of dark hair that had fallen across his forehead.

"How…how kind of you to join me," Jessup said. "Please, let me introduce you to—"

"They're there, did you know that?" Blake demanded. "The countess and her daughters three, but it seemed like three hundred when they all assaulted me at once with their chatter and batting of eyelashes. I thought I'd suffocate from the scent of their rose toilet water."

"Would…would you care to join me and my friend Mr. Barker for dinner? We've not yet been served."

"What I want is to know is why you sent me to that town house knowing those women were there?" Blake demanded.

"I was not aware of that, my lord. I apologize for not checking again. Last week when I received the message that you'd be arriving, I had the town house in Mayfair opened up and aired and servants hired in anticipation of your arrival. The countess must have come to London since."

Blake tightened his grip on his thoroughly wet hat and looked away, giving himself a moment to let his anger subside. They were in a dining room of one of the many gentlemen's clubs in the city. This one appeared old and well-established, and though it was not as well-furnished as some he had visited in Boston and abroad, it did have a certain air about it. The scent of tobacco and hickory wood seemed to permeate the air of the dark-paneled rooms.

"I truly apologize for the inconvenience," Mr. Stowe repeated, pulling himself up to his full height, which was still nearly a head shorter than Lord Wessex's.

Blake scowled, but he was not as angry as he had been when he stormed out of the town house into the rain and had been unable to hail a carriage for a full block. "I suppose it could not be helped."

"No, my lord, it could not be," Stowe answered firmly. "If you wish, I shall bring about proceedings first thing tomorrow morning to have the countess removed from your property."

Blake caught sight of the butler hovering in the doorway. "Get me a scotch," he grunted.

"Certainly, my lord." The man rushed forward.

"Could I take your wet things now, my lord, and then bring you a meal, as well?"

Blake handed him his hat and the scarf and coat. "Thank you, but nothing to eat. Just the scotch. I've another engagement, but I think I'd best fortify myself before I go."

"Yes, my lord." Calvin bowed. "Just let me get you a chair, my lord."

"I can get my own," Blake grumbled, grabbing an upholstered chair from the nearest empty table. "Nice to make your acquaintance, Barker." He placed the chair at the linen-set table and thrust out his hand to shake Barker's. "I suppose you're a barrister, too. You've got the same barreled abdomen as Stowe and a dozen like you. Comes from sitting behind that desk all day."

"Yes, my lord." Mr. Barker pumped Blake's hand enthusiastically, and all three men took their seats.

"Damn it, tell me what the hell I'm to do now, Stowe. And don't tell me it's my prerogative to throw these women out on the street." Blake gave his head a shake. "I knew I should never have made this journey. I knew it would be nothing but trouble." He accepted the glass the bartender brought him and impolitely lifted it to his lips, not waiting for the other two men before he drank. "Tell me what you advise concerning the countess and her frog spawn, else they'll be sleeping in your bed tonight, sir."

After two scotches, Blake was able to catch a hackney—even in the rain—thanks to the butler at the men's club. He arrived at the address of one of his business associates more than two hours beyond the engraved invitation's specified time, but was nonetheless greeted by a flurry of activity and fuss. He had gained overnight status as a celebrity of sorts and everyone addressed him as Lord Wessex. The party was in celebration of his associate Mr. Todd Warrington's daughter's eighteenth birthday, but Blake barely gave her a moment's notice beyond propriety's perfunctory waltz. He preferred his women a little older, and certainly more experienced.

A brandy in his hand, Blake wandered out onto the granite balcony that overlooked a lush garden. The rain had stopped and a crescent moon had risen high in the sky. As he gazed upward he realized that the night sky was different here in Europe, different in a way that made him yearn for Boston.

"Good evening."

Blake turned at the soft voice to see a woman close to his own age dressed in a pale pink gown, her light blond hair upswept in an elaborate coiffure, a heavy string of pearls hanging above a well-rounded bosom. He immediately understood the tone of her voice due to his many late-night balcony experiences, with women who stood alone in the darkness while a lively party ensued inside. They were sad women, vulnerable.

"Good evening," he replied with a smile.

Hesitantly, she moved toward him, offering her hand. "Elizabeth Barclay...Mrs. Williams," she corrected herself, as if on second thought.

"Blake Thixton." He took her hand, kissing it...lingering. She smelled of lilacs and utter femininity.

"I know who you are, Lord Wessex."

When he lifted his head, he saw that she was smiling at him. Not exactly a coy smile, but an honest one, a sad one. He had read her tone correctly.

"And I believe I know you, Mrs. Williams. New York, right? Your husband is Jefferson Williams, in iron?" He recalled meeting Williams once in New York City, an ugly man twice his wife's age with an even uglier disposition.

"That's correct." She withdrew her bare hand; she wasn't wearing gloves like all the other women.

"Your husband is here in London on business?"

She nodded, coming to stand beside him to gaze down into the garden below. She shivered, and Blake reached out to draw her matching silk wrap around her bare shoulders. When she turned, her mouth rested half open, as if longing to be kissed by someone younger than sixty.

Blake set his brandy on the balcony's rail and drew her against him with the arm he had raised to cover her shoulders. She gasped and stiffened in surprise as he touched his lips to hers, but when his tongue entered her mouth, she surrendered.

Blake knew Elizabeth Williams had never made love to a stranger on a balcony, but he had done so many times. Holding her in his arms, covering her mouth, her neck, her breasts with hot kisses, he led her to the darkest corner of the balcony, beyond the musicians' waltz and the bright gas lamps that flanked the double doors that led inside to the ballroom.

Elizabeth struggled for breath, clearly shocked by her reaction to him. He thrust his hand into the bodice of her pink gown and felt her nipples harden instantly at his touch. She moaned. She was starved for a man's touch. He lowered his head, taking one nipple between his lips and tugged gently with his teeth.

She groaned aloud, leaning against the damp stone

wall, both arms above her head in utter surrender to her need. Lifting her skirts without further preliminaries, he pulled aside her silk encumbrances, penetrated her roughly and deeply, and satisfied them both.

Only afterward, as he fastened his wool trousers and smoothed her silk skirts and bodice, did he see a single tear slip down her pale face.

"Don't cry," he murmured as he kissed her cheek.

"I...I've never done this before," she said breathlessly.

"You're a beautiful woman, a woman whose needs must be met—"

"Mrs. Williams, are you here?" called an older gentleman.

She flinched at the sound of the door opening onto the balcony.

Blake kissed her, whispering against her lips. "Come see me in Boston."

By the time Mr. Jefferson Williams stepped onto the balcony to retrieve his wife, Blake was at the rail again, sipping his brandy, looking into the garden. If Williams saw him, he paid him no mind.

"Are you ready to go, Mrs. Williams? I have an early morning appointment."

"Yes, of course, Mr. Williams."

The hem of her gown almost brushed Blake's polished boot as she glided past him. Either Mr. Williams didn't see him or he didn't care what his wife did on balconies with strangers.

Blake smiled. Yet another reason to be in no hurry to wed...

5

"Ah, there you are, *ma chère.*" Lucia swept into the bedchamber Sapphire and Angelique were sharing on the third floor of Lord and Lady Carlisle's town house near Charing Cross, dressed for the afternoon in a pale green and lavender barege gown, gloves and a beribboned straw bonnet. "Are you certain you won't join Lady Carlisle and me for tea at Lady Morrow's?"

"No, thank you, Auntie." Sapphire glanced up from her book of Lord Byron's poetry, trying to appear fatigued. "I'm afraid I'm still tired. My horseback ride this morning with Lord Carlisle was long and I think I'd rather just stay here and cozy up with my book."

"Very well, puss." Lucia sighed as she adjusted her new bonnet with its upturned brim that made her look years younger. "I can stay with you if you like, though. I don't really want to go visit with Lady Morrow. Nearly a month on the ship with her was enough to last me a lifetime, but I was just going so we could stop at the Royal Exchange on the way home."

Sapphire, wearing a ruffled, ribboned blue dressing gown, was seated in a chair under the window, her legs tucked beneath her. "Don't be silly, Auntie. I wouldn't want you to stay on my behalf, especially when you have the chance to shop." She smiled mischievously.

"Well, I suppose Angelique will be here with you should you need anything."

"Mmm-hmm," Sapphire intoned, pretending to read again.

"Where is Angelique, anyway?"

"I believe she might be taking a walk in the gardens." Sapphire licked her fingertip and turned the page of the book without looking up. "Or did she say she was going to the stables to see those new kittens again? I can't recall."

"Well, all right." Lucia rested her hand on the glass doorknob. "You're certain you'll be fine?"

"Of course—now go and don't worry about me. A little reading, perhaps a nap, and I'll be fine by dinner." Sapphire smiled sweetly.

"All right, dear." Lucia opened the door to go, then turned back, her hand still on the doorknob. "I do hope this has nothing to do with my not allowing you to go immediately to Lord Wessex's residence. I understand your impatience with wanting to meet your father, but we've not even been here a full day and there are channels to follow, society rules to oblige. This is far too important to make a muck of it."

"I understand. You're right, absolutely right." Sapphire turned another page and reached for her teacup on the table beside her. "Have fun, and do buy yourself a hat. The one you're wearing today is delightful."

The door closed and Sapphire glanced up over the

top of her book, listening as her guardian's footsteps echoed in the hallway, then down the stairs. She took a deep breath, still listening, as she rose and set the book down, using a piece of wide hair ribbon to mark her place.

Walking to the bed, she knelt, pulled her mother's old leather casket out and gently lifted the lid. Smiling tenderly, she drew her fingers over the brittle love letters given to her mother by her father when they were courting—letters she had reread a hundred times during the journey to London. Also inside was her mother's locket, worn in her days in New Orleans, and a small curl of Sapphire's auburn hair. Deeper in the small, leather-bound trunk she found pressed flowers, a tiny silver hairbrush that had been Sapphire's as a baby and one of Armand's old handkerchiefs. Digging beneath the lining at the bottom of the casket, her fingers found the velvet bag she sought. Sitting back on her knees, she opened the drawstrings of the bag and lifted the cold, smooth gem from the soft folds of the fabric.

Sapphire's breath caught in her throat as she lifted the jewel toward the window and the sunlight struck it, lighting it with a blue brilliance that was almost blinding. After all these years, she was going to meet her father....

"But I think our meeting will not be what you imagined, Mama," she said, pressing a kiss to the glittering jewel. "I've a thing or two to say to this man, I'll warrant you." She eased the sapphire into the black velvet bag, tightened the string and returned it beneath the casket's worn burgundy velvet lining, so that even if a nosy servant did open the box, she would never suspect the treasure hidden inside. To the unknowing eye, the old, battered leather casket looked simply like a box of worthless female keepsakes.

Sapphire pushed the trunk back under the bed and got to her feet, her fingers untying the ribbons of her dressing gown. Confident Lucia was in Lady Carlisle's carriage by now, she stripped off the gown to reveal the dress she'd bought as soon as they'd arrived in London, the dress she would wear when she confronted her father.

Sapphire placed the dressing gown on the bed and turned toward the floor-length oval mirror. The dress was actually of two pieces, a skirt and a front-buttoning jacket with a short basque in a brilliant jewel-blue challis. The sleeves were narrow, as was the latest fashion, and dainty new square-toed black leather boots peeked from beneath her petticoats.

She smiled at her reflection, knowing that the moment her father saw her eyes—one blue, one green like his—he would know who she was.

But she realized she had no time to waste if she was going to escape the house undetected, meet Lord Wessex, and then be back before Lucia and Lady Carlisle returned. She went in search of the bonnet she wanted to wear. It was her plan not to tell Lucia what she had done, and then, when they were formally introduced according to the plans Lady Carlisle and Lucia were making, there would be no scene. Once she had given him a piece of her mind privately—out of respect for her mother and Armand—she would be cordial, if not remote, publicly.

The door opened as Sapphire lowered her bonnet over her auburn curls, and she whipped around to see Angelique walk in, her dark hair mussed and the bodice of her peach-colored day gown slightly rumpled.

"What do you think you're doing?" Angelique demanded.

Sapphire turned to the mirror, adjusting the hat before drawing the ribbons under her neck. "Me? What about you? What do you think *you've* been doing? Though why I bother to ask, I don't know."

Angelique sighed and threw herself on the bed. "His name is Robert and he's the stable master's eldest son. He thinks I'm the most beautiful woman he's ever seen."

Sapphire glanced doubtfully at her companion, then back at the mirror, attempting to achieve just the right tilt of her bonnet. "We spoke of this before we left Martinique, Angel," she chastised. "You cannot kiss every young man you run into."

"And why not? I won't be in nearly as much trouble for kissing Robert if I get caught as you will be for sneaking off to Lord Wessex's."

"I'm not sneaking." Sapphire spun around. "I'm walking right out the front hall, out the front door and hiring a hackney to take me to Mayfair."

"Does Aunt Lucia know you're going?"

Sapphire frowned as she opened the drawer of a chifforobe to retrieve a pair of scented travel gloves.

"Are you going to tell her where you've been when you return?"

Sapphire didn't answer.

"Then you're sneaking."

"He's my father, Angel. I will not have our first encounter in front of hundreds of people at some formal ball or another."

"Let me go with you, then."

"You're not going with me." Sapphire traversed the

bedchamber to the door, tucking a stray pincurl beneath her bonnet. "You're going to stay here and cover for me in case my father and I fall into a lengthy conversation and lose track of the time." She glanced back at Angel. "Although I think that is highly unlikely, considering what I have to say to him."

"Just don't say I didn't warn you. Aunt Lucia is going to be furious." Angelique followed her into the hallway. "Are you nervous?"

Sapphire shook her head, biting down on the soft flesh of her inner lip. It was a lie, of course, even Angel knew it, but saying she wasn't nervous somehow made her feel stronger, bolder. "Cover for me if you must, but don't get yourself in trouble. I wouldn't ask that you lie for me." Sapphire gave her friend a quick peck on the cheek and, seeing the third-story hall was empty, hurried for the staircase, raising a gloved hand in farewell. "I'll be back before you know it."

London was noisy, smelly, dirty and deafening. There were so many sights to see—churches, elegant town houses, narrow shops, public buildings—that she couldn't decide where to look next. Throngs crowded the streets: butchers' boys carrying huge sections of beef, mutton and pork; ladies' maids hurrying by on errands; beggars; plump merchants' wives; clergymen; farmers in wooden clogs and straw hats; bewigged judges and uniformed soldiers, all threading their way past riders on horseback, hackneys, carriages, ale wagons and wicker carts, not to mention the stray dogs, pigs and occasional chicken. The carriage ride from Charing Cross to the fashionable West End of London was not nearly as long as Sapphire would have liked, and before she knew it her coachman reined in his horse in front of the marble steps of an elegant town house— one she had discreetly discovered was her father's home when he was in the city.

"Would you like me to wait, miss?" the driver called from the high seat of his hackney.

Sapphire put on a false smile, lifted her chin a notch and tried to imagine how an earl's daughter would behave around common working men. "No, thank you, sir. Good day." She passed him what she hoped was the correct fee for his service.

He grinned, tugged at his forelock and nodded. "Thank'ee, miss." Then he cracked his whip over the horse's back and the hired carriage rolled away, leaving her no choice but to lift the ornate lion's-head knocker on the paneled walnut door that was wide enough for two broad-shouldered men to pass through side by side.

The door was opened almost at once, startling her.

"May I help you?" a slender, middle-aged footman in a spotless black coat inquired, looking down at her through the lenses of his eyeglasses.

"Yes, thank you, sir." Sapphire felt as if she couldn't breathe as she stepped into the front hall without waiting to be asked. "I'm here to see Lord Wessex." She was amazed how true and clear her voice sounded; it was without a hint of waver.

"And may I ask who is calling?"

Sapphire could tell by his tone of voice that he did not approve of her arrival without a proper invitation. In the day they had been in London, she had learned that English society life was quite different from the laissez-faire existence in Martinique among the wealthy French and English landowners. Here, there were rules concerning proper etiquette for visiting involving calling cards, morning invitations and evening invitations and even the length of sleeve appropriate. It was her lack of a proper calling card, presently at the printers, that probably made the footman suspicious of her.

"His daughter." She smiled sweetly.

The footman could not hide his surprise. "Miss?"

"You ask who calls on Lord Wessex. I am his daughter." She plucked off a glove, amazed at how easily she could fall into the role of Lady Sapphire Thixton. "Please tell him that I'm here. I haven't but a moment."

The butler gave a half bow, still looking as if he did not believe her. "Would you care to sit down while I see if his lordship is available?" He indicated a row of white and gold brocade chairs along one wall of the large, ornate receiving hall.

"No, thank you." She hoped he would interpret her smile to mean he should hurry along.

"One moment, miss."

He bowed again and disappeared through an arched doorway. The town house did not appear especially large from the outside, but she could now see that it was immense. Her father was not only titled, but obviously quite a wealthy man.

Sapphire exhaled slowly, pressing her hand to the knot in her abdomen, staring at the huge formal portraits of balding men that lined the walls.

Only a moment more, she told herself, *and we'll meet face-to-face.*

* * *

Blake heard the first knock at the door to the study but ignored it. The knock came again and he peered up irritably from behind the desk that had belonged to the late Lord Wessex. "Yes, what is it that is so urgent?" he barked. "Did I not say less than half an hour ago that I did not wish to be disturbed unless the house was aflame? I don't care what color livery the footmen wear today and I don't care if we have the eel pie or the tripe soup because I will not be dining in this house tonight! Not if it were the last table of food on God's earth," he finished.

The paneled study door opened and the butler, Preston, stood at attention, his eyes downcast, until Blake completed his string of insults. "My lord."

"Yes?" Blake groaned.

"There is someone to see you here, my lord."

"Who?" He half rose from the chair, pressing the heels of his hands into the polished wood of the desk.

"A young lady, my lord, who says…"

"She says what, Preston? Come, now, I grow old before your eyes."

"She says she is your *daughter,* my lord."

"My daughter?" Blake exploded. "I haven't got a damn daughter. What in God's name—" He broke off before completing the sentence when he realized what was going on.

Word apparently spread fast in London when it came to inheritances, and people had been pouring out of the woodwork all week, claiming the previous earl owed them money. Perhaps a few *were* owed, considering the state of Edward Thixton IV's accounts, but mostly these scavengers were on his doorstep hoping to take advantage of a grieving widow or an aged, addlepated heir.

"Would you like me to turn her away, sir?"

Blake thought for a moment as he tightened the tie of the silk dressing gown he wore over a pair of silk trousers. The earl's daughter? At least this claim was more inventive than an unpaid receipt for a wig or an evening coat. "No, no, Preston, I'll take care of this one myself." He wasn't properly clothed to receive a caller, but he didn't care.

"Right this way, miss," the footman said as he led Sapphire down a hall and into a receiving parlor.

She couldn't help but take in the room, the walls painted a pale green, the heavy drapes in stripes of a complementary hue. The furniture was old but well kept and far more attractive and elegant than some of the newer styles she had seen in the Carlisles' home. She sighed, then whispered to herself, "I'm here, Mama, at last."

"His lordship will be in directly," the footman said, backing through the doorway and closing the double pocketed mahogany doors behind him.

Sapphire turned toward one wall to study a large seascape hung in a gilt frame. She could just make out the name *E. Thixton* scrawled in the bottom right corner of the painting. It was really quite good. Had her father painted it? Taking a step closer, she admired the bold strokes of blue and green that seemed to bring the sea pounding against the rocky shore to life.

The doors behind Sapphire slid open and she turned.

For a moment, Blake found himself speechless. Preston had said it was a girl come to call, claiming to be the daughter of the Earl of Wessex, but he had fully expected a malnourished chit with bad teeth, dressed in a cheap gown and ugly hat.

But standing before him was a full woman with glossy dark red hair, an expensive, fashionable gown and eyes he would fantasize about for many nights to come. She had the creamiest, most luscious skin, with a sprinkling of freckles across her straight nose and a charming chin with the slightest cleft. But it was her mouth, even more than her shocking eyes or lustrous hair, that mesmerized him most. Hers was the mouth of a courtesan—perfectly shaped with a thin upper lip and a full, sensuous lower lip, a mouth his own suddenly ached to taste.

Only when she blinked was Blake jolted back to reality.

"What do you think you're doing?" he demanded.

"Pardon me?" she replied angrily, her mind racing in confusion. He was young, certainly too young to be her father, who would be close to fifty. Who was this rude man and what was he doing in her father's house?

"You heard me," he said as he strode in. He was a shockingly handsome man, perhaps ten or twelve years older than she was, with a shock of ebony hair and the most intense brown eyes she had ever seen.

"I suppose I should ask you the same thing." She took a step toward him, lifting her chin as she crossed her arms over her fitted jacket.

"I don't know who you are or what you want but I will not tolerate any false claims from fortune hunters or thieves. Now, whatever you might believe is owed to you will be paid, if it is indeed owed to you," he said. "I will provide you with the name and location of my barrister and all bills will be submitted to him and only him. I'll not pay a pence until your claim is investigated."

Sapphire stepped back. The man's words didn't make sense. Who was he calling a fortune hunter and what bills was he talking about?

"What have you to say for yourself, young lady?"

The stranger strode across the room. He was so close, she could smell his shaving lotion and the masculine scent of his skin.

"Who are you?" she asked. "I'm looking for Lord Wessex, the Earl of Wessex who owns this house."

"*I* am Lord Wessex, and I am the owner of the property, young lady. Now I suggest you remove yourself from said property before I call the constable."

Sapphire made a sound of protest but it caught in her throat. "No, you can't be the Earl of Wessex! My father is the Earl of Wessex, Edward Thixton."

He scowled. "The late Edward Thixton, Earl of Wessex, had no issue."

She stared at Blake. "Where is he?" she heard herself whisper.

"The graveyard, I suppose. Now go," he said coldly as he stepped aside. "Make haste and I won't call the constable, but if you attempt to appropriate money from me or this estate again, it will be off to Newgate Prison with you."

Sapphire looked up once more at Blake and her eyes became cloudy with tears. Confused, hurt beyond reason, she stumbled forward and ran for the door. She rushed down the hallway and out the broad front door, ignoring the footman as he tried to call a carriage for her.

She rounded the corner, halting to grasp the pole of a gas lamp on the stone-paved walk. "He's dead," she murmured as she squeezed her eyes shut in disbelief. "Oh, Mama, he's dead."

6

"There, there," Lucia said, sitting on the edge of the four-poster bed, smoothing back Sapphire's hair. "Would you like me to get you a cup of tea, perhaps even a little sherry?"

"No, I'm fine, really." Sapphire dabbed at her tear-swollen eyes with a sodden handkerchief. "I'm sorry, Auntie. I've behaved badly." She sniffed. "You shouldn't sit here with me any longer. You should go to the theater with Lady Carlisle as you'd planned."

"Nonsense. What reason does an old woman like me have to go to the theater? It's nothing but a place to see and be seen." She pushed a dry handkerchief into Sapphire's hand. "And what's even more nonsensical is you thinking there's anything wrong with having a good cry. You've just been told that your father passed away. I'd think something ailed you if you didn't cry. I'm only sorry that Lord Carlisle didn't hear at his men's club until this afternoon after I'd left the house."

Sapphire dabbed at her eyes again and stared up at the painted white ceiling above the bed. It was almost dark outside and Angelique had pulled the pale blue damask draperies across the windows and lit two oil lamps, which now cast shadows on the ceiling.

"Remember what it was like when your mother died?" Angelique sat on the other side of the bed. "We cried for days."

"I know, but that was Mama. I...don't know why I'm so upset when I didn't even know my father. I'd never even seen his face and it's not as if I was looking forward to it. I was so angry at him for what he did to my mother that mostly I think I just wanted to tell him how much I despised him."

"*Non, ma petite!* How many times do I have to remind you that your mother was very clear that she didn't think Edward ever knew what happened to her."

"I don't care. He *should* have known. If only that...that *man* in my father's house had not been so hateful to me," she said, her anger rising. "He was simply abominable."

"Abominable or not, it seems he is the heir to your father's estate. He is Blake Thixton, an American and a distant cousin of your father's, Lord Carlisle has learned." Lucia, dressed in elegant evening clothes, rose from the bed to walk to the table where she'd placed the bottle of sherry.

"An American?" Sapphire spat. "Why didn't Lord Carlisle know sooner?"

"Now, now, puss." Lucia poured herself a healthy dose of the sherry meant for her charge. "You cannot blame the messenger. We only arrived yesterday. How was Lord Carlisle to know? Edward passed away six

months ago of natural causes, but Lord and Lady Carlisle have been out of the country seven months, escorting the baron and baroness on their honeymoon tour of
Europe. And, truth be told, you would have heard of
your father's passing in a far gentler manner had you
not stubbornly gone against my wishes and set out on
your own to meet him."

Sapphire sat up on the bed and pushed her long hair
out of her face. "Why do you always say I'm stubborn
with that tone in your voice? After all, had Mama not
been stubborn, she might have met her demise those
first lonely days in New Orleans—alone, with child and
nowhere to live."

"Still, you don't want to go back to Martinique, do
you?" Angelique asked.

Sapphire glanced at her.

"I...I don't mean to sound selfish," Angelique went
on quickly. "And I'll fully admit I prefer to stay because
I like the excitement of London, but really, Sapphire,
what has changed? Yes, the Earl of Wessex has passed
on, but you're still his daughter."

"You're right, Angel. That fact hasn't changed, and
that detestable man cannot alter that."

"No, he cannot." Lucia lifted her cordial of sherry in
toast and took a sip.

"Of course, I have no legal right to my father's en-
tailed property. I'm female. English law doesn't allow
me to inherit from my father unless I am specifically
named in his will. Since he was unaware of my existence, it isn't possible that I have been."

"Why did you come, *ma chère?* Did you come to England for land or money?"

"I came because Mama—"

"That wasn't what I asked," Lucia interrupted as she approached the bed, the cut-crystal glass still in her hand. "I loved your mother as dearly as anyone, but you are Sophie's daughter and I know very well you did not come just to satisfy her dream."

Sapphire rested her hand on her forehead for a moment, taking time to think before she responded. Yesterday she had felt like a young woman, barely more than a child, and yet today…this evening, she felt years older. "I came because it was my mother's wish," she said evenly, "but I also came to satisfy my own desire to be acknowledged."

"And…"

She met Lucia's gaze. "I wanted him to acknowledge that my mother was indeed his legal wife, not for him to accept me as his daughter." She hesitated. "So I suppose, in a way, I did come for her, but not for the reasons she thought I would."

Lucia tipped her glass and smiled over the rim. "Now, there is the Sapphire I know."

"He's dead, I know, but I am still Lord Edward Wessex's daughter and Sophie Barkley was still his wife," Sapphire said, throwing her legs over the side of the bed. "And heir or not, that man must recognize me as such. He must make an announcement to London society and formally acknowledge me. Even upon my father's death and the passing of his title, I do possess the right to retain his name." Sapphire set her jaw with the stubbornness her aunt accused her of possessing. "Aunt Lucia, did Lord Carlisle not tell you that my father left a widow who is hosting a reception Saturday evening for her husband's American heir?"

"That he did!"

"How improper would it be for us to attend this reception?"

"I'm certain Lady Carlisle could acquire an invitation for us. It seems all of London society has received one since the dowager is apparently quite eager to show off the new heir. They say he is not only handsome, but quite wealthy."

"Why on earth would you want to attend a reception in honor of the man who has insulted you?" Angelique asked in surprise.

Sapphire turned to her companion, a furtive smile on her lips. "How else can I demand my title due me, but to see the knave again in person?"

"Are you certain you want to do this?" Aunt Lucia asked Sapphire, placing her ringed hand on her god-daughter's forearm as she emerged from the Carlisles' carriage.

Sapphire stared up at the doorway she'd run from less than a week earlier and swallowed hard. For days she'd been rehearsing what she would say to Mr. Blake Thixton, but all those words escaped her and she was left with nothing but her determination.

The great front doors opened and the same footman Sapphire had encountered previously appeared.

"Say the word and we'll go," Lucia whispered in Sapphire's ear. "Say the word and we'll be on the next steamer to Martinique, to Hong Kong, to California in America. You name the place, my dove, and we shall leave all this poppycock behind and go on the adventure of a lifetime."

Sapphire looked down at Lucia, her heart pounding in her chest. She felt that something was about to change, something that would alter her life forever. "I can never thank you enough for all you've done for me, but no, I have to do this. For Mama, for me."

Lucia gave her an understanding pat on the arm and turned toward the steps. Lord and Lady Carlisle had already entered the residence and the butler was now staring down at Sapphire and Lucia with great interest.

"Are we going in?" Angelique murmured, so excited she could barely contain herself.

Sapphire grasped the skirting of her new shoulder-baring apple-green silk gown and started up the steps. "Of course we're going in," she said confidently. "I haven't come this far to turn back now."

"The Viscount Carlisle," announced the footman stiffly. "Lady Carlisle."

Sapphire handed the footman her newly printed calling card so that she could be announced.

"Miss Fabergine."

Sapphire glided across the glittering hall and entered the receiving line behind Lord and Lady Carlisle, who were speaking with a painfully thin woman—the dowager Lady Wessex, her father's wife, she surmised. Sapphire smiled. The dowager had never legally been his wife because he had, until her death, still been married to Sophie.

"Miss Fabergine." The butler announced Angelique and then took Lucia's card. "Mademoiselle Toulouse."

Sapphire met Lucia's gaze over her shoulder one last

time, smiled and turned to be introduced formally to her father's so-called widow.

"And this is Miss Fabergine," Lady Carlisle said. "The young girl you and I spoke of, Lady Wessex. Her stepfather was such a dear, a handsome Frenchman. It would have been impossible for me to deny his request to escort his stepdaughter to London."

Sapphire curtsied. "Lady Wessex, thank you so kindly for the invitation."

The widow barely acknowledged her.

"And Lady Wessex's daughters," Lady Carlisle continued, moving down the receiving line. "The eldest, Miss Camille Stillmore."

Sapphire curtsied and smiled at the daughter who appeared to be a year or two older than herself and looked a great deal like her mother. She was most certainly not an attractive woman, and her pale ivory gown overrun with ruffles did not improve her appearance. "It's very nice to meet you."

Miss Stillmore glanced at Sapphire with the look she knew too well after being in London for two weeks. It was the look, Aunt Lucia had explained, that ugly English girls gave the pretty ones as they realized they were no match.

"Miss Portia and Miss Alma," Lady Carlisle said, completing the introductions.

The two younger girls, who were more comely than their elder sister, bobbed curtsies, seemingly more interested to meet the new arrival. Portia appeared to be the same age as Sapphire, and Alma only a year or two younger.

"It's very nice to make your acquaintance," Sapphire said, returning their smiles.

"Is he here?" Lady Carlisle asked the youngest daughter, leaning closer so as not to be overheard by those passing in the hall.

"*He,* my lady?"

"Why, Lord Wessex, of course," the older woman hissed under her breath. "I expected to meet him in the receiving line. That is why we were invited, was it not? To formally meet the new Earl of Wessex?"

Alma snatched a quick look at her sister, then returned her attention to Lady Carlisle. "He's here, my lady, only…he says he prefers not to stand in the receiving line."

Lady Carlisle raised her plucked and painted eyebrows so high that Sapphire thought they might reach her receding hairline. Then, spotting an acquaintance, Lady Carlisle fluttered her fan and walked into the next room, her husband in tow.

Sapphire waited for Angelique inside the doorway of a large parlor a little farther down the hall. Exquisitely decorated with stylish furniture and rich-hued draperies, the sound of clinking glasses and restrained laughter came from inside.

"So, my chicks, shall we stick together?" Lucia asked, putting one arm around Sapphire and the other around Angelique. "Or shall we scatter?"

"If you'll excuse me," Angelique said, narrowing her gaze and pursing her plump lips seductively. "I believe I recognize that gentleman under the window."

Sapphire looked at the man and lowered her voice as she spoke. "Angel, how can you know him? We've barely been here long enough to—"

"Find me if you need me," Angelique said, moving off in her new lavender and white silk evening gown.

Lucia and Sapphire watched Angelique cross the room, and then Lucia turned to her goddaughter. "So what will it be, my dear? Shall we corner this scoundrel together?"

"Thank you, but no. I can do this on my own."

"Very well, puss." Lucia pecked the air close to Sapphire's cheek with her rouged lips and walked away, lifting her hand to Lady Morrow who stood beyond them. "Lady Morrow," she called in her French accent, "so good to see you again, *ma chère.*"

Sapphire's pulse raced and she felt butterflies in her stomach. She leaned against the wall for a moment and watched the stylishly dressed guests come and go. There were at least two hundred guests socializing in the two parlors to the right of the front hall and the large drawing room on the left that seemed to have been cleared of furniture for dancing. She was overwhelmed by all the sights and sounds: the glittering jewels hanging from slender necks and earlobes, the stiff white cravats gentleman wore around their necks, the hushed voices, the lively strum of instruments as the musicians struck up a lovely dance.

Sapphire watched as couples moved opposite one another, advancing and retreating, locking arms and then separating to weave their way among the other dancers. She tapped her kidskin slipper beneath her gown, remembering how Armand and her mother had hosted parties at Orchid Manor. They had danced half the night in the tropical garden where Armand had built a platform for such occasions. How her mother had loved dances…. When Sapphire closed her eyes, she could almost hear Sophie's laughter, see Armand draw an arm around her and whisper in her ear. She remembered dancing with Maurice, as well, and the feel of his arms around her…

"You would care to dance? Excellent."

Sapphire's eyes flew open as a man closed his hand over hers and pulled her into the drawing room to join the other dancers. Before she could open her mouth to speak, Blake Thixton released her, pushing her onto the dance floor in the direction of the other ladies as they and their partners separated. Sapphire realized she knew the steps from lessons in Martinique; it seemed as if her mother had spent her whole life preparing her for this introduction to London society. The dance was a variation of the Roger de Coverley and she took her place across from Thixton, staring at him.

She forced a smile, advanced, retired and curtsied to his bow. The moment they joined hands to begin the figure, he spoke harshly beneath his breath. "I thought I warned you not to come here again."

To the many men and women who lined the walls of the drawing room to observe, or to the other dancers, it must have appeared that Sapphire and Thixton were conversing pleasantly as they danced. She would certainly not be the first one to disclose otherwise.

"I must speak with you," she said, loathing the fact that he was holding her so tightly when he rested his hand on her waist. Loathing the fact that her eyes kept straying to his mouth, that strange waves of heat washed over her each time he spoke.

"Let me guess—you must see me so that you can tell me more about how you are Wessex's daughter and what the estate owes you."

"Yes." The dancers parted and he released her. "I mean no," she said in his ear, and then sailed away.

It was a full minute before they were joined again, and as they danced he watched Sapphire with impenetrable brown eyes. It was something near to hatred she felt for those eyes at this moment. "I don't want money," she said under her breath. "I want to be acknowledged. I want my mother, who was Lord Wessex's legal wife, to be acknowledged."

He spun her around, proving to be a superb dancer. "Surely you jest."

She was forced to move away from him to remain in step with the music, but the moment he took her hand again, she met his gaze with determination. "I assure you, sir, I do not jest."

The dance came to end and all the dancers bowed, curtsied and clapped.

"I want you to go now," Thixton said, his disdain for her obvious in his voice as he looped her arm through his and escorted her off the dance floor. "Go now or you will find that it is *I* who does not jest." In the hall, he released her. "As I told you before, there are laws against fortune hunters like you, and the constable will be more than happy to take you to prison where you belong."

"Fortune hunter! Sir, I don't know who you think you are, but I—"

Thixton turned and strode down the hall and entered a room, closing the door behind him.

For a moment, Sapphire stood there seething, her gloved hands pressed to her sides as she tried to catch her breath. Another dance had begun and the sound of the orchestra seemed to swirl around her in the twinkling candlelight.

Her gaze shifted to the door where Thixton had gone. There were no guests in the hall. It was completely inappropriate for an unmarried woman to follow a man into a room without a proper chaperone, but without considering the consequences, she hurried down the hall, drew back her hand and rapped hard on the door.

When she got no response, she knocked even harder. "Mr. Thixton, I'm not through with you!"

The door jerked open and Thixton looked down on her. "Did you not hear what I said?" He knew she was trouble, had known it a week ago when she'd shown up on his doorstep trying to see what she could squeeze from the stone of his *inheritance.* And she was even more beautiful tonight—her rich auburn hair glossier, her eyes even more beguiling and her mouth—it took his breath away. The curve of her sensuous lips made him hard at once, made him want to take her there in the doorway the same way he had taken the sad Mrs. Williams that night on the balcony. But something told him she would not be such an easy conquest and certainly not as easy to forget.

"Sir, it is you who are apparently hard of hearing!"

"Get in here."

He pulled her into the room and closed the door behind them.

They were in a dark-paneled, masculine-style room dominated by a large billiards table. A billiards room that smelled of tobacco, leather and *him.*

Taking a step back, Sapphire rested her hand on the edge of the walnut table. "You have to listen to me."

"I have to do no such thing."

He strode toward her and she realized then that he had removed his coat. The white shirt beneath his black waistcoat was impeccably pressed, as was the cravat at his neck. He wore his clothing well.

She took another step back, confused by the ridiculous thoughts that were popping into her head. "Yes, you do have to listen to me. I was—*am* Lord Edward Thixton's legitimate daughter and—"

"Wait a minute." He pointed his finger at her, still walking straight toward her. "Were you sent here by that cousin? What is his name?" He snapped his fingers, the side of his mouth turning up in a half smile. "Charles," he said. "Charles something. He said he knew the best ladies of the evening."

His hand snaked out, and before she could get out of his way, he grabbed her wrist again. "Why didn't you say so in the first place? Why this game, hmm?" He pulled her close to him, gazing down at her with an incredibly smug smile. "You do clean up nice, I'll give you that. A prettier whore I don't believe I've ever seen."

"Let go of me, sir," she said as she struggled to remove herself from his grasp. But he overwhelmed her, not just with his physical force, but with his nearness— the smell of him, the heat of his body in the places where it touched her.

Instead of getting away from him, she somehow managed to entangle herself further in his arms. "Let go of me," she insisted, pushing against his chest as her heart pounded.

"One kiss," he said. Holding her close, inhaling the fragrance of her hair, her skin, he could smell the depth of the unrest she could unleash on him. He could *feel* it and he knew he would be able to taste it in her mouth. "Just a sample of your wares first before I put out any hard-earned money."

"Sir!" she spat, so angry now that she could barely focus on the face hovering over her as she bent backward in order to keep his body from touching hers any more than it already was. "I assure you I am no—"

His mouth came down hard over hers, muffling her last words. She'd been kissed before, by Maurice, and by a few other young men on Martinique, but never like this. His mouth was merciless, searing her lips like a flame, forcing them apart. He held her with one arm around her waist, the other around her shoulders, crushing her. When she tried to move her head to escape, she felt his hand slide upward until his fingers brushed the nape of her neck, holding her trapped in his arms.

Sapphire's legs went weak. She couldn't think. Her mind was screaming but she could make no sound. To her horror, Blake thrust his tongue into her mouth, and as she grasped a handful of his waistcoat to loosen his hold, she somehow rose upward, deepening his kiss even further, forcing little whimpers from her throat.

She feared her pounding heart might burst from her chest. He was smothering her, filling her with heat.

Suddenly, there was a sound.

Thixton jerked back, glancing over his shoulder, but did not release her.

7

"Pardon me, Lord Wessex." The intruder cleared his throat. He stared at Sapphire, who was trying to extricate herself from Thixton's arms. "I hadn't realized you were—" he cleared his throat again, obviously amused "—occupied." His hand on the doorknob, he backed out the door, smiling lasciviously at Sapphire.

He thought she was some sort of wanton, as well! "Wait," Sapphire cried, flustered, trying to smooth the bodice of her gown. She still couldn't catch her breath. "This isn't how it appears, sir. I only—"

"Lord Wessex." The intruder, still smiling, bowed to Thixton and paid no attention to Sapphire as he pulled the door closed behind him.

"How could you do such a thing?" Sapphire demanded as she took a step back from Thixton, still trying to straighten her gown. Then, realizing a thick lock of her copper hair had fallen from its fashionable upsweep, she tried furiously to return it to its place, but when she pulled out a pin to fasten the stray lock, more hair came tumbling down.

Thixton just stood there staring at her, seeming a little perplexed. "You really aren't a harlot, are you."

"Certainly not." She pushed back a lock of loose hair and then gestured angrily in the direction of the door. "Little good the truth will do me now! That man…that man will go out there and tell everyone I was here alone with you."

"And that you were kissing me?" he asked, taking a step toward her, smiling again.

She wiped her mouth with the back of her gloved hand. "I was *not* kissing you, sir," she spat.

He took another step toward her and she sidestepped him by going around the other side of the billiards table.

"I…I must talk to you about my father. About Edward Thixton," she said, attempting to gather her thoughts and remind herself of the reason she'd come here tonight in the first place. Only now she could think of nothing but *him*. Of nothing but the feel of his mouth on hers. The taste of him…

"But…but," she stammered indignantly. "A more public place might be more appropriate as you are *obviously* not to be trusted as a gentleman."

He surprised her yet again by not leaping to the defense of his honor as any decent gentleman would have. Rather, he tilted his dark head back and laughed.

"How dare you laugh at me! I am not through with you, Mr. Thixton," she threw at him as she turned and rushed for the door.

"I hope not," he called after her, still laughing.

Sapphire stormed out of the billiards room, slamming the door behind her. As she pushed her hair from her eyes and hurried up the hallway toward the music, she looked up to see guests lining both sides of the wall, staring at her.

Sapphire strode past them, down the hall and directly into the entrance hall. Without even looking for Aunt Lucia or Angelique, she continued out the front door.

"There you are."

Lucia couldn't resist a smile as she looked up to see Jessup Stowe hurrying toward her. He was quite handsome for a middle-aged man, bald pate and all, and they had shared a turn on the dance floor as well as a very engaging conversation earlier in the evening.

"Please tell me you weren't going to run off without saying good-night, my dear Cinderella. I don't believe I could have slept tonight without bidding you a fond farewell."

She offered her hand and watched as he bowed formally and brushed his lips across the back of it. She giggled. "Mr. Stowe, you're certainly smooth with *les dames*."

"Only with ladies as beautiful and charming as you, my Cinderella."

She smiled, genuinely flattered. "Now I know you're being insincere. There are plenty of women in this house tonight more appealing to the eye and certainly younger than I am."

"But it is you, Mademoiselle Toulouse, who has caught my fancy. I don't often meet women as interesting as you."

"I must go, Mr. Stowe." With everyone at the ball gossiping about Sapphire and Lord Wessex, she needed to be certain Sapphire was all right.

"I wish you wouldn't. One more dance? A walk in the garden, perhaps? " Stowe's broad brow furrowed. "Or if you're tired, we could—"

"Tired?" Lucia scoffed as she thrust one slippered foot from beneath her new gown. "I could dance all night on these feet. I could dance most of these young women in their silly heeled shoes right off the dance floor."

"I bet you could, couldn't you, Mademoiselle Toulouse?" He grinned.

She narrowed her eyes. "Are you certain you are unmarried, Mr. Stowe?"

"I am afraid I am. A widow, these past three years."

"Did you love your wife?"

"I did. A great deal and I miss her."

"Good answer. Now, I must be on my way, but because you have passed the test, you may come for me Sunday afternoon and take me for a ride in Hyde Park." She walked toward the door and the footman opened it.

"To think I didn't even know I was taking an examination and I've apparently not only passed it, but won the prize," the barrister called after her, his face red with glee.

"Good night, Mr. Stowe." Lucia walked out the door, feeling lighter on her feet than she had in years.

"Sapphire. Sapphire? Puss, I'm coming in."

The door opened and Lucia entered, but Sapphire didn't sit up. She just lay there staring at the ceiling. She'd managed to get out of her shoes and gown, petticoats and stays without any assistance, but she was still wearing her drawers and new chemise.

"Are you asleep?"

"How could I be?" Sapphire asked miserably. "It's a scandal. I'm sure you heard. I'm sure all of London has heard by now."

"Ah, they have nothing better to do with their lives than gossip."

Sapphire groaned in frustration. "And now everyone in London will speak poorly of me and call me terrible names. My reputation is ruined. I came to London for my mother's sake and look how I've shamed her, how I've shamed my father."

Lucia sat on the edge of the bed. "Poppycock," she said softly. "I have to ask, though, puss—were you a...*participant,* or did Lord Wessex take unfair advantage of you?"

Sapphire felt heat rise in her face. "It was only a kiss. He didn't...didn't—"

"I know this is delicate, but I must know, puss. I of all people would never judge you. Participant or victim?"

"He didn't hurt me, Aunt Lucia."

Lucia was quiet for a moment while she smoothed Sapphire's hand in hers. "Did you speak to him of your father?"

"I tried, but he wouldn't listen to me. He...he—"

Aunt Lucia patted Sapphire's hand and released it. "The new Lord Wessex is quite handsome. Unmarried."

"He was abominable again."

"Was he, now?" Lucia asked. "The party was rife with tittle-tattle, everyone was speaking of how handsome he is. They say his interest may lie with the dowager's eldest daughter. Were he to marry her, the money would stay in the family."

"Well, her interest might lie in his direction, but I can warrant you he'd not be interested in a shrew like her!"

"Really?" Aunt Lucia rose from the bed. "Well, dear, it's late. I just wanted to be sure you were all right and to say good-night." She glanced at the empty side of the bed. "I suppose you've seen no sign of our Angel."

"No."

Lucia sighed. "Certainly not surprising. She had several suitors tonight." She walked toward the door. "I'm going to turn in, if you're certain you're all right."

"I'm fine."

"We'll talk more tomorrow when you're rested, puss. Good night."

"Good night," Sapphire called, knowing full well it would not be a good night because memories of Blake Thixton's kiss would keep her awake until the early hours.

"Good morning, Lucia." Lady Carlisle sat at the head of the dining table set for breakfast, dressed for an outing in a striped gray and white taffeta morning gown, her hair pulled tightly in a matronly chignon.

Lucia noted that Lady Carlisle didn't look at her when she spoke. "Good morning, Edith," she replied cheerfully, moving to the buffet table that had been set up along the wall of the dining room so that one could dine at one's leisure. "Did you sleep well?" She accepted a plate from a maid standing as inconspicuously as possible beside the serving table, gaze fixed on the polished floor.

"I did not."

Lucia took her time placing several lamb sausages on her plate, knowing exactly the direction this conversation was headed.

Lady Carlisle cleared her throat.

Lucia lifted the lid of a pottery serving bowl but rejected the dish of sardines. "I'm sorry to hear that you didn't sleep well, Edith. Were you feeling poorly?" She took several corners of toast and heaped blackberry jam on the side of her plate.

"You could say that." Lady Carlisle set her fork down firmly on the table. "Lucia…Mademoiselle Toulouse," she said, taking on a more formal tone. "I must speak frankly with you."

"So early in the morning?"

"Pardon me?"

Lucia turned from the buffet, a smile placed strategically on her lips. "I said, 'a moment, darling.'" She took a seat at the dining table.

"Coffee, mum?" the servant asked Lucia, eyes downcast.

"Thank you." Lucia smiled sweetly and then picked up her napkin and tucked it into the neckline of her brightly colored caftan. "Now, what were you saying, dear?" She lifted her gaze, batting her lashes.

"You heard what they were saying last night? The rumor?"

"Which one? I heard that Lady Thorngrove had lost three thousand pounds sterling at whist, that Baron Birdsley's wife had run off with the Italian he'd hired to paint her portrait, and that eighty-year-old Lord Einestower's son and heir had been born with hair as red as his Scots gardener's when both Einestower and his nineteen-year-old bride had hair as black as any chimney sweep."

"You know very well which one," Lady Carlisle said haughtily. "Your goddaughter, Miss Fabergine, was seen in a compromising situation with Lord Wessex."

Lucia shrugged, spreading jam on one of her toast points. "She kissed Lord Wessex. Rather, he kissed her. I'll guess you did as much when you were nineteen, Edith. I wouldn't put it past you to have done so since."

"How dare you!"

Lucia took a bite of her toast. "It was a kiss, nothing more."

"She was seen, alone, in the billiards room with a man."

"For heaven's sake, Edith, if you want to evoke these preposterous unwritten rules of London society, one could say Lord Wessex is a distant cousin."

Lady Carlisle patted the corners of her lips with her napkin. "We have absolutely no proof of that. I never heard a word last night at the party about your goddaughter having any connection whatsoever to the Wessex family."

Lucia tossed her toast on her plate. "Edith Carlisle, are you calling me a liar?"

"I am Lady Carlisle to you and I would not presume to say who speaks the truth and who does not. I'm simply stating that there is no proof that Sapphire Fabergine is related to the Thixton family in any way, and now that she has been caught in an unfortunate situation that could reflect badly on Lord Carlisle and me…"

Lucia could feel her face beginning to burn with anger. "Because we're staying here?"

"I have no issue with you or Miss Angelique. She's quite sweet, but…"

"But what, Edith?" Lucia demanded. "What are you trying to say? That Sapphire is no longer welcome in your household?"

"I asked Lord Carlisle to handle this unfortunate situation, but he was unable to—" she gulped water from a crystal glass "—remain here this morning to discuss the matter with you."

"So you are putting us out, then?" Lucia exclaimed. "Simply come out and say it why don't you."

"As I said, I have no issue with you or—"

"So you would put out a girl not yet twenty years old?" Lucia leaned forward, pressing her hands on the polished table. "And where would you have Sapphire go? What would you have her do?"

Lady Carlisle leaned back in her chair as if unsure what her houseguest might do. "That really isn't my concern. I suppose if she needs finances, she could set herself up as a woman in need of a protector. Obviously she's that kind of young woman, as I suspected when we first met in Martinique."

Lucia shoved her chair under the table. Armand hadn't sent them with enough money to live on their own; such a need hadn't been anticipated. But she didn't care about the money. She'd prostituted herself once and she could do it again if she had to. She'd do that before she would allow Sapphire to be treated this way. "How dare you! We shall leave by noon."

"You understand, she left us with no other recourse," Lady Carlisle said.

"What I understand is that you, Edith, are not fit to

wash Sapphire Thixton's underclothing." She whipped around to walk out, and then thinking better of her exit on an empty stomach, turned back, grabbed a toast point covered with jam and walked out of the dining room.

8

"What else can I do for you, Auntie?" Sapphire asked, a leather valise in her arms. "This is the last of our belongings from the Carlisles'."

"You can't do a thing but sit here and have a cup of coffee with me and some of these divine pastries from Mrs. Partridge's shop on the corner, *ma chère.*" Lucia patted the floral settee.

The apartments Lucia had located to rent were in Charing Cross, only a few blocks from the Carlisles' town house. Though located on the second floor, which forced them to walk up a narrow flight of stairs, the residence was large. It had two bedrooms, a parlor, small drawing room, kitchen and dining room and it came with kitchen staff. Set as it was over a dressmaker's shop, the soft hum of voices could be heard from below during business hours, but Sapphire adored the large casement windows that ran the length of the apartments and opened up onto the street where she could see the activity of the day. They'd only been here four days, after staying in a rooming house for two nights, but it already felt like home to her.

"Just let me put this away and I'll join you," Sapphire said.

"Put it down, you've done enough—too much," Lucia insisted, waving her arm. "We must have a personal maid and I intend to see to it directly. I won't see you running up and down those stairs as if you're one of the servants."

Sapphire lowered the valise to the floor. "I blame myself for everything."

"Pish!" Lucia tapped the seat beside her again. "I was sick to death of that Edith Carlisle. You simply provided the perfect excuse to get us out of that house."

Sapphire lowered herself onto the soft piece of furniture and made herself more comfortable. "No coffee for me, but I'll sit while you have yours. Did you send Papa a note informing him we've moved?"

"I did."

"Do you think he'll be angry? He arranged for us to stay with Lord and Lady Carlisle thinking it would be the best for us. I hate to disappoint him."

"Armand has a good heart but he's still a man, dove." Lucia sipped her coffee served in a tiny china cup. "How was he to know Edith was such a poor hostess and a gossip to top it off? No, he would never want you to remain in that household."

Sapphire's eyes flashed. "That horrible man—"

"I don't want to hear it," Lucia interrupted, sweeping one graceful hand. "Coffee beans already on the floor. What we need to do now is decide how to proceed from here." She glanced at her goddaughter. "What *you* need to decide, dear, is if you would still like to pursue the matter of your birth."

"Of course I would! Just because that man was rude, and coarse—" Sapphire rose and began to pace in front of the table set out with the coffee service "—that doesn't mean he's frightened me off. I am not about to be bested by some...some American upstart! Mr. Blake Thixton may be the legal heir to my father's title and possessions, but he has no authority over me, and if he won't listen to me then I'll...I'll take my cause elsewhere. I will be heard and I *will* be acknowledged!"

Lucia smiled slyly. "Which was my thinking precisely. I just wanted to hear you say it."

The door opened at that moment and Angelique blew in like a fluttering leaf from the park. "What in heaven's name are you two doing sitting here like two old spinsters?" she demanded, sweeping off her bonnet and patting her wind-blown hair. "I've just had the most pleasant carriage ride through the park."

"With whom?" Sapphire rested her hands on her hips.

"Just a gentleman." Tossing her bonnet on a chair, Angelique sashayed to the table and picked up a small, round cherry-topped cake from the china platter. "What have you two been up to?" She glanced around. "Settling in, I see."

"You could have stayed and helped," Sapphire offered.

"And you could have gone to the park with me. There's a Mr. Krum who's been inquiring of you all about town."

"Me?" Sapphire brushed the bodice of her pale blue

morning gown. "Why ever would someone want to in-
quire about me?"

"He saw you at the 'Change, in the park, somewhere.
I suspect he's wife-shopping."

Sapphire shook her head, choosing not to continue
the subject. "We were discussing what I'm to do now
that Mr. Thixton will not listen to me in person. He refused to accept the letter I sent to him yesterday."

"Really, Sapphire, I don't know why you care about
all this. The city is full of handsome men like Mr. Krum.
Surely you could find a husband to suit you."

"Angel, this isn't about finding a husband," Sapphire
snapped. "Haven't you been listening to what I've been
saying all these weeks? It's about who I am!"

"And not about Blake Thixton?"

"Certainly not!" Sapphire turned her back to them,
feeling her cheeks grow warm. "I would appreciate it if
you would refrain from mentioning him in my presence."

"We were just saying that we need to go elsewhere
to make Sapphire's plea," Lucia explained as she added
two pastries to a tiny china plate rimmed with lavender
blossoms.

"Elsewhere?" Angelique licked the sweet icing from
her fingers. "Is this your idea, Sapphire?"

"Actually, it was Lady Carlisle's suggestion."

"I want no part of anything she has to say," Sapphire
declared, turning to face them, her arms crossed obsti-
nately. "She insulted us both, me by suggesting I had
done something illicit and you by suggesting you were
somehow responsible."

"Now, now, smooth your feathers. I'll warn you, this
is not a conventional approach."

"We adore unconventional, don't we, Sapphire?"

Sapphire sat in one of the upholstered chairs at the tea table. "I'm listening."

"The question is, exactly what is it you want from Lord Wessex?"

"All I want from *Mr. Thixton* is for him to acknowledge that my father was married to my mother and that I am his legitimate daughter."

"Which makes the Dowager Lady Wessex what?" Angelique giggled. "A kept woman?"

"I don't care." Sapphire leaned forward in her chair, threading her fingers. "I want all of London to know I am Sapphire Thixton, daughter of the late Edward Thixton, Earl of Wessex."

"Even if the American is willing to admit you could be Edward's daughter, the dowager is going to want proof." Angelique reached for another cake.

"But we don't even know where to start looking for this proof. Aunt Lucia has had no luck so far finding any record of a marriage of anyone in the Wessex family in Devonshire in the past one hundred years. She's been told such records would have been destroyed," Sapphire said.

"But perhaps we would not need the physical proof," Lucia said, "not if we stir up enough trouble." She sipped her coffee.

"Trouble?" Sapphire repeated.

"Well…" Lucia's gaze flitted from one girl to the other as her voice rose with excitement. "You see, when I said you had nowhere to go, Lady Carlisle suggested that you set yourself up in search of a protector."

"Oh!" Sapphire cried. "That despicable woman!"

"Now listen." Lucia held up a finger. "I understand that the eldest daughter—the one with the bad complexion—is hoping to wed soon. What if we were to initiate a scandal that the dowager would be eager to squelch?"

"Like the late Earl of Wessex's daughter being put out on the street and forced to seek a protector in order to survive!" Angelique said.

"I don't know," Sapphire said, stalling.

"Oh, come now, it would be so much fun!" Angelique continued. "Can you imagine? The men would be lined up on the street outside the dress shop just waiting to leave those silly calling cards. We could go to a ball or the theater every night, and during the day there would be horse races, picnics—"

"It sounds so outrageous!"

"So outrageous, it just might work." Lucia winked. "I heard at the cook shop down the street that the dowager's middle girl—what is her name? Polly, Porridge, Petunia?"

Sapphire couldn't help but laugh. "Portia."

"Yes, that's it." Lucia reached for another cake. "I understand her mother is expecting a particular gentleman caller to ask for her hand any day now."

"Lord Carter?" Angelique asked, turning back to Lucia. "You mustn't be serious."

"You know him?" Sapphire asked.

She smiled. "I would think so. He was the one who took me riding this morning, with his brother and a cousin."

"You were riding in a carriage with three men, unescorted?"

Angelique rolled her eyes. "One of them brought a

little sister along. Of course, I'm not sure how that would matter if we're talking about setting ourselves up as courtesans."

"Women in need of protection," Lucia corrected.

"You know," Sapphire said, looking to her god-mother, "I couldn't really—"

"I could." Angelique grinned.

Lucia met Sapphire's gaze. "I don't expect you to sacrifice your virtue, sweet. What kind of woman do you think I am? I'm only suggesting that you allow others to think you might consider it, under the right circumstances. First we let it be known that you ladies are both in need of protectors because Lady Carlisle has put you out and I'm too old and feeble to care for you." She drew the back of her hand dramatically across her forehead. "And then—" she popped up "—once you are the toast of London, people will hear the tragic truth—that you are a Thixton, forced to set yourself up as a kept woman because your family is unwilling to take you into their loving bosom…"

"Lady Wessex wouldn't want that hanging over her head. It could prevent her daughters from making proper alliances." Angelique smiled. "It's a perfect plan!"

"A perfectly outrageous plan," Sapphire agreed, sitting back. "Just outrageous enough to work."

"Here, driver," Lucia called, tapping the seat of the open hackney with the new walnut and copper walking stick she'd purchased at the 'Change. The late spring sun shone warm on her face and she resisted the notion that she should turn the brim of her hat down to prevent freckling. What did she care at her age? The sun felt divinely good; it made her feel alive and full of hope. "Down this street, closer to the wharves."

"Missus." The tiny man perched high on the driver's seat glanced over a hunched shoulder. "Ye sure, missus? Rough lot down Water Street."

"I know," she said merrily. "I was once employed there." She rapped on the seat with the cane again. "Onward, man. Look at these wrinkles! Can you not see I grow older by the minute?"

"Aye, missus." The driver clucked between his teeth and urged the two-seater carriage down a narrow street.

The stench of fish and brackish water filled Lucia's nostrils and she breathed deeply, letting memories return to her. Never for a moment had she missed this place, but she'd always thought it was good for the soul to revisit old haunts. It made a woman who had come as far as she had better appreciate her good fortune.

The street narrowed even further and antiquated frame buildings rose up on both sides, partially blocking the sunlight. Sewage ran in an open gutter along the rutted street, adding to the stench of the Thames. This portion of London that ran along the public docks was like its own city, swarming with the noonday crowd of black-toothed women bartering their wares. "Cream, fresh cream," someone called. Tarred pigtailed sailors wound their way around fish carts, wagons and a herd of goats being driven down the center of the street. Lucia realized she hadn't been here in twenty-five years, yet nothing seemed different.

"Here, missus?" the driver called.

"A little farther," Lucia encouraged, waving the walking stick. Ahead were the taverns and alehouses of the working class, filled with patrons, even at midday. Spotting a decrepit wooden sign marked with a hare wearing a top hat, she rapped the stick excitedly. "Here," she called. "Let me off here."

"Missus?"

Lucia rose and grabbed the side of the carriage, even before it rolled to a halt. "I want to get off here."

The driver pulled the brake, wrapped the leather reins and scrambled down from his seat to offer his hand to assist her.

"I won't be but a minute," she said, dropping a coin into his dirty palm. "Wait for me and there'll be two more like it."

"Aye, missus." He tugged on the torn brim of his wool hat. "'Course, missus."

Smiling, Lucia walked up the street to the corner of Water and Front. As if she were stepping back in time she approached the Hare of the Hat tavern and the women who loitered at the door.

Lucia walked up to the woman closest to her, the one wearing a pink silk chemise, her thin shoulders bared, her small breasts spilling out over the garment that would have been more appropriate beneath a dress, had she been wearing one. She appeared to be close to forty years old but could have been as young as twenty; it was hard to tell under the mop of tangled hair.

The woman looked Lucia up and down and spat a stream of chewing tobacco. "Can I 'elp ya, mum?"

Two women behind her cackled. Another stared, but didn't seem to see the well-dressed lady standing before her or hear her cohorts.

"Perhaps." Lucia moved closer to inspect the other

women, taking care not to step in the stream of tobacco juice on the wooden walk. The one with the vacant stare was out of the question. Lucia knew that stare—the woman was too far gone. The other two women were possibilities, but she liked the redhead immediately.

"Ya lookin' fer yerself or yer man?" The redhead stepped closer, squeezing her arms together to display the pink of her areolas.

"Myself."

The prostitutes behind her snickered.

"I ain't usually one fer the *laddies*," she said. "Cost ya extra."

"What's your name?" Lucia studied the woman's brown eyes. It was the eyes that reflected a person's soul.

"Whatcha want it ta be?"

"Come, come, I haven't time to waste with nonsense," Lucia said. "Tell me your name."

She gave Lucia the best sultry look she could manage. "What the boys calls me, or what ya can call me?"

Lucia ignored the continued laughter. "What your mother called you, dove. Come now." She reached out and took the whore's hand between her gloved ones, meeting her gaze.

The redhead stared for a moment, and then spoke, the bravado sudden gone from her voice. "Avena," she whispered, sounding forlorn. "Avena Croft."

"Avena, what a lovely name."

"Been a long time since someone call me that," she said, looking down at the grimy walk.

Lucia smiled. "Would you like a job?" She didn't wait for an answer. "A real job, as a lady's maid to me and two young ladies."

Avena stared. "I...I ain't no *laddie's* maid, mum. I'm a ho'."

Lucia smiled, not the least bit offended. "But you can learn, can't you, Avena?" She brushed a lock of dirty hair from the girl's face. Now Lucia could see that she *was* young, midtwenties, probably. "And I bet you clean up nice. A decent gown and bodice, a hot bath, some food to put a little meat on these bones." Lucia reached out and eased a strap of the chemise back up on Avena's shoulder.

"Ya ain't serious, mum?"

"Completely." Lucia took a step back and looked up and down the street. Avena's companions had moved down a few steps to talk to some sailors in sailcloth shirts, oilcloth bags thrown over their shoulders. "I've need of a lady's maid, but our household is a bit unconventional."

"I...I could learn, mum."

"I bet you can." She turned and indicated the waiting hackney. "So, shall we go?"

"Aye, mum." Avena hurried after her.

"Don't you want to say goodbye to your friends," Lucia asked over her shoulder.

"Nah. They ain't my friends no how, mum."

"I'm certain she'll be back directly, Mr. Stowe." Sapphire smiled, settling on the settee across from the balding, middle-aged barrister. "I really can't say what's taking her so long."

"Oh, that's quite all right. I still have a bit of time."

"And you say she was expecting you?"

"Well, yes...and no." He glanced up anxiously. "I... She was expecting me on Sunday afternoon, but when I went by Lord and Lady Carlisle's as she requested—"

"Oh heavens," she sighed, clasping her hands, finishing his sentence for him. "We were already gone."

"Lady Carlisle indicated she didn't know where Mademoiselle Toulouse had gone," he explained.

Sapphire rose with indignation. "What a witch, that Lady Carlisle!"

"I'm sorry." He glanced up, startled by Sapphire's outburst.

"No, no, I'm the one who should be sorry." She sat down again. "Aunt Lucia didn't tell me she was expecting a gentleman. It all happened so fast and I'm responsible for—"

"I won't hear another word of that," Mr. Stowe interrupted, his voice surprisingly stout. "I would never speak ill of a lady, but suffice it to say fewer believe Lady's Carlisle's words than she thinks."

"That's kind of you to say, Mr. Stowe." She studied his sincere-looking face.

"Things are said at these parties, my dear. No one believes a word of it. By next week another person will generate even more gossip and no one will remember the Dowager Wessex's party at all."

Mention of the dowager suddenly made her uneasy. "Lady Carlisle told you about the party?"

"Actually, I was there."

She rose from the settee again, mortified. "You were there?"

"Yes, that's where I met Mademoiselle Toulouse, your godmother. She's a lovely woman," he went on, his cheeks reddening as he grew more excited. "You know, I don't usually invite women for rides in the park. I'm…I'm a widower, you understand."

Sapphire nodded.

"In fact, I can say I've never done this before, and I don't mind admitting, Miss Fabergine, that I'm more than a little nervous." He began to fiddle with his hat. "I truly do...admire your godmother and I hope... heavens, listen to me, I don't know what I'm hoping for."

At that point Sapphire realized he was far more concerned with seeing Lucia again than with whatever nasty gossip Lady Carlisle or anyone else had offered. She relaxed a little, easing back onto the settee. "Are you certain I couldn't get you some tea, Mr. Stowe, or perhaps some coffee? My godmother is quite fond of her coffee."

"Is she now?" He looked up. "Why, I am, as well. I adore coffee, though it isn't very English, is it, my dear?"

Sapphire couldn't help but smile. Mr. Stowe truly was a pleasant fellow and she could see why Lucia would fancy such a man. "We grew coffee on Martinique."

"Martinique!" Mr. Stowe exclaimed. "A world traveler. I just knew Mademoiselle Toulouse was a world traveler!"

"Mademoiselle Toulouse is a what?" Lucia exclaimed as she burst through the door.

The barrister shot out of his chair. Sapphire rose, pleased by the thought that the gentleman could be so enamored with Lucia. She liked him more with each minute that passed. "Auntie, Mr. Stowe came to call on you."

"Mr. Stowe, I was beginning to wonder what had become of you," she said, sweeping off her bonnet and ushering in a thin, dirty woman dressed in underclothing.

Mr. Stowe had eyes for no one but Lucia, but Sapphire couldn't help but stare at the other woman, who now appeared frightened.

"This is Avena, Sapphire, our new lady's maid," Lucia explained. "Didn't I tell you I'd find us a lady's maid, and that old bat Carlisle claimed there wasn't a decent one left in the city? I want you to take her up to the servants' quarters and see that she has everything she needs for a bath, and then, if you don't mind—" she plucked off a white glove, taking her time in doing it "—could you run down to the dressmaker's and see what she has for Avena."

"'Fank ya, mum," Avena declared tearfully.

"While you do that, Sapphire, dear, Mr. Stowe and I will take a cup of coffee—won't we, Mr. Stowe?" She offered her hand and he took it, kissing the freckled, wrinkled skin as if she were the queen.

"I hope I'm not intruding," he gushed, red-faced again.

"Certainly not." Lucia led him back toward the chairs and settee, her French accent very light. "I told myself, if you could find me after our unanticipated change of lodging, Mr. Stowe, you'd be worthy of a second look. I'm so pleased you found me."

Sapphire walked over to the young woman huddled in the doorway appearing both frightened and overwhelmed. She was afraid to ask Lucia where she'd found this "lady's maid." "Avena," she said kindly, "do come in and let me show you upstairs. Would you like some tea and bread and cheese? We've more than enough."

"'Fank you, miss." Avena nodded. "This is like…like a dream come true. I got to keep pinchin' mysef to see it's real."

"If you'll excuse us," Sapphire said as she ushered Avena to the rear of the apartments. But Lucia and Mr. Stowe never heard her, since they were already too engrossed in their private conversation.

9

"Could you tighten the stays on my corset?" Sapphire asked, turning her back to Angelique.

In less than an hour, several gentlemen would be arriving to escort them to the theater, and Sapphire was as nervous as she had been the first day of school with the nuns in Martinique. Sapphire still remembered the smell of her mother's hair as Mama leaned over to kiss her goodbye, and she recalled her own excitement…and fear that she would not succeed. And it was fearing that she would not be able to pull off this ruse that made her palms damp and her stomach flutter. Would Aunt Lucia's far-fetched plan work?

"Your stays are tight enough." Angelique gave them a tug and then spun Sapphire around to face her. "If your waist was any smaller I'd find it difficult to ever speak to you again. Now, calm down. This is going to fun, you'll see."

"I don't know that it's going to work. I don't know

if I can do it." Shaking her head, Sapphire took a seat on a velvet-covered stool in front of the charming dressing table and gazed into the oval mirror, studying the serious young auburn-haired woman with one green eye and one blue who was looking back at her. "What if the men don't believe I need a protector? Or that I'm willing to take one?"

"They'll believe it because they want to, and it doesn't take much to bait men this age." Angelique sat on the edge of the bed and began to roll on a silk stocking she'd just removed from a sheet of tissue. "They're already randy. One look at you, that hair, those eyes, that mouth of yours, and they'll be lining up on the street."

Sapphire's fingertips went to her mouth and she stared at the mirror, frowning. "What's wrong with my lips?"

"Not a thing except that they haven't been kissed enough."

Blake Thixton's face flashed in Sapphire's mind and she remembered the feel of his lips against hers, the heat that raced between them. "I can't do this," she cried, drawing her fingers away from her mouth as if she could somehow erase the memory of him.

"Don't be such a goose!" Angelique ran her hands over the smooth stocking that covered her shapely leg and reached for a ribbon garter. "It's easy. Smile. Laugh deep in your throat, like this." She demonstrated a husky laugh that exuded sexuality. "Men like a husky laugh." She gave a wave of her hand. "Simply say things they'll find flattering."

Sapphire dusted her nose with a little rice powder, still wondering what was wrong with her lips. Was it the fact that her lower lip seemed larger than her upper? She grabbed a brush to pull through her long hair, which she'd washed and perfumed earlier with Avena's help. "I don't know what flatters men. How many men have I actually known besides Maurice and a few other boys on Martinique?"

"Just say anything complimentary to them, true or not." Angelique picked up the other new stocking from its wrapping. "You're thinking too much about this, Sapphire. This is supposed to be fun. No one is going to make you do anything you don't want to do. Even Aunt Lucia is having fun with it."

Sapphire exhaled, meeting Angelique's gaze in the mirror. "We're relying on the power of gossip to get word back to the countess and Mr. Thixton, and in the meantime, look at all the money we're spending." She picked up the glass container of rice powder and set it down, then indicated her own new silk stockings on the dressing table. "If this doesn't work, if it doesn't force Mr. Thixton—"

"Ah, we're back to Mr. Thixton again, are we?"

"Whatever is that supposed to mean?" Sapphire rose and walked to the open bedchamber door, poking her head through the doorway. "Where has Avena gotten to? She said she'd pick up the dresses at the dressmaker's and be right back. I hope the gowns are completed. I really love the blue *fichu-pelèrine*." She stepped back into the room, glancing at the porcelain German clock on the fireplace mantel. "Our escorts will be here soon and we're not even dressed."

"We're nearly dressed and they won't be here for another half an hour." Her stockings secured just below her knees, Angelique stood, letting the stiff fabric of her petticoats fall until they almost brushed the floor. "And I have an idea it's not the dressmaker that is keeping Avena, but rather her son the tailor."

"Avena has eyes for the dressmaker's son?" Sapphire smiled. Once fed, deloused, bathed and dressed, Avena had thrown herself wholeheartedly into her new occupation of lady's maid, immediately earning the respect of them all. And although she was certainly different from the lady's maids found in Lady Carlisle's home, Sapphire thought Avena was wonderful. She was helpful and efficient and always willing to throw a sage tidbit of advice into any conversation—advice that sometimes sent Sapphire into peals of laughter, and other times made her turn red with embarrassment.

"Haven't you noticed how many times this week she's gone down to check on the gowns since our fittings?" Angelique stepped into a pair of new gold kidskin slippers. "Sometimes twice in one afternoon."

"I suppose I haven't noticed. I've been selfishly too busy with my own thoughts," she admonished herself. "It just makes me so angry to think that I am forced to do all this, to fight some…some *American* for the right to my father's name." Sapphire walked back toward the dressing table, clenching her hands. "And every time I think about that Mr. Thixton, I just…I just—"

"Do you spend a great deal of time thinking about Mr. Thixton?" Angelique raised an eyebrow suggestively.

"Certainly not in that way!" Sapphire turned hastily to check herself in the mirror, again sweeping up her hair, which was still slightly damp. "Up high, or lower?" she asked, first bringing the locks high on her head, then lowering them to a more ordinary chignon.

"Oh, high, definitely." Angelique came up behind her, wrapped her fingers around Sapphire's knot of curls and began to twist them artfully one way and then another. "Pins. I need pins."

Sapphire grabbed a handful of tortoiseshell pins from a silver dish on the dressing table and began to hand them one by one to Angelique. In a matter of moments, she watched her hair transformed from a wave of unruly curls to a fashionable, sleek coiffure.

"Like it?" Angelique asked, taking a step back to admire her creation.

"It's beautiful. Thank you."

"*You* are beautiful, and I believe Mr. Thixton is quite aware of that fact."

Sapphire frowned. "I was finally calm and now you have to mention him again? He thinks nothing of the sort. He only kissed me to…to humiliate me."

"Perhaps, but all in love play," Angelique cooed. "This is a complicated man, your Mr. Blake Thixton, the American."

"He is not *my* Mr. Thixton!" Sapphire strode to the open door again. "If Avena doesn't get here soon, I'm afraid I'm going to have to parade down the street in my underclothes to get the gowns myself!"

"Leave the strumpin' work to the likes a me," Avena announced, hurrying down the hall toward Sapphire, her arms filled with the gowns wrapped in bleached muslin to prevent them from being soiled in transport up the dirty street.

"Was Master Dawson there?" Angelique asked, taking her gold gown from the maid's arms as she entered the bedchamber.

"That 'e was." Feet planted in the used shoes Lucia had bought her, the prostitute-turned-lady's-maid sashayed her hips, blushing like a schoolgirl.

"He *is* handsome." Sapphire smiled.

"Ya seen 'im?" Avena carried Sapphire's gown to the bed and began to uncover it carefully.

In the center of the room, Angelique clasped the shoulders of her gown and shook it eagerly, sending the muslin cover floating across the floor.

"I can 'elp ya in a minu'," Avena said.

"I can do it myself. You help Sapphire, Avena. She's got her drawers all in a twist between worrying she can't play this game with these fops, and thinking of Mr. You-Know-Who."

"I am *not* thinking about him and I don't know why you keep bringing him up."

"Stan' still, puddin', else yer gown'll never go on right." Avena wrestled the yards of exquisite blue fabric over her charge's head.

Sapphire groaned and forced herself to stand stock-still, arms in the air, as the maid slid the gown on. "I'm just not as good at this as you are, Angelique." She pouted, the room suddenly dark as her eyes were covered by the bulk of the gown. "But you're right. I know I can do it. I know I can make these men want me."

"'Course ya can." Avena gave the gown a tug and Sapphire's head popped out. "Every woman go' the talens if she dig down deep."

Angelique chuckled. "Avena, I really think you should take Sapphire up on her offer to help you speak properly. I haven't the patience for it, but I'm certain she does. She did much better with schooling than I did."

Sapphire turned so Avena could button the back of her gown. "Because you were too busy sneaking away from the nuns to play hide-and-seek with all the village boys."

Angelique grinned as she squirmed, tugging at her gown until it lay just right over her breasts. "We all have our *talens*."

"We'll begin tomorrow, Avena." Sapphire smiled.

"Really? 'Cause then maybe ol' Avena get up the narve to speak to 'im."

"You haven't even spoke to him?" Angelique exclaimed.

"No, too scart."

"Too scared?" Sapphire asked, enunciating carefully.

"Aye, too scared." Avena mimicked Sapphire almost painfully in her attempt to pronounce the words correctly. "'E's gonna be a 'ailor, out on his own soon. Why, 'e's likely to have 'is own shop one day!"

"Wouldn't that be something?" Sapphire smiled at Avena. "You, Avena Croft, the tailor's wife."

Avena blushed and drew her bleached white apron up over her face. "No man good as Dawson would want no ol' 'ho like me."

"Well, I heard from the baker's daughter yesterday, the little one with the red pigtails, that he was *asking about you*," Sapphire sang, walking to the floor-length mirror to get the first glimpse of herself in her new gown.

"No!" Avena slid the apron down from her face and then comically pulled it up again. "Yer lyin' sure as yer speakin'," she giggled from beneath the apron.

"I'm not." She glanced at Avena over her shoulder.

"Tomorrow we start our lessons in earnest, and I will not take no for an answer."

"Aye, Miss Sapphire." Avena curtsied, walked toward the door and curtsied again, her face flushed.

After days of cajoling, they had learned that Avena was actually only eighteen years old. It was tragic what a short time on the streets could do to a woman. The longer Sapphire lived in London, the more she discovered that while there were many exciting and beautiful things for the privileged, for most of the city there was abject poverty, pestilence and even death. It was terrible that there could be so much grief and sadness in such a wonderful place.

"Girls!" Lucia called from down the hall. "Are we almost ready? Your escorts will be here any moment and Mr. Stowe has arrived!"

"Bad news, monsieur?"

Armand looked up from his chair on the terrace to see Tarasai standing over him, her lovely face lined with concern. He realized then that the sun was about to set and darkness about to fall over his jungle home. He wondered how long she had been there, how many times she had spoken before he heard her. He glanced down at the letter on his lap, fingering it absently. "No. I don't believe so, *ma chère*. At least I hope not."

"I brought you a blanket," Tarasai said, raising a lovely multicolored patchwork quilt made from squares of homemade native cloth.

"I'm not cold."

"Put it on anyway," she said in her lovely, lilting voice. "The breeze is cool tonight." She took the letter

from his lap, laid the quilt over his bony knees and returned the letter to him without looking at it. Not that
it would mean anything to her; like most of the native
people of Martinique, she could not read.

"Is this letter from your daughter?" Tarasai asked,
walking to a burning torch near the French doors that
opened into the house. She took a dry blade of grass, lit
it and walked back to light the oil lamp on the small table beside him.

Armand realized he spent a great deal of his time on
the terrace these days. At first, when his Sapphire, Lucia and Angelique had left, he had tried to go back to
his daily routine, visiting villagers, walking the fields,
checking in on the drying warehouses, but he no longer
had the strength. As his illness grew more severe, and
with Tarasai's gentle nudging, he had begun staying
closer to home. Mostly he read, worked on his moth and
butterfly collection and simply sat on the terrace listening to the jungle, watching its ever-changing beauty. In
the year after Sophie's death, he had shared his bed
with many women—mostly native girls—but lately
there had been only Tarasai. Tarasai was the only one
he wanted, the only one who did not look upon him
sadly, already thinking toward his death rather than
celebrating his life.

The oil lamp cast light onto Armand's lap and the letter. "Are they well, monsieur?"

"Yes." Again, he looked at the letter, then up at her
face—such a sweet face with round, dark eyes. And
skin the color of coffee with just a little milk added to
it. "Well, I think."

She waited.

He adjusted his glasses and reread one of the lines Lucia had written. "They are no longer staying with Lord and Lady Carlisle—they have struck out on their own. I will have to send more funds at once."

"Of course, monsieur."

"She...says that, sadly, our Sapphire's father is deceased and there is a new Earl of Wessex, but that they are hopeful the matter of her birth will be resolved." He said this with more enthusiasm in his voice than he actually felt. For the hundredth time he wondered if he had made the right choice in sending Sapphire away. Just one more year and she would have been wiser, perhaps not quite so innocent and trusting. But this was what her mother, his Sophie, would have wanted.... He had vowed that he would fulfill his dead wife's dream and he could not lie peacefully in his grave if he did not keep his word.

"You should not worry so much, monsieur. Miss Sapphire is a smart young woman. She will find what she wants. She will have all she wants and more. She is lucky, that one, born under lucky stars."

He smiled, squeezing her hand. "I would like to write a letter and send it along with a draft from one of my accounts in London."

"You sit, monsieur, and enjoy your garden." She rose. "I will bring you ink and pen and paper and then I will bring you soup."

Armand wasn't hungry; he was never hungry anymore, but he knew better than to argue with Tarasai. It was easier to just take a few sips from the spoon and pour some out into the garden if he found the opportunity. "That would be nice," he said, watching her go. "Thank you."

She turned in the doorway. "You do not have to thank me, monsieur. I thank you for giving me a home and that which I carry under my heart." She smiled, drawing her hand over her breast and down to her slightly rounded belly.

Armand smiled. It was hard to believe that at his age and in his rapidly failing health, he could still father a child.

Sapphire alighted from the four-horse carriage onto the street in front of the Drury Lane Theatre with the aid of a handsome young baron. Lord Thomas, one of the first suitors to appear on her doorstep after hearing the rumor that the Fabergine sisters were in need of protectors, was presently a student at university, or at least he was, he had explained to her, as long as he was not booted out next week for his latest antics. His father, the Earl of Crumpton, was a member of the House of Lords, his family having served there for more than two centuries.

"Miss Fabergine, have I told you how truly bedazzling you look tonight?" Lord Thomas declared dramatically, pressing his lips to the back of her gloved hand, his smile utterly roguish.

Spreading her skirts, Sapphire glanced down at the jewel-blue fabric of her off-the-shoulder *fichu-pelèrine* gown and smiled to herself, feeling much like a princess tonight. Her gentlemen escorts were charming and the gown was the grandest she'd ever worn. She just hoped it wasn't too expensive, especially when she had ordered three more evening gowns from the dressmaker. "You must look the part to attract the caliber of man you're in search of," Lucia had explained, seeming to forget that Sapphire's goal was to gain not a protector, but a family name.

Lucia had written to Armand telling him of their change in housing and was certain finances were forthcoming, but their pile of bill receipts kept inside the desk in their new parlor was growing taller by the day. Armand had sent them with adequate funds to stay with the Carlisles, not to live on their own in London where rents were exorbitant and the price of a pound of tea would have purchased a wagonload of fruit and vegetables in Martinique.

"Lord Thomas!" Angelique called as she appeared in the doorway of the carriage, beckoning him with a fan painted with dancing naked cherubs.

Sapphire turned to see Angelique throw out both arms, allowing the young baron to lower her to the street, his hands spanning her tiny waist, her hands planted on his broad shoulders. Four more gentlemen piled out of the carriage, all dressed similarly in dashing black frock coats and silk top hats. Behind their carriage was another, smaller one, from which Lucia was being escorted by Mr. Stowe.

"Allow me to escort you, Miss Fabergine," Mr. Carl Salmons insisted. He was a young widower who, though untitled, was supposedly one of the wealthiest men under thirty years of age in the city. He had made his money in the import business and had brought Sapphire a gift of a Chinese painted fan that matched her new gown almost perfectly. A man who had taken the time to discover what color gown a woman intended to wear was the kind of man Sapphire thought she might like to know better. And not only was Mr. Salmons clever, but he was funny and articulate, as well. It was obvious that Mr. Salmons was in search of a woman to keep, but he would certainly take a wife again, she reasoned. Once she was acknowledged as the late Lord Wessex's legitimate daughter, and the entire "in need of a protector" rumor was squelched, Mr. Salmons might be the kind of man who would call on her…or might even request her hand in marriage.

"Hey, Salmons, I had her first!" Having passed Angelique to the arm of Lord Carter, one of the most eligible young men in London, Baron Charles Thomas took Sapphire's gloved hand again and wrapped it possessively around his arm.

"Perhaps you could both escort me," Sapphire soothed with a bright smile, offering her free arm to Mr. Salmons.

Angelique winked at Sapphire as she took the dashing Lord Carter's arm. She had met Henry that night at the reception at the Wessex town house and he had begun calling on her regularly, even before the outrageous rumor that Angelique and Sapphire were searching for patrons reached London's parlors, men's clubs and the Royal Exchange.

Lord Carter's family had made it known that their son would soon be marrying, but it was evident that young Henry was not the least bit interested in settling down with a wife and children in the country. A schoolmate of Charles Thomas, he was too busy drinking, gambling and womanizing, activities that seemed to endear him even further to the adventurous Angelique.

"What are we seeing tonight? I know you chose something we'll enjoy," Sapphire said flirtatiously, remembering Angelique's advice.

"One of de Pixerécourt's melodramas," Lord Thomas said, jumping in. "I've already seen it twice and it's quite charming. I've reserved a box, of course. And then, if you ladies would be so inclined, Lord Carter has reserved a private dining room above our favorite tavern, the Cock and the Screw."

Sapphire lowered her lashes, demurring at the words, but she had to be careful because she had not actually told any of these men she was searching for a protector. Since all was insinuated and nothing stated outright, it would be easy to wiggle out of the situation when the truth was ultimately revealed.

"Or elsewhere, if you prefer," Lord Thomas went on quickly, patting her gloved hand with his. "And of course, Mademoiselle Toulouse and Mr. Stowe are invited, as well."

Sapphire found it all very amusing how this game worked, as Lucia had explained it to her. Women could let it be known they were need of a protector who would keep them in apartments, pay their lavish dressmakers' bills and escort them to the theater and balls. In return, a woman was expected to be the man's lover, at his beck and call day and night whether he was married or unmarried. In Sapphire's eyes, this was clearly a form of prostitution, yet a kept woman still behaved as if she was a pillar of genteel society.

"I think a late supper with these handsome gentlemen would be divine, don't you, Miss Fabergine?" Angelique piped in as they passed between the marble pillars into the theater's extravagant entrance hall.

Sapphire tightened her hold on both gentlemen's

arms, smiling at one and then the other. "I agree entirely, Miss Fabergine."

"And you two are sisters?" Mr. William Hollington asked, hurrying to catch up with the group. He looked at Sapphire and then Angelique. "Or are you cousins?"

Sapphire smiled coquettishly. "Tell me, Mr. Hollington, what do you think?"

The Earl of Wessex leaned back in his velvet chair, propped his ankle on his knee and let his gaze drift lazily over the crowd of theatergoers settling into their seats in the mezzanine below. The play had just begun but he was no more interested in the story line than the rest of the audience. The English theater, he had learned, much like the theater in Boston or New York City, was not so much a place to see a play as a place to see and be seen by others.

Blake had been practically kidnapped and dragged to the Drury Lane Theatre on the insistence of the Countess Wessex and was now seated next to her and found that her only talent seemed to be her ability to whine incessantly.

Blake shifted his attention to the elaborate set on the stage below and to the lovely actress presently speaking. She was tiny, appearing to be no more than twenty, and had a full head of pale blond hair and remarkable green eyes.

He thought at once of another young woman with green eyes—one green eye, actually—and a familiar sensation rippled through him. He felt his groin tighten. He could almost smell the scent of her hair and could have sworn he heard her voice.

Blake groaned and shifted in his seat, redirecting his focus to the actress below. When she finished her line, she looked his way, lifting her dimpled chin, meeting his gaze. She smiled.

Blake smiled.

Twice more he caught her openly looking at him, and when the intermission came, before he could excuse himself and make his way downstairs to purchase a double scotch, a boy brought him a note and Blake unfolded it with amusement.

My dressing room after the show was all it said in a woman's flowery script.

He crumpled the note in his hand with a wry grin as he took the stairs down to the foyer.

A few moments later, Blake was turning from the bar, idly sipping his scotch, when a commotion of laughter behind him made him turn around with curiosity. A group of young gentlemen in expensive frock coats surrounded two young women as they laughed gaily, pushing each other as young men do, mocking, retreating and advancing as they jockeyed for positions closest to the two beauties.

Damn! It was the chit with the red hair. Sapphire Fabergine, he had learned when she had sent him a note after that night at Lady Wessex's party. He had returned the message without reply because he would not play her games or entertain her false hopes. Not even as lovely as she was.

Sapphire, a remarkable name for a young Englishwoman, he mused. He could still taste her lips on his. And now he could hear her voice, husky, deep, filled with seductive promise. So it had not been his imagination when he thought he had heard her earlier in the theater. Amid close to a dozen swains, with no chaperone anywhere to be seen, it was obvious she was some variety of exactly what he had accused. She was remarkable, all right, a woman out to extract whatever wealth or prestige she could from unsuspecting males.

He drank from his glass and savored his scotch, and the smoky flavor somehow reminded him of her, of the taste of her mouth. He was just about to walk away when she turned.

He drew a breath. She was even more lovely than he recalled, dressed in an exquisite blue gown the color of her name, filled out in all the right places. She had good taste, he would give her that. With that rich auburn hair, her unusual eyes and that full, sensual body, she was a woman begging a man to make love to her.

She met his gaze directly, almost in challenge.

He smiled lazily, lifting his glass in toast as if to commend her for her achievements here tonight. The redhead stared at him for a moment longer, then turned her back to him in an act of dismissal.

Blake felt his jaw suddenly tighten. Women didn't usually turn away from him, though he had no idea why he cared about this one. She was a cheap adventurer.

He strode away, leaving the glass half-finished on a waiter's tray, and walked out onto the street to smoke a cigar. He couldn't stand another moment of the cloying theater, the countess, her daughter or the play.

More than an hour later, men and women began to pour from the theater. Voices rose in the early summer night air, now scented with perfume. Blake entered the alley along the side of the theater and took the first open door inside, which led him down a long hall. When he bumped into one of the players, the young man pointed him in the direction of the lead actress's dressing room.

"Whatever took you so long?" she said when he knocked on the door and walked in. "I was afraid you wouldn't come."

"I would never keep a lady waiting."

10

Lamplight danced off the whitewashed walls of the small dining room, softening the time-worn edges of the painted woodwork, and thankfully, Lucia mused, the lines on her face. Sipping from her wineglass, she studied the barrister, thinking she felt younger tonight than she had in years.

"Did you enjoy the play, Mademoiselle Toulouse?" Mr. Stowe asked as he cracked a walnut and offered her the sweet meat from the center.

They had shared an exquisite meal of turtle soup—an expensive delicacy in London—oyster-stuffed partridge with a jellied wine sauce, pork and peas pudding, and fresh bread. A serving girl had just cleared the table, brought another bottle of wine at Mr. Stowe's request and served them a plate of fresh fruits and nuts.

Lucia plucked the meat from the nutshell and popped it into her mouth with a smile, washing it down with more ruby-red wine. The small room where the host had seated them was actually a hall-way leading into a much larger dining room where Sapphire, Angelique and their group of young men dined in the rented rooms above the Cock and Bull Tavern. With the door left open, the dining arrangements were considered perfectly acceptable and her young charges were considered chaperoned, which amused Lucia to no end considering what the girls were up to. Somehow, the four gentlemen who had come to take them to the theater had become five by the time they arrived on Drury Lane, and had expanded to nearly a dozen by the time they reached the tavern.

Lucia wasn't concerned about the girls' safety, even in a group of men so large—not that she ever worried about Angelique, a girl who had been born old. Tonight, even Sapphire seemed to be enjoying herself, playing the role of the flirtatious new girl in town. And, Lucia realized, she was certainly enjoying herself, too.

Her gaze returned to Jessup Stowe's jolly face. Lucia had made love to many men over the years, been loved by many men, but she had never been in love. She'd always teased her dear friend Sophie, claiming there was no such thing as love. Now, after all these years, she wondered if she had been wrong. Jessup Stowe was nothing like the men who paid such high prices for her affection in New Orleans, or like the men she had affairs with in Martinique. He was certainly nothing like the handsome Armand, whom she had come to care for a great deal. Perhaps that was what made Jessup Stowe all the more fascinating to her.

"Come now, Mr. Stowe, I think it's time we dispense

with society's decrees and use first names, don't you?" Lucia set down her wineglass.

He lowered the iron nutcracker to the table, glanced at her, then began to tidy up the table, sweeping nutshells into his hand. He seemed pleased but unsure how to take her suggestion.

"Jessup, I like you a great deal." She reached out and rested her hand on his until he looked at her. "And I think you have feelings for me. Let's face the truth—neither of us is getting any younger. Need we really waste our time with all these ridiculous rules when we could be moving on to something...more mutually satisfying?"

His eyes widened slightly, and then narrowed as she leaned over the table until her lips met his. A heat danced between them at once, a heat Lucia had feared was gone from her life forever, and when she opened her eyes to look at him, he was smiling.

"That was nice," he said softly, taking her hand between his and smoothing it. His eyes filled with moisture. "It...it's been a very long time, Lucia, since I kissed anyone."

"Pretty good for being out of practice," she teased as she leaned over the table again. Only this time, she let him take the lead—and she was not disappointed.

Jessup was less hesitant with his next kiss, and his touch sent a delightful shiver of pleasure that she felt from her eyebrows to the balls of her feet. Their lips brushed once, twice, and then she tasted the tip of his tongue.

"I think I should go home with you," Lucia murmured, searching his eyes. Then she smiled mischievously, drawing her fingertips under his clean-shaven chin. "You don't seem as shocked by my proposal as I would have expected."

He took her hand in his. "Nothing shocks me any-more, my dear Lucia." He chuckled, turning his head to gaze through the open doorway where several of the young gentlemen had begun a game of cards. Angel-ique and her Lord Carter were dancing to the strum of a hired minstrel's lute. "I do, however..."

"You what?" She clasped his hands, drawing him close again. "There must only be honesty between you and me, Jessup. I don't have time for any drivel."

He grinned lopsidedly and Lucia thought she caught a glimpse of the young man he had once been—hand-some with dark hair and a devil-may-care smile.

"The young ladies." He cleared his throat. "I'm not certain that..." He stopped and started again, seeming uncomfortable.

Lucia waited, even though she was fairly certain what he was about to say. What he wanted to break gently to her was that he could not be associated with such scandalous young women. It was bad for business and his clients would never stand for it.

"If it's money you need, Lucia, to care for you and the young ladies, I have more than enough. My sons are both ungrateful louts and they don't deserve a pence of what is mine. I'd be happy to spend it all before I die, if I could figure out how to do it." He met her gaze again. "It's not necessary that these young ladies do this. They could marry—I could perhaps offer them a small dowry—"

Lucia turned away and laughed. That was not what she had anticipated. She had thought he would say something about having to keep their affair private so his business would not be affected. But his offer to care not only for her, but also for her chicks, was a pleasant surprise.

Now it was her own eyes that filled with tears, and Lucia was not a woman who had time for tears. "Jessup—"

"I mean what I say, dear Lucia. What is money if it cannot make a person happy? It means nothing to—"

"Jessup, listen to me. This is not as it appears. Despite the gossip you hear or what you may believe you see, my charges are not really looking for protectors."

He glanced through the doorway again. Angelique was now perched on the edge of the dining table, flashing more than a little calf as she swung her legs with the hapless lightheartedness of a child. Sapphire sat in a chair, fanning herself madly.

Jessup looked back at Lucia again.

"I'm going to tell you a story," she said, "and I'll warn you, it will sound far-fetched. I'll also warn you that if you don't believe what I say, you and I will have a nice tumble tonight. I'll sleep with you until dawn and I'll probably come to your bed again, but we will never have any more than that."

Jessup swallowed hard and nodded.

"This—" she pointed in the direction of the larger dining room "—is a ruse. A way to get the American, Blake Thixton to listen to my Sapphire. You see, she is also a Thixton, and we journeyed from Martinique so that she might claim her legitimacy."

"I don't understand. His lordship is only nine or ten years older than Miss Fabergine. He could not possibly—"

"Just listen, Jessup, and let your supper settle." Lucia withdrew her hands, poured him more wine, then sat back and told the tale.

"Such a claim would be very difficult to prove now that her father has passed away, Lucia," he said when she had finished.

"Sapphire has letters written by her father to her mother. Love letters. And a jewel. An exquisite sapphire that belonged to the Thixton family. Surely there must be written records of the stone being lost or stolen at the time Edward gave it to Sophie."

He shook his head. "Probably not, as the family would have guessed where it had gone—they already knew about his love affair. It would be an embarrassment to announce one's eldest son and heir had given away one of the family jewels to a dairy maid."

"She was his wife," Lucia stated insistently.

"There, there." Jessup patted her knee. "I'm only telling you what the courts would say. And I still don't understand what Miss Fabergine's claim has to do with all this." He indicated the merry party going on in the next room.

"Why, we're going to embarrass the family into acknowledging her! Isn't that a delicious idea?" She clapped her hands with delight. "Sapphire has let it be known she's in need of a protector and intends to go into keeping. Once we leak the truth of Sapphire's birth, the family name will be in jeopardy. The countess and Mr. Thixton will both wish to preserve the integrity of the name."

"But for the countess to recognize Miss Fabergine, she would have to concede that she herself was never legally wed to Lord Wessex."

"That's makes no difference to Sapphire. At this point, the countess will care about what most women her age care about—her daughters and seeing them properly wed." She raised a finger. "The fact that Edward was married to Sophie and therefore couldn't marry the countess won't matter to the American. It will only mean she isn't really of the house of Wessex. His primary objective will be to save the family from scandal."

Jessup lifted a bushy brow and indicated the other room with a hook of his thumb. "And *this* is not a scandal?"

"Oh, posh, yes, but a different kind of scandal. Every Englishman and woman loves a tale of romance. What would it mean to the American to simply acknowledge her in name? Nothing. She doesn't want any of his blasted money!"

Jessup flinched at her last words.

Lucia frowned. "What on earth is wrong? What did I say?"

He shook his head. "Nothing, dear Lucia, it's only that I'm just not certain your plan will work. It might be better to find the original marriage certificate and legally prove that Edward married Sophie."

"And where would I find that? Jessup, they were married twenty-one years ago. I don't even know where. Not in London, certainly. Some hill or shire, I would imagine, in a potato patch or some country church."

He tapped the table thoughtfully and then looked up at Lucia. "Let me see what I can do."

She smiled, leaned forward again, and this time took

his hand to rest it on her knee. "That would be wonderful. In the meantime, I think I'll let the girls continue with our plan."

"Just one more question."

"Certainly."

"Miss Fabergine—the other Miss Fabergine…"

"Angelique, yes."

"You say she is no blood kin to your goddaughter."

"She is not. Only a dear friend, something better than blood kin sometimes."

"Then why is she pretending she is in need of a protector?"

"Oh, just for the thrill of it!" Lucia reached for the wine bottle. "Now, what will it be for you, sir?" She lowered her lashes seductively. "More wine or another kiss?"

Seated on Blake's lap, Rosalind threw her arms around his neck and kissed him fully on the lips, brushing her nearly bare breasts against him. The other diners in the rented room above a popular tavern, the Cock and Screw, burst into bawdy laughter, clapping and whistling. Her friends were an eclectic group, mostly actors and actresses, a few gentlemen, a Frenchman on holiday, several orange girls and a brunette who was obviously a courtesan. Blake was the only American, the token guest of the evening, he presumed.

After he and Rosalind had coupled on the floor of her dressing room, they had talked while she removed her stage makeup and dressed for supper. She had informed him that he was already quite famous among the unmarried ladies of London and their mothers, and everyone wanted a chance to be considered a potential wife of the new Lord Wessex. When he asked her teasingly if she, too, was looking for a husband, she only laughed. "Why pay for what I can get for free?" she declared with a wink.

Rosalind rose from his lap and he slapped her bottom playfully; she laughed and danced across the room into the arms of a fellow actor. Blake leaned back in his chair until his head rested against the wall. He lifted his glass to his lips and drank deeply of the English whiskey, wishing it was scotch. He'd had quite a bit to drink. Enough. He was tired, tired of the party, of Rosalind and her vulgar friends. He wanted to go to bed, but that would mean returning to the Mayfair town house, and he wasn't quite ready to do that.

Beyond the wall he leaned against, he could hear that there was another dinner party going on. He could hear the rattle of dice, the clink of glasses and boisterous male laughter. He could also hear the voices of women.

He kept thinking he heard Sapphire Fabergine's voice. He thought he heard her husky laughter, and when he closed his eyes, he could feel her mouth on his. God, he really had had too much to drink.

He opened his eyes, sat up and set his glass on the table as he stood. That little fortune-seeking strumpet was invading his thoughts too often and he found it worrisome. All these years he'd managed to keep any woman from getting under his skin—why this one?

"Where are you going, Blake?" Rosalind called out to him when she saw him walking toward the door. She tried to escape the arms of her dance partner, but he held her tightly, pressing his lips to her breasts bared by the low-cut bodice of her gown.

"Home."

"Don't you want to come home with me?" she asked, pursing her rouge-stained lips. "Worn you out, have I?" she teased loud enough for several of her companions to hear her.

They chuckled.

Blake offered a perfunctory smile. "Precisely. Thank you. Good night." Grabbing his coat and hat from a hook near the door he slipped out onto the stair landing. He glanced down the hall in the direction of the lute music and the voice he kept thinking was Sapphire's. He couldn't hear her now; maybe it had been his imagination.

At the very end of the dimly lit hall was a small table with a middle-aged man and woman seated at it, their backs to him. He frowned and turned away as he punched his arms into his coat sleeves. They ought to know better at their age. There was no such thing as love—anyone with sense knew that. There was only lust.

Blake lowered his top hat to his head and started down the narrow back staircase. Hearing someone approaching from below, he attempted to move to the side, but the stairwell was narrow. He could tell it was a woman from the sound of her light footsteps. A woman in heeled slippers. Another actress or orange girl, probably. They'd been coming and going with men all evening.

At the landing halfway between the upper rooms and the main room over the tavern, the staircase turned sharply and Blake nearly collided with the woman skipping up the steps.

"I..."

One green eye. One blue. She stared up at him, as

shocked to see him as he was to see her. Her cheeks were flushed and her lips rosy, her hair slightly tousled as if she'd been dancing...or kissing. It *had* been her voice he'd heard.

Sapphire found herself staring up at Blake Thixton, breathless, her heart pounding. She tried to step back to put space between them, but on the small landing there was no place for her to go. He was holding both of her forearms tightly—she could not escape him.

"Why wouldn't you accept the letter I sent to you?" she demanded, feeling her cheeks burn. "You have to give me a chance to explain my situation to you."

"No, I don't."

"Yes, you do! I am Sapphire Thixton, daughter of—"

With a quick movement, he covered her mouth with his hand, turning her so that her back was pressed against the wall of the stairwell.

She wanted to scream when she felt his weight against her, his whole hard, lean body molding to hers. He held her immobile against the wall, taking his hand from her mouth only long enough to kiss her savagely.

Sapphire tried to push against him with her free hand but there wasn't enough space between them; with his body pressed so intimately against hers, she couldn't get any leverage. She tried to call out, but he only kissed her harder, forcing her mouth open with his tongue.

She thought she was going to faint, but at last he slid his mouth from hers, only to draw it along her cheek to her ear.

"What's the matter?" he murmured. "Those tiresome

fops good enough for you, but I'm not? I'm wealthy enough to buy and sell them all, damn it."

"I don't know what you're talking about," she panted, turning her face away from him.

"I think you do. I saw you tonight at the theater, flirting with those men, strutting your wares before them. I heard you upstairs laughing. Really, Sapphire, all those men, what do you do, move from lap to lap?"

Sapphire stiffened and turned to stare at him. "What is it to you?" she demanded, feeling her eyes blaze with hatred for him. "Now let me go," she ordered. "Let me go, or—"

"Or what?" His voice took on a teasing tone. His breath smelled of scotch. She could still taste it in her mouth. "What will you do to me, Miss Fabergine? Make me kiss you again?"

"Don't be ridiculous!" she snapped. "Let me go. Someone will come looking for me and then—"

"And then they will see this for what it is. You've been upstairs all evening with a bevy of male suitors. You and I are doing nothing you weren't already doing upstairs with them."

She tried to breathe deeply, tried to slow her pounding pulse. "I can assure you those men are all too kind, too gentlemanly to take advantage of a women in that way."

"Is that right?" He cleared his throat. "That's interesting because that's not what I heard. I heard that the Fabergine ladies are in search of protectors, and those gentlemen upstairs were all vying for a chance to be the fortunate fellow to take one of them into keeping." When she didn't respond, he went on. "What is your price, my dear? I know—lavish apartments, an account with a dressmaker, the hatter, the usual female requirements—but how much are you asking a month in stipend?"

He still held her against the wall, allowing her no chance to escape. "It doesn't matter because the offer is not open to you, Mr. Thixton!"

He laughed aloud and his laughter startled, then angered her.

"Don't flatter yourself, Miss Fabergine." He let go of her so suddenly that she fell back and her head hit the wall. "I'm not interested personally." He grabbed his hat off the landing where it had fallen and started down the steps. "Just asked out of curiosity," he called over his shoulder as he lowered the top hat to his head and disappeared around the bend of the narrow staircase.

"Sapphire? Dear?" Lucia called from upstairs.

Sapphire took a deep breath, forced a smile on her face and, grabbing handfuls of skirt, hurried up the stairs. "Coming!"

Lucia and her Mr. Stowe were waiting for Sapphire at the top of the steps. "Where have you been?" she asked, frowning with concern. "You're flushed." She reached out, placing her cool hand on Sapphire's forehead. "Are you feeling all right, dear?"

Sapphire pulled back. "I just went downstairs to the ladies'." She glanced at Mr. Stowe and gave Lucia a quick smile, laying her hand on her forehead. "I'm getting a bit of a headache, though. Do you think it's time we go?"

"I've been telling Angelique that for half an hour. She wants me to leave her here, but I told her it was out of the question. We must, after all, keep up *some* appearances."

"I'll call the carriage if you two lovely ladies will excuse me," Mr. Stowe announced, skirting around them and starting down the stairs.

"Are you certain you're all right?" Lucia asked Sapphire again. "The young men who escorted you tonight all seemed pleasant enough, but you never know with men."

"Aunt Lucia." Sapphire turned to her. "I'm fine. Just tired, I've a headache and…" She hesitated. "I ran into Mr. Thixton when I was coming up the stairs."

"Dear me." Lucia sighed. "I wondered if you might. He was in the dining room next to yours, with the actors and actresses from the play tonight."

Sapphire lifted a brow, knowing that actors and actresses had a reputation that was not always tolerated by polite society, though she didn't know why it should surprise her that Blake Thixton would be comfortable in those surroundings. Nothing about that abominable man would surprise her.

"I don't suppose you had a chance to ask him if he might reconsider addressing your claim?" Lucia asked, watching her carefully.

Sapphire didn't meet her gaze. "No. No, I didn't. He had his chance. I'll not approach him again on the matter. Next time it will have to be him coming to me." She rested her hand on Lucia's shoulder and walked past her. "Let me go and find Angelique. Mr. Stowe will be waiting with the carriage. I'll drag her out by her hair if I must."

Lucia laughed. "You might just have to, puss."

11

Lady Wessex drew the veil down over her new broad-brimmed Parisian hat and entered the church, her three daughters in tow directly behind her. The crowd in the elaborate marble vestibule parted to allow her, a woman of obvious of high status, to pass through so that she could take one of the better seats in the chapel.

"Hurry," Lady Wessex said without turning to her daughters, "or we'll be late again. No man likes a woman who is perpetually late."

"How can I possibly hurry?" Camille whined, taking little trotting steps in an attempt to catch up with her mother. "This new gown is too small and I can't get my breath. I told you it was too small when the dressmaker came last week for the fitting."

"I'll take it back if it's too small," Portia whispered loudly, catching up to Camille and leaving the youngest sister to trail behind them. "I've been asking for a new gown for weeks, Mother. I'm certain Lord Carter—"

"Oh, who cares about Lord Carter?" Camille snapped, turning to look at Portia as she walked beside her. The organist had already begun to play the introit. They were officially late. "I'm to be married first. Mother has already promised."

"And precisely who do you intend to marry?" Portia asked. "You scare off every man who comes to call with your constant complaints."

They entered the chapel by the broad center aisle as organ music filled the cavernous room. "It's not true— is it, Mother?" Camille demanded in her high-pitched voice. "I don't scare off the gentlemen—it's only that we're being so particular, isn't it?"

"That's enough, young ladies." Lady Wessex lifted her thin nose beneath the broad brim of her hat and marched directly to the front, despite their tardiness. "We are in the house of the Lord where you should be reckoning your hearts and finding the proper attitude of humility required for the Sabbath." She slid into the third pew from the front on the left. While there were no family pews per se, this had been the Wessex pew at St. George's for more than a hundred years, according to her late husband.

Just as Lady Wessex and her daughters sat, the priest entered and the congregation rose to sing. Refusing to appear flustered, she took her time to find the proper page in the hymnal she carried under her arm before turning to her dear friend Lady Wellington.

"I feared you were ill," Lady Wellington whispered, staring straight ahead as if her full attention was on the first hymn selection.

"Late, I know. So much to do now that there's a man in the household again," Lady Wessex explained.

"Lord Wessex the American, yes. Is he very demanding?"

Lady Wessex smiled patronizingly. "Not more than any man, I fear."

Lady Wellington lowered her voice, glancing in Camille's direction. "Is Lord Wessex as smitten with your Camille as all the other young bucks who come to call?"

"Oh, quite," Lady Wessex agreed, and then sang the last words of the verse, beginning in midsentence.

"Good morning, Lady Wessex," Lady Marlboro greeted from the pew behind her.

Several parishioners glanced at the women in obvious reprimand. Lady Marlboro, though a dear friend of Lady Wessex's, was hard of hearing and therefore always spoke louder than necessary, even about Mr. West's slightly off-key organ playing.

"Good morning, Lady Marlboro," Lady Wessex called over her shoulder. Then, hearing Camille still whispering under breath to her sister about her dress, she gave her daughter's ear a quick tug.

"Ouch!"

"Shh," admonished a woman in the pew in front of them.

"Did you see them?" Lady Marlboro said loudly into Lady Wessex's ear.

The congregation continued to sing one of John Mason Neale's hymns that he had translated from Latin, but Lady Wessex didn't like the hymn anyway. Parishioners all around eyed them with disapproval, but they didn't dare suggest Lady Wessex and her friend cease talking. Each one of the ladies was too important in London right now, for one reason or another, to offend.

Lady Wellington's husband had the new King William's ear, they said, and would talk of a new reform bill to redistribute seats in the House. He was not a man to cross. Lady Marlboro's husband was currently an important man in the Court of Faculties and Dispensations, a person one wanted to remain on good terms with should one ever wish to be granted privileges one was not entitled to by law. And Lady Wessex was the talk of society since her husband's heir arrived. Everyone wanted to remain on her good side in the hopes of being invited to one of her teas, balls, or perhaps even a daughter's engagement party—if there was any truth to the rumor that the American heir had his eye on Camille, Lady Wessex's eldest daughter.

Lady Wessex leaned back. "Do I see who, dear?"

"Those young ladies who attended your reception for Lord Wessex." Lady Marlboro's voice took an accusatory tone. "The redhead, the pretty one caught with Lord Wessex. Her so-called sister is here, too, but they couldn't possibly be sisters. Look at the color of her skin!" She pointed with a perfumed handkerchief to a pew across the aisle and one forward of Lady Wessex's. "Didn't you hear?" she said loudly.

The hymn came to an end, at last, but then the organist moved directly into another.

"That Lord and Lady Carlisle were forced to ask them to leave? Yes, of course." Lady Wessex sniffed.

"Noooo," Lady Marlboro cried excitedly, grabbing her large brimmed hat so that it wouldn't strike Lady Wessex's as she leaned forward over the pew. "I can't believe you haven't heard! Didn't you see them at the theater last night?"

"Come, come, what is this dreadful news?"

"Because Miss Fabergine and her godmother were put out of the Carlisles', she and the one with the dark skin have been forced to go into keeping!"

"No," Lady Wessex breathed.

"No," Lady Wellington chimed in.

"God's truth," Lady Marlboro swore. "She's looking for a protector, taking *offers*."

"Shocking." Lady Wellington rested her hand on Lady Wessex's arm, peering into her face. "It's just as well the Carlisles distanced themselves from the whole lot of them. Can you imagine the scandal?"

"It's a good thing she has no family in England, that's all I have to say," Lady Marlboro continued, now full of herself and her news. "Such scandal could put a family name in ruin in a matter of weeks."

"And to think you invited Miss Fabergine into your home." Lady Wellington squeezed Lady Wessex's hand before releasing it. "But of course you had no idea what kind of woman she was when you extended that invitation."

"I had no idea," Lady Wessex agreed. "They were houseguests of the Carlisles', just come from Martinique. How was I to know? I was only doing what was de rigeur, extending my invitation to them."

"How was *anyone* to know?" Lady Marlboro insisted. "It's scandalous."

The hymn came to an end and, at the priest's direction, the congregation took their seats. Lady Wessex sat down on the cushioned pew and glanced at her daughters sitting in a row beside her. *Poor Lady Carlisle*, Lady Wessex thought. She had to be beside herself, knowing she had let such undesirables into her home. Thank goodness her children were all married and gone.

Closing her hymn book, Lady Wessex folded her hands neatly on her lap as the rector began his sermon. Though his sermons tended to be long and tedious, she was thankful for this peaceful time each Sunday. It gave her the perfect opportunity to plan her week's menus in her head.

"I appreciate your taking the time to see me, Lord Wessex," Jessup Stowe said, clearing his throat. "I hope your stay in London has been pleasant so far."

"It has not." Blake took the same leather chair he had occupied the last time he visited the barrister's office. "Lady Wessex is the most irritating woman I have ever met. She does not shut up long enough to let a man think, no less speak."

"But what of her daughter Camille?" The barrister smiled knowingly, looking over his wireframe glasses. "I understand you have interest in that direction. Very wise. Though there's no longer any money in that family. Her father, Lord Danby, Lady Wessex's previous husband, was not only a powerful man, but well-respected. His entailment also went to a distant relative, I understand."

"What are you talking about?" Blake demanded. He wasn't sleeping well and he was eager to return home to Boston. He had cancelled a business meeting to come here in the hopes that Stowe would have news that would assist in seeing him on his way. "I'm not even certain which one is Camille." Blake frowned as he tried not to think about the bony young women with their thin hair and bad complexions. "I barely speak to Lady Wessex's daughters and none have certainly ever spoken back."

Stowe returned his gaze to the documents before him on his desk. "Yes, well…"

"Yes, well, what?" Blake commanded. "You called me for a reason. Papers to sign, more bills to pay, perhaps?"

"Yes, yes, of course. A few documents, but also…" Stowe looked up, then down and then up again. "A delicate matter that has come to my attention."

Blake waited.

"There is a young woman who—" Stowe's Adam's apple bobbed as he attempted to find the right words "—who claims she is the late Lord Wessex's legitimate daughter."

Blake shot out his chair. "She's been here, too?" he asked. "That little conniving…" He wiped his mouth with the back of his hand, staring down at the waxed wood floor as he walked around the back of the chair and began to pace. "Persistent little minx, though, isn't she?" he said as much to himself as to Stowe.

"Then you've spoken with her, my lord?"

"She's a charlatan, just like the others who have darkened my door since my arrival in London, laying claim to monies or favors owed."

"This…" Stowe caught his breath and then went on. "This young woman asks for no monies, or even favors. She simply requests that she be acknowledged as Lord Wessex's legitimate daughter."

"How the hell could that girl be Wessex's daughter? His first wife, the first I know of, died in childbirth with their first child eighteen years ago. He was only married to this one, his supposed second wife—" he hooked his thumb over his shoulder, continuing to pace "—ten or twelve years."

"This young woman, her name is Sapphire Fabergine—"

"I know what her name is," Blake snapped. "She's been plaguing me for weeks."

Stowe was silent for a moment and then continued. "She claims her mother was legally wed to Lord Wessex approximately twenty years ago. Her mother was a poor, uneducated country girl, so the family was, of course, completely against any union between them. She asserts that when the Thixton family discovered the couple had married, they had the young woman kidnapped and sent to America, where she gave birth to Edward's daughter, the young Miss Sapphire. Apparently the Dowager Wessex would be his third wife…of sorts."

"It's a preposterous story! A lie built upon lies to help the girl move up the ladder of London society."

"Yes, my lord, it sounds preposterous, but sometimes the most outrageous accounts are the ones that are true. This would not be the first time a good family has attempted to erase a bad marriage from the annals of history. With this in mind, I was wondering if you would object to my researching the girl's claim. At my own expense, of course," Jessup added quickly.

Blake halted, resting one hand on the soft, rich leather of the chair. Stowe had surprised him again and he liked being surprised by people because it happened so rarely. Jessup Stowe was a man of stronger character than he appeared on the surface. "I'm telling you, the whole story is ridiculous. I don't care what this girl says she wants, she's just more cunning than the others. She wants money, which you and I both know doesn't exist."

"Just these few documents have need of your signature, my lord." Stowe pushed them across the desk and offered an ink pen.

Blake came around the chair and leaned over the desk to scrawl his signature.

Stowe waited until the documents were signed and Blake had slid them back across the table. "So you have no objections to me making a few inquiries?"

Blake turned to stroll out of the office, raising one hand. "Do what you like, Stowe. Just get this paperwork done so I can get the hell out of England."

"Where are you going, love?" Jessup put out his arms, watching Lucia in the candlelight as she crossed his bedchamber completely unclothed. His heart felt like it would pound right out of his chest. Never in their entire life together had his dearly departed Emma ever allowed him to see her nude. "Come back," he beckoned.

"I told you, Jessup, my chicks. I must go home." She picked up a silk dressing robe from the chair in the corner of the room and slipped it around her shoulders, giving him one more glimpse of her pale, lovely breasts before she covered them.

"But what will I do when you go? I'll miss you too much to bear it."

She laughed and walked back to the bed to sit on the edge. "What will you do? The same thing every man does after he makes love to a woman. You'll roll over in your comfortable bed and be asleep before my carriage departs downstairs."

He took her hand, lifting it to his cheek. She smelled so good to him, felt so good, that it truly was hard for him to let her go, even for the night. Especially for the night. He had slept too long alone and he didn't like it. "Just a few more minutes, Lucia. I'll take you home myself."

"You'll do no such thing this time of the night. I'm too independent a woman to allow it." She leaned down to touch her lips to his. "Though I must say it is nice to be so desired."

"I don't just desire you," he said quietly. "I love you, Lucia."

She smiled down on him, wishing she could believe him, but she knew better than to believe any man. "Perhaps I can come back tomorrow night. Sapphire and Angelique were invited to some party or another. They want me to go along, but I thought I might stay in a night. All these parties—they're tiring for a woman of my age."

"Your age?" He kissed her hand. "You're twice as beautiful as a woman half your age."

"And how do you know my age?" she asked, lifting a brow.

He smiled. "I can guess."

She smiled in return. "You can guess, but I'll not tell. Now I really must go, but I'll come back Saturday night. I promise." She started to get up but he pulled her back.

"I've something to tell you. Something I think will please you. Will you stay long enough to hear?"

"What do you want to tell me? Lord Wessex has come to his senses and agreed to give my Sapphire an audience?" She lifted one finger, touching it to his nose. "Better yet, he has denounced the Countess of Wessex, declared Sapphire's mother to be the true wife of Edward and eagerly awaits the opportunity to acknowledge Sapphire amidst all of London society?"

He looked down at the bed. "It's not that good, but it is more realistic, Lucia darling."

She softened and reached out to stroke his cheek, which at this hour was rough with stubble. "Do tell."

"I saw Lord Wessex today on another matter, and while we were conversing, I brought up Sapphire."

Lucia stood up abruptly. "You know Lord Wessex personally and you didn't tell me?"

"You know very well a barrister does not discuss his clients with others."

She scowled. "I'm not *others*, Jessup. You just made passionate love to me." With a jerk, she tightened the silk tie on her robe. "You just claimed you loved me and now you tell me that Lord Wessex has been a client of yours and you failed to tell me?"

Jessup leaned against the headboard, readjusting his pillows. "Do you want to hear or not?"

She studied him for a moment. He had more spine than she had thought. Most men, after making love to her, could easily be crushed, certainly more easily manipulated. "Tell me."

"Sit down." He patted the bed.

She reluctantly complied with his request but only sat on the edge, her arms still crossed over her chest. "I'm listening."

"While Lord Wessex does not believe there is truth to Sapphire's claim—"

"How would he know? An American, just come—"

"Are you going to let me finish or not, dear?"

Lucia pressed her lips together and nodded.

Jessup cleared his throat and began again. "While Lord Wessex does not believe there is reason to think her claim to be true, he is willing to allow me to look into the matter."

"Jessup, that's superb!" Lucia leaned forward, throwing her arms around him. "Why didn't you just say so in the first place?"

He smoothed her hair tenderly and brought his lips across hers. "Because you wouldn't give me a chance, love."

"What a silly man," Lucia murmured, covering his face with kisses. "You really should pay me no mind and speak up." She drew her mouth to his and their kiss deepened.

When she pulled away, her heart pitter-pattering in her chest, she looked up at him through her lashes. "Would you like me to stay a little longer?" she whispered, slipping her hand under the coverlet to stroke his bare thigh.

"Just a little longer," he answered, a twinkle in his eyes as he slid her hand farther up. "And maybe I'll have something else for you...."

"Don't go," Clarabelle begged, sitting up on her knees on the four-poster bed, drawing the coverlet over her pert, bare breasts.

"Not so soon," Clarissa, her twin sister chimed in, coming to her knees beside Clarabelle. Like Clarabelle, she had waist-length red hair that fell in thick curls down her back, but unlike her sister, she had a mole to the right of her sensuous mouth, allowing him to tell them apart.

Blake watched a ringlet of hair fall at Clarissa's pale nipple and he contemplated their request. He'd been in their apartment for hours and had certainly enjoyed the pleasure of them both, but still, there was something unsatisfying about them, separate or together. They had relieved his tensions in several creative ways, but he still found himself restless, thinking of another redhead while he made love to the two in his arms.

"We'll miss you." Clarabelle pouted, dropping the coverlet to reveal her nakedness.

Blake watched as she slowly slid her hand over one full breast and down her belly to the patch of dark curls at the apex of her thighs. She tilted her head back, closed her eyes and glided her hand up and down to pleasure herself while her sister watched.

Stirring, but not stirring enough. Blake stepped into his trousers, which he had left folded neatly over a Louis XIV chair. He had to admit that the courtesans had good taste in both clothing and decor. They were wealthy, indeed, thanks to the frequency with which they were apparently summoned to the king.

After slipping into his white shirt, Blake sat down on the chair to pull on his stockings. It was after one in the morning and he was tired. He'd had too much to drink, too much rich food. He'd scheduled an appointment in the morning with a steam-packet agent and he needed a clear head by then. He had decided that whether his business was completed here in London or not, he was ready to go home. He would simply give Stowe permis-

sion to sign whatever needed to be signed and sell whatever needed to be sold. His life was in Boston and it was
time he returned to his business.

"I can't believe you would leave us alone in this big
bed," Clarissa simpered, looking at him with her large
blue eyes.

He leaned over to slip one foot and then the other
into his boots. Standing, he grabbed his waistcoat and
coat and walked toward the door. "I left money beside
the bed," he told the sisters.

Clarabelle was on the stack of bills in an instant. "Will
you come back tomorrow night?" she purred when she
realized how large a sum he had left.

He didn't care. It was only money and he had more
than enough to last him a lifetime. "Good night." He
lifted his hand in farewell and let himself out.

Twenty minutes later, Blake entered his town house
in the West End of London. The butler, asleep on a chair
in the front hall, leaped to his feet as Blake walked in
the door.

"Lord Wessex," Preston greeted, trying to appear as
if he had not nodded off.

"Go to bed, Preston. I've no need of your services. In
fact, you may always go to bed if I have not returned
by eleven at night." He tossed his hat and coat to the
butler.

"My lord?" Preston said as Blake walked past him.

Blake rubbed his temples. He could feel a headache
coming on that would last well through noon tomorrow.
"Yes?" he asked, not bothering to turn back.

"Lady Wessex, my lord." He sounded uncertain.
"She waits for you in the parlor."

Frowning in confusion, he turned around to look at the butler. "At this time of night?" he asked incredulously. "It's nearly two."

"Yes, my lord." Preston bobbed his head, keeping his gaze fixed on the polished floor.

With a groan, Blake walked away. He had half a mind to just go to bed and let the old biddy sit up all night waiting for him, but he walked down the hall toward the parlor where he had first met Sapphire. He didn't know what made him think of her as he turned the doorknob. "You needed to speak with me, Lady Wessex?" he asked, trying not to sound more interested than he was, which presently was not at all.

Unlike Preston, she had not been dozing while she kept vigil. She flew up out of her seat, dabbing at her eyes with a handkerchief. "My lord, thank heavens you've returned. I received the most disturbing news today and I knew you would want to know at once."

He stared at her for a moment and rested a hand on the back of a horsehair couch as he let her words sink in through the fog brought on by the scotch he'd consumed. He couldn't imagine the dowager had any news of importance, but he asked the expected question anyway. "And what is that?"

"Well," she began, "you know that young woman who was staying with the Lord and Lady Carlisle but had to be put out because of her inappropriate behavior."

He felt his forehead wrinkle. "No, I have no idea who you speak of."

She drew closer to him, lowering her lashes. "The young woman who was seen alone with you, my lord."

"When?" he asked impatiently.

"Sapphire Fabergine is her name."

Suddenly Lady Wessex had his attention and he looked up, the fog clearing.

"Pardon me first for even having to bring up such a delicate subject," she went on.

He motioned impatiently to her to get on with her story.

"Two weeks past, perhaps three, she made it known that she was setting herself up in keeping." Lady Wessex didn't look at him. "Looking for a protector to care for her."

"Yes, yes, I suppose I heard that—but what does it have to do with me?" He didn't bother to hide his irritation.

"My lord." Her eyes filled with tears. "She is spreading a nasty rumor that she is my late husband's legitimate daughter," she said, suddenly looking faint.

He groaned, seeing her sway. "Lady Wessex, perhaps you should sit down," he said as he reluctantly came around the chair.

She put her hand out to him, leaving him no choice but to take it. "I *am* feeling a little light-headed."

He helped her sit down on the settee.

"I…don't know what to do. It's untrue, of course." She wiped her mouth with her handkerchief. "But I would never want you to think our family, my daughter Camille—"

"What in God's name has your daughter Camille got to do with this?" he interrupted.

"My lord, if you're serious concerning your interest in my eldest daught—"

"Interest in your eldest daughter!" He stared at her. "Madame, I don't mean to insult you or your daughter, but I don't believe I have ever even spoken to her. I'm quite sure she hasn't spoken to me and I'm not even sure which one she is." Then he thought about the fact that Stowe had mentioned Camille, too. Was this more gossip being spread, that he was calling on Lady Wessex's daughter? Exactly what did Lady Wessex think she was doing?

"My lord, I know this is a delicate matter," Lady Wessex went on, seeming not to have heard what he said. "But I assure you there is no truth to this young woman's claim. She's merely out to see what she can gain from my husband's leavings."

"Of which there are none," he said wryly.

"But I want you to know, this should in no way alter your feelings for my daughter. Any intentions you might have—"

"I have no intentions for your daughter! Would you listen to me, woman?"

Lady Wessex began to cry. "Such a scandal, even if it is a lie. I just knew it would be the ruin of us. I just knew—"

Blake turned away and walked toward the door.

"My lord, where are you going?" she cried, rising to her feet.

"I don't know," he shouted back. "Just away from here."

12

"Ah, hell and fire," Angelique muttered as she gazed at the Irish case clock standing against the wall. "I should go."

"Don't go," Henry said sleepily, draping one arm over her waist and kissing her bare shoulder.

"If I don't, Sapphire will be up all night worrying." She ruffled his hair and started to climb over him to get out of the high tester bed.

"Are you leaving us?" A hand reached out to clasp her arm and she glanced over her shoulder to see Charles lift his head from the rumpled pillow and gaze up at her, red-eyed, his voice scratchy with too much drink and not enough sleep.

"Charles," she said impatiently. Though the man had a great deal more money than Henry, she simply didn't like him as much. He was positively a goat in bed. "I told you I couldn't spend the entire night." She glanced down at her arm and he released her. "You really could use a bath."

"But I want to make love with you again," he whined.

She rolled her eyes. "You're so greedy, Charles."

"But I want to make love with you again, too," Henry joined in, trying to catch her around the waist as she climbed over him.

She slapped his hands away playfully, landing barefoot on the worn Safavid carpet. "Then you're both greedy little boys, greedy little piglets who are never satiated. You know what we do with greedy piglets in Martinique, don't you?" She stood beside the bed, naked in her glory, and poured herself some sherry from a nearly empty decanter. "We put them in the stew pot and eat them for Sunday supper." She took a long drink and passed it to Henry, who drank, then passed it to Charles.

Henry flopped onto his back and watched Angelique walk across the room to gather her clothing. Henry and Charles both rented rooms in the same boardinghouse in the Temple Gardens district of London, run by a Mrs. Talbot, who Angelique knew for a fact was willing to accept sexual favors in return for missed rent payments. The young university men all thought she was crazy, and though most of them had sired themselves out to her on at least one occasion to prevent her from contacting their fathers, they all scorned her privately. Angelique rather admired her; she was a woman who could financially take care of herself and gain a little pleasure in the task. How could any independent woman not love her?

"Did you speak with Sapphire about the ball?" Angelique asked, turning up the flame on the oil lamp beside the chair she had perched on. When Charles didn't answer, she turned toward the bed as she rolled up one pink silk stocking. "Charles, did you ask her?"

"A hundred times," he groaned, drinking to the bottom of the sherry glass before dropping it on the floor beside the bed. He lay back, closing his eyes. "I must confess, Angie love, my patience is wearing thing. I've spent a fortune dining, attending plays, buying her trinkets, and I've got nothing out of her but a taste of her lips."

"I told you," Angelique said impatiently. "I told you from the beginning, she isn't like me."

"You can say that again," Henry chuckled, adding a sexually explicit phrase under his breath.

Charles laughed. Angelique didn't. "Do you want her or don't you?" she asked, rolling on her other stocking.

"I do. You know I do. Damn her, she's got my balls so blue, I actually half proposed to her the other night."

"Did you really?" Angelique stood up, stepped into her shoes and reached for her wrinkled chemise. "She didn't tell me. But surely she will accept your invitation to the ball."

"I don't know." He frowned and rested his forearm on his forehead. "She seems fond of Salmons."

"Salmons doesn't hold a candle to you, Charlie." Henry gave him a good-natured slap on his bare belly.

Charles knocked his hand away. "I'm just not used to not getting what I want, when I want it."

"Did you mean it?" She dropped the chemise over her head and picked up her stays. "I mean the part about being willing to marry her?"

Charles shrugged. "I suppose I must marry someone, and marrying her would certainly infuriate my parents, considering her reputation. That alone would be worth it, perhaps."

"Because marriage is what she wants. Marriage to a good man."

"I'll vouch for Charlie. A finer chap I've never known." Henry went to hit him again, but Charles caught his hand in time to stop him.

"I just don't know if you're the right man for her," Angelique said, stepping into her rumpled pink gown and slipping her arms into the sleeves.

"And what's that supposed to mean? My family—"

"Your family," Angelique interrupted, "made its wealth less than a hundred years ago off the bad fortune of others. Her family, without money or not, is descended from Anglo-Saxon kings."

"I've yet to see any proof of her claim," Charlie said airily.

"You'll not speak of my Sapphire that way, Lord Thomas," Angelique fumed as she marched over to the bed while struggling to straighten her bodice. "Take it back this moment or I'll tell Sapphire just where you were tonight, in this bed, performing those unlawful acts."

He frowned and crossed his arms over his bare chest like a little boy scolded by his mother. "And she would be angry with me and not you?"

"Sapphire loves me."

"I love you," Henry said sweetly, reaching out to take her hand and bring it to his lips.

She smiled down at him. "I know you think you do, dear." He must have brought his own furnishings to these rooms, she mused. The case clock was an Alex Kelt, and he had two lovely rugs, worn, but still very nice. Henry might not be flush, but he did have substance.

"No, I mean it." He sat up. "I would marry you. Portia Stillman be damned, my parents be damned. I would give up my inheritance to marry you in a minute."

"And what on earth would make you think I would marry you without your inheritance?" With a smile playing on her lips, she turned her back to him and sat on the edge of the bed. "Lace me up, will you? I really must go."

Henry laced up her gown and she leaned over and kissed him soundly.

"Will I see you tomorrow night?"

"It's already tomorrow," she said as she thought to herself that she liked Henry much better than she ought to.

"Will you see *me* tonight?" She shrugged her slender shoulders. "Very likely." She leaned over Henry and kissed Charles on the lips. "Bye, sweet."

"Tell Sapphire I was asking for her, and do put in a good word for me," Charles said.

Angelique grabbed her silk wrap and reticule and skipped toward the door. "I will. Sleep tight, gentlemen." She gave them a wave and was gone.

"You want me to see 'bout that green ribbon, Miss Sapphire?" Avena asked, taking great care to enunciate each word correctly. "I could run down to the dress shop and get you more."

"And see Bixby Dawson at the same time?" Angelique teased from the stool where she sat in front of the vanity, twisting her hair into fat curls with the aid of a hair iron Avena had heated for her.

Lord Carter was coming for Angelique at noon and they were attending boat races on the Thames. Sapphire had also been invited by several of the young men courting her, but she had feigned fatigue out of desire to stay home for just one day. It seemed as if it had been months rather than weeks since she'd had a chance to sit and read a book or go for a walk without worrying about entertaining the fawning gentlemen who constantly surrounded her.

Avena smiled mischievously, color appearing on her cheeks. "Not yer business if I do see Mr. Dawson, Miss Angel."

"No, I don't suppose it is. Nor is it my business if you sneaked out late last night to meet him."

Avena's smile turned into a broad, proud grin. "We didn't do nuthin'...*anything* but take a walk in the moonlight. I'm a good girl, now." She giggled behind her hand as if she were a schoolgirl. "Bixby's been wantin' a piece of tail so bad, he asked me last night if I thought he was the kind of man I might be willin' to marry."

"Sounds romantic," Sapphire told Avena, genuinely happy for her. "You will say yes if he asks you, won't you?"

"Can't imagine bein' married to a man like that," Avena murmured dreamily. "Me, Mrs. Bixby Dawson, a tailor's wife!"

"He'd be lucky to have you as his wife, Avena," Sapphire said, unable to suppress a twinge of something akin to jealousy. It wasn't that she wanted any part of Mr. Bixby or any man like him, but she did find herself longing for someone who cared for her the way the tailor seemed to care for Avena. "If you wouldn't mind going down the street, I would like some more ribbon for my costume for the masquerade ball Saturday evening. Another three or four yards would be wonderful." She sat on the bed, her mother's wood and leather casket beside her. She waited until Avena had gone and then opened the lid.

Angelique watched Sapphire in the mirror. "You seem quiet this morning. What's the matter? Why aren't you more excited? You'll be the belle of the ball Saturday night."

"You mean *you* will," Sapphire corrected, carefully setting aside her father's love letters to locate the precious sapphire in its velvet bag.

Angelique set down the curling iron and rose, crossing the room to sit beside Sapphire on the bed. She wrapped an arm around her. "Tell me what's wrong. You've been having such a wonderful time these past few weeks, meeting all these exciting men. Men you would never have had the opportunity to meet in Martinique. Why, they say half the eligible men in London are madly in love with you." She giggled, giving Sapphire a peck on the cheek. "And a few who are not eligible, I understand."

Sapphire lifted the gem out of the small trunk and held it in her palm, feeling its weight. "I can't continue to string these men along this way. They're beginning to press me for a decision. I knew this was a bad idea." She looked up, her tone full of introspection. "Angel, they think I'm going to accept money from them to allow them to…" She couldn't finish her sentence, and not just because of the subject. She'd been feeling guilty for weeks.

Everyone in London was buzzing about who she was and who she claimed to be, but still she had heard nothing from Mr. Thixton. She had heard that he moved out of the Wessex town house and into a hotel. Then yesterday she had heard that he proposed to Lady Wessex's eldest daughter, Camille, and that a whirlwind wedding was being planned before he returned to America. Somehow, Sapphire had a difficult time imagining Mr. Thixton with someone like Camille—but who was she to say and what did she care? She despised the American blackguard and Camille Stillmore could have him!

The dilemma for Sapphire, however, was that if Blake Thixton left without allowing her to at least discuss the matter of her birth with him, she didn't know what to do next. Aunt Lucia said that her Mr. Stowe would find proof of Sophie's marriage to Edward, but Sapphire didn't know what she was supposed to do in the meantime. It had never occurred to her that she might not accomplish what she'd set out to do, and now she felt as if she were drifting in a dinghy without sail or oars on the vast ocean they had traversed to reach England.

"So you can't string them along much longer. Fine," Angelique said, resting her hands in her lap. "Then perhaps you should take one of them up on their offer."

Sapphire turned to stare at Angel.

"It wouldn't be such a bad life, you know," she said playfully.

At some point during the past week, Angelique had decided to bestow her favors solely upon Lord Thomas, Portia Stillmore's previous beau. She'd not moved out of the rented apartments she shared with Sapphire and Lucia, but she and Henry were making daily ventures into the city to search for the perfect place for them to reside together. Henry said his parents were threatening to cut off his inheritance if he didn't cease his behavior, cut all ties with the Fabergine *demimondaine* at once and return to Miss Stillmore's side. Angelique said her Henry was not the sort to take kindly to orders, even if his father was providing three hundred pounds a year in allowance, and paying his debts, besides.

"I can't take a lover, Angel, and you know it." Sapphire set the heavy velvet bag in her lap and reached out to take her friend's hand in hers. "It's not what I want. It's not who I am."

She shrugged. "So tell your suitors you've changed the price. Women do it all the time. Tell them you want one of them to marry you."

"What?"

Angelique rose to pace in front of the bed. "If marriage is the price you want for your virginity, tell them so. Didn't Lord Thomas ask you to marry him yesterday at the horse races?"

Sapphire rolled her eyes, then picked up the velvet bag to move it from one hand to the other. "He wasn't serious. You saw him—he was quite tippled."

Angelique snickered. "Weren't they all?"

Sapphire smiled. She had enjoyed herself yesterday, first at a garden party where she had played croquet with half a dozen eligible men all vying for her attention, then at afternoon tea at the horse races where the gentlemen had overindulged in a rum punch. "I'm not in love with Charles," she said. "I don't want to marry him."

"So what about Mr. Salmons or Mr. Cortez?" Angelique asked expectantly. "Lord Raleigh?"

Sapphire shook her head.

Angelique threw up her hands and returned to the stool at the vanity. "You and your silly notions of love. I thought you'd given them up for more reasonable desires—companionship, compatibility." She glanced in the mirror, her eyes twinkling. "Lust."

"Now you're just making fun of me." Sapphire walked to the window to look down on the street full of activity, with carriages and wagons and two-seater hackneys rolling in both directions, merchants and buyers hustling up and down. "Is it so wrong to want more than you have?" she mused aloud, thinking about Avena's dreams and how they might just come true.

"Certainly not." Angelique dropped the curling iron on the vanity. "Cold," she muttered. "It will have to be heated in the coals again." She spun around on the stool to face Sapphire. "It's not wrong to want things, to dream, but it's wrong not to enjoy life as it comes. It's wrong to never take pleasure in today, in anticipation of what might happen better tomorrow."

"It's not that I never take pleasure in what I do." Sapphire tossed the velvet pouch up and down with one hand. Suddenly, all she could think of was Mr. Thixton and her secret, one she hadn't even shared with Angelique. Just thinking about it made her cheeks grow warm.

She had to admit, at least to herself, that a part of her had enjoyed his kiss that night in the tavern when he cornered her on the stairs. As on the night in the billiards room, he had frightened her, angered her, but he'd also… She didn't know the right word for how he had made her feel, not just in the pit of her stomach, but deep inside.

Her breath caught in her throat and she turned her back to Angelique, covering her discomfort by making an event of returning the pouch to its place in the trunk. She didn't want to talk about this with Angelique, not with anyone. Blake Thixton was the enemy. He was the one person who could give her what she needed and he would not even listen to her.

Maybe Angelique was right. Maybe she had to consider her options. Even if Mr. Stowe did find proof of her legal descent, it could take weeks, years even. The utterly dislikable Mr. Thixton would return to America with his new wife—and where would that leave Sapphire?

She hadn't yet accepted anyone's invitation to escort her to the ball on Saturday. Perhaps she should agree to Lord Thomas's and seriously consider his marriage proposal. He was wealthy, his family was well-respected, he was a good man who would make a good husband and provider. Blake Thixton thought Sapphire was nothing but a penniless fortune seeker, a liar, a whore and a woman without a family name. If she married Thomas and became Lady Thomas, he'd certainly reconsider his assumptions, wouldn't he?

"Lord Wessex, what you're asking is unfeasible. The ship can't possibly be ready to sail for another week. We're still loading cargo and we've a shipment from China to transfer that isn't even due in until tomorrow."

Blake paced the tiny, sparse room above a warehouse on the London docks, only half listening to the shipping agent, Mr. Klaus, whom he'd been dealing with for weeks. Out a filthy, smoke-streaked window, Blake could see the Thames below and across the street. Along the dock beside the ship, men loaded the hold full of merchandise, new gowns of the latest Parisian fashion, coffee beans from the Caribbean and silks from the Middle East, in preparation for the voyage back to Boston.

He didn't exclusively ship merchandise meant for wealthy Bostonians, of course; he was too good a businessman to count too heavily on one market. He imported sugar, molasses, bananas, tea, gypsum, chalk, sulfur, guano, soda, iron, wool, hemp, liquor, fur and flax among other goods. And on the return voyage, he would export fine New England timber, fabrics and whale oil, if he was lucky.

"Surely you'd be more comfortable on one of the new passenger steamer ships, my lord. They're equipped with far better accommodations," the tall, thin man with gray sideburns and a thick mustache implored.

"*People.*"

"My lord?"

Blake hooked his finger around his cigar and removed it from his mouth, beginning to pace in front of the desk again. As he walked the length of the room, he tried to remain patient. "Will there be people on board, Klaus?"

"Yes, of course, my lord. It's a passenger ship, meant to transport people across the Atlantic. With the improvement in steam engines, my lord, we are able to—"

"I understand the advances we're making in steam engines, Mr. Klaus," Blake snapped. "It's what I do for a living. What I'm saying is that I don't wish to travel with any more people than necessary. The cabin you've had prepared is more than adequate. I just want a little peace!"

Mr. Klaus drew back, his slender fingers twitching on the desk. "Yes, my lord. As you wish, my lord."

"I've seen the tide charts. We sail Sunday morning."

"Lord Wessex, as I stated previously—" now his heavy mustache was twitching, as well "—I cannot possibly have the ship loaded properly and ready to sail by—"

"Sunday, six in the morning," Blake reiterated, walking toward the door. "The ship leaves at six a.m., Mr. Klaus. Good day."

Wisely, Mr. Klaus did not follow Blake to his carriage. Outside in the sunshine, Blake's nostrils filled with the stench of the shipyard and he felt an odd twinge of nostalgia. He and his father, Josiah Thixton, had never gotten along, not when Blake was a child and certainly not when he was an adult. But one memory that Blake considered close to being a fond one was that of walking the Boston harbor docks with his father late in the afternoons. Ships loaded with America's best timber and fibers bound for exotic lands would line up, ready to sail on the next tide. He would trot behind his father who was busy finalizing details, who spoke not only to the shippers, shipping agents and captain on the docks, but to the crewmen, as well. He had been a real bastard to his family, but to the men who worked for and with him, he was probably an entirely different man—the smiles, the inquiries as to how this new baby was doing or if that wife had recovered from an illness... His father's feigned—or perhaps it was even real—interest in these men's lives made them give him their very best, and thus improved his already booming business.

Too bad Josiah Thixton would return home to his mansion and beat his ten-year-old son with his fists.

The fine French cigar suddenly tasting sour in his mouth, Blake spat it out and ground the glowing end with the heel of his boot. Stepping up into the carriage, he called out an address to the driver and slammed the door shut.

Twenty minutes later, Blake was in Stowe's lobby. "I don't care if he's presently occupied," Blake told the clerk. "What I have to say will only take a moment."

"A-an appointment c-c-can be m-made," the clerk stuttered from behind his high desk.

"As much as I'm paying Mr. Stowe for as little I'm reaping, I think he can give me two minutes of his time." Blake strode past the desk toward the hall that led to Stowe's office.

The clerk leaped off his stool, hurried down the hall and somehow managed to put himself between Blake and the door to Stowe's office. "M-my Lord Wessex, p-please, allow me to at l-least announce—"

Blake scowled at the distraught clerk. "He has a client in there?"

"Y-yes, well, n-no."

"Which is it?" Blake demanded. "Either he has someone inside or he hasn't."

The door suddenly swung open, the knob resting in Mr. Stowe's hand. "Lord Wessex," he said sternly.

The clerk's jaw worked up and down. "I…I…"

"It's all right, Turnburry," Stowe said. "Go back to work and I'll see to Lord Wessex."

Blake grasped the lapels of his fine black wool coat and tugged. "I told him you would see me. Whatever client you might have is surely able to wait the five minutes it will take for me to speak to you."

"Actually, Lord Wessex—" Stowe blocked the door with his rounded body "—it's not business. It's personal."

Blake lifted a brow, now amused. "A lady friend, is it?" He attempted to peer around the paneled walnut door. "Didn't know you had it in you, Stowe. You Englishmen are a sly—"

"Jessup, have you a client, *mon chèr?*" The woman had an interesting accent, one that appeared French, but he recognized it as actually being French-Cajun out of New Orleans.

An American? Stowe had an American lady friend? Blake's interest was definitely piqued now. His homesickness made him long for the sound of an American's voice, even if it was an older woman's.

"That's quite all right, dear," Mr. Stowe called over his shoulder, and then, returning his attention to Blake and still holding firmly to the door, he barred Blake's entrance. "Lord Wessex can wait."

"Lord Wessex?" she exclaimed. *"Mon dieu!"*

Her tone changed, intriguing Blake further. Apparently she knew him, even if he didn't know her.

"Invite him in."

"Really, dearest," Stowe hedged. "I don't think that—"

"The lady wishes to be introduced," Blake insisted. "I never disappoint a lady."

The moment he pushed past Stowe and met the mystery woman's gaze, he knew who she was. They had not met, but he recognized her all the same. He had spotted her frequently in the past few weeks, at the theater, at balls, at the races. She was Sapphire Fabergine's aunt, godmother, chaperone, something.

"Mademoiselle Lucia Toulouse," Stowe said reluctantly as he followed Blake into his office. "Lord Wessex. Lord Wessex, the woman I hope to make my wife very soon if she'll have me, Mademoiselle Lucia Toulouse."

It didn't get past Blake that Stowe first introduced him to the woman, an obvious fault in proper protocol—done intentionally, he was certain. The slight amused him. Mr. Stowe was obviously smitten.

Blake turned to Lucia and bowed, then offered his hand. She curtsied and allowed him to lift her gloved hand to his lips. "Mademoiselle Toulouse," he said in perfectly accented French.

"Lord Wessex, a pleasure."

He released her hand. She was a pretty woman for her age—stout and well-rounded with a relatively unlined face. He couldn't guess how old she was. Forty-five? Fifty? Fifty-five? "A pleasure, indeed. I cannot help but notice your accent, madame. It's not from France—New Orleans?"

She chuckled, seeming to know she was caught. "I was actually born right here in London, but I passed through New Orleans, once upon a time," she said with a smile.

Blake was tempted to move the conversation right along and ask her what the hell her charge, Miss Sapphire Fabergine, was doing making claims to a dead man's name, but he decided against it. In three short days he would be gone from London, gone from all this nonsense, and who she or Sapphire Fabergine was wouldn't matter to him any longer.

"I apologize for barging in this way," he told Stowe, who had taken his seat behind his desk. Mademoiselle

Toulouse had returned to the red leather chair in front of the desk. "I only wanted to inform you that I'll be sailing for Boston Sunday morning. Any paperwork you might require of me in order to give you full access to my properties, the right to sell in my stead, and whatever other business that needs to be transacted, you must have prepared by tomorrow."

"You're leaving London?" Madame Toulouse asked, sounding alarmed.

Blake looked at her sternly. "I've been here over two months dealing with some business matters as well as a personal affair, as you well know, but I can remain in London no longer. I must return to Boston, mademoiselle."

She scowled, lifted her chin and made a show of looking away, dismissing him.

Stowe's gaze darted from Blake to Madame Toulouse and back to Blake again.

"My Lord Wessex—"

"Stowe, I've made up my mind. I cannot possibly remain in England another week. I've one engagement I must fulfill, some ridiculous masquerade ball, but then I'm off and there will be no further discussion on the matter." He started for the door. "I've work in Boston I've ignored too long." He didn't say he was leaving to get away from a redhead with one blue eye, one green. He hadn't even realized the truth until he'd met her aunt, until the lie had come out of his mouth.

"Lord Wessex." Stowe rose from his chair, hurrying after Blake. "We've matters to discuss and decisions to be made."

"I trust you completely, Stowe."

"But, my lord..." Stowe lowered his voice until Lucia could not possibly hear what he was saying. "I realize this is not my place to say, but what about the Dowager Lady Wessex's situation? If I sell the homes, she'll have no place to go."

Blake scowled, knowing all too well he couldn't just throw them out on the street. "You're right, it isn't your place to say. I inherited the damn house, but..." He hesitated. He just wanted to be gone. "Give them the place in the country," he snapped, now impatient to be out of the barrister's office.

"My lord?"

"You heard me. They don't need the town house in London. It's the least I can do to spare Londoners having to listen to what I've heard these past weeks, but they can go to the country. The cows can listen to them."

"And the town house, my lord?" Stowe asked, looking at Blake as if he had taken leave of his senses. "You want me to sell it, or keep it for your next trip to England?"

"I don't know. Let me think about it." He replaced his top hat on his head. "Good day, Stowe."

"Good day, my lord," Stowe replied, standing at his office door as he watched Blake leave.

"And, Stowe..." Blake glanced over his shoulder. "Nice-looking woman you have there." He winked. "I like redheads, too."

Lucia was out of her chair by the time Jessup closed the door. "I'm terribly sorry about that, my dear. I don't care who he is or what title he possesses, he had no right to barge in here like that."

"Now, now," Lucia said, looking at the door where Mr. Thixton had just made his exit. "He's a blustery young man, obviously used to getting his own way. You probably behaved the very same way once upon a time when you were a young man, before you found your senses."

"I don't care. It's inexcusable," Jessup repeated, tugging on the hem of his waistcoat.

"Do you think he'll really return to America without hearing my Sapphire out or waiting to see what you've uncovered?"

"My love." Jessup sighed, reaching out to rest his hand on her shoulder. "I told you, it could take me months to find anything, if there *is* anything to prove that the late Lord Wessex was Sapphire's father."

"I know." She gazed into his eyes. She and he were of equal height and she liked that—not being looked down upon by a man. "It's just that—"

"I know. He was never willing to hear her out, and for that I'm sorry. But men like Lord Wessex, like Blake Thixton," he said, "can be obstinate." He hesitated. "That doesn't mean they're bad people."

Lucia tried to think what he meant by that comment. "It's not just that," she said softly.

"Then what is it?"

She didn't want to tell Jessup what she was truly worried about now, but if she was serious about wanting to spend the rest of her days with him, she knew she needed to trust him in a way she had never trusted another man, even dear Armand. "I'm concerned…that Sapphire may have feelings for Mr. Thixton."

He raised a bushy eyebrow. "I see. Well, that could complicate matters, couldn't it?"

"Perhaps." Lucia smiled, reaching up to smooth the

frown lines around Jessup's mouth. "You know, *mon chèr*, you're very handsome when you wear that concerned look on your face."

"It's only that I would not want to see her hurt if he doesn't feel the same for her, which perhaps he does not," he said gently, "since he obviously intends to make his departure shortly."

"You never know what will transpire. You haven't seen the way Thixton looks at my Sapphire," she continued. "Across a ballroom, from across the theater. I don't care what he says, I know men and I know he's attracted to her. Fiercely, I suspect."

"My love, I don't recall Sapphire saying she was any too fond of him. What was it she called him the other night when his name was brought up in conversation? An arrogant, blustering—"

"Blockhead," Lucia finished for him, leaning to brush her lips against his. "I'm off to shop now, but I will see you Saturday evening if that still suits you. Your house." She drew her finger under his chin teasingly as she walked away. "Your bedchamber…"

13

"Good lord a'mighty, Hattie, did you see 'im?" Odelia hurried behind her companion down the narrow, dark servants' hall, balancing the heavy tray of dirty glasses in her arms. The sound of the orchestra in the ballroom playing a waltz could be faintly heard behind them.

"It's no wonder all the ladies is faintin' left and right," Hattie agreed excitedly over her shoulder. "I don't know if I've even seen a man as good-lookin' as that." The unwieldy tray in her arms tipped slightly. "Whoa," she cried, turning back to rebalance it. "I jest don't see why m'lord don't pay for candles in the halls, much as he's worth, the old skinflint."

"Can't be buyin' candles," Odelia offered. She had a terrible itch under her nose, but she couldn't scratch it and balance all the dishes on the tray. If she broke a single glass, Mrs. Paxton, the housekeeper, would have her hide and a month's pay, too. "Not when he's got to be payin' for all them 'spensive gowns the missus is always buyin'." Odelia tried to wiggle her nose to relieve the itch. "You see what she was wearin' tonight?"

"I seen it, all right. Scared me, all them feathers. Look like she was gonna take off flyin' down the grand staircase or somethin'." Hattie halted at the door at the end of the dismal hallway that smelled of mildew and rodent droppings. Balancing carefully, she lifted one foot and kicked the door twice and a third time for good measure. Then she backed up and leaned her shoulders against the wall to try to relieve the ache in her arms from the weight of the tray, which was now more of an annoyance than her itchy nose.

Hattie had been carrying these heavy trays of glasses and fine china back and forth from the pantry or the kitchen to the main house since dawn, first to set all the tables in all the rooms. Lady Harris liked her guests to be able to enjoy their refreshments in every room. Now Hattie and Odelia were to clean up dirty glasses and replace them with new ones until the party ended, which would probably be at dawn. Hattie didn't understand why these haughty-taughties couldn't drink from the same glass more than once, but it wasn't her place to say so.

"What I also seen," Hattie continued, "was that floozy Miss Fabergine, the one that's got all the single gentlemen in the city all hot and randy. She was wearin' practically the same fancy white silk dress. Same mask on a stick, too, with all them feathers, but she looked a sight better than the lady, I'll warrant you that." She opened her mouth wide and then closed it in an unsuccessful attempt to relieve the itch on her nose. "What was they supposed to be?"

"I don't know, some kind of white duck or something, I s'pose." Odelia planted her feet farther apart to keep her tray balanced while she waited to gain entrance to the busy kitchen. "You think that girl copied Lady Harris' dress?" Her eyes now adjusted to the dark, Odelia looked at her companion, authority in her voice. "You know these society women, always tryin' to best each other. I hear they pay a lot a money to their fancy dressmakers just so they can show up in a dress the same as someone else and make a fool of 'em."

"Nobody even knows if Miss Fabergine *is* society." She paused. "You heard, right?"

"That she says she's the old Lord Wessex's daughter?" Odelia whispered loudly.

Hattie nodded. "Wouldn't that be somethin'!"

"It's a lie. Always is, but 'bout that gown, didn't you hear Tula the other day?"

"Tula?" Hattie eyes widened until they were as round as the dirty plates she carried. "Who's Tula?"

"One of the missus' handmaids. The one with the harelip."

"That's right. I know her." Hattie nodded, her mobcap beginning to slide over her forehead.

"She said the lady sent one of the livery boys all over town with a little bag a money, tryin' to find out what Miss Fabergine was wearin'."

Odelia snickered. "Like the missus was ever gonna look like *that* with them ham hocks for thighs. I don't think I ever seen a prettier woman than that Miss Fabergine, I don't care if she is indecent."

"It's the red hair, ya know. My mama always said the redheads was the floozies. Born like that." Hattie nodded as if it was the gospel and then turned to face the door and shouted, "Somebody comin' to let us in, or are we gonna die out here!"

"Hold yer herses," a muffled voice called from inside the kitchen.

"You think one of these glasses is his?" Odelia asked, her eyes dreamy as she studied the tray that was beginning to make her arms hurt.

"Who?"

"Lord Wessex. I swear by the Saints alive and dead, he's a fine-lookin' man. An American, they say."

"Don't matter what he is. He ain't never speakin' to you."

"I know that," Odelia sighed. "But a girl can dream, can't she?"

The door opened and they were immediately assaulted by the heat and noise of the kitchen. One of the kitchen boys, wiping his hands on his dirty apron, stepped into the hall to hold it so they could enter.

"You ought to be dreamin' about somebody who can feed ya and keep a roof over yer head, that's what you ought to be dreamin', Odelia. A fine man like my Denley." Hattie looked at the kitchen boy as she passed him. "You got a brother, don't you? Elwood?"

The boy, who couldn't have been more than nine or ten, blushed and nodded, keeping his gaze fixed on the stone floor. "Works in the stables, ma'am."

"Now there's a man a woman can dream about," Hattie instructed, walking into the kitchen. "A decent man who could take care of you, Odelia."

"Elwood in the barn?" Odelia wrinkled her nose as she followed Hattie, who was the more experienced of the two when it came to men. Nearly seventeen, Hattie was marrying a sailor just as soon as he returned from sea. "Ain't he the one who got the blind eye that rolls around crazy-like when he talks to ya?"

"Eh," Hattie called over her shoulder. "The eye ain't so bad if you don't look right at it...."

"Something to drink, my darling?" Lord Thomas asked Sapphire, drawing his face inappropriately close to hers.

They stood in an alcove off the Lord and Lady Harris's ballroom and Sapphire was feeling a bit light-headed. The rooms were too warm and too loud, and after being there for hours, she was tired of smiling and laughing and playing this part she was no longer convinced she could play.

The cream of society, bejeweled and gowned, had attended the annual masquerade ball, including members of parliament and court, dukes and duchesses, barons and baronesses. There was word even King William might make an appearance before dawn on his way home to the palace after one of his infamous nights of drinking and carousing the streets of London.

Having taken the throne after the death of his brother the previous year, the king was well-received by his people. Though Sapphire did not entirely understand the principles behind the Reform Act that gave parliament more power and the monarchy less, it was being said in newspapers that the king was "playing a difficult hand with considerable finesse."

Sapphire drew back slightly since Charles's breath smelled of whiskey or some other type of strong drink. He and the other gentlemen had been none-too-secretly passing a silver flask around earlier. Apparently Lady Harris did not serve anything stronger than a good Madeira in her home, which presented the gentlemen with a dilemma when it came to accepting the annual invitation.

"A drink would be nice, thank you," she told Charles. She deliberately let her eyes sparkle in the provocative manner Angelique had taught her and then lifted her mask to her face.

She was still playing the game, but Charles had been acting strangely all night, pressing her to accept his generous offer to take her into keeping. He'd only tried to kiss her once in the past few weeks, but tonight she was finding him more difficult to handle. Three times he'd managed to get her in a corner alone, and while she'd previously been curious about what it would be like to kiss him, she was less interested with each passing hour. Logic told Sapphire that Charles truly was an appropriate suitor, but there was something about him that bothered her, something in him she hadn't seen before.

"I'll only be a moment, my beautiful swan," he told her, bringing her hand to his lips to kiss it before releasing her.

She offered a quick smile. He'd been attentive all evening, obviously pleased that she had accepted his invitation over the others' to escort her to the ball. Obviously he thought the acceptance of his invitation meant she was seriously considering his offer of financial support. "I'll wait right here and then perhaps we could go for a stroll in the garden," she said. "I understand it's spectacularly lit with thousands of candles."

"A fine idea. I'll be right back. You'll be all right here alone?"

Sapphire nodded and let out a sigh as she watched him weave his way through crowds dressed in exquisite gowns and black frock coats and elaborate masks on sticks raised to conceal their faces. Sapphire had chosen the white and black mask of a swan and her gown was a delicious white silk that felt sinfully smooth against her body. Charles, in honor of her costume, had also chosen an avian persona, but was a peacock, of all things, his mask made of bright green and blue feathers.

"Sapphire!"

Sapphire looked up at the sound of Angelique's voice, attempting to spot her in the crowd.

"Sapphire, we've been looking all over for you!" Angelique called from a short distance down the hall. She stood on her tiptoes amid bears, jesters, Egyptian princes and princesses, and waved her green mask, ignoring their stares and whispers of impropriety. Tonight she was a mermaid dressed in an emerald-green gown with a green silk mask. "There she is, Henry. I knew she hadn't left without saying good-night."

Angelique made her way to Sapphire with Henry on her arm.

Sapphire lowered her mask and leaned forward to greet Angelique and was disturbed to find that she smelled of whiskey, as did Henry. Henry, in fact, was bleary-eyed, red-faced and appeared to be quite inebriated.

"I'm so glad you didn't leave," Angelique continued at the same unladylike volume. "This is a wonderful party. Isn't it a wonderful party, Sapphire?"

"It is," she murmured.

"Where's Charles?" She looked around. "Surely he hasn't abandoned you."

"I should speak to him about his manners," Henry piped in quite sternly, despite the slur of his words. Then he broke into laughter.

Angelique laughed with him, running her hand up and down his arm. He had discarded his black frock coat somewhere and was no longer carrying the mask Sapphire had seen earlier, that of a lion. He held up a pink lady's mask that sported genuine pearls hanging down one side so that it appeared he was wearing an earring. "Isn't this a divine mask?" he asked Sapphire, leaning forward to peer through it at her.

She put her hand on his chest, gently pushing him upright. "Divine," she said. Then she looked to Angelique. "Perhaps you should go," she said softly. "Henry's parents are here. I was introduced to them only a short time ago. They shouldn't see him like this."

"See me like this?" he demanded jovially. "Like what, Sapphire, dear? Happy? In love? I've asked my Angel to marry me, you know, at least a hundred times."

Sapphire looked to Angelique in surprise—she hadn't said a word!

"And I've refused him a hundred times," Angelique explained. "Why on earth would I want to marry him? I like him too much."

"Oh, you'll come around." Henry grabbed her roughly by the waist and pulled her against him, lifting her feet off the ground. Both of them burst into laughter again.

"Henry," Sapphire chastised quietly. She looked to Angelique again.

"What can I say?" She raised her hands. "He can't be controlled. See you later, darling."

Sapphire watched them sail off as Angelique fluttered her ivory fan, a recent gift from Charles, in front of her face. She was hot and suddenly felt as if she couldn't breathe. There were too many people in the alcove, all jostling her as they went by. Now all she wanted to do was find Charles and have him take her home. She was turning to look for him, rising on her toes to try to see over the crowd, when she felt someone approach from behind her.

"Charles?"

She knew at once that the man wearing the plain black silk mask and standing so near to her was not Charles; he was too tall, his shoulders too broad.

"Not Charles," said the man as he leaned over her.

She recognized the voice and scowled. "Mr. Thixton, what kind of costume is that?" she asked.

"The kind a man wears who does not like masquerade balls."

She fluttered her fan, the heat now seeming to come in waves over her. "And who are you supposed to be?"

"Myself." He removed the mask, slipping it inside his coat. "I don't suppose you were ever an ugly duckling."

"Excuse me?"

He rested one arm possessively on her waist. "Hans Christian Andersen. The fable of the ugly duckling who became the swan." He smiled, a reckless slant to his lips.

She attempted to take a step back from him, but two gentlemen stood behind her arguing heatedly with another gentleman.

"I don't know what you're talking about," she snapped, trying to hold her breath so that her chest would not expand to brush against him.

"You don't know Hans Andersen?"

"Of course I do!" She exhaled, feeling dizzy. "I only meant—"

"Are you feeling badly? You look pale." He frowned, tightening his grip around her waist, making her feel even warmer than she already did.

"Sir…my lord." She closed her eyes for a moment and then opened them. The room's candelabras seemed to be spinning around her, the bright light turning into blurred lines like shooting stars.

"Why don't we step outside?" He was already moving her through a crowd that parted like Moses' Red Sea.

Everyone was looking at them. At her. Talking about her, no doubt repeating the scandalous gossip about them they'd heard weeks ago. She didn't care. She just needed some air and to put some distance between her and the American. But feeling too weak at the moment to refuse his assistance, she allowed him to escort her down the long, marble-floored hall, through a salon and out onto a veranda.

"This…this will be fine," she said, her hand on her forehead, as she wondered why her heart was racing and her palms were damp.

"There are too many people here," he grunted, pulling her down the steps into the garden.

Many guests were enjoying the garden, as well, sitting on benches and walking the stone paths. But there was a cool breeze outside and people were not bumping into her or smothering her with their heavy douses of rose water or French perfume. Blake Thixton led her to an unoccupied carved stone bench near a pecan tree.

"Sit down," he ordered.

She sat, setting her mask beside her, and gazed up. From this secluded spot in the garden, she had a spectacular view of the Harrises' mansion. Every window in the house glittered with candles, and from her seat, in the dimmer light, she could see people in almost every room, hear the music drifting from the open windows.

"Better?" he asked after she took several deep breaths.

She nodded, her gaze shifting to a small stone statue of a girl beside the bench. "I feel foolish." She fiddled with her fan. "I don't know what happened inside. I was fine and then—"

"Too many people. I get the same way. It's not like this in Boston, probably even less so in Martinique."

She glanced at him, surprised he knew where she was from. "I suppose an event such as this can be overwhelming," she heard herself say. Then, remembering that Charles had gone for a drink for her, she looked back at the stone mansion. "I suppose I should go back inside. Lord Thomas, my escort, will be looking for me."

Thixton continued to watch her and it was obvious from his expression that he didn't approve of Lord Charles Thomas. "He's a bright boy," he said dryly. "He'll find you."

She did not care for his tone of voice. "Lord Thomas received his education at Oxford, sir, and his family is quite wealthy."

Thixton scowled. "His family, *exactly*. The boy probably hasn't worked a day in his life. Of course, perhaps that's precisely what you're seeking, a woman like yourself looking to better her situation." He raised an eyebrow.

Feeling a little more clearheaded, Sapphire stiffened her spine, choosing to ignore his barb. "And what, might I ask, is wrong with family money, sir? I understand you inherited from your father in America."

"And in six years, I've made it twice what it took him fifty," he told her, his tone clipped. "And I'm smart enough to know that this kind of profit won't always exist in shipping. I've other ventures, as well."

"Other ventures? Like what?"

"You honestly want to know?"

"I wouldn't ask if I didn't." Her tone was as curt as his.

For a moment she could have sworn he smiled.

"Petroleum—rock oil."

"Rock oil?" She laughed.

"It comes out of the ground."

She refused to break eye contact with him despite his smoldering stare. *"Obviously."*

"It will be the new fuel that will not only burn our lamps cleaner, but run machines more efficiently. Rock oil will transport us more efficiently across the sea, the land—who knows, perhaps even the sky."

She laughed again and covered her mouth with her hand. "Oil from rock? Machines that fly in the sky? *Really*, Mr. Thixton, I know that I am naive, raised on a remote island, but surely you do not also think me addle-witted."

He looked away, running his hand across his mouth. Sapphire found herself strangely drawn to the gesture. Her gaze settled on his mouth and she remembered when it had touched hers, what she had felt. How he had made her feel.

He plucked a leaf from the pecan tree. "I'd like to make you an offer," he said, staring into the garden behind them.

"An offer?"

His mouth twitched and he suddenly seemed angry with her. "Twice what the boy has offered. Anyone has offered."

Against her will, she felt her cheeks grow warm with embarrassment and something else she couldn't identify. "I do not accept."

"And why the hell not?" he asked, turning to her. "It makes perfect sense. You're in need of a protector and I—"

"You what, sir?" she demanded, barely able to contain her rising anger.

"It's simple enough." His voice was without emotion, as if he were making a business deal or purchasing a cigar. "I desire you. And someone needs to teach you a lesson. You come to London spreading your lies—"

"They are not lies!"

"Parading your attributes before all these young men. You're nothing but a tease, Miss Fabergine, and it's time you learned where teasing will get you."

She shot off the bench. "I'm feeling much better now, sir," she declared coolly, reaching for her mask. "And this conversation is over. Thank you for your assistance."

As she stepped away from him, she saw a group of men and women gathering on the garden path. They were all staring up at the second or third story of the house, murmuring.

Blake turned toward the house first. Something registered on his face, and as Sapphire turned to see what everyone was looking at, he attempted to step in front of her to block her view. She dodged him, grabbing her white satin skirt in both hands to keep from stumbling. She gazed upward, looking from one window to the next. Nothing seemed extraordinary on the first two floors: people dancing, men smoking, women gossiping. She was about to turn back to Blake to ask him what he saw when movement on the third floor caught her attention.

For moment she wasn't certain what she was looking at. She saw a man and a woman. The woman's gown and underclothing were pushed down around her waist, her bare back pressed against the glass casement. The man faced her and the onlookers below. He moved toward the woman, then back, then toward her again, thrusting his body, pushing her again and again against the glass.

Sapphire felt the blood drain from her face as she realized not only what they were doing, but who they were. She knew that bare back. She knew the green silk gown. "I have to go," she whispered, stepping back.

"Not like this." Blake caught her arm. "Let me take you—"

"Excuse me, sir." Charles appeared out of nowhere, a glass of punch in his hand. Obviously he had no idea of the spectacle taking place in plain view of the guests. "Miss Fabergine, is there a problem?"

"No, no problem," she heard herself say as she took another step back, wishing she could fade into the garden or become stone like the statue beside the bench.

How could Angel do such a thing? Make such a public display of herself?

"You should take her home," Blake said.

"Sir, I'm perfectly capable of knowing what's to be done for Miss Fabergine."

"Charles, please," Sapphire managed to say, reaching for his arm to steady herself. "Might we just walk around front and call for your carriage?"

Charles set the glass on the bench and, covering her hand with his, turned her around and headed for the gate. Sapphire didn't look back. Blake Thixton was sailing on the morning tide the next day. She would never see him again, and even that would be too soon.

In the carriage, Sapphire slid to the center of the bench and Charles climbed in behind her. As the groom closed the door, she glanced at Charles, unsure why he had sat down beside her rather than across from her as he usually did, but she was so upset about Angelique that she didn't give it another thought.

"I'm sorry I took so long to find you, dearest," Charles said. "I hope the American wasn't behaving too crudely. I—"

"It's all right, Lord Thomas," she murmured, wishing he would just be quiet. "He isn't what's upset me. I can certainly fend for myself when it comes to men like Mr. Thixton."

"Please, I've asked you to call me Charles." He moved closer, sliding his arm over the back of the smooth leather carriage seat until his hand rested on her bare shoulder.

She realized then that, in her haste, she had forgot-

ten her gown's matching white silk wrap. She must
have left it in the ladies' parlor.

"I was hoping you might allow me to call you by
your given name." He lowered his head and leaned
over her, his voice deeper than usual.

She could feel his hot breath on her bare skin.

"In private, of course," he said.

Annoyed that Charles couldn't tell that she was obviously upset about something, she laid her hand on his
chest to make him stop. He must have misinterpreted
her gesture because, before she realized what he was doing, he'd pushed her down on the bench and was climbing on top of her.

"My lord!"

He pressed his mouth between her breasts, dragging
his wet tongue over her hot skin.

"My lord, you're hurting me!" Sapphire cried out,
trying to push him away. "Please...Charles, no!"

"Enough games, you thankless chit. We've been playing this for weeks," he said angrily, grasping the shoulder of her gown and pulling it down. "We both know
what I want. I'll give you whatever you want in return—money, wedding vows if I must—but I will not
be turned away. Not any longer. Not tonight."

The carriage turned the corner, swaying, and Sapphire was thrown against the back of the seat. As the
conveyance came back around, she used the momen-
tum to shove Charles away from her. "Charles, please!"
she demanded, barely able to see him in the dim light.

Charles's knees hit the floor, but he still managed to
keep his arms around her, pinning her to the seat. With
a growl of rage, he climbed back on top of her, shoving

his knee between her legs, grabbing her wrists and forcing them over her head.

"No—"

He crushed her mouth with his, silencing her, and though he was no rougher than Blake Thixton had been with his kisses, there was something about Charles that she found repulsive.

He thrust his tongue into her mouth and she gagged. His mouth was sloppy with saliva and he tasted of cheap whiskey and smoked fish.

No, this cannot be happening, she screamed inside her head. *I won't let this man take the one thing I have to give freely.*

Charles released one of her wrists and dragged his hand down over her bare shoulder. Grasping the bodice of her beautiful silk gown, he jerked the fabric, and she heard it rip.

"Please," she begged. "Charles, please don't do this."

"It's what you've wanted from the beginning, isn't it?" he said as he violently squeezed her half-bared breast. "A rich cock to keep you in your coop?"

Her anger spurned her on even more than the pain he was inflicting. With her free hand, she slapped his face, then grabbed a section of his hair and yanked as hard as she could.

"Ouch!" he cried, jerking back in shock. "You little bitch!" He slapped her hard across her cheek.

Just then, the carriage turned again, this time in the opposite direction, and when it swayed, she threw her entire weight against Charles, knocking him onto the floor. She landed on top of him, her cheek still stinging where he had struck her, and scrambled to get up.

"Let me out! Stop the carriage!" she screamed as she grasped one of the leather loops that hung from the ceiling in order to keep herself from falling on top of him again. The coach slowed and she thought she heard the driver call out.

Sapphire grabbed the doorknob.

"Oh no, you don't!" Charles shouted. "I'll have what's rightfully mine!" Up on his knees, he lunged for her, tearing her skirt before closing his fingers around her ankle.

The door flew open.

Giving her leg a hard kick backward, she struck Charles in the shoulder, freeing herself from his grasp, then leaped out the open carriage door.

14

Sapphire landed on both feet, but her ankle twisted as she hit the cobblestones. Blinding pain shot up her right leg and she pitched headfirst, falling to her knees. Planting her hands on the ground, she slid forward but successfully came to a stop before falling over on her side. She heard a driver shout and horses' iron-shoed hooves grinding on the stones behind her as the carriage slid to a halt, the horses stopping only a few feet from where she lay.

"Y'all right, ma'am?" someone called.

"Get back in here at once!" Charles shouted at Sapphire. "Before you make a spectacle of yourself and embarrass me further!"

Trembling, heart pounding, Sapphire pushed up off the street with her raw hands and saw Charles's polished shoes approaching her.

"What the hell is going on here?"

Sapphire sat up, her head spinning, her body aching in so many places that she wasn't sure she could stand. She knew the second voice. By the light of the carriages' oil lamps she saw Blake Thixton striding toward them.

"This is none of your concern, Wessex," Charles shouted, his voice rising in pitch. Halting beside Sapphire, Charles thrust his hand out for her to take it, never removing his gaze from the American. "Let's go, Miss Fabergine. Now!"

"I'd rather lie here and die on the street than go with you," Sapphire spat as she slapped his hand away. Then, realizing the entire bodice of her gown was torn, exposing most of her breasts, she gathered the tattered silk and attempted to cover herself.

Blake took one look at Sapphire, stepped forward and struck Charles in the chin with his fist.

Sapphire gave an involuntary cry as Charles flew backward from the impact of Blake's blow. Thixton took another step, leaned over Charles and grasped the lapel of his expensive frock coat, lifting Charles off the street. "If you ever touch this woman, ever *speak* to her again, I swear by my mother's God that I will personally kill you—do you understand me, Charles?"

"My lord," Charles cried in fright.

"Do we understand each other?" Blake repeated from between clenched teeth.

Charles nodded.

Blake released him and Charles fell back on the street, stunned. Sapphire could only sit there in shock. She'd never witnessed such rage, never seen two men fight before....

"Are you all right?" Blake asked, leaning over her.

Tears suddenly welled in her eyes and all she could do was nod.

He reached down and lifted her into his arms. She wanted to protest and tell him she could walk, but she wasn't entirely certain she could. Her ankle was throbbing badly. Instead, she pressed her face into his coat and tried to stifle the little sobs rising from her throat.

"Take us to The Arms at once," Blake barked to his driver.

Sapphire's eyes tightly closed, she felt him carry her to the carriage. Inside, they sat, Blake still holding her in his arms. Again, she wanted to object, but suddenly she was so afraid for herself, for what could have happened, and was so ashamed she had allowed herself to get into such a situation, that all she could do was bury her face and cry.

"It's all right," he hushed, his voice uncharacteristically kind. He stroked her hair that had tumbled from her coiffure in her struggle with Charles. "You're going to be fine. I won't let anyone harm you again. I swear it."

A short time later the carriage halted. "No, drive us to the back," Blake ordered the driver. "No need for anyone to see you in this state," he told her quietly.

She nodded. She'd stopping crying now but couldn't bring herself to sit up and look the American in the eye. She was so embarrassed, so stunned that Charles could have…would have… It was almost too much to absorb, that she could have judged the man's character so badly. When she remembered the names he had called her…the assumptions he'd made… Where…how had everything gone so terribly wrong?

The carriage rolled a short distance, and when the

door opened, Blake stepped out into the darkness, still holding her in his arms. Sapphire hid her face, mortified to be seen in this state even by the groom or the driver. She kept her eyes closed and her face against Blake's coat until he gently lowered her to a bed.

"Sapphire, can you hear me?" he asked, helping her to lie back on several pillows.

She nodded, her eyes still squeezed shut.

"I have to ask you."

She felt the bed sink with his weight as he sat on the edge.

"Did he—"

She didn't wait for him to finish because she knew what he was going to say. "No. But he tried to. That…that was why I had to jump." Another sob rose in her throat and she fought to stifle it.

"Shh, it's all right," he whispered. "Pretty brave of you." He drew his hand down her cheek and she instinctively turned toward it, needing the comfort of another human being.

"Where does it hurt?"

"What?" She opened her eyes. They were in a beautiful bedchamber with dark wainscoting and heavy, lavish, hunter-green bed curtains and drapes, and the room was lit only by an oil lamp beside the bed and another on the far wall on the fireplace mantel.

"There's blood," he said gently.

She looked down to see that her beautiful white gown was streaked with crimson. For a moment she felt a sense of panic, fearing she was more injured than she had realized, but then she remembered scraping her hands and trying to cover herself. She turned her hands palms up to show him the abrasions, only now feeling the pain of the deep scrapes. "From when I fell," she whispered, feeling as if she were in a dreamlike state.

None of this seemed to be possible. Not Angel and Henry in the window committing that indecent act…not Charles trying to rape her, and her jumping from the carriage. Not Blake being there at just the right moment. Not being here with him alone now like this….

She could feel her pulse flutter, her heart beating in her chest.

"Ah, it's not so bad," he told her, taking her hands gently in his and uncurling her fingers to have a better look. "Where else?" he asked after a moment.

"My right ankle," she whispered. "And…my knees."

He slid down toward the end of the large four-poster bed and removed her right shoe, then her left, taking more care with the right.

Sapphire winced as he twisted the second slipper off and slid his hand gingerly over her stocking-covered ankle.

"Swollen a little, but not so bad," he said. He glanced up at her. "Probably sprained, but not broken."

He pushed the hem of her gown up farther and she stiffened at once, reaching out to try to push him away.

"I just want to see your knees," he chastised as if she were a child. "Come now, Sapphire, you were nearly raped. That street was filthy; horse manure, offal and Lord knows what else. You could be seriously injured. This is no time for modesty."

Tears stung the back of her eyelids as she lay back on the pillows again. She felt the silk fabric of her gown slide up her leg, felt the heat of his hand as he drew it over her shin, and then he pushed down one stocking that had come loose from its garter. She winced.

"Pretty scraped up," he said as he brushed his fingertips over her knee. "Nothing too serious." He looked up at her. "Anything else hurt? Your neck? Your arms?"

She shook her head.

"Good." He rose and walked to the far side of the room where a washbowl rested on a washstand. He removed his frock coat, rolled up the sleeves of his fine white shirt, removed his cravat and poured water from an earthenware pitcher. He carefully lathered his hands with a bayberry scented soap, rinsed them, dumped the soiled water into the pottery receptacle on the floor beneath the stand, and refilled the rose-patterned washbowl. Grabbing a clean, folded linen towel from the stand, he carried the bowl and towel to her bedside.

It wasn't until he dipped the towel into the bowl, wrung it out and leaned over her that she realized he meant to clean her wounds.

"No," she whispered, lifting one hand as if she could fend him off in her state. "I can do that, really…there's no need for you to—"

"Don't be ridiculous." He brought the cloth to her cheek. "There's some dirt, here," he muttered.

She closed her eyes as he drew the soothing, cool cloth over her face, wiping away the grime and her tears. He had such a gentle touch.

"There," he said after he had wrung out the cloth and wiped her face again. "Doesn't that feel better?"

She nodded.

"Good."

He took one of her hands and opened it in his. The

first touch of the wet cloth made the wounds smart, bringing tears to her eyes again, but after a moment, her hand actually felt better. He took his time cleaning one and then the other, and slowly the stinging pain gave way to a strange warmth that seemed to spread from his hands to hers and then through her entire body.

"I don't think these need to be bandaged, but we'll see in the morning." He dropped the cloth into the porcelain washbowl with a splash.

She felt him rise off the bed and opened her eyes to watch him cross the bedchamber, which she now realized was a room in an inn or a hotel. From a small table beside the fireplace he picked up a crystal decanter and poured a dark liquid into a glass. He brought it to her. "Brandy," he said, sitting on the edge of the bed beside her. "It's all I have. Drink it."

She lifted her lashes to look at him and said stubbornly, "I don't want to."

He pushed the glass into her hands sternly. "Do it anyway. You've had a shock. Such things can be worse than physical injuries."

She held the glass with both hands and tipped it, first drinking hesitantly, then less so. The taste was strong and biting, but surprisingly not unpleasant. The liquid burned a fiery path to her stomach, filling her with warmth.

"Easy there," he warned, closing his hand over hers.

She coughed.

"Maybe a little bit at a time would be better." He took the glass from her and set it on the elaborately carved rosewood bedside table. "I want to have a look at that ankle. I need to take your stocking off." He met her gaze. He was neither smiling nor frowning. "Is that all right, Sapphire?"

She nodded slowly, still not feeling fully conscious. Maybe it was everything that had happened, or maybe it was the brandy.

Blake was being so kind to her, this man who was her enemy, this man who kept her from what she wanted most in the world. It didn't make any sense. Charles had said he loved her, and yet he had behaved in such a despicable manner toward her. And this man, who would not even respond to her requests to talk with him, was caring for her injuries as tenderly as any beloved nursemaid might do for a mischievous child.

"Do it if you must," she heard herself say.

Blake held her gaze with his penetrating eyes as he untied her white velvet garter ribbon and slowly began to roll down what was left of her silk stocking.

He's done this before, she thought, feeling as if she were floating. *Removed a lady's stocking.* Already the brandy had eased the pain in her hands and knees and ankle and she was feeling only its warmth and the security it seemed to offer…warmth and an unfamiliar tingling in the pit of her stomach.

When he reached her ankle, she flinched.

"Pretty tender," he said as he slipped the torn, soiled stocking off her foot and sent it sailing to the floor.

"It's…not broken, is it?"

He turned it one way and then the other and she gritted her teeth against the pain, determined not to cry.

"Move your toes."

She wiggled them.

"Point your foot."

She grimaced but complied.

"Good. No, I don't think any of the bones are broken." He reached back for the cloth in the washbowl, wrung it out and then laid it over her ankle, wrapping his fingers around it.

She closed her eyes and pressed her lips together to keep from crying out.

"The cool water is good for it," he told her, moving his hand to rest it on her shin. "It will help keep the swelling down."

All she could do was nod.

"Have some more brandy."

Again, it wasn't a request but an order and she found herself obeying him. As she drank, he removed the cloth from her ankle, rinsed it in the cool water and applied it again to her swollen ankle.

She had finished the brandy by the time he rinsed the linen cloth a third time and began to slide it up her shin. Sapphire felt herself relax as she sank deeper into the soft pillows beneath her. She felt her eyelids flutter and she parted her lips slightly, sighing. The cool cloth felt so good, his warm hand almost better.

When he reached her knee, though, she tensed again. The cloth suddenly felt rough and it smarted as he tried to gently scrub away the bits of dirt embedded in the flesh.

"Good thing you were wearing all this clothing," he said teasingly as he pushed away a billow of silk skirt and ruffled petticoat. "Otherwise, you might have been more seriously injured."

She felt her mouth turn up in a half smile. "I...I want to thank you for—"

"I don't want to hear it. Honestly, I can't believe you would agree to be alone with a man like him. In a group, I'm sure he's fine, but—" Rather than finishing what he was going to say, he frowned and dropped the cloth dotted with her blood into the washbowl. "Some of these scrapes are rather deep, and I suppose that the responsible thing would be to call a physician and have him treat the injuries, but we could hardly do that without drawing attention to ourselves, could we?" He swirled the cloth in the water, then squeezed it out with one hand. As he went through the motion that was now familiar to her, she found herself staring at his muscular forearm.

She knew he owned a shipping company in Boston, but she hadn't suspected he'd ever done any physical work. Though Armand was a wealthy plantation owner he had made a point of going to the fields or the drying house to toil side by side with his workers. He said it kept him close to the land and to the coffee that provided the luxuries he reaped with his profits.

Blake's forearms were the arms of a man who could lift a heavy weight and carry it a long way. She wondered if he worked on the docks or in the warehouse with his hired men. Had he ever trimmed the sails on a sailing ship or rowed a boat to shore?

The words to ask him about his experiences were on the tip of her tongue, but she couldn't bring herself to speak. It was as if she were under some spell. His spell.

Again he was beside her; she could feel the warmth and pressure of his hip pressed against hers. As he drew the cloth over her shin to her other knee, she caught his eye. Suddenly her heart was pounding, not from fear this time, but something else.

Blake leaned over her, his hand on her knee...perhaps even a little higher. "You've intrigued me, you know," he said, his voice barely audible. "From the day you showed up in my parlor claiming you were Wessex's daughter."

"But I am Lord Edward Wessex's—"

"Hush, Sapphire, I'm speaking. Surely you know it's rude to interrupt when another is speaking. No doubt the nuns on that tropical island of yours reprimanded you on more than one occasion for that."

She pushed her elbows into the soft tick, propping herself up. "How did you know—"

"You're doing it again, Sapphire. I'm still speaking."

She lay back again, pressing her lips together. He leaned so close to her that she could feel his breath on her cheek. "Fortune hunter or not—"

"I'm not—"

This time he laid his free hand on her mouth to silence her. "Do I have to gag you to be permitted to speak?"

She felt her eyes widen and suddenly she was a little fearful of him as she remembered his rage on the street. She shook her head.

"Good." He slid his hand off her mouth and let it rest on the pillow just beside her cheek.

"What I wanted to say was that you've intrigued me and that...against my will, I find myself desiring you, as I stated before in the garden." He smiled. "You're really not my type, you know."

"Mr. Thixton, I—"

This time he silenced her with his mouth. Sapphire had opened her own in protest and he had covered it with his, pushing her down into the bed.

"Sapphire," he said as he raised his lips from hers to draw them across her cheek.

It came out more as a groan, sending a shiver of apprehension through her body.

He drew his mouth to her earlobe and whispered again. "Sapphire, a jewel of a name. So sweet…"

She heard herself moan as he raised his hand higher up her leg. He pushed back the tattered fabric of her gown to expose her bare breasts.

I mustn't…I can't let this happen, she thought somewhere in the back of her mind. And yet there was a part of her…that wanted him the way that she knew he wanted her.

Before she could say anything, his mouth found the hollow between her breasts and her breath caught in her throat.

Blake covered her breasts with his hot kisses, and every time she opened her mouth to protest, he kissed them again, stifling the words she tried to utter.

Blake slowly slid down over her, and by the time he traced the taut buds of her nipples, she felt drained, unable to stop him. Her pulse was racing, her breath coming in short bursts. She whimpered each time he covered her nipple with his mouth and tugged.

And all the while his hand rose farther beneath her silk skirts and petticoats. The cool linen cloth was gone—where she didn't know. Now it was only his hand, hot, seeking…

She turned her head one way and then the other, her eyes shut. She wanted to tell him no, but as he moved his hand farther up the tender inside of her thigh, she couldn't find the strength.

She was so confused. She hated this man, and yet she wanted him…the way she now understood Angelique wanted men. A hot twist in her stomach seemed to be flaring outward, burning her, making her writhe beneath him.

Again, he was kissing her breasts, her neck, her mouth. He barely had to tug at the fabric of the tattered silk gown for it to fall away. His fingers found the laces of her stays, and then they were gone, too. She watched through half-closed eyes as he sat up and slipped her gown off, first pushing it down to her waist, then carefully pulling it over her feet. She shivered as she felt the fabric slip away, her last defense with it. He threw it carelessly to the floor; it didn't matter, she thought dreamily. It was ruined anyway.

There was nothing between them now but her thin white chemise and eyelet drawers. When he found her mouth again, his hand caressing her breast, his thumb gliding over her sensitive nipple, she kissed him back. Against all reason, all logic, Sapphire kissed him back, aching to know what this was between a man and a woman.

Still completely dressed, Blake stretched out over her, pinning her to the bed, one leg thrown possessively over her. She felt his mouth on her neck, her breasts, her belly, and even through the fabric it burned a fiery path.

He took her mouth with his and she felt his hand on the waistband of her drawers, and she was defenseless against him. All she could do was kiss him back, making sounds deep in her throat.

When he pushed the undergarment down over her feet and raised his hand along her bare calf, then her inner thigh, she felt her body tense.

"Don't," he whispered, easing her legs apart. "You're so beautiful, Sapphire, your body is made for a man to make love to. Let me."

His deep, rumbling voice seemed to draw her on a wave that first splashed on the shore and then tugged her outward into the darkness, the unknown.

His fingertips brushed the apex of her thighs and she cried out incoherently, fighting the pleasure.

"Shh," he murmured, resting his cheek on her abdomen.

Another moment and she forgot who she was, who she was with. He just kept stroking her, moving upward and then back again, and she found herself straining against him, desiring...what she didn't know. Needing him, his touch more than anything she had ever known.

Sapphire reached down to run her fingers through his dark hair, her eyes closed, her body moving with his touch. "Blake," she heard herself moan. "Blake." The aching filled her, consumed her, and time seemed to stretch until it stood still. Suddenly her entire body shuddered, burst, and a second later she felt as if she were floating, slowly falling to earth again.

"I didn't know," she whispered, half ashamed, half joyful, tears in her eyes.

He stretched out beside her, a smile on his lips, as he cradled her in one arm. "I told you your body was made for loving." He pushed back a lock of her hair that had fallen over her cheek.

She drifted on the last waves of the pleasure he had given her.

"I...should go home," she whispered.

"Not now." He kissed her mouth lightly, almost lov-ingly. "Sleep now and we'll talk in the morning."

Sapphire knew she couldn't stay, not here in his bed, not undressed, not like this—but she couldn't stay awake another moment.

15

At the sound of movement in the room, Sapphire opened her eyes drowsily. She knew at once where she was; the lamp still burned on the nightstand, but Blake was no longer in bed beside her.

He was seated in a chair near the fireplace, pulling on a pair of tall leather boots. He wore a woolen patterned coat that appeared more a working man's garb than the elegant frock coat he had discarded after the ball. There was a wool cap on his head and several leather satchels on the floor beside him. He appeared to be leaving....

She almost smiled. Of course he was leaving. Blake Thixton was more of a gentleman than she had first given him credit for. He would say nothing of what had passed between them in this bed, this mistake, error in judgment, whatever it had been. He would slip out the back of the hotel, bribe any servant who had seen them enter earlier, and she would wake in the morning and return home with some tale to protect herself and her virtue.

At that thought, she almost laughed aloud. How could her virtue possibly matter at this point? Half of London believed she was a courtesan!

"Ah, you're awake. I'm sorry. I tried to be quiet." Blake rose from the chair, pushing the cap farther back on his head as approached the bed.

Suddenly shy with him after her earlier response to his touch, she pulled up the light blanket until it touched her nose. She realized she was completely unclothed beneath the coverlet and she looked around quickly, in horror. Every stitch of her clothing was gone—the beautiful white gown, her petticoat and chemise, even her eyelet drawers.

"Where are my clothes?" she whispered accusingly, wishing she could take back her thought that he could be any sort of gentleman.

He gave her that half smile that had been attractive earlier but now only infuriated her.

"They were quite ruined, beyond repair."

Tightening her grip on the edge of the blanket, she stared up at him. "But…but I have to have something to wear home."

"You're not going home."

"What?"

"My offer. You've accepted."

"What offer?" she breathed.

"To become my mistress."

"I did no such thing! Why, I would not…not if you were the last man on this Godforsaken—"

"You see," he interrupted, picking up a leather billfold from the bedside and slipping it inside his coat. "I knew you were going to make this more difficult than it had to be."

She sat up in the bed, still covering her nakedness as best she could with the blanket. "What are you talking about?" she asked, staring at him. "Surely you didn't save me from Charles only to—"

"Sapphire, I'm not going to rape you." He frowned. "I'm not the kind of man who needs to rape in order to have a woman." Again, that smile. "They come to me of their own accord."

She sucked in a breath, speechless in her rage. "You…you are the most conceited, the most self-centered, most egotistical man I have ever had the misfortune to meet! What are you going to do with me?" she demanded. "What are you talking about? What will I make more difficult than it need be?"

He picked up a small leather case with a wide strap and dropped it over his head and one arm. "I've decided to take you with me."

She tried to push herself back farther with her feet, attempting to put more distance between them, but the simple movement sent pain shooting from her injured ankle up her leg.

"Lie still before you injure yourself more." He leaned over the bed and began to pull up the corners of the sheet beneath her.

"I demand to know where you're taking me, Mr. Thixton!"

He continued his task, folding the sheet and blanket around her. "Mr. Thixton again, is it?" He raised an eyebrow. "Seems to me it was Blake not long ago, but then we were more intimately engaged, weren't we."

She wanted to reach out and slap that ridiculous smile from his face. "You can't do this," she spat. "You can't...kidnap me."

"I'm not exactly kidnapping you. After all, you've touted your wares over most of London these past few weeks waiting for the highest bid. I've made the highest bid and you're going to accept it."

"I'm going to do no such thing," she hissed.

He began to draw the blanket over her shoulder and around her and she lashed out at him, trying to slap away his hands.

"Really, Sapphire," he muttered. "This is completely unnecessary. Where are you going to go like this, stark naked and barely able to walk this time of morning? Not to Lord Thomas, I'll guarantee you that. Your offer was that of a virgin's."

"I'm still a virgin," she sputtered as he lifted her into his arms.

"A technicality, but who would believe you?"

"Oh!" she cried, her eyes filling with tears of frustration as she tried to reach out, to claw his eyes out or something equally harmful, anything to shut him up. But wrapped tightly in the sheet and blanket, she couldn't get her legs free, and now he had her arms pinned inside, as well.

"There, there, darling," he soothed, lifting her from the bed.

In his arms, he drew her against his chest, forcing her to look up at him. "In time you'll get used to the idea of being my mistress. I think you'll even come to like it."

"Let me go!" she shouted, glaring at him. "Let me go or I'll—"

"You'll what? Scream? Who would come? I bring women back with me most nights. Some whores, but mostly respectable ladies who prefer to be discreet. No one will come if you scream, my dear. Anyone who might hear you will just assume it's all part of our early morning love-play."

Sapphire gritted her teeth.

"Or did you intend to free yourself and run? Wouldn't that be a pleasant sight, you running stark naked down the middle of the street? Of course, with that bad ankle, you'd have to hobble. And that wouldn't be quite so lovely a picture, would it? Tarnished lady hobbles through the streets of London. I'm afraid you'd be ruined, my dear, all value of your charms lost to anyone of quality—once they stopped laughing."

"I'm not going with you, wherever you're going," she said quickly, suddenly afraid of what she had gotten herself into. "Last night...it was all a mistake. I...I had too much to drink, I—"

"You keep telling yourself that. Now be quiet while I get you out of here, or I swear by my father's gin bottle, I'll set you loose on the street and I'm taking my blankets with me."

"Oh!" was all Sapphire could manage to say before he covered her face with the blanket, silencing her and leaving her in darkness as he walked out the door.

When Angelique entered the apartments at dawn, Lucia was seated on the couch in her bedclothes, drift-

ing in and out of sleep. At the sound of the door opening, she leaped up. "Sapphire?"

"Aunt Lucia, what are you doing awake at this time
of morning?" Angelique, still in her gown but wearing
a man's frock coat over it, her ebony hair down over her
shoulders, closed the door behind her. "Are you ill?"

Lucia rushed toward her, taking both her hands.
"Sapphire never came home last night. I hoped she was
with you."

"With me?" Angelique drew back. "Certainly not. I
was with Henry. We went back to his parents' home. He
had this ridiculous idea to tell them he was marrying
me with or without their consent." She pulled away
from Lucia and walked toward the kitchen, tossing the
man's coat on a chair as she went by. "Or mine, apparently, for that matter."

Angelique pushed through the swinging doors into
the small utilitarian kitchen and Lucia followed her.
They ordered most of their meals out from the cookshop
down the street, so it was perfectly adequate. Though
Avena had become an excellent ladies' maid, a cook, Lucia had quickly learned, she was not.

Angelique opened a cupboard and poked around,
finding a plate covered in cheesecloth. "I'm starved."

"Have you any idea where she might have gone? I'm
worried sick. Could she possibly be with Charles?"

Angelique plucked the cloth from the plate to find a
slab of yellow cheese. She drew a knife from a drawer
and sliced a piece off. "With Charles? I think not. We
saw him around three at a pub near Westminster, and I
must say he was in a foul mood." Leaning against the
wooden table beneath the cupboard, she bit into the

cheese. "Apparently they had some sort of row. He wouldn't say what had happened, but I can tell you he was not pleased with her. He kept asking me what she had told me and finally, when I convinced him we'd not spoken since the ball, he began to ramble about not believing anything she said. About her being intoxicated and misinterpreting his intentions." She fluttered her hand. "It was all a bunch of nonsense and I had no idea what he was talking about."

"Dear me." Lucia sighed, drawing her hand to her mouth and glancing away. "I can't imagine where she's gone, then. This isn't like her. She's never stayed out all night before."

"Actually, it could be my fault." Angelique sliced another piece of cheese, hesitating. "She and Charles left rather quickly, a result of a commotion Henry and I inadvertently caused at Lord and Lady Harris's ball last night."

Lucia lifted an eyebrow.

"Don't listen to the gossip. None of it is true." Angelique raised a slender, bare shoulder. "Most of it isn't, at least."

"You think Sapphire could have run away?"

"Run away? Certainly not. Where would she run to? You don't give her enough credit, Aunt Lucia. Our little Sapphire has a mind of her own and she can take care of herself. Everyone seems to forget she was the one who saved me from those wild dogs all those years ago." Taking the last of the cheese, she walked out of the kitchen.

"Where are you going?" Lucia called, following her into the parlor.

"To bed." Angelique turned to her. "Where you should be going."

"I couldn't possibly sleep." Lucia worried her hands. "Armand left her in my care and now—"

"Aunt Lucia." Angelique grasped her shoulders. "You're getting yourself worked up over nothing. Who knows?" She released her. "Perhaps she met up with the dashing Lord Wessex. She's half in love with him, you know, and he with her."

"I know no such thing!"

"Well, do what you like, but I'm going to bed. Henry said he'd be here by noon." She flashed a grin over her shoulder. "Though he'll probably be here closer to three. I told him to sober up and apologize to his parents. I'll not have him penniless."

Lucia glanced up at her. "Is that unfair? He will apparently have you penniless."

"I'm not penniless. I have what Sophie left and my own devices." She chuckled and gave a wave with the piece of cheese, disappearing down the hall.

Lucia shook her head at her adopted niece, who knew less about love than she thought. It came so seldom in life. She just prayed Angelique wasn't missing it right under her nose. Despite Henry's immaturity and blithe attitude, Lucia could tell that he truly did love Angelique, and she hated the thought that Angel might let true love pass her by. But Angelique had been uncontrollable since childhood—as uncontrollable as her Sapphire—and right now she was most concerned about Sapphire. Turning, she went into her room, grabbed a cloak and her reticule and hurried out of the house, hoping it wouldn't take her long to find a hackney so early on a Sunday morning.

* * *

"Lucia, love, what's wrong?" Meeting her in the front hall, dressed in a silk nightshirt, Jessup opened his arms to Lucia.

"It's Sapphire," she cried, her eyes filling with tears as she threw herself against him. "She never came home!" She peered up at Jessup, knowing now that she was more distraught than she had realized. "I'm so sorry to wake you, but I didn't know where else to go, who else to turn to."

"There, there, don't be ridiculous." He ushered her down the hall and into the parlor. "Malcolm," he called to his butler who had let Lucia in and was now lighting lamps as fast as he could. "Have Ella put hot water on for tea."

"I believe she's not come in yet for the day, sir. It being Sunday."

"Then put it on yourself! Now here, darling, sit down." Jessup guided Lucia to his favorite chair in front of the fireplace, an old, down-stuffed brocade that had seen better years. "Look at you in your nightclothes," he said, perching on the footstool at her feet, covering his knobby knees with the old, thin flannel dressing robe he wore. "You should have sent Angelique or Avena."

Lucia frowned. "Angelique thought my worry heedless." She met his gaze. "But this is so unlike my Sapphire."

"Yes, yes, of course." He rubbed her hand between his. "There's a chill in this room, don't you think?" He turned to call over his shoulder. "Malcolm! Get us a fire going in here at once!" Jessup turned back to Lucia as he ran his fingers through his thin gray hair. "You say she never came home last night, and am I to understand that Angelique doesn't know where she is?"

"Sapphire went to the Lord and Lady Harris's masquerade ball with Lord Thomas but he never brought her home."

"Don't take this the wrong way, my dear," Jessup said carefully, "but do you think she could have…gone home with Lord Thomas?"

"Certainly not! I told you, Jessup, that was a ruse from the beginning." She dropped her hands to her lap. "And it was all my idea to begin with. What if something's happened? I could never forgive myself if—"

"Lucia, listen to me." He captured her hands again. "Nothing has happened to her. I'm certain there's a logical explanation and I mean to get to it at once."

"You'll find her?" Lucia asked in relief.

Jessup rose and leaned to press a kiss to her forehead. "Of course I'll find her. Now you sit here and have a cup of tea and I'll get dressed."

"I'll go with you." She started to rise.

He pushed her gently back into the chair that smelled of him and his pipe tobacco, a comforting scent to Lucia. "No, you won't. Unless, of course, you'd like me to take you home. You look as if you haven't slept a wink."

She shook her head. "I haven't, but I couldn't possibly go to bed." She clasped her hands. "Oh, Jessup, do find her."

"I will, my sweet."

After a great deal of jostling, a carriage ride and being carried again like a side of meat for what seemed like hours, Sapphire finally felt Blake drop her unceremoniously onto a bed. The moment he released her, she scrambled free of the tangle of bedclothes. "You can't do this," she cried, quickly taking in her new surroundings.

They were in a small room that was crudely paneled in knotty pine and she was resting on a narrow bed meant only for a single person, built into the wall. Beneath her, she felt the floor shift slightly and she knew that what she had been praying wasn't true was indeed true. The moment he'd stepped foot out of the carriage she had thought she smelled water, and she knew now that she was on board a ship. He was kidnapping her and taking her to America!

"Do you hear me?" she yelled, rising to her knees, ignoring the pain that shot through her right ankle.

Blake stood at the closed door of the small cabin, one side of his mouth turning up. "Honestly, it's hard to listen to anything you say when you're putting on such a spectacular exhibition, my dear."

Sapphire glanced down to see that she had dropped the corner of the blanket to reveal one bare, pink-tipped breast. "Oh!" she cried as she jerked up the blanket to cover herself, so angry that tears welled in her eyes. "You cannot be serious about taking me with you."

"I am entirely serious." He walked to a built-in desk and slipped the leather case off his shoulder, dropping it onto the surface. "You wanted a protector, and now you have one." He raised both hands matter-of-factly.

"I wanted you to acknowledge me as Lord Edward Wessex's daughter!"

He opened the case and began to remove several books and a worn leather-bound journal. "You know, we would get along much better if you would give that notion up. Obviously I'm not going to fall for it. You are what you are, Sapphire, a beautiful young woman trying to make your way in the world. I'm not the kind of man to see anything wrong with that in a mistress. I congratulate you, in fact. You have the right idea, you know—a man generally treats his mistress far better than his wife."

Sapphire sat with her back against the bulkhead to relieve the pressure on her ankle. She could not believe what he was saying, could not believe the situation she found herself in. "A fortune hunter! You still think I'm a fortune hunter?"

He considered her words and then nodded. "Yes."

"Oh," she cried again, her shoulders slumping against the cool wood of the bulkhead.

Sounds outside the cabin suddenly caught her attention. She could hear shouting, footsteps, and feel the unmistakable sensation of the ship moving. "We're sailing?" she asked. "We can't be! I can't—my Aunt Lucia, she won't know what's happened to me. Please," she begged.

When he made no response, she glared at him. "I can't believe you're doing this," she accused, fighting her tears. "You're...you're kidnapping me!"

"Not really. The door's unlocked. We've already pulled away from the dock by the sound of the commotion outside, but you could probably dive over the side and swim to shore. Someone would fish you out, I suspect. You can swim, can't you?"

"I was raised in Martinique—of course I can swim," she said, drawing herself up indignantly.

"Then be my guest." He gestured toward the door.

"But I'm naked," she protested, staring longingly at the door.

"Yes, you are."

She looked at the door for a moment and then, with a groan of frustration, threw herself facefirst onto the bunk and drew the blanket over her head.

"It's fine with me if you take that attitude," she heard him say, the sound of his irksome voice muffled by the blanket. "It could be a long trip, depending on the winds, but it's up to you, really."

Sapphire could hear Blake continue to unload his bags.

"You can spend the next two weeks sulking under that blanket or we can enjoy each other's company, nice dinners with the fine wine I'm transporting, chess, reading…and then there are other activities we could amuse ourselves with."

Even through the blanket she could hear the huskiness in his voice, and knew what he meant.

She lifted the blanket and hurled at him a curse word she'd never dared to utter before.

As she dropped the cover over her head again, his laughter ran though the cabin.

After Jessup had gone and she had taken a cup of tea, Lucia decided to accept at least half his advice and try to sleep. Instead of returning home, though, she climbed the stairs of his comfortable town house and crawled into his bed, where the sheets smelled of Jessup and offered at least some comfort. If the butler, Malcolm, thought it odd that she was there in his master's bed, he gave no indication.

To Lucia's surprise, she drifted off to sleep almost at

once and didn't wake until she heard someone in the room. Her eyes opened. "Any word?" she asked, as Jessup entered his bedchamber, still in his overcoat.

He shook his head. "I went to the Lord Thomas's London house." He removed his coat and then hung it on a hook on the back of the door. "Not terribly welcoming, that family. I say Sapphire's done herself a favor if she's cut ties with that young man." He approached the bed. " I could barely make heads or tails of what Charles was saying, but apparently he attempted to escort her home and she threw some sort of temper tantrum and got out of the carriage right on the street."

"Sapphire, a temper tantrum?" Lucia sat up and wiped the sleep from her eyes. "I find that difficult to believe."

Jessup perched on the edge of the bed and looked at her. "As do I."

She took his hand, peering up at him. "You think Charles was lying?"

"I think he was not telling me the entire truth. Apparently, your wild colt, Angelique, and Lord Carter put on quite a spectacle at the masquerade ball last night."

She gave a wave of dismissal. "Yes, yes, she already told me."

He raised a bushy eyebrow. "She told you what she did?"

"Not exactly, but I don't I care. What I care about right now is finding my Sapphire. I want to speak to that upstart Charles at once! How dare he allow her to get out of the carriage alone in the middle of the night! Has he no idea what kind of danger can befall a young woman, unescorted on the streets of London at night?"

"Darling." Jessup took Lucia's hand in his. "I've thought of one possibility."

"And what's that?"

He hesitated.

"Please," she begged, squeezing his hand. "If you know something else, no matter how terrible, you must—"

He smiled kindly. "Are you always so dramatic, my love?"

"I am and that's why you love me."

"What I wanted to say is that Lord Wessex sailed for America this morning at dawn."

"Lord Wessex!" She exhaled the words as she glanced down at her hands, which appeared more wrinkled than she remembered. "Angelique mentioned the American, as well." She looked up into Jessup's kind, brown eyes. "Do you think he could have had something do with her disappearance?"

He shrugged. "You did say that you thought they were attracted to each other, only you weren't certain either one was aware of it."

"But if they were going to go away together, my Sapphire would have come and told me. She would never have run off like this." She inhaled sharply. "Do you think he could have taken her against her will?"

"I find it hard to believe anyone could force your Sapphire to do anything against her will, but..." He stopped.

"But what?" She continued to gaze into his eyes.

"Blake Thixton is a man used to getting what he wants."

She clasped her hands. "I only pray that she is with

him and that she's all right. Do you believe he will do right by her—I mean, if she has run off with him on some impulse?"

"You mean marry her?"

She nodded.

He thought for a moment before replying. "I can say honestly, my dearest," he told her, taking her hand in his, "that he is one of the most honorable, respectable men I have ever had the privilege to meet."

"So you think she'll be all right?" she asked softly.

He smiled, drawing her hand to his lips. "I think she'll be just fine."

16

Sapphire lay on the bunk with her head under the blanket until it got stuffy and perspiration began to gather above her upper lip. At first, as the minutes ticked by and she listened to Blake move about the room putting things away and settling at the desk, all she could think of was what an awful, hopeless situation she had found herself in. But as her self-imposed prison grew warmer and warmer, the wool blanket itchier against her bare skin, her self-pity blossomed into anger.

How dare he? How dare Blake Thixton do this to her! Sapphire didn't care if he'd gone to Boston's Harvard, she didn't care what a successful businessman and entrepreneur he was, or that he was the Earl of Wessex and her father's heir; she wouldn't have cared if he was the king of England. He had no right! He had no right to kidnap her and take her from her family and she did not have to submit to such treatment. What was he? An American. Nothing more than a merchant masquerading as a gentleman. Who was he to think he could treat the daughter of an English nobleman like a common strumpet?

Sapphire flung the cover from her head and scrambled from the bunk, ignoring the pain in her ankle. As she hit the floor on her one good foot, dragging the sheet behind her to cover her nakedness, Blake looked up from his desk. "You have no right!" she shouted as she hobbled the short distance toward the desk.

Blake rose, obviously startled, but he still had that ridiculous smirk on his face.

"I don't want to go with you, do you understand?" she yelled, grabbing a book off the corner of her desk and hurling it at him. "I don't want to go to America!"

He ducked and took a step back. "You'll get used to the idea. Boston is a wonderful city, very different from London but exciting in its own way. As my mistress, you'll accompany me to the theater, to the symphony, to dinner parties with the richest, most successful men and women in the United States."

"I don't want to be your mistress. I *will not* be your mistress," she shouted, grabbing another book and heaving it at him.

This time, either her aim was better or he wasn't quick enough, and the missile struck his shoulder before hitting the polished wooden deck with a *thump.*

"You'll get used to the idea. I can really be quite charming." His eyes sparkled. "Some say I have a way with women."

Hopping toward him, she grabbed a boot and flung it at him. "I certainly will *not* get used to the idea!"

"Ouch!" Blake cried when the heel of the boot struck

him in the forehead. "Sapphire, stop it! One of us is going to get hurt."

"Oh, one of us is going to get hurt, all right, but I can assure you it won't be me." With one hand clutching the sheet to cover her breasts, she grabbed a leather satchel off the floor with the other and attempted to steady herself on her one good foot as she lifted the heavy case over her head.

"That's enough!" Blake dove forward, throwing both arms around her waist, knocking her off balance. The satchel flew from her hand and she felt a sting of pain on the bottom of her good foot as she fell backward. She didn't tumble to the floor because Blake held her securely in both his arms, pulling her against his body.

"Let me go!" she screamed. "Let me go!"

He held her tighter against his body, effectively pinning her arms to her sides, molding the entire length of his muscular form to hers. In an effort to escape his embrace, Sapphire threw her weight backward and they both lost their balance and fell onto the narrow bunk, Blake on top.

"Oh!" Sapphire blurted as the sheet slipped and she felt Blake's unshaven cheek brush against the sensitive skin of her breast. "You're heavy!" She turned her face away from his.

"It doesn't have to be this way," Blake said, shifting his weight over her, his tone softening as he purposefully lowered his mouth to her breast and she felt the heat of it. "You and I were meant to be together like this, Sapphire. You know it. I know it."

His lips…his tongue…his teeth were doing unspeakable things to her…wonderful things that made pinwheels of pleasure radiate through her from the crown of her head to the tips of her toes….

"No," she whispered, and yet she could feel her blood race as every inch of her body responded to his touch. This was wrong—it had to be wrong. She wanted him in the same way he wanted her, and suddenly she was resolved to it. All that seemed to matter at this moment was his touch and his quiet, husky voice that drew her closer.

She ran her fingers through his soft, dark hair, which had grown longer since the day she first met him almost two months ago. He pulled the sheet down and she felt the brush of his slightly rough fingertips.

He kissed his way to the tip of her puckered nipple, kissed the hollow of her throat, the line of her collarbone, continuing on until his mouth met hers. Slowly the warmth of his body and his mouth seeped into her and she kissed him back. As she kissed him, his heat seemed to spread through her limbs, spurring her own inferno, igniting every fiber of her being until she could feel her heart pounding in her chest, her breath coming in gasps.

Burying his face in her hair strewn across the pillow, she felt him slide his hand over her breasts and down the length of her body, exploring her curves and hollows.

When he thrust his tongue into her mouth, she put up no resistance to his exploration. Blake was right; this was meant to be from the beginning, from the first time they met in her father's parlor just after she had arrived in London. It didn't matter that she was now bound for Boston against her will. She didn't know where these actions would lead her or what sorrow it would bring. All she knew was that she needed this man. She needed to feel his touch, needed him to show her what it meant to be a woman.

Blake shifted in the narrow bed, sliding off her to lie on his side beside her, keeping her pinned with one leg. Every limb of her body quivered as she felt his mouth on her breast again, his lips and tongue teasing her nipples until her skin felt as if it were on fire. She heard herself utter a muted, strangely incoherent sound.

"Blake," she moaned. "Please...I want..." She didn't know what to say or how to tell him. How could she explain what was happening to her when she didn't understand it herself? She felt the pressure building inside her like the air of her island home before a hurricane, and without knowing how or why, she was being swept into the storm.

"Relax," he whispered. "I know what you want." He chuckled huskily, moving his hand lower. "But the more time we give it, the better it will be."

As he slid his hand over her belly down to her inner thigh, she relaxed into the soft tick, surrendering to her own desires as heat pooled inside her.

"Uncross your legs," he whispered.

Mesmerized by his voice, by his touch, she did as he ordered. "I...I don't know what I'm supposed to do," she admitted.

"Do as I say. Just relax, let yourself feel it."

He slid his hand between her thighs and began to stroke the soft flesh, and her body recalled, at once, how good it had felt only a few hours ago.

"That's it, that's right, love," he breathed, teasing her earlobe with the tip of his tongue, his caresses gentle and unhurried.

Sapphire turned her head to look away from him, letting herself go, imagining herself floating until he again lifted her higher, moving faster until every muscle in her body tensed and then released. She cried out, threading her fingers through his hair, struggling to catch her breath.

"What is that?" she panted, arching her back one last time as the sensations washed over her. "I don't—"

"You talk too much," he interrupted, amusement in his voice as he brought his face close to hers.

Her lashes fluttered and she opened her eyes to meet his brown gaze, stormy and unreadable. She wished she knew what he thought of her, beyond his lust.

"But that's not it, love. There's more," he murmured. "I want you to undress me."

She tensed, suddenly afraid of him, of herself. She could feel her cheeks growing warm with embarrassment. To let him do this to her was one thing, but to actually participate... "No, I couldn't."

"You could," he told her, holding her with his eyes, grasping her hand and bringing it under the hem of his shirt. "And you will."

Looking up at him, she drew her finger tentatively over his bare chest. Just one stroke. Then another. Then another, and in a matter of moments, she found herself marveling at the muscular hardness of his male body and the strangeness of it. When she brushed her fingertips over one of his nipples and heard him catch his breath, she smiled to herself, fascinated by the thought that she could arouse him the way he could arouse her.

Blake lowered her hand to the waistband of his trousers. She drew her hand back as if burned.

"No need to be shy now," he whispered. "Surely you're curious, my virgin jewel."

She watched through her lashes as he leaned back, pulled his shirt over his head and then found the button of the only piece of clothing left between them. She gasped as she watched him spring forth from the fabric.

"Harder for a man than a woman to hide his desires," he teased as he tossed his clothing to the floor. "Go ahead. Touch me."

Biting down on her lower lip, she hesitantly reached down, drew back and then reached again.

She heard him groan and recalled something Angel had once said about the power a woman held over a man. All at once, she understood.

"Like this," he breathed, guiding her hand up and down, his skin amazingly soft. "That's right," he whimpered, lifting his mouth to hers. This time his kiss was neither gentle nor unhurried, but almost brutal, and the thought that for this moment she had such control over him made her brave.

As they kissed, she continued to explore, stroking first the flat muscular hollow of his belly, then his upper thighs, then that place again. So smooth and yet so powerful…warm silk over marble…but larger than she'd imagined…so big…too big to ever…

"Sapphire," Blake gasped when she stroked him again. "Easy, love, or we'll be done before we've started." He covered her hand with his, burying his face in her hair as he slowed her motion. "That's right," he whispered. "That's right."

He nudged her onto her back and her hands fell to her sides as he began to kiss her again. When he parted her thighs with his knee, she gave no fight. She wanted to know what this was all about, this act that in the history of the world had toppled kings, set brother against brother and brought about wars.

Blake grasped her hands and slid them upward until they were over her head, stifling her moans with his mouth as he slowly began to penetrate her.

At first his movements were slow, gentle, but then he thrust into her and she cried out in pain, her eyes flying open. "Ow!" she cried, snatching her hand from his to slap him on the back. "That hurt. You didn't say it would hurt," she accused, panting hard.

He chuckled, deep in his throat, covering her face with kisses as she tried to turn her face away from him. "It will never hurt again, my love, I swear it. From here on out, it only gets better."

He kissed her mouth gently, caressing her breast with his free hand as he began to move inside her, and she began to move with him. After a moment there was no more pain, only an incredible sense of urgency, increasing with every breath she took. As before when he had touched her, the sensations began to build, one on top of the other until they burst inside her, fanning outward in a release of pleasure she had not imagined possible. Blake thrust one last time, his body tensing as he groaned, and she knew he, too, had found release.

Later, when he had withdrawn from her and she lay in the crook of his arm, weak-limbed and unable to do anything more than try to catch her breath, she realized that she finally understood Angelique. Understood what it meant to be a woman. To be a lover.

"So sweet," he whispered, kissing her bare shoulder,

his eyes closed. "You see, I told you we would get along well."

Without responding, she turned onto her side, pushing her bare bottom against his groin as she pulled the rumpled sheet over them, and then she fell asleep, content, at least for a moment.

Sapphire woke later to find herself alone in the ship's cabin. Blake was gone, but on the desk she spotted a small tray with bread, cheese, an apple and a pewter mug. Suddenly starving, she wrapped the sheet around herself and hobbled the three steps to the chair at the desk. Once seated, as she tore off a piece of bread and stuffed it into her mouth, she found a note. It was the first time she had ever seen Blake's handwriting, which was bold, the lines of ink thick and purposeful.

Nourishment was all it said, but the single word made her smile. Nourishment for what? To recover from their heated lovemaking? To prepare for more?

Sapphire was shocked that her thoughts could be so sexual. The first time she had ever been with a man and she was already thinking about the next time?

She sawed off a piece of cheese with the small knife he had left her, and wrapped it in a piece of bread, wondering where these indecent notions had come from. She expected such behavior from Angelique, but never herself. Not before today, at least.

Perhaps all this pretending was the cause. Play the whore long enough and you become one?

She almost laughed. *What a ridiculous thought.* Despite what she had led Charles and the other young men to believe, she had never done anything more than most of the young women her age. In fact, if truth be told, she knew she had done far less than many. She heard the whispers in the women's salons, heard her beaux talking among themselves when they thought she wasn't listening. London's young women were not as innocent as they liked their parents and guardians to believe.

Sapphire sliced off a bit of apple and pushed it into her mouth as she reached for the mug. The cider was cool and crisp and she gulped it so fast that a trickle ran down her chin.

The door opened and she spun around, tightening the sheet around her bare breasts, swallowing the last gulp of cider.

"Ah, you're awake," Blake said, ducking through the door.

She chewed the last of the apple in her mouth, unsure of what to say.

"I see you found the food. I thought you might be hungry." He came toward her, a smile playing on his lips. When he stopped in front of her, he reached out and caught the dribble of cider on her chin and drew his finger to his mouth.

The simple gesture left her insides trembling, and she looked away to cover her discomfort.

"Why, Miss Sapphire Fabergine, I don't believe I've ever seen you speechless."

"I want my clothes back," she said, reaching for the rest of the apple as she rose from the chair, backing up toward the bunk while trying not to put too much pressure on her injured ankle.

"Which is why I brought you these." He held up a

bundle of clothing, but it appeared far too compact to be her gown and underclothes.

She stared at the bundle tied with twine. "I want my own clothes."

"Sorry." He frowned. "I told you they were torn beyond repair. Besides, silk gowns and ruffled petticoats are not terribly practical on the open sea."

She studied the bundle of clothing again and realized anything was better than wearing this sheet. Once she was clothed in *something*, she'd feel less vulnerable. That thought in mind, she put out one hand and sat on the bunk.

He lifted the bundle by the string and let it dangle from his finger, staring at her, making no attempt to hide his lust. "Then again," he said, "I must admit I like you this way."

She tightened her grip on the sheet around her. "Please?"

He smirked and tossed the bundle to the bed, turning to the plate on the desk. "For such a slender woman, you certainly eat a lot." He tore what was left of the bread in half and began to cut off a piece of cheese for himself. "This was supposed to be my breakfast, too."

She set the apple on the bed and reached for the clothing. Untying the twine, she found that he had brought her a pair of boy's canvas breeches and a white cotton shirt. "That's it?" she asked incredulously. "This is all you could find me?"

"I'm sorry, we're now on the open sea. Not many dress shops."

"Surely you can't expect me to wear these. It's indecent!"

"Hardly more indecent than what we did here not so long ago."

"Oh, you really are a cad."

"If I was a cad, I'd keep you in the blanket. But...if you'd rather remain in the *natural,* I could take these things back—"

"No." She shook out the shirt and managed to lower it over her head without dropping the corner of the sheet. "You think you're so superior," she snapped from under the shirt. She popped her head through. "Maybe you should have thought of bringing proper attire for me when you kidnapped me!"

He cut off another piece of cheese. "And maybe you should have thought before you hurled yourself from that coach into the street and ruined your gown. You're lucky you only twisted your ankle. It's a wonder you didn't break a bone or get trampled by my coach's horses."

She scowled at him as she slipped her bare feet into the pant legs and stood on her good foot to draw them over her hips. The soft, worn canvas pants tied at the waist and fit her almost perfectly. She didn't drop the sheet until she'd laced them.

He took a step back. "Best-looking cabin boy I've ever seen."

"You stole these from a cabin boy?" She pulled her hair back over her shoulders.

"I bought them from Ralphie. You'll like him."

"Probably not," she said tartly, retrieving her apple and taking a big bite; she had no intention of sharing it with him.

Blake just stood there eyeing her.

"What now?" she asked when she could no longer stand the silence or his stare.

He appeared bemused, which annoyed her further.

"What now, what?"

She felt her nostrils flare with resentment. "What am I supposed to do, stuck on this ship with you, against my will?"

"We could make love again," he offered with a shrug of his broad shoulders. "I heard no complaints at the time."

She was tempted to throw the apple at him, but she was too hungry to give it up.

The look on her face must have given him a hint of what she wanted to say because he went on.

"Or," he said, "we could read. Play cards. I brought a chess set. Do you play chess?"

She crossed her arms over her chest, sitting back on the bunk again, finishing off the apple. "Of course I play chess. My stepfather, Armand, taught me." She arched her brows. "I'm really quite good."

"As am I. At a number of things, which brings us back to how we could occupy our time. We could make love."

She glared at him.

"Suit yourself. Or maybe, if you're up to it later, I could carry you topside. It's a beautiful day to be sailing."

"A walk, yes, that would be wonderful," she said quickly, wondering if they were still close enough to shore to be passing other ships. Perhaps she could get someone's attention on another vessel, maybe even gain the assistance of one of the sailors on the boat.

"Don't get your hopes up. No one on board this ship is going to help you escape, row you ashore, or anything as equally dangerous or stupid." He licked his fingers and reached for the pewter tankard. "I hired this ship to take my goods and me back to Boston. It's no one's business if I have an elephant in my cabin, and no one on this ship would dare question it."

Finishing the apple, she wiped her mouth with the back of her hand. "Surely you must have given some explanation." She gestured with the apple core. "The captain must have questioned why he thought he was sailing with one passenger this morning and now he has two."

Blake finished the last of the cider. "I told him the truth."

"That you kidnapped me?"

"No. That you are my mistress."

Sapphire threw the apple core at him and she didn't miss.

17

"Monsieur."

Armand heard Tarasai call from behind him, but he did not turn to her.

"Monsieur, I go to the village only for a short time and you flee the house. You are like a child I cannot leave alone." She came to his side on the dock and draped a coat over his shoulders, the wind whipping at the tiny plaits of hair that fell around her face. She tucked her hair behind a delicate ear. "Armand, do you listen to me? You should be in bed," she said softly, and then she kissed him lightly.

He drew the coat closer, shivering inside as he continued to watch the dark waves crashing onto the dock. He had been here in this spot for more than an hour, and despite the warmth of the season, his feet felt like ice and he was light-headed, but he could not tear himself from the sight of the churning sea. "The water is rough, Tarasai, don't you think? Very rough for this time of year."

"A summer storm," she said gazing at the sea for a moment, then dismissing it as she slipped her arm through his. "Armand, *mon chèr,* you must listen to the *docteur* if you are to get better."

He sighed, feeling worn to the bone. Defeated. "Tarasai," he said gently, turning his head to look into her liquid-dark eyes. "We both know, you and I, that I will not get better."

"Non." She gripped his arm tighter, then drew her other hand over her barely rounded belly. "The medicine the *docteur* gives you, it is making you stronger. Stronger for *l'enfant.*"

"It's not making me stronger," he whispered sadly. "This illness, it's eating me up inside."

"But, *mon*—"

He pressed his finger to her sweet lips, silencing her. "Tarasai, I am getting weaker. Look at me. I cannot even walk my jungle paths any longer. I must have men to carry me." He pointed to the two teenage village boys who stood back discreetly and waited to be summoned to take Armand back to the house in the sedan chair he had had built from one of his grandmother's old dining room chairs.

"Non, non," she repeated, closing her eyes and rubbing her face against his arm, breathing in his scent.

"Shh," he soothed. "It is not so bad, really. I'm much older than you. I've led a good, full life." He kissed the top of her head, her hair braided in black plaits. Then he stared out at the rough sea again. "I only wish it did not take so long to hear from England. I sent the funds weeks ago, the moment I heard from Lucia and the girls, but I have heard nothing since."

"They are fine, your *chères filles*," she assured him.

"I keep telling myself that." He watched a wave break at the dock's pilings and water splash and wash toward him. "And yet I have this feeling about Sapphire that I cannot shake." He drew his free hand into a fist. "I sense…I don't know. Unrest. Fear." He looked into her eyes. "I know it sounds foolish, but I'm afraid she has gotten herself into trouble and she needs me."

"It does sound idiotic, coming from a man like you. A learned man," she said, smiling up at him. "So enough *sottise*." She tugged on his arm. "Come, let us take you home and put you to bed."

"You're right. I know you are. But I could do this, you know. Give in, die peacefully, if I just knew she was safe."

"No more talk of *mort!*" Tarasai wrapped a small arm around Armand and led him off the dock, making a sign with her hand she often made to ward off evil spirits. "Come to bed, Armand, *mon chèr*, and I will join you."

"You never come to bed in the middle of the day."

"For you, *mon amour*, I will. Just until you fall asleep."

"That would be nice," he said, suddenly so overcome with weakness that he could barely walk. Taking one last look over his shoulder at the raging sea, he pushed his worried thoughts of Sapphire away and allowed himself to yield to Tarasai.

The moment Lucia heard the knock at the door, she was on her feet. "Avena," she ordered, waving her hand.

Avena hurried to the door. "Mr. Stowe, welcome," she said in carefully pronounced English as she extended her hand. "Please come in."

"Have you heard anything?" Lucia asked, rushing toward Jessup.

He opened his arms to her, breaking into a grin. "I have. There was a message there waiting at my office when I arrived this morning." He kissed Lucia's forehead. "I cancelled my first appointment and came straight over."

"Where is she?" Lucia clasped both his pudgy hands in hers, thinking to herself what a treasure this roly-poly man was. "Is she safe? When can I see her?"

"She is safe." He nodded and then turned to Avena. "Some tea, please."

Avena bobbed a curtsy and disappeared into the kitchen.

"She's fine," Jessup continued, "but apparently young Lord Thomas was not entirely forthright in his conversation with me the other night." He led Lucia to the settee and helped her sit before taking his place beside her, holding her hands.

"Whatever do you mean?" Lucia said, beginning to lose patience with him. "If that young man has harmed a hair on my Sapphire's head, I swear—"

"Now, now," Jessup soothed. "Don't get your feathers all ruffled."

She put her hands on her hips. "I don't have feathers—now tell me what has become of my goddaughter."

He hesitated, then took a deep breath and reached for her hand. "It's as I guessed. She's gone to America with Lord Wessex."

Tears sprang to Lucia's eyes and she turned away. Her darling had gone. She'd always known it would happen someday, but so soon? She hadn't expected it to be so soon. "I don't believe you. She would never leave me without saying goodbye, without telling me where she was going."

"But you see, she did leave word. Lord Wessex sent me a note. It was only because they sailed on a Sunday that we didn't know sooner." He patted her hand. "The message was delivered to my office, rather than my home, by mistake."

She turned back to him. "Sapphire sent a message?"

"Lord Wessex did."

Lucia wasn't sure what to make of this and found herself immediately suspicious of the note. "And he said…"

"The note was rather brief, mostly instructions for me concerning the business of his inheritance."

Lucia's eyes narrowed. "What about Lord Thomas? What does he have to do with all this?"

"Well, I'm not entirely certain, but I have a feeling that Lord Wessex rescued your Sapphire from Lord Thomas and in a moment of impulsiveness—you know how impetuous these young people in love can be, dear—she agreed to run away with him."

A smile crept across Lucia's face. "I see, an adventure," she murmured. "They fell madly in love and, after having a row with Charles, she impulsively boarded the ship with Lord Wessex, unable to go another moment with him."

"Something like that, I think," Jessup agreed, smiling. "Very romantic, isn't it?"

"Mostly foolish," she said, looking at him. "But it sounds like my Sapphire. I knew that when she truly fell in love, she would fall hard." She frowned. "But what of this business of her needing to be rescued from Lord Thomas?"

"That was not information I gained from Lord Wessex's note, but from a far more reliable source."

"And that source being?"

He offered a sly grin. "One of my servants. Apparently my housekeeper's daughter's husband's brother is one of Lord Thomas's coachmen, and he was a firsthand witness to Sapphire's—" he paused "—flight."

"Good God, Jessup, you're making no sense," Lucia said. "What flight?"

"It seems that Lord Thomas did not leave her on the street so much as she left him."

Lucia arched a brow.

"From what the driver could gather—" he cleared his throat "—there was a bit of a tussle inside the coach and Sapphire simply…got out."

Lucia chuckled. "Tussle, was there? Sounds like my girl, my Sophie's girl. Sapphire has always been one to make her own decisions. But she wasn't harmed? Tell me that she wasn't harmed."

"No one was harmed except Lord Thomas, who gained a broken jaw from Lord Wessex somewhere in the process."

"Serves him right." Lucia sighed with relief. "I'm just thankful she's safe. And this Lord Wessex, he will take good care of her, won't he?"

"I must tell you again, my dear," he said, "a finer gentleman I do not believe I have ever met. Oh, a little arrogant perhaps, a little too full of his own accomplishments and capabilities—but what successful man isn't, at his age?"

She smiled. "Thank you," she said, lifting his age-spotted hand to kiss it. "Thank you so much. You told me you would get to the bottom of this and you have."

He patted her hand. "So, I suppose there's no need for me to go any further with my research concerning Sapphire's father."

Lucia pulled her hand away from him. "Whatever do you mean?"

He looked at her in obvious confusion. "It's…it's just that if she has gone with Lord Wessex, who her father is or is not is of little consequence, don't you think?"

Lucia rose to her feet. "I think nothing of the sort, Mr. Stowe."

"I…I don't—" He pushed himself off the couch.

"Who Sapphire was—*is*—is just as important today as it was last week. It will be even more important if she is to wed this Blake Thixton. She'll go on her adventure, explore the United States and then she'll come back, most likely Lord Wessex's wife, but she'll still want to be recognized as her father's child. It will be important to her children." She stared at Jessup. "What? You don't think she'll come back?"

"I…"

"You're wrong!" Lucia declared. "I know my Sapphire, and while she may have gone off impulsively, she will not forget us, nor will she forget who she is. She'll be back, and if you don't believe this to be true, Mr. Stowe," she said contemptuously, "then perhaps Avena should show you to the door."

For a moment Lucia thought he might burst into tears.

"No, no, no," Jessup said, reaching out to her. "I only said that because I wasn't certain—" He looked down at the floor, then up at her. "Lucia, love, if you want me to continue researching Sapphire's parentage, I'll do it. I'll find the truth for you if it takes me the rest of my days, if that's what you want." He dropped his hands to his sides. "Please do not be angry with me. I can't bear to have you angry with me."

She fell silent at his plea. "It's what I want, Jessup."

"Then it's what I want," he said softly, offering his hand to her. "Now, come sit beside me and we'll enjoy a cup of tea before I must return to my office."

"Gone? Whatever do you mean she's gone?" Henry asked, standing before a gilded floor-length mirror, trying to tie his cravat.

Angelique lay on her belly across his bed in nothing but her shift, a plate of berries and a bowl of sweet cream in front of her. She dipped a berry in the cream and popped it into her mouth. "She's gone to Boston with the American."

Henry turned away from the mirror, his fingers tangled in the fabric of the cravat. "Sweet, innocent Sapphire has run away with Lord Wessex?" he asked in wide-eyed amazement.

She dipped another berry, licked the sweet cream off it and dipped it again. "Wessex, Thixton, whatever you want to call him, left a note for his barrister, Mr. Stowe. That's my aunt Lucia's Jessup. He didn't say much, but he did say that Sapphire was with him and not to worry."

"I'll be damned," Henry mused, turning back to the mirror. "You think the chap is, you know, *safe?*"

Angelique shrugged. "Safe enough." She cut her eyes coquettishly. "Safe as you, Lord Henry Carter."

He chuckled at her reflection in the mirror. "Just not what I expected from our Sapphire. Charles said she wouldn't give him so much as a squeeze of a teat."

"She was in love with Wessex even though she said she hated him." Angelique rolled her eyes. "Her and her romantic notions. It's from reading that silly poetry— Keats, Byron, Shelly."

"I don't think it's silly to be in love with someone." He looked at her in the mirror. "I'm in love with you, Angel."

She licked her sticky fingertips and frowned. "Don't say such things. You're in love with my body and what it can do for yours."

"I am in love with your body *and* your heart."

She rose from the bed and strolled toward him. "Have you been reading poetry, too?" She reached around him, pushed his hands aside and finished tying his cravat for him. "You're going to be late for your parents' dinner if you don't hurry."

"You should go with me."

"That would certainly go well with the roasted pheasant your mother is serving. Didn't you say your grandparents will be there? Lord and Lady Carter, the lady's parents, Lord and Lady Bottlewait, the heir apparent Lord Carter...and his whore, Angel."

"You're not a whore." He turned in her arms, wrapping his around her waist. "I love you, Angel, and I want to marry you."

"That will wear thin once your father disinherits you." She gave his cravat one last tug and then stepped back to view her handiwork. Satisfied, she gave him a nod. "Now go, before you're late."

He sighed, grasped her arm and kissed her soundly on the lips before releasing her. "You'll wait up for me?"

She smiled, returning to the bed and her strawberries and cream. "Of course." She dipped one finger into the cream and began to lick it off seductively. "I'll even save you a little dessert."

He removed his frock coat from the coat rack near the door and slipped one arm into it. "You'd better."

Henry was always saying he loved her, but every man she had ever made love with proclaimed his undying love. She knew men didn't mean it and she never held it against them. Life was too short for falling in love only to end up brokenhearted.

That was usually what happened to women, Angelique thought. She had witnessed it from a young age. Her mother had loved the white planter who had come to their hut nights, her father, whose name she had never known. Then he had cast her mother aside for another. She died of a terrible fever when Angelique was five, but the old women in the village said she'd died of a broken heart.

"Angel?"

Henry's voice broke into her thoughts and she looked at him, smiling.

He opened the door as he reached for his top hat. "I want us to have our own apartments. I want us to be together."

"And if your parents disown you, how will we pay for these grand apartments?" she asked.

"They won't disown me. They're just testing me to see if I really do love you." He lowered his hat to his head; it was a rather handsome hat, she had to admit. "You let me worry about money. Let me worry about everything."

"Have no fear of that," she teased, dropping onto the bed. "You're already doing a fine job of it."

He kissed her hand and drew it from his mouth. *"Adieu, mon amour."*

"Your French is atrocious," she laughed, trying to lighten the conversation.

"And you love me anyway." He held on to the door. "Say it, say you love me, Angel."

"Go. You'll be late." She waved him away.

"It isn't enough."

There was something in his voice that hurt her. She met his gaze. "For now, it will have to be."

Sapphire sat cross-legged on the bunk, as far from Blake as she could get. She watched him read, but whenever he turned his head to look at her, she pretended to be interested in her nails or the pattern of threads in the blanket.

Hours passed. She napped, relieved herself when he discreetly excused himself from the cabin, ate in the afternoon, and napped some more. Now it was growing dark outside the single porthole and the fact that she was going to America was beginning to sink in. The silence in the cabin had begun to wear on her. She fidgeted. She made the bed, then remade it. Twice Blake offered her a book. Both times she declined.

When it grew too dark in the cabin to read, Blake lit two swinging brass lamps that were attached to the bulkhead and another that was cleverly attached to the built-in desk, which swayed along with the ship.

"Are you going to sulk all the way across the Atlantic?" he asked, startling her when he finally spoke.

"I'm not sulking."

He closed his book. "Yes, you are. Which is fine, if you're enjoying yourself.

She folded her arms. "I am most certainly not enjoying myself. I've been taken against my will and am being dragged across the ocean toward the wilds of America.

Blake rose from his chair. "All right, all right, enough." He extended a hand to her, turning his head as if to protect himself from her next attack. "We've already gone over this. I know you're here with me against your will. The question is, how are you going to deal with it now that you find yourself in this position?" When she said nothing, he went on. "Because that really tells me what mettle a man is made of, how he reacts to a bad situation he finds himself in."

"I'm not a man."

The corner of his mouth turned up in a smile. "I, of all people, am well aware of that."

She almost laughed. She stared at her feet for a moment, her arms still crossed over her chest. "I'd like to go up to the deck before it gets too dark. I'd like to see the ocean."

"Would you like to dine topside?"

The thought intrigued her. "We can do that?"

"I paid the ship's owner well for this crossing. I can do whatever the hell I please."

"Do you always get your way?" she asked, letting her hands slip to her sides. "Do you just buy your way through everything?"

"Usually."

"That's pretty arrogant," she said.

"It's the truth."

She let her gaze fall to the floor.

He waited.

She reluctantly lifted her lashes to look at him. He was handsome in this flickering lamplight, dressed in simple breeches, linen shirt and the tall boots of a working man, perhaps even more handsome than in his frock coat and top hat.

"I'd like to have dinner on the deck...preferably without you," she added quickly.

"Not an option. We dine together topside or we dine together here." Walking to the bed, he opened his arms and waited.

Sapphire hesitated and then slowly scooted toward him, taking care with her ankle. A truce. At least for tonight.

Much later, after a meal of fresh fish, rice with Caribbean spices just the way Sapphire liked it, and a bowl of fresh fruit, she and Blake stood at the ship's rail, looking out onto the dark ocean.

They talked about nothing in particular; he had been curious about Martinique and she found herself telling him things about the island, about Armand and her mother—things that she had never discussed with anyone aside from her immediate family. She asked him about Boston and America and he painted a picture that she found most intriguing. She discovered that Blake was not only a businessman but also a bit of a philanthropist, though he tried hard to hide it. He spoke excitedly of the changes taking place in the shipping and manufacturing industries due to the steam engine, and also of his concern over the treatment of the laborers. He was an interesting man. Indeed, she was learning she had to peel away the layers to find what was inside.

As they stood at the rail, she balanced on her good leg while he rested his hand on her waist to steady her. She watched the dark ocean that was outlined by whitecaps, the cool, salty breeze tugging at her hair and loosening it from the ribbon that tied it back off her face.

"My mother's God..." she said quietly.

"Pardon?" He looked at her.

"You said earlier that you swore by your *mother's God*." She turned to look at him. "Why is He your mother's God?"

"It's just a phrase."

He shrugged as if it meant nothing, but the tone of his voice told her differently.

"Your mother is a religious woman?"

"Was. I didn't know her. She died when I was a child and I was raised by a stepmother. But those who knew her..." Again, he shrugged. "They say she was a good woman whose faith ran very deep."

"And your faith does not?"

He laughed.

"You don't believe in God?"

He thought about this. "I believe in hard work. In convictions. In honesty."

"But not God?" she mused. "But how can you look at this ocean—" she gazed up into the dark sky "—these stars and not believe in a Creator? How can you see an old woman and an old man, walking arm in arm, or see a baby in a carriage and not believe in a God?"

The oil lamp on the table behind them cast a faint light on the profile of his face.

Blake took his time to answer her. "Sapphire, from the things you've told me tonight, you grew up in a house where children were treasured. Your stepfather cared deeply for your mother. My life growing up was not so…idyllic."

She didn't know about his childhood or what kind of life he'd had, so instead of speaking the first thoughts that ran through her head as she usually did, she stayed quiet. Something in Blake's voice made her sad for him. Every child deserves to feel loved, and while she sensed that much had been provided for him, love might not have been one of them.

"Do you think that love changes things?" she asked, breaking the silence.

He tightened his arm around her waist. "I think that making love can change things." He took her hand and brought it to his mouth, kissed it and then drew it along his cheek.

Sapphire could feel her face growing warm, her breasts beginning to tingle. As much as she would have liked to deny her desire for Blake, she could not. She felt as if she were teetering on a precipice. "So are you saying you've loved many women?"

"You could say that."

"But isn't that hard? To love and let them move on, back to their husbands, to other men?" she asked, truly wanting to understand.

"Not really." He kissed her hand again, then pushed up the sleeve of her shirt and began to plant light, fleeting kisses across the delicate skin of her forearm. "If you expect nothing from anyone, it's easy to walk away. No one gets hurt that way."

So what did Blake mean, Sapphire wondered as he tipped her chin and brushed his lips against hers. Was he saying that as long as she expected nothing from him, he wouldn't hurt her? That they could have this time together and then she could walk away, unharmed?

Was Blake saying that he could never love her?

It was a sad thought, but perhaps one she needed to consider.

18

After the first night on ship, Sapphire and Blake settled into a routine that she might have found utterly enjoyable under different circumstances. The early August weather was excellent each day and they took most of their meals on the deck at the small table Blake had transported for just that purpose. On the stern, it was breezy but not overly so, and the warmth of the sun was splendid. Sapphire spent much of her day reading from Blake's eclectic collection of books, playing chess or cards with him, or simply enjoying the fresh air. While used to being more active, after a few days of adjustment she was able to relax and accept her time here with Blake as it was, while allowing her ankle to heal. Ten days into their journey and more than halfway there, she was able to walk on her own and it only pained her slightly.

Except for the cabin boy, Ralphie, who served the meals and saw to any of their personal needs, Sapphire rarely saw the sailors on board, except from afar. Blake had left strict instructions not to be disturbed and the crew respected this request, probably out of fear of him, she guessed, for he could truly be an intimidating man.

The captain, a Bostonian named Jeremy Pottle, would make his daily report to Blake, telling of the expected weather, the number of miles they had covered the previous day and the number they hoped to cover that day. Sometimes he and Blake discussed the workings of the steam engine, but he never dallied. He spoke clearly and quickly and never stayed a moment longer in Blake's presence than absolutely required.

This morning as Sapphire watched Captain Pottle make his retreat from their table on the aft deck, dressed in a navy wool coat with shiny buttons and a cap, she nodded in his direction. "What did you do to him?" she asked Blake.

"Pardon?" Blake glanced over the top of the book he'd been reading—something he had acquired in England about the latest developments in the different types of fuel used to run engines similar to the one powering the ship they were on. He sat facing the sun, one boot propped on the table, his shirt half-open, and she found herself having to control her thoughts.

They had already made love this morning before coming up for breakfast. What kind of a wanton woman would Blake think she was, desiring him again? She was no better than her beloved Angel, whom she missed very much. That thought made her laugh. It was pretty obvious what kind of wanton woman she was and she had no wish to repent of her sins. Not today, at least.

"I don't understand the question," Blake said, interrupting her mischievous thoughts.

"Captain Pottle—he acts as if he's scared to death of you. Why?"

"I have no idea what you're talking about." He reached for a stoneware mug filled with fresh coffee. They might have been traveling on a transport ship, but Blake liked his amenities: fresh fruit, fresh vegetables, daily baked bread and Caribbean coffee, strong and black.

"You don't see the way he acts around you, as if he's afraid you might lash out at him at any moment?"

Blake frowned. "I hadn't noticed."

"No, I don't suppose you would." Blake was a strange man, so arrogant, so egotistical in so many ways and yet in others, he was clearly unpretentious.

She rose.

"Where are you going?"

"To the cabin to get the chess set—the waters are still calm enough to play on deck. You may have beaten me yesterday, but it was only a fluke." She walked past him in her bare feet, drawing her fingers along the back of his neck as she went by.

Below deck, in the cabin, Sapphire sat down on the floor in front of the bed she shared with Blake and pulled out the drawer built beneath it. As she retrieved the carved ivory and onyx chess set in its wooden storage box, she thought about another box under another bed so far from her, the casket that had been her mother's.

Tears filled Sapphire's eyes as she thought of the box left under the bed in the apartments her aunt Lucia had rented. Heavens, but she missed that box. And her family.

Feeling foolish, she wiped her eyes.

She was so confused by her emotions. How could she sit there on the deck with Blake and laugh and share breakfast with him, when he had taken her from her aunt who had no idea what had become of her? And worse, how could she make love with him when he still maintained she was a fortune hunter, still refusing to believe she might really be the late Lord Wessex's daughter?

Perhaps that was why she yearned for her mother's box. The precious casket was her proof—if not to him, then to herself—that she *was* Edward's daughter, and that her mother had been married to him, that she was *someone*. She was not the daughter of a whore, but of a wealthy, titled man and his beloved wife. She was no fortune hunter, but a woman of title and lineage, one who deserved to be loved, could be loved by a man like Blake Thixton...

Loved by Blake Thixton? Where had that thought come from?

Fresh tears ran down her cheeks. She didn't want Blake's love! He had made it plain to her that he was interested in nothing more than a tryst. She was only making love to him because...because...

The tears fell harder on her cheeks. Just because she had given herself to him did not mean she was his mistress. She would never be that. She deserved more.

What Blake Thixton didn't realize was that she was only biding her time until they reached America. Once they were there, she would set him straight. She would flatly refuse to be his mistress and demand he put her on the next ship to England. He hadn't even allowed her to address the subject of who she really was, and with each passing day she became even more determined to prove her claim to him. Blake was right too often. When he had kidnapped her he'd said that it was time someone taught her a lesson. In time, Sapphire intended to be the one teaching *him* a lesson.

"Sapphire? Are you all right?"

The sound of Blake's alarmed voice out in the passageway startled her, and she pushed herself up to her knees, reaching blindly through her tears for the box containing the chess set. "Y-yes. Coming!"

But he was already in the doorway behind her. "I was afraid you had fallen or twisted your ankle again when you didn't come back."

When she heard the cabin door close, she released the wooden box and wiped her eyes with both hands. "No, I'm fine, I just—" Her lower lip trembled and she let her hands fall to her lap.

"Sapphire, what is it?" In an instant he was at her side, on his knees, grasping her shoulders, forcing her to look at him. Some emotion passed across his face when he saw her tears, one that Sapphire had never seen before. "You fell again, didn't you."

She shook her head and turned away from him, ashamed of herself for crying over a silly box of old letters.

"Let me see," he insisted.

"No!"

"Sapphire, if you're hurt—"

"I'm not hurt," she said, but it wasn't true. Her heart ached.

Blake grabbed her around the waist and made her sit back, but she refused to look at him. He wrapped his hand around her right calf, just above the injured ankle. "The swelling is completely gone. Can you stand?"

"It's not my ankle," she said, unable to meet his gaze. "It's...my aunt Lucia." It was only a half lie. "She must be so worried about me. She might think I'm dead."

Blake looked away, his tone suddenly distant. "She won't think you're dead."

"No, you don't understand." Sapphire kept shaking her head. "When my mother died, Aunt Lucia—"

"Sapphire, this is foolishness." He turned her by her shoulders, forcing her to face him. "I sent a letter to Jessup before we left England. We'll be in Boston in another three days. You can send a letter to Lucia and tell her you're fine." He paused. "That you're with me."

"But it will take so long to get to them. I should write to Armand, as well, in case Aunt Lucia has sent him a letter. He would be so worried."

"It won't take as long for the letters to cross as you think. Look how quickly we've crossed the sea with this fancy steam engine." He drew close to her, his mouth almost brushing her cheek, his tone gentle again. "I'll put your letters on the fastest ship leaving the Boston harbor the day we set anchor."

Sapphire felt overwhelmed—by her emotions, by his proximity, the feel of his hand on her bare ankle, his warm breath on her cheek. He did care for her. She could hear it in his voice. He *did* care.

"Would you like to do that?" Blake asked. He caught her chin with his fingertip and forced her to look into his eyes.

She nodded.

"We'll do that, then." He kissed her. "We'll send the

letters and then I will show you the finest things in Boston, the finest buildings, the finest ships, I'll introduce you to the finest men...and women." He kissed her again. "Would you like that?"

She was mesmerized by the sound of his deep voice, the feel of his lips against hers. "I'd like that," she whispered, raising her hands to rest them on his shoulders.

"I'll buy you the most beautiful gowns in Boston, jewels if you like." He kissed her again, harder this time, and she found herself kissing him back. Her anguish, her fears were all slipping away. Once again, nothing seemed to matter but her pounding heart and how Blake made her feel when he touched her.

"You'll dress in the most fashionable gowns and we'll attend all the best parties. You'll be the toast of the town." He drew her into his arms, brushing her hair off her face so that he could gaze into her eyes. "You'll forget London and Charles in no time."

"What if I don't like Boston?" she asked.

"Then I'll send you back to London to your aunt Lucia."

She nodded, but she almost wished he had said he would not let her go. *Could* not. "No more talk," she whispered, covering his mouth with her fingertip, then replacing it with her mouth.

"Ah, Sapphire," Blake groaned, wrapping his arms around her and pulling her into his lap. "I can't get enough of you."

He thrust his tongue into her mouth and Sapphire closed her eyes as the kiss deepened. When she drew back, breathless, her mood had changed. She was light-headed, lighthearted. "You're not afraid of me?" she teased.

He leaned over, taking her with him, and then they were lying on the hard floor. "Afraid of you?" He laughed as his fingers found the buttons of the cabin boy's shirt she wore.

She nodded, lifting her arms, allowing him to remove the shirt. "In the village near my home, there were men and women who were afraid of me." She gazed into his eyes.

She had once read that the eyes were the windows to a person's soul and she found herself wishing that she could see something in Blake's. But as always, his eyes were cloudy, swirling flecks of brown as unreadable as the stormy sea.

"Afraid of you?" he crooned, cradling her in his arms again. He tugged on the ribbon that held her waist-length red hair back, and watched as her hair fell over her shoulders like a curtain.

"One blue, one green," she managed to say as a ripple of pleasure radiated through her body. "A sign of evil spirits." She opened her eyes wide as if to frighten him.

He laughed and lowered his head to kiss the valley between her breasts before dragging his warm mouth to her nipple. "I think your eyes are beautiful—they make you seem mysterious. Unpredictable."

He touched the tip of his tongue to her nipple and she gasped. "Unpredictable?"

He nodded. "It's why I like you. What first caught my eye...besides the red hair." He teased her nipple into a hard nub, taking his time before speaking again. "I never know what to expect from you. What you will say. What you will do. I'm tired of predictable women."

She laughed. "You'll be pleased to know that I find my own actions and thoughts unpredictable, as well, these days."

With a sigh, Sapphire relaxed as he drew a path of hot, wet kisses over her belly and then lower. She put up no protest when he unlaced the boy's pants she wore and slipped them off. And as he slid his hand between her thighs and found the soft folds, she parted her legs, her breath catching in her throat again and again as he moved his mouth lower. In a moment's time she surrendered to his hand, to his mouth, letting his fingers do what they would, lifting her higher and higher.

Blake knew her too well, what made her laugh, what made her moan, and he used every bit of his talent each time they made love. He teased her to the very edge and then let her drift back until she found herself arching her back, raising her hips to meet his hand.

"Blake, please," she begged. She was so close…

"Come sit on my lap," he whispered, rolling onto his back to remove his trousers.

She shook her head, feeling her cheeks flush. "I wouldn't know how to… I don't know what to do," she panted.

"Ah, I think you do. I think you were born knowing how to please a man." He kissed her earlobe, her cheek, and she turned to meet his mouth, accepting it hungrily.

"I think you were born knowing how to please me," he muttered hungrily.

Before she could protest, Blake lifted her up and onto his lap and she found herself seated astride him, her knees on the floor. Her boldness matching her need to find fulfillment, she lifted up and settled over him, finding a certain pleasure in his groan.

"What were you saying about not knowing what to do?" he teased, his eyes heavy-lidded with passion.

"Hush," she told him as she leaned over to kiss him, her hair falling around them.

Again he groaned, her movement further arousing him. "To think you were almost wasted on that dandy—"

"Did you hear me?" she commanded, pushing the heels of her hands into the floor on either side of his head and then lifting and lowering herself again.

His response was just what she had hoped for.

"Damn, but you're a fast learner," he moaned, his eyes closed.

She lowered herself, flattening her body over his, trying to remain in control of his mounting pleasure and her own. "Hush," Sapphire whispered in his ear, teasing it with the tip of her tongue.

And then she sat up again and began to move over him. She said she didn't know what to do and she didn't, at least not in her mind, but her body seemed to know. She moved rhythmically, slower, then faster, then slowly again.

"Roll over," Blake ordered gruffly after some time, resting both hands on her hips.

But she only smiled, slowed her movement and covered his face with light kisses. "How will I learn if I don't practice?" she teased.

So once more she brought him to the brink, but this time, she let her own control slip. She moved faster and faster, laying her body out flat over his, molding her soft curves to his hard form. When she cried out and heard him echo her, waves of pleasure crashed over her, leaving her shuddering, panting.

"Shh," Blake soothed as he eased her to the floor, rolling onto his side and drawing her against him. He kissed her closed eyelids, her cheek, her chin, the tip of her nose.

"No one ever told me it would be like this," she said when she finally found her voice. Her eyes were closed still, and she reveled in the feel of Blake's arm securely around her, his warm breath on her skin.

"It isn't usually," he murmured, kissing her shoulder.

She wanted to ask him what he meant, but she didn't. Maybe because she was afraid.

The day before they were scheduled to reach Boston Harbor was a rainy one, so Blake and Sapphire spent it alone in their cozy cabin, reading, sometimes aloud to each other, making love and just talking. It was late afternoon and Sapphire lay on the bed in only her shirt, which was so long that it hung past her hips. She rested on her side, reading one of Blake's books by a James Fennimore Cooper called *The Prairie*. She was enjoying it a great deal as it gave a fascinating look at America and the adventures it had to offer.

But Sapphire was bored of reading, bored of being cooped up in the cabin all day, and was a little anxious about arriving in Boston tomorrow. She and Blake had not talked about what would happen when they got there. He'd promised he would send her back to England, so she'd considered staying a few days, perhaps a week or so. He'd talked so much about Boston and New York that Sapphire was curious about both cities and saw no reason why she shouldn't see them after coming such a long way. But they needed to discuss the fact that she had no intention of being his mistress, no matter how much she enjoyed his company in or out of bed.

She laid the book down on the bed and looked at Blake. He was reading with one bare foot propped on the desk. A breeze came through the porthole and ruffled the hair around his face, giving him a relaxed, almost carefree appearance.

Sapphire realized that she hadn't brought the subject up because she didn't want to fight with him. At least for a little while. For a short time it had just been the two them and this cabin, this ship, their books, their laughter and their lovemaking. But time could not stand still and nothing that had taken place in this bed could change who she was. Or who she was determined to be.

"Blake," she said.

He continued to read.

"Blake," she repeated a little louder.

"Yes?"

"Blake, I need to talk to you."

He must have noticed the seriousness of her tone because he sighed and slowly closed the book. "Yes?"

"I want you to come here." She patted the bed. "Sit with me."

"I'd rather stay here," he said stubbornly.

Still lying on her side, her head propped up by one hand, she patted the bed again.

Another sigh ensued as Blake slowly rose and came to sit on the edge of the bed. He looked at the door, not at her.

"We need to talk about what's going to happen when we get off the boat tomorrow."

"We're going to my home. I think you'll like it. It's built on the shore with an amazing view. I told you many of the rooms are not yet furnished, but I was hoping you might help me with that. I just have the time to consider what a room needs and then—"

She laid her hand on his forearm, his dark hairs teasing her palm. "Blake, you know I'm not talking about the house. I'm talking about me. You. You know I cannot be your mistress."

"Can't or won't?"

This time, it was Sapphire who sighed. She withdrew her hand from him and lay back on the bunk. "Both," she said, imitating Blake's method of speaking slowly, taking time to decide exactly what she would say. "I am Lord Wessex's only child, the daughter of Edward and Sophie Thixton. I can be no man's whore."

He frowned, rising from the bunk, shoving his hands into the pockets of his trousers. "You know, you don't need to do this. I know you're a bright woman, Sapphire. Clever. Amusing. A bit of an entrepreneur yourself." He began to pace between the door and the bunk. "But this claim of yours is not going to work with me. In fact, it angers me. It angers me that no matter what I offer you, you say it's not enough. You're greedy."

"I am not greedy," she said, trying to control her emotions. She stared at the low ceiling as she listened to him pace. "I only ask for what is mine. All I ask is that you acknowledge the truth."

"And all I ask is that you *tell* the truth."

She fought the urge to snap at him; anger had gotten

her nowhere with Blake Thixton. She needed to remain as calm as he was. "When we disembark tomorrow, I'll need clothing fit for a woman of my station," she instructed. "Once we arrive at your home, where I will sleep in a room separate from yours, we can discuss this matter further."

"Fine," he said.

She rolled onto her side to look at him. "Fine?"

"Fine." He opened the door. "I'm going topside for some air."

She glanced at the porthole left slightly ajar and it was wet. "It's still raining out."

"I'll be back in a little while."

Sapphire wanted to go with him, but instead she just rolled onto her back again and listened to the retreat of his footsteps down the passageway. Listened, and refused to let herself cry.

19

By the time Sapphire woke the following morning, Blake was gone, as were the letters she had written to Armand and Aunt Lucia to be posted the moment they hit dry land. They had sailed to the mouth of the harbor in the middle of the night, and after standing on the bow together, watching as the few lights of the city grew closer, they had retired to their cabin. They'd made love, but Blake had remained emotionally distant from her, and that morning she rose and prepared for the day with great trepidation.

She drank the coffee Blake had left her but only nibbled on the bread, her stomach too nervous for anything more. She could feel the motion of the ship as it was towed to the docks in the harbor, but she did not go topside for fear someone might see her dressed in cabin boy's clothes. Once she stepped foot off this ship, no one would know her or what had taken place this last fortnight. She intended to resume the life she had before Blake had carried her onto the ship in the middle of the night.

Retrieving Blake's silver-handled hairbrush from the chest he had packed the previous day, she sat cross-legged on the bed and brushed her hair, waiting for the clothing Blake had promised he'd send for by dory first thing this morning.

Time seemed to drag. She could hear the rush of the water against the hull, the frenzied activity on deck and the excited shouts of sailors as the ship docked. She wanted so badly to be topside and see all there was to see in Boston Harbor, but she would not give in to her own inquisitiveness; she had to be dressed properly to go ashore as Lord Wessex's daughter, rather than some dockside trollop.

At the sound of Blake's familiar footsteps in the passageway, Sapphire dropped the brush and quickly drew her hair back in a simple knot. By the time he came through the door, she was standing in bare feet, hands behind her back, waiting anxiously.

"We can disembark as soon as you're dressed," he said, tossing a bundle on the bed beside her. He had donned a pair of dark trousers and coat and wore a bowler-style hat on his head. With his creamy white shirt and scowl, he looked every bit the entrepreneur and respected businessman that he was, and nothing like the man who had held her in his arms a few nights ago, twisting her hair around his finger, than pulling to watch the curl bounce. "The carriage is already on the dock, as is my assistant."

Sapphire turned to stare at the bundle of clothing that could not possibly be a lady's gown and petticoats;

it was too small. "Your assistant?" she asked, stunned by the parcel on the bed.

"Mr. Givens. He was my father's assistant. Not a terribly jolly fellow, but a good worker. He's very loyal." He said this without any emotion.

Sapphire tugged at the string tied around the parcel and the paper fell away to reveal a woman's plain gray woolen skirt, a long-sleeved cotton blouse that had seen better days and an apron. There were black stockings, a pair of worn black shoes and a mobcap, as well. Maids' clothes—and not even clothing fit for a lady's maid. This was the uniform of the lowliest household servant—the scullery girl. She stared at the clothes for a moment, then turned to Blake, her eyes blazing. "What is this?" she demanded.

"Clothes," he answered plainly.

She gritted her teeth. "I can see that."

"You ask for clothing befitting of your station, Sapphire." He raised a hand. "And I have provided them, as promised."

"You son of a—" She caught herself before the words slipped out and she could not take them back. Ladies did not curse, no matter how angry they might become. "I'm not wearing these," she said stubbornly. "I am Lord Wessex's daughter, I am not a maid, and I will not wear those clothes!"

"So wear what you have on." He laid his hand on the doorknob.

"I can't wear this!" She stepped back, spreading her arms. "I can't be seen on the street in men's clothing. I...I'd be arrested for indecency." She indicated the transparency of the shirt by tugging on it. "I can't enter your house, be seen by your assistant, your household staff in this. What will they think of me?"

"Sapphire, the carriage is leaving for Beacon Hill in five minutes, with or without you." He opened the door and stopped, turning back. "Unless, of course, you're just Sapphire Fabergine, a clever girl who has caught my eye." He raised his brows. "My mistress."

Five minutes later, Sapphire walked over the gang-plank behind Blake and onto the dock dressed in the maid's clothing, so angry that she thought the fire in her eyes might set the back of his fancy coat aflame.

"Good to have you back, sir," greeted a man some years older than Blake who stood next to the large and obviously quite expensive carriage. He would have been pleasant enough looking had he not been scowl-ing worse than Blake. He did not speak to her, nor did Blake make introductions.

Inside the roomy carriage, Sapphire sat as far from Blake on the leather bench seat as she could get. As they rode down the bustling city street, she looked out the window. Like London, the avenues were teeming with vehicles and pedestrians. There were fancy carriages like the one they rode in, but also simple wagons pulled by sway-backed nags and handcarts being steered by boys. There were common men and women dressed in simple clothes, carrying sacks, bags, sides of beef and buckets of coal. But walking beside them were men dressed like Blake in tailored black suits and women in elegant morning gowns, wearing bonnets and carrying parasols to protect their skin from the summer sun. De-spite the fact that they were at the harbor—usually the poorest, most run-down district in a city—these Americans had a different air about them. The venders selling meat pies, the slave boy carrying a parcel of letters, even the dockworkers seemed less dirty, less desperate. There was none of the filth and stench of London. Pigs ran loose in the streets, as did chickens, and she even saw a nanny goat standing atop a pile of barrels, but the streets were relatively clean, and most of the boys chasing one another among the bales and boxes wore shoes. She hadn't known what to expect in Boston, but the seemingly good conditions of the common people was a welcome surprise. She'd found London exhilarating but a little sad, and her first glimpse of Blake's city revealed promise.

The skyline rapidly changed once they were away from the docks, and Sapphire found herself craning her neck, so fascinated that she pushed aside the brocade curtains to get a better view. The buildings were tall, beautiful and so clean compared to the soot-sullied structures of London. And the architecture was remarkable. Sapphire had never seen herself as a student of architecture, though Armand had insisted she be knowledgeable about a host of subjects women did not normally familiarize themselves with, and architecture had been one of them. "My goodness," she heard herself say. "The buildings are so beautiful. That's Greek Revival, isn't it?" She pointed as they passed an institute of banking.

Blake and Mr. Givens had been talking about various matters of business. Now Blake turned to her. "Yes, it is," he said, seeming surprised by her knowledge.

"And look at that." Without thinking, she rose on

her knees on the bench. "What is that? The gold dome is so exquisitely beautiful."

"Our state house." Blake pinched the pleat of his trouser pant leg and crossed his legs.

"Neoclassical?" she asked, turning her head as they sailed by the newly constructed building.

"Yes, I suppose it is." Again, he sounded surprised. "The architect was Charles Bullfinch. He designed many buildings here in Boston. Fascinating man. You would like him. I could introduce you—he's quite a conversationalist."

Sapphire saw Mr. Givens give Blake a look, as if questioning why he would speak to a serving girl this way. She had half a mind to defend herself but decided she wouldn't give Blake the pleasure of hearing her try to explain why she was wearing these ridiculous clothes. She'd let Blake win this game, but once they arrived at the house and he found her some decent clothing, Mr. Givens would learn the truth of who she was.

"I'd like to see some of those buildings," she told Blake. "Armand had some sketchbooks on Greek Revival architecture, and I must admit I'm partial to that style." She half smiled. "Perhaps because of my penchant to Greek tragedies."

Again, Givens's thin brows arched.

"If you like Greek Revival, you will truly admire the house." He lifted a finger to point ahead. "We're approaching it now. This place is called Beacon Hill and it is bordered by the Charles River. In the 1780s they actually burned fires up here to warn ships of how close the shore was. Bullfinch and a partner cut about sixty feet off the top of the steep hill where you see the houses there. Town houses were just finished a few years ago there at the top at Louisburg Square."

"And your house is there?" she asked, a little amazed a single man would choose such an exclusive area of a city to build a house in.

He nodded, glancing away from the window. "The architect's name is Alexander Parris. He's probably considered the best in America today. He stopped building houses a few years ago as he's engaged with federal work, but he did this as a favor. He and my father were friends."

The carriage was slowly climbing the hill and Sapphire struggled to try to see to the top. "Which house is yours?"

"The one with the gray stone and the double bays rising above the roofline." He nodded in the direction of a magnificent house built of granite with its rusticated front wall that gave it a monumental tone. There were cartouches on the bowed front, which Sapphire thought to be French in design, but somehow the house still seemed to fit among the neighboring federalist-style homes.

"It's just called the Thixton House. We Americans are not like the English, naming houses with creativity." The carriage pulled up to the front door of the massive three-story house overlooking the bay, and several servants ran to catch the horses' harnesses. "And here we are."

The moment the carriage rolled to a stop, the door swung open. "Welcome home, Mr. Thixton," said a young man dressed in a smart green livery.

"Thank you, Billy." Blake stepped out of the carriage and Mr. Givens followed, leaving Sapphire to exit on her own.

They entered the house through massive double cedar doors which were opened by another male servant, also in dark green. "Welcome home, Mr. Thixton."

The same greeting was uttered with equal respect half a dozen more times before Mr. Givens left them in the enormous front hall. The moment they were alone, she pulled herself from the fascinating seascape oil paintings that hung on the walls in the entry room to confront Blake.

"All right," she said quietly. "You've had your fun. You've humiliated me in front of your assistant and your servants. I'd like proper clothing and I would like it now, please."

"You asked for clothing to fit your station, and I provided that. You are a simple girl, attempting to better yourself in the world, to rise above your birth…or are you my mistress?" He lifted an eyebrow.

It took a moment for Sapphire to realize what he was saying. She could hear footsteps on the slate floor and the jangle of keys as someone approached from the long corridor. She lifted her chin to meet Blake's eyes, and the determined look on his face angered her.

"Say it," he whispered. "That's my housekeeper coming. Her name is Mrs. Dedrick and she's a stickler for propriety. Maids don't stand in the front hall talking with the master of the house." He paused. "Not even maids I've brought with me from my new home in London."

She was so livid that she could barely speak. How dare he do this to her after what they had shared. How dare he! "I am not your mistress."

"My mistress would sleep in an elegant bedchamber

on the third floor." He indicated the wide, spiraling marble staircase in front of them. "She would wear gowns of the latest fashion and accompany me to the dinners, receptions and balls I am required regularly to attend as well as play hostess to the affairs I hold here in my home."

When she didn't immediately respond, he went on. "My maids, however, sleep in the attic where there are dormitories. I've only been up there a few times, but there are just small windows, so I imagine it's a little warm this time of year. And of course, you already know what my maids wear." He looked down at her shapeless, worn clothing with disdain. He paused. "Feel free to take some time to think it over." He glanced down the hall. The sound of footsteps was growing louder. "But not too much time."

"I am not your mistress," she repeated again.

"Fine." He turned away.

"Mr. Thixton, welcome home," a small, thin woman in a gray dress said as she approached them. She wore a belt from which a ring of keys hung—the jangling Sapphire had heard. "And what 'ave we 'ere?" she asked, taking one look at Sapphire and lifting her nose scornfully.

"This is Sapphire. I have inherited several homes in London and I...found this poor orphaned young woman on the street. I thought she had promise as a maid, though she has no such experience, so I brought her back with me. I apologize for not asking you beforehand. If you don't have room for her on the kitchen or house staff..." He let his last words hang in air that seemed to crackle with tension.

"Cehtainly not, sih," she said.

The housekeeper's speech sounded strange to Sapphire's ears. In each place where an *r* should have been pronounced, she used something akin to an *h* sound.

"This way, gihl," she said sternly. "I'm cehtain the masta wishes to rest and not be bathehed by the likes of you."

Sapphire glanced at Blake but he had already turned away, headed for the staircase. "I'll be in my study, Mrs. Dedrick. Could you send up some coffee and perhaps a little something sweet, like some of Mrs. Porter's cinnamon rolls?"

Sapphire's mouth watered. She'd had nothing but half a cup of coffee this morning and her stomach was now protesting.

"Of course, Mr. Thixton. Baked fresh this mauhin', just come out of the oven, I believe in anticipation of your retuhn."

Blake rested his hand on the smooth, carved mahogany banister and started up the curved staircase. "Excellent."

"Well whatayou stahing at?" Mrs. Dedrick asked Sapphire.

Sapphire shifted her gaze from Blake to the housekeeper, and for a moment she did not register that this was the way a housekeeper might speak to a new servant. At a loss for words, she stammered. "I...I..."

"Best you keep youh mouth shut," Mrs. Dedrick interrupted. "I shall call you Molly. Shaffire is not a proper skivvies name. Follow me, Molly." Mrs. Dedrick whipped her shoulders around and marched back down the corridor, leaving Sapphire with no choice but to follow.

As Sapphire passed the staircase, she looked to see Blake on the first landing. He was standing there watching her, grinning triumphantly.

Sapphire turned away, and hurried after the housekeeper. She'd rather sweep hearths and wash dishes than concede to his fancy.

Later that night, Sapphire lay on a narrow cot in the women's dormitory in nothing but an old, thin cotton chemise that a kitchen girl named Myra had loaned her after taking pity on her. As Blake had predicted, it was stiflingly hot on the fourth floor, and although she had a long and physically exhausting day, she could not fall asleep. She was too upset to sleep, too angry with Blake, with herself. She should never have given in to her desire for him. She should have dived off the ship stark naked while they were still in London Harbor. Anything would have been better than seeing that smug smirk on his face when she followed Mrs. Dedrick to the kitchen to begin learning her "new position."

Sapphire had expected Blake to come to her all day. She thought he might take the broom or the wet clothing from her hands and lead her upstairs to a lady's bedchamber where she could take a cool bath and dress in a light, summer gown, then join him on the beautiful veranda that overlooked the bay. But he had not come, and as the hours ticked by, her hands became redder, her back starting to ache and she became more determined not to give in to him.

Tomorrow, she decided, she would tell him she was going back to London. He had promised he would send her home and she was going to call him on his word.

She wanted to see Boston, to see the beautiful buildings more closely. She wanted to meet this architect whom she already admired, but the only way she would meet Mr. Bullfinch now would be if she were promoted from her kitchen job and permitted to answer the front door as one of the housemaids!

A lump caught in Sapphire's throat but she refused to allow herself to cry. Instead, she rolled over on the lumpy mattress, said her prayers and closed her eyes, willing herself to sleep.

"Manford." Blake rose from his chair in his study where he'd been reading and offered his hand to one of the few men he could genuinely call his friend.

"Blake." The tall, slender man shook Blake's hand and then wrapped his other arm around him. "Or should I say, Lord Wessex?"

Blake frowned and stepped back, always a little uncomfortable with Manford's physical displays of affection. They had met at Harvard, where Manford had been an instructor at the time. His family was also in shipping, originally out of Baltimore, but after marrying a Boston socialite, Manford had remained in the city and eventually took over the family business, moving the center of operations to Boston after his father passed away.

"Can I interest you in a brandy?" Blake asked.

Manford laughed. "Have you ever known me to turn away a good brandy? Or a bad brandy, for that matter?" He loosened his cravat, pulled it off and tossed it onto the brocade chair that Blake had been sitting in before his arrival. "Sorry I couldn't get here sooner, but Elizabeth had another dull benefit ball we were forced to at-

tend." He rolled his eyes. "I escorted Clarice, as well."
He waggled a finger. "You know, she had several invitations from perfectly respectable young men her own
age, Harvard men, I might add, but she refused them."
He accepted the crystal glass Blake offered him. "She
said she'd rather go alone than go with any of those
boys. I think she's rather smitten with you, my friend."

Blake covered his discomfort by raising his glass.
"Yes, an appropriate toast, to old friends," he said.

"And getting older by the moment." Manford
brushed his fingers against the graying hair at his temples, then lifted his glass into the air and tipped it back
to sample the brandy. "Let's go out on the veranda,
shall we? Hot as Hades in here."

Blake added some more brandy to his own glass,
taking his time before following Manford through the
French doors that opened onto the veranda. The one
good thing about his lengthy trip to London had been
escaping from Miss Clarice Lawrence, Manford's
daughter. Though more than ten years his junior, she
fancied herself in love with him, and despite Blake's
best attempts to extricate himself from her clutches, he
found himself escorting her more and more often to social events. At first it had been simply a favor to Manford—a ball here, an art exhibition opening there—but
by the time he had set sail for London, half of Boston
had been gossiping about the expectation of an engagement between Clarice Lawrence and her father's best
friend and occasional business partner, Blake Thixton.
Clarice was a beautiful, slender blonde with the face of
Athena. She had the looks, the education, the social etiquette of the kind of woman Blake knew he should

marry; the problem was that the moment she opened her mouth, all was ruined. She was immature, short-sighted, ill-tempered and…dull.

As he walked through the doors, it occurred to him with sudden surprise that Sapphire was probably no older than Clarice.

But that was irrelevant, he told himself firmly.

"So," Blake said, walking to the marble railing to stand beside Manford, who was taking in the view of the bay. "Mr. Givens has given me all the news of what's going on in the Boston shipping business, but I want to hear the real news." In an unusual gesture of affection, he slapped Manford on the back. "So tell me everything, old boy."

Manford laughed and sipped his brandy. "Good to have you back, Blake."

Blake exhaled, ignoring his thoughts of Sapphire lying upstairs, and gave his friend his full attention. "Good to be back."

20

Sapphire quickly deduced that her work would entail anything not assigned or completed by another scullery or housemaid, which meant she had to perform the most difficult, dirtiest duties in the house. By midmorning of her second day in Boston, she had already washed, dried and put away a sink full of dirty dishes, swept the kitchen floor, scrubbed the front steps, polished six silver candelabras and the entranceway doorknob and knocker, and carried table and kitchen scraps to the compost pile behind the garden shed. Now she'd been ordered by the laundress to collect the bed linens from the four bedchambers on the second floor, as well as the dirty towels from Mr. Thixton's bathing room.

Sapphire's first mistake was attempting to use the front staircase, and after a proper scolding from Mrs. Dedrick, whom she could still barely understand, she slowly made her way up the narrow rear servants' stairs carrying a large basket given to her by the laundress. Her second mistake was allowing her mind to wander.

Towels from the bathing room? Blake had a room in his house devoted to bathing?

She had discovered that Blake was far wealthier than she had presumed and that he lived a life of luxury she had not even realized existed. Armand, who had plentiful servants and slaves, had been a wealthy man, but his success could not even begin to compare to Blake's. In London, all of society had been impressed by his inheritance of the homes and titles belonging to her father, but no one had realized how the new Lord of Wessex lived in his own country.

His house, built on a cliff over the bay, was not, as he had warned her, entirely furnished, but the rooms that he had completed were magnificent. Blake mixed old with new, such as the Louis XIV pieces in the parlor, referred to as the downstairs keeping room, and plain, cherry pieces in a style she'd been told by one of the housemaids was called Shaker, in an office. But each room blended perfectly, from the fabrics on the chairs to the beautiful paintings on the walls, with themes dominating each. While the small dining room had a definite Asian feel, with Oriental carpeting and china on display, the larger dining room housed a table that was distinctly eighteenth century and French in design.

And Blake spared no expense—not just in the design and construction of the house, but in the decorating of it, as well. While Armand had two carpets on the floors at Orchid Manor, a fairly new fashion, Blake had at least two in every room, some of Chinese design, others Turkish, each one more beautiful than the next. He had authentic artwork in every room, some she recognized as works by Jean-Antoine Watteau and Anton Raphael, but some she suspected were American artists. And there were sculptures, as well, and glassware and pottery that must have come from halfway around the world.

As Sapphire climbed the narrow staircase with the cumbersome laundry basket in her arms, she could not help but wonder what was in this bathing chamber of Blake's, and what had possessed him to build such a grand house.

But she didn't even know whether she'd have the opportunity to ask him. Since they had parted the previous morning, Blake had made no attempt to contact her, and even if her so-called duties had not prevented her from seeking him out, she didn't have the faintest idea where to look for him. She'd heard, by way of Myra's boyfriend who worked in the stable, that Mr. Thixton had left early for his offices in the shipyards. If she was going to find him and give him a piece of her mind, she didn't want anyone to notice her missing because she didn't want to be the one to explain all this foolishness. He had created this farce; it would be up to him to explain it to his staff. For now she intended to complete her duties as best she could, despite the blisters on her feet from the crude, ill-fitting shoes and the calluses developing on her hands from the unaccustomed housework.

The first bedchamber Sapphire entered had obviously not been used recently, but she stripped the bed linens, anyway, as instructed. Just inside the second bedchamber door, she realized that this was the bedroom Blake used. Not only did it look like him—dark wainscoting, dark green brocade bed curtains and drap-eries—but it smelled like him, too.

Sapphire left the laundry basket in the hallway and walked to the bed, but instead of stripping off the lin-ens, she leaned over a pillow and inhaled deeply. She felt her pulse flutter as she breathed in Blake's scent, and images flashed through her mind. She remembered ly-ing beside him in the tiny bed built into the wall of the ship's cabin, the taste of him, the feel of his hand on her bare hip as she drifted off to sleep in his arms.

She cursed him under her breath and yanked the bedcovers off. "I don't know who you think you are, Blake Thixton, but you are no match for me," she mut-tered as she balled up one of the sheets and tossed it in the direction of the door. "Have me carry your slop bucket, wash your sheets, polish your silver, why I—"

The sound of Blake's voice outside the bedchamber door startled Sapphire and she froze.

"Give me half an hour, Givens, and I'll meet with you in the downstairs office," he said.

Sapphire felt her heart leap in her chest. She wasn't ready to see him yet; she didn't have her speech prepared.

"I'm sorry," he said, catching a glimpse of her as he walked in the door. He took a step back. "I can come back in a second."

"No, please," Sapphire said, tossing the pillow onto the bed. "By all means, come in, my lord. I'm almost done here."

It wasn't until she began to speak that he actually looked at her. Then he seemed as startled by her sud-den appearance as she was by his. "Sapphire."

She let her hands fall to her sides.

He glanced at the bed and the sheets strewn on the floor. "What are you doing here?"

She suddenly felt very vulnerable. She'd spent every day for more than two weeks with Blake and now she missed him. Not just the way he touched her or the way he made her feel, but the sound of his voice, his presence. Their conversations, their laughter. "What am I doing? What does it look like I'm doing, Mr. Thixton? Laundry, of course. A task befitting of my station, apparently."

He reached behind him and closed the door. She watched it swing shut.

"All you have to do is say it, Sapphire," he told her quietly, walking toward her. "All you have to do is admit that you sought me out for my money, for my title. That's all you have to do. It's very simple, really. You want something from me." He touched his chest. "I want something from you. It's a business agreement, pure and simple."

Sapphire shook her head. "That's not true. I sought you out because you are my father's heir, because I knew no one else to plead my case to."

He halted, looming over her. "There are courts for such pleas."

"I know, but until I have tangible evidence, evidence beyond the letters my father wrote to my mother—"

His voice was cool and matter-of-fact. "None of which state they were married."

"None of which state they were married," she agreed reluctantly. "But—"

"Sapphire. This is absurd!" He grasped her arms. "Look at you!" Letting go of her, he jerked at the hem of her apron, stained earlier by the rotting vegetables in the slop bucket. "This isn't you. You should be wearing the finest gown money can buy. That *my* money can by. You should be sitting on that balcony right now—" he pointed to the double glass doors on the far wall "—sipping lemonade and deciding how the ballroom should be tiled when the Italian arrives in the fall." He clenched his hands into fists at his sides, his face reddening. "Just say it, damn it!"

She held firm. "I will not. You demand that I be false to what I know is true. Well, you've met a woman you can't bend to your whims, Blake Thixton. I won't do it. I'd rather die!"

He glanced away, scratched his chin, then looked back at her again. He was so close that she could smell his shaving tonic; she could see the tiny wrinkles that creased each side of his mouth as he frowned.

"You are the most stubborn, most—"

Suddenly Blake was kissing her, pulling her roughly into his arms. She lifted her hands up to push against his chest, keeping her lips tightly pressed together. She had no intention of letting him do this to her, not again. But the scent of his skin, the feel of his arms around her was too much, too much for her to fight—and she knew that he knew it.

A sob escaped from her lips as she threw her arms around his neck, parting her lips and thrusting out her tongue to meet his. "I hate you," she said as she pulled away, breathless. "I hate you!"

Everything happened so fast.

Blake snatched off her apron, nearly tearing it from around her neck. He pulled the blouse out from the waistband of her gray skirt, and finding the buttons down the back, lifted it over her head. Kissing him again and again, Sapphire removed his cravat and tossed it onto the floor. She unbuttoned his pressed shirt until she could slide her hand beneath the fabric and caress the bare, silk-and-steel muscles of his chest.

Blake groaned as her thumb found his nipple and she rubbed it, wanting to torture him, taunt him the way he taunted her.

Drawing his mouth across her cheek to her earlobe and down her neck, Blake tugged at the waistband of her skirt and she shimmied out of it. As he grasped her around the waist, they fell onto the bed, their arms and legs tangled, their mouths meeting in passionate kisses.

Blake fondled her breasts and then kissed his way to one hardened nipple, and even through the fabric of her shift, she could feel his hot, wet mouth.

"The door," she gasped, writhing beneath him. "Blake."

"I closed it. No one would dare open it in this house—not Lucifer himself," he panted.

Her desire...no, it was more than that. Her *need* for him, was too great. She could no longer deny this strange, physical desire she had for him. Her logical thinking had vanished, gone on the warm breeze that played at the open drapes on the doors that led off to the veranda.

Sapphire slid her hand over Blake's hip and cupped the evidence of his desire for her. He groaned and fumbled with his trousers. As he arched his back, she lifted her shift, pulling the fabric up around her waist. With no drawers, there was nothing between them now, no clothing, no disagreement.

Blake took her quickly and she cried out in pain, joy and emotions she couldn't identify and didn't want to. A part of her was ashamed of herself, ashamed that she could not resist him, but none of that mattered, not right now. He stifled her cries with kisses until they were little more than sighs of contentment.

"Blake," she sobbed, digging her nails into his back.

His lovemaking was rough and without tenderness. She clung to him, wrapping her legs around his hips, lifting off the bed to meet him each time he thrust into her. At the end Sapphire felt her entire body tense and then found release, and a moment later, Blake collapsed on the bed beside her.

For a moment Sapphire just lay there on his elegant, massive bed and stared at the vaulted ceiling. She couldn't catch her breath and her mind was shooting in a thousand directions at once. Was she being foolish? If all he wanted her to say was that she was a fortune hunter in order to release her from her servitude, couldn't she just say it?

No. She could not say what wasn't true. And what would be the point in the end? They would enjoy each other's company for a few weeks, a few months, perhaps even a few years, but the only thing he had offered was to care for her in return for her agreement to become his mistress. Blake didn't love her. He never would. And somewhere, deep in her heart, Sapphire knew she wanted him to.

She sat up and reached for her blouse.

Blake rolled onto his side and grabbed her bare arm. "Where are you going?" he asked quietly.

She pulled away from him. "I have to get these sheets downstairs or the laundress will have me by the ear."

"Why are you being so stubborn, Sapphire?" He stood up, raising his trousers. "You don't have to do this."

"But I do." She dropped the ugly blouse over her head and reached for her skirt. "I do until you make arrangements for my transportation back to London."

Leaving his trousers open, he started to button up his shirt, and when he couldn't line up the buttons, he growled in anger and ripped it off. "Damn thing's wrinkled, anyway," he muttered.

Sapphire stepped into the skirt and began to tuck in the hem of the blouse.

Blake walked to a wardrobe on the far side of the room, opened a drawer and pulled out a freshly starched shirt, identical to the one he'd discarded on the floor.

"You said you would let me go home if I didn't like it here, and I don't like it here."

"Of course you don't like it here!" he exploded. "Not like this! I didn't intend for you to be doing my laundry, Sapphire. You were supposed be my—"

"Your whore," she said, tears stinging her eyes.

"No, that wasn't what I was going to say. That's not what I want."

She spun around to face him, refusing to release the tears that threatened to run down her cheeks. "That's exactly what you want. You want me to be your whore." She flung the words at him. Dressed, she grabbed his shirt and the sheet she had left on the floor. "You want me to serve as your entertainment. You want to put me on display like all your lovely artwork. You'll never love me. You don't want to marry me!"

"Marry you?" he said, his voice surprisingly soft. "Where did that come from?"

Horrified at what she had blurted out, Sapphire jerked open the bedchamber door, threw the dirty clothes in the basket and rushed down the hall.

"Sapphire," Blake called from his open doorway, obviously trying to keep his voice down.

She ignored him as she passed the grand staircase in the direction of the servants' stairs.

"Damn it, come back here!"

Sapphire heard him start down the hallway after her, and then he halted, obviously changing his mind. "Fine," he hollered after her. "Wash laundry, polish the silver for a few days, and then we'll see if you've come to your senses!"

By the time she made the turn in the hall to go down the steps, Blake had retreated back to his bedroom.

Once on the staircase, Sapphire leaned against the wall and, holding the heavy basket in her arms, fought the sobs that racked her body. How could she have laid her emotions out like that to him so that he could trample them?

Love? There had never been any talk of love between them. Not once had Blake insinuated that he'd felt such a thing. And she didn't love Blake. She *didn't!*

After another minute or two, Sapphire sniffed, wiped her eyes with her sleeve and started down the stairs. Blake had promised he would send her back to London and she was going to hold him to it. Next time, however, she'd be more careful about her own vulnerability. It was stupid to have allowed herself to be taken in by his charms, to have yielded to her own base desires.

But next time they met, next time, she'd be sure she had the upper hand.

* * *

Sapphire saw no sign of Blake for the next several days. She wrote a carefully worded letter to Aunt Lucia and Angelique and another to Armand and pinched pennies from the desk in Blake's office, getting one of the stable boys to post the letters for her. She made no mention of the relationship between her and Blake in the letters, but made it sound as if her trip to America was turning out to be a great adventure. She promised to write again soon and told them not to worry, that she would have great stories to tell when she saw them all again.

Mrs. Dedrick kept her busy with an endless number of household chores. Sapphire never thought she had taken her servants in Martinique or London for granted. She had always spoken kindly to them, had never been a harsh mistress and had never purposefully left a mess thinking another would clean up after her. But she realized that she hadn't fully comprehended the role of a servant. She hadn't understood how hard they worked, or, interestingly enough, how they moved about a household almost invisibly, learning the most intimate details of the lives of those they worked for.

Sapphire's newfound friend, Myra, who had been working at Thixton House for a little over a year, was quick to tell her all about her last employer. Mrs. Sheraton was having an affair with her husband's cousin, while the husband was having an affair with his business partner's wife. In the meantime, Mr. and Mrs. Sheraton's only daughter, engaged to one man, had been making assignations with a married man, and when the daughter became pregnant, she was forced to seduce her fiancé so that he would think the child was his.

Despite her depression over her own situation, which she did not reveal to Myra, Sapphire found herself laughing as she went about the chores assigned to her.

Six days after her arrival in Boston, Sapphire and Myra worked together in the larger of Thixton House's two dining rooms. As they polished the brass detail of the fireplace, Myra entertained Sapphire with tales of her previous employers' odd likes and dislikes and told the story of how one of the sons had half fallen in love with her, and that was why she had been "loaned out" to work at the Thixton mansion. Apparently, Mrs. Sheraton did not want Myra in her home, influencing her seventeen-year-old son, but she knew too well that she couldn't simply fire her.

"You should be ashamed of yourself, Myra," Sapphire teased as she settled on her knees at the hearth of the fireplace large enough to roast a steer. "Taking advantage of that poor, smitten boy."

Myra giggled, the dark curls that peeked from beneath her mobcab bouncing as she lowered herself to her hands and knees and began scrubbing the inside of the fireplace with a hard-bristled brush. "He's the one who started it to begin with," she protested good-naturedly. "I told him it wasn't fittin' to fall in love with your mother's maid." She dunked the brush into the pail and pulled it out, streaming with water. "'Course, look where it's got me now. I'm back to scrubbin' floors. A *demotion* is what John called it. He was crazy mad with his mother when she sent me packin', I can tell you that much."

Sapphire couldn't help but smile. Myra was not educated, but she was bright, witty, attractive and, most importantly, she had a good heart. From the first day Sapphire arrived, Myra had gone out of her way to welcome her and make her feel more comfortable in her strange new surroundings. Myra would make some man a good wife, even if he was not a wealthy man's son. Perhaps a wealthy man's son didn't deserve her, Sapphire thought wryly as she dipped her rag in the paste used to polish the brash, then began to rub the tarnished ball that sat atop a fireplace iron. Not if they were all as arrogant as Blake Thixton.

"Tell me about the master here," Sapphire asked softly. There was no one else in the dining room or the adjoining keeping room, but she was learning that there were ears everywhere.

"Not much to tell." She shrugged with ambiguity, but then looked up with excitement. "'Cept to say he's got to be the best-lookin' gentleman in Boston. 'Course you already knew that, him takin' you in in London when he found you on the street."

Sapphire had to look away and bite her lip to keep from saying what she wanted to say about Blake Thixton. Instead, she polished the andiron harder. "What's he doing in this big house all alone?"

"I wondered the same thing when I first come." Myra sat down on her bottom to take a break, which she did as often as possible without being caught by Mrs. Dedrick. "Works hard, that man does, a sight harder than Mr. Sheraton, I'll tell you that. Leaves early in the morning, comes home late at night. Girls in the kitchen who knew girls who worked here before them say his father was the same, only he weren't so nice as this one." She arched her brows knowingly.

"Do tell," Sapphire whispered, copying a phrase she had heard Myra use. Taking Myra's lead, she tossed down the rag.

"Foul man, the elder Mr. Thixton." She wrinkled her nose. "A drunk, too. Some say he beat the young Mr. Thixton when he was a boy. Liked to smack his servants around, too, which is why there ain't nobody left here who actually worked for the old Mr. Thixton. Just Mr. Givens, only he ain't one of us." Myra placed her palm on the smoothly polished wood floor and leaned over, lowering her voice even further. "Why, you can take one look at that man's face and tell *he's* an unhappy soul. Don't know if the old Mr. Thixton was mean to him 'cause his wife left him for a fisherman like they say or 'cause he swallowed a turd, but he's got himself a foul disposition, that man has."

Sapphire covered her mouth with hands that stank of polish to keep from laughing out loud. Myra had a way with words, and though she might speak crudely at times, there was no denying her meaning.

Myra giggled again and then reached out to tap Sapphire's hand. "Truth be told, I think Mr. Thixton works so hard 'cause he got nothin' else. I see him at night, though, sittin' all alone on that balcony of his, lookin' out over the water. He's lonely is what he is, and I think he didn't build this house to show off like some say. I think he built it 'cause somewhere inside him, he's hopin' someone will love 'im. Someone will come here and love 'im and give 'im babies."

Myra's words struck a chord in Sapphire and she had to glance away. She was so angry with Blake right now that she could barely stand it, but she still felt a sadness for him. "Is he...does he see women?" she found herself asking.

"Oh, we got plenty women comin' and goin' in this house, but all but one by the back door, if you know what I'm sayin'." Myra winked. "Mrs. Sheraton bein' one of them."

Sapphire knew she should have been shocked, but she was too tired to be. "You said all but one. Who doesn't come by the back door?"

Still seated on the floor, Myra rested her hands on her shapely hips and swayed. "Miss Clarice Lawrence. Mr. Thixton's got a business partner, Mr. Lawrence, nice man who always cleans his plate." She gave a nod of approval. "Been friends for years, they say. It's his daughter got her sights on him. She has her way, she'll be the one sleepin' upstairs in that big bed, orderin' us around."

Sapphire raised herself to her knees, pressing her hands to the tops of her thighs. "Does...is Mr. Thixton—"

"Who's to say? She's sour as early grapes, but she got the beauty of one of them women in his paintings." She pointed to the dining room wall where hung a nearly life-size oil painting of one of the Roman goddesses, painted in rococo style.

Sapphire felt a lump rise in her throat. Of course Blake wasn't interested in anything in her beyond what she could offer him in his bed. When he could have a woman like Clarice Lawrence—she eyed the painting— why would he want a woman like Sapphire who was without money or family lineage?

A sound in the connecting keeping room startled Sapphire and she snatched up her polishing rag. At the same time, Myra popped up onto her knees, grabbing the brush that bobbed in the dirty bucket of water.

"This way, Miss Lawrence," Sapphire heard Mr. Danz, the day butler, saying.

"I hope that Mr. Thixton will not be long," a high-pitched female voice announced, her tone close to a whine.

Two sets of footsteps echoed in the keeping room, one masculine, one feminine.

"If you'll wait here," Mr. Danz said firmly, "I am certain Mr. Thixton will join you momentarily."

"It's her," Myra whispered with great facial animation. "You got to see how she acts with him. It's a wonder she don't climb right into his trousers on the settee."

Sapphire lifted both brows. She didn't have to pretend to be curious.

"Runnin' over here all the time when her papa ain't lookin'," Myra continued in a hushed voice, leaning into the fireplace to scrub again. "Little trollop is what she is. Just can't get Mr. Thixton to drop his drawers, but not for want of tryin'. You just wait a minute, listen in, you'll know what I'm talkin' about."

The sound of the bristles on the hearth stone echoed loudly in Sapphire's ears as she used every bit of might she possessed to polish the brass fireplace ornament. "You mean he hasn't—" She struggled to find the word.

Myra giggled. "No, not as far as anyone here knows, and I can tell you nothin' happens in Boston, least not Beacon Hill, that Myra Clocker don't know about."

Sapphire had to smile. "How do you—?"

"Shh, here he comes—gimme a rag." Myra snatched a clean cloth from Sapphire's hand and ripped it in half.

Giving Sapphire the other half, she motioned for her to follow her.

The two women slowly crept closer to the doorway, Sapphire, like Myra, dragging the rag along the chair rail to appear as if she were dusting it.

As Sapphire sneaked up on Blake to listen in on his conversation, a part of her felt guilty for being devious, but a part of her thought it might be for his own good.

21

"Miss Lawrence," Blake said, "how kind of you to call."

Sapphire faced the dining room wall, but looked through the arched doorway into the keeping room. Just out of the corner of her eye, she could see Blake take a fashionably gowned blond woman's gloved hand and bring it to his lips.

Sapphire gulped, shifting her gaze to the wall in front of her. Myra had not been exaggerating, as she sometimes did, when she described Clarice Lawrence. Clarice was as beautiful as any woman Sapphire had ever seen, with long golden blond hair and clear hazel eyes. Her face was classically exquisite with a short, pert nose, high cheekbones that were slightly flushed and a perfect chin. Sapphire sighed heavily. Clarice Lawrence could only be described as stunning.

Self-consciously, Sapphire tucked a greasy lock of her hair that had come unpinned and tucked it up under her mobcap. On the ship, she had bathed almost daily in a tin tub that Blake had brought for that purpose, but there were no bathing facilities available to servants here beyond a washbowl she had to carry up four flights of stairs to the dormitory, or the hand pump in the kitchen courtyard. Most of the young women employed here either washed at home, or if they lived on the premises, simply stripped to the waist in their shifts and washed their hands and faces each morning in the August sunshine. Sapphire hadn't had the time—or the energy, for that matter—to carry water upstairs after her long day was done.

After a moment, she stole another peek into the keeping room. Myra had continued along the chair rail and was now boldly dusting the painted white molding that framed the arched doors leading into the next room. If Blake or Miss Lawrence had noticed Myra's presence, they gave no indication. Of course, servants were, by nature, invisible, and now it seemed that Myra was the most invisible of all.

Myra caught Sapphire's eye and curled a finger, beckoning her closer. Sapphire could see that Blake and Miss Lawrence had taken a seat side by side on a fine example of an eighteenth-century Italian settee upholstered in a green and brown brocade with a classic hunt scene woven into the design.

"Really, Miss Lawrence. There was no need for you to travel here in the heat of the day. Your father has invited me to dinner tomorrow evening. I could have seen you then."

Sapphire eased closer to the doorway. Blake sat stiffly on the settee, his hands on his lap so that no part of his body or his garment touched her, but she was leaning closely. Even from fifteen steps away, Sapphire could smell her rose-water perfume.

Blake looked tired. Apparently he had been working long hours, but perhaps he did that so he could avoid the house and her.

"I just couldn't bear to wait until tomorrow night." Miss Lawrence pouted, leaning closer to Blake. "I know it's forward of me, but I can't begin to tell you how much I've missed you all these months, Mr. Thixton."

He glanced away. "Please call me Blake. You and I have known each other since your father dandled you on his knee. It seems silly that we should not be using given names."

She giggled and Sapphire nearly groaned out loud. Miss Clarice Lawrence was the type of woman she despised. She had known several of her kind in Martinique—planters' daughters out fishing for the best catch in the pool of single males. And the Miss Lawrences had been as thick as fleas in London, all sweet-talking, coyly flirtatious and as manipulative as the female of the species could be.

Blake was a man who spoke only truths. He believed in hard work and honesty. For all his wealth and education, he was a simple man. He could never love a woman like Clarice Lawrence. She doubted he could even abide an evening with her.

Sapphire looked down at the rag in her dirty hand and then back at Miss Lawrence, dressed in her mint-green gown, white straw boater's bonnet and thin white lace gloves. The contrast between Sapphire and Miss Lawrence was both unnerving and unfair, and there was nobody to blame for the outrage but Blake Thixton.

"Tell me you missed me, Blake dear," Miss Lawrence continued in a simpering voice.

Sapphire almost laughed. It was humorous, really, Miss Lawrence trying to entice Blake while Sapphire, who had made love to Blake more times than she could now count, dusted the molding in his dining room. It was so amusing, Sapphire didn't know whether she wanted to laugh or cry.

"I'd really like to have you stay and visit with you," Blake said, rising from the settee and stepping away from his partner's daughter, just as she reached for his arm. "I apologize, but I've an important matter I must attend to before the end of business today."

"Work, work, work. It's all you men do," Miss Lawrence cooed as she rose. "Papa does the same thing, leaving early in the morning and staying at his office late into the night. Why, he's just like you, *Blake*." She fluttered her eyelashes. "Which is probably why I'm half in love with you."

She reached out to him, but he smoothly sidestepped her yet again. "Mr. Danz," he called. "Could you see Miss Lawrence to the door?"

"What did I tell you?" Myra whispered, slipping back along the wall to return to her work without anyone seeing her. "Nothing but a whore, virgin or not. And them hoity-toity ones is the most dangerous. I'm just afraid Mr. Thixton is going to end up getting caught in her web whether he likes it or not."

The next day, Sapphire accidentally ran into Blake in the second-floor hall; it was late, but she had thought he was still out, which was the only reason she had agreed to run upstairs and leave fresh towels in his bathing room. The bathing room, she had learned, was a magnificent space with a huge white tub and a rather interesting *necessary* that used a series of pipes and simple gravity to rinse the bowl clean with each use. Sapphire had been dying to ask Blake about the amazing invention, but she refused to allow her curiosity to get the best of her.

She was just about to enter through his open bedchamber door when he stepped out, wearing the same silk dressing robe he had been wearing the first morning she met him in London.

Sapphire took an unsteady step back as she clutched the thick white towels in her arms. "I'm sorry, sir," she murmured. "We didn't realize you'd returned home." One look into his eyes and she felt her stomach tighten and her throat go dry. She was so miserable without him. But she knew that she would be miserable with him, too. She could not be this man's mistress, or any man's; she would not tarnish the memory of her parents in such a way. Yet nothing could quench her need for him.

"Sapphire, it's all right." He reached out but did not touch her. "I've been meaning to come find you."

He was wearing silk lounging trousers and Oriental tapestry mules on his feet. She clutched the towels tighter. "You've been busy. A company to run, dinners and parties to attend, Miss Lawrence to escort."

He chuckled. "Is that jealousy I hear in your voice, Miss Fabergine?"

"Certainly not," she snapped. "If Miss Lawrence wants you, she's welcome to have you. Of course, perhaps I should forewarn her. If she finds herself in your bed, she may soon find herself washing your laundry and emptying your chamber pots."

"I don't believe, *Molly,* that anyone in this house has emptied chamber pots. The necessary that I had installed at great expense put an end to that. And personally, I haven't used a pot since I was out of leading strings." Again, he chuckled. "Is this your way of saying you've had enough?"

"I'm saying what I said days ago. I want to go back to London."

"Sapphire, you're being childish."

He grasped her arm, pulling her into his room. She tried to fight him, but he was too strong.

"Look at you. You look no more like an under parlor maid than…than President Jackson!"

"You're hurting me," she said stiffly.

He sighed and loosened his grip on her arm. "There's got to be some way we can settle this, you and I." He hesitated. "I miss you." He reached out to draw his fingertip along the outline of her jaw and she suddenly could not breathe. "I miss you in my bed. And I know you miss being there, too."

Sapphire felt her lower lip tremble. All she had to do was lift her chin and look into Blake's eyes to have him take her into his arms. He would close the door and carry her to his bed. Even though it would not settle anything between them, for that short time, she would be happy. She would feel safe. Almost loved.

"No," she said, setting her jaw with determination. "You're not going to do this to me."

"Do what?" he said, his voice husky. "Make love to you?"

The sound of that deep, baritone voice sent shivers through her. And he knew that. That was why he spoke to her that way, and that was why he touched her the way he was touching her now.

"Here, your towels," she said abruptly, thrusting them into his arms.

"Thank you. I thought I would take a cool bath. You know, there are holding tanks in the attic that allow the water to flow through pipes directly into the tub. Wouldn't a cool bath be nice right now, Sapphire? I could soap your back...I could soap you all over." He reached out for her again, but she jerked her head back.

"Good night, Blake," she said. And using every bit of determination she could muster, she turned in the worn, oversize shoes that gave her blisters and stalked out of his room.

"You'll tire of this game," he called after her, almost cruelly. "You'll tire and then you'll come to me. To my bed. On my terms," he added.

"Never again," she muttered under her breath as she hurried down the hall.

For the next three days, Thixton House was in an uproar. Blake was hosting an intimate dinner party for sixteen and Mrs. Dedrick was determined the Beacon Hill mansion would be cleaned top to bottom. Every bed was remade with fresh linens, every marble fireplace swept, every piece of furniture dusted, even rooms still void of furniture were aired and the floors scrubbed and polished. Sapphire's task on the night of the party was to remain in the kitchen at Mrs. Porter's side, but less than an hour before the guests were to arrive, Myra, dressed in a new black maid's dress with a white apron and mobcap, came rushing into the kitchen.

Myra bobbed a curtsy in Mrs. Porter's direction and then addressed Sapphire, who was practicing her hand at making butter curls. "Molly, you must come at once and change! Mrs. Dedrick's orders." She talked in excited bursts, her cheeks bright red with exhilaration. "You're to serve with me in the main dining hall tonight. Felicity isn't feeling well." She cupped her hand around her mouth and leaned to whisper. "The one always making eyes at Mr. Thixton. Everyone says she's free with her favors, if you know what I mean. Sick to her stomach. Morning sickness, they say," she hissed. "If you ask me, she's got a little coachman growing under her apron."

Sapphire glanced at Mrs. Porter and then back at Myra. She shook her head. "No," she said softly, taking a step back. "I don't want to serve. I'm supposed to be here, helping Mrs. Porter."

"Unfahseen changes occuh," Myra announced, drawing herself up stiffly as she folded her hands in front of her, doing her best Mrs. Dedrick imitation. "Household staff must adjust." Then she broke into a wide grin, reaching out to take Sapphire's hand. "Come on—it will be fun. And Miss Lawrence is coming," she whispered in Sapphire's ear.

Sapphire didn't know what to say. She didn't want to be humiliated by serving Blake his baked duck with truffle sauce. But perhaps she was looking at this all wrong. She hadn't asked to be dragged all the way to Boston, torn from the arms of her loved ones, and she didn't ask to become the lowliest servant in his mansion, either. Perhaps he was the one who should be embarrassed to have her offer the soup tureen. Besides, it would give her another chance to see that shameful Miss Lawrence.

Sapphire looked to Mrs. Porter, who was busy straining grease from the truffle sauce.

"Go." She shooed with her hand, only mildly annoyed. "She likes doing this, you know, Mrs. Dedrick— showing me she's first in command. Taking my girls right from under my nose. What are you standing there for, silly miss? Go! Dress in a proper serving uniform. But mind you, you behave yourself and don't spill gravy into the master's lap or you'll be back in here scraping scraps off the floor!"

Myra grabbed Sapphire's hand and the two young women raced for the door that led to the rear hallway and the servants' stairs. "We'll have to hurry," Myra insisted, taking the steps two at a time.

Half an hour later, Sapphire was at Myra's side, back in the kitchen. Dressed in Felicity's starched cotton black dress that was a tad long and a fresh white apron and small mobcap with a tiny black bow, Sapphire held a silver serving tray out for Myra, who was placing tall, slender glasses on it.

"I thought we were only serving dinner," Sapphire whispered nervously. The stiff gown itched at all the seams, and she feared that she would trip on the skirt while she was carrying the heavy tray and send the glasses of lemonade flying.

"First, refreshments on the veranda," Myra explained. "Then dinner. Then the men adjourn to Mr.

Thixton's office on the first floor and the ladies go into the keeping room for a nip of sherry, or the veranda, if it's a warm night like this. Mrs. Sheraton will be the one who decides. She always does."

Sapphire nodded, trying not to fidget and wishing she had shoes that fit properly. If she wasn't careful, she'd step right out of these ragged boats.

"There we are," Myra announced. "Now you carry and I'll serve." She turned to head for the kitchen door where Mrs. Dedrick stood waiting for them, tapping her foot, her keys jangling.

"Miss Clockah, make haste," she ordered sternly.

"Ready?" Myra whispered, looking Sapphire in the face.

Sapphire swallowed. "Ready."

"Coming, Mrs. Dedrick," Myra sang.

Sapphire followed her out the door and down the hall, watching the round silver tray as it tilted slightly one way and then the other with each step she took. "I can't do this, Myra," she whispered loudly.

"Yes, you can." She slowed her pace. "Eyes up. Never look at the tray."

Sapphire lifted her chin and concentrated on keeping her shoes on.

"Look straight ahead. Mouth soft. Neither a smile nor a frown. And, oh," she added quickly, "never make eye contact. Even if a guest speaks to you."

Sapphire nodded. "I know. I'm invisible. And if Mr. Thixton speaks to me?"

"Oh, he won't. He never does," she assured her.

At the door of the keeping room, Myra halted. "Are you ready?"

Sapphire could hear voices that were so familiar she felt a twinge of homesickness. She heard men and women talking in their funny New England accents, and an occasional laugh. The room was filled with dancing lamplight and strains of music drifted from the end of the veranda where the hired musicians played. A party. Oh, how she missed parties! And Aunt Lucia. And Angelique. This was all wrong. Why couldn't Blake see that she should be the one dancing…the one having all the fun.

Myra led the way through the keeping room, and just as she stepped out onto the veranda, Blake passed her coming into the house. He barely glanced at Sapphire, who had stepped aside to allow him to pass, but when he realized who it was, he looked behind him to be sure no one was near and backed her away from the door so no one could see them in the keeping room.

"What are you doing?" he demanded, his tone angry but hushed.

Sapphire, as ordered by Myra, kept her gaze fixed ahead of her, the tray of glasses balanced in her hands. "Serving lemonade to your guests, I believe, Mr. Thixton," she said haughtily.

"Damn it, Sapphire."

"It's Molly here, remember. And I'm just following your housekeeper's orders, sir."

He took a step closer, but she refused to allow him to intimidate her. She stood rigidly the way Myra had tutored, attempting to ignore the scent of his freshly bathed skin, trying to pretend he was not strikingly handsome in his starched white shirt and black frock coat.

"This is ludicrous!"

"I have no idea what you speak of, I assure you, Mr. Thixton."

"I think you do, _Miss Fabergine._" He leaned closer, over the tray she held between them, so close she could feel his breath on her mouth. "Manford Lawrence is a business associate, but he is also my dear friend. If you say anything to embarrass me—"

"And what of Miss Lawrence?" she asked, staring at him. They were so close she could have kissed him. Or smacked him across the face. "Hmm?" she asked. "Is she also your _dear friend?_"

He sat back on his heels, his eyes suddenly turning a stormy gray. "I think you're jealous."

"Absurd."

"I think you miss me," he whispered, leaning close again. "I think you miss my touch." He brushed her waist with his fingertip in a light caress and then withdrew it.

It was just enough to set her skin beneath the rough fabric aflame and he knew it…just enough to make butterflies flutter in the pit of her stomach.

"I think you want to kiss and make up, but your foolish pride is what stands in the way between you and me and a very…mutually satisfying arrangement."

Sapphire felt the tray of tall, frosted drinks tip slightly in her hands as she peered at Blake. "You know what you are," she whispered. "You are a conceited, manipulative—"

"Mr. Thixton?" a woman called from the veranda.

Sapphire took a step back just in time to see an attractive dark-haired woman dressed in a lovely rose satin gown glide through the doorway into the keeping room from the veranda. Mrs. Sheraton, Sapphire thought.

Myra had pointed her out on the street the day before as her previous employer and one of Blake's neighbors.

"Oh, there you are, Blake dear." Her last words were soft enough for only Blake and Sapphire to hear. She acted as if she didn't even see Sapphire standing there. "I was wondering where you had gotten to. I want you to tell Mrs. Carter about the Italian painting you procured. It isn't hanging yet, is it?" She slid her arm through Blake's and took a glass of lemonade from Sapphire's tray as she led him back onto the veranda.

Sapphire stood there for a moment, frozen in her old, beat-up shoes. Myra poked her head around the corner and waved frantically. Sapphire found her feet and hurried for the door.

"What did the master say to you?" Myra whispered. "Is there a problem with the lemonade?"

Sapphire shook her head, not trusting herself to speak yet.

"Come along, then." Myra gave another quick wave. "The ladies are waiting on their drinks. 'Course Mrs. Sheraton has already asked me if there isn't something stronger before dinner." She winked and then turned to the first female guest they came upon on the veranda. "Lemonade?" Myra asked, already lifting a glass from the tray to offer it.

Once Sapphire and Myra had served the drinks, they did not return to the kitchen as Sapphire had hoped they would. Instead, they stood at attention, backs to the stone wall of the house, waiting to see if they could serve more lemonade or take the glasses.

"This is the best part," Myra whispered out of the side of her mouth. "It's like we ain't even here."

Sapphire tried to stay focused as she looked out over the veranda that hung over the cliff. Even at dusk, it was a spectacular view. She could still see the ripple of dark water and whitecaps far below, and there was a twinkle of lights on the small slice of land that was the shore. By this time of evening, there was little movement on the water; all the ships that had anchored would burn lamps through the night in order to be seen by those insistent upon sailing in the darkness.

"So, has he asked?"

A young woman with ebony ringlets holding Clarice Lawrence's hand led her in front of Sapphire and Myra as they lowered their heads in private conversation. "Has he?" the woman repeated.

Both young women were dressed elegantly in nearly identical off-the-shoulder evening gowns of white silk; Clarice wore a pale lavender ribbon belt, and the other woman a pink one. Both had their hair swept up with fresh flowers tucked in one side of their coiffures, and Sapphire felt herself longing for one of the white gowns, for clean hair and the ivory pins she would need to sweep her hair off her neck. The privileged young women appeared so cool, so comfortable, while Sapphire's uniform was itching her fiercely at the neckline. But no matter how badly it itched, she knew she couldn't scratch. She *would not* scratch, not in front of Miss Clarice Lawrence, even if it killed her.

"Well, when *is* he going to propose?" the dark-haired young woman asked. "I thought you said you were certain he would ask you the day he returned from London. What did you say? I remember, it was 'now that he is a titled lord, he would have need of the perfect wife.'" The last words were almost hissed and most certainly accusatory in nature.

Myra sank her elbow into Sapphire's side and cut her eyes in the women's direction to be certain her companion was listening, then continued to look straight ahead.

"If he doesn't ask you soon," the dark-haired debutante went on, "you might as well start looking elsewhere, because you are certainly not the only woman setting her lace cap for Mr. Blake Thixton, Earl of Wessex."

"He'll propose," Clarice insisted, tapping open an ivory lace fan with one hand, sipping her lemonade. "Have no fear of that."

"I understand Mrs. Sheraton has been discussing her daughter with him. She's eighteen next month, you know. Younger than you and some say prettier."

"He'll marry me if my father tells him he must," Clarice whispered hotly.

"And exactly how will your father be in a position to insist Blake Thixton—"

Sapphire heard a gasp from the dark-haired twit, then a giggle. "Miss Lawrence, don't tell me you have surrendered your virginity to Mr. Thixton!" She sounded both properly shocked and excited at the same time.

"Not yet, I have not, Miss Breton."

Sapphire couldn't help it; she had to look. She shifted the silver tray in her hands and turned slightly.

More giggles.

"Don't tell me you plan to seduce Mr. Thixton."

Clarice clasped the other woman's hand and moved closer to her. Sapphire could feel anger building in the pit of her stomach as she clenched the tray tighter in her hands.

"Tomorrow night," Clarice explained. "My parents and I are supposed to attend some benefit or another at the new art gallery on Trudeau. Mr. Thixton declined the invitation, pleading too much work to be done." She rolled her hazel eyes.

"Which means he'll be home alone tomorrow night," the woman whispered in a conspiratory tone.

"I'll come to him with one excuse or another. I'll allow him to seduce me." Clarice tapped her companion on the shoulder with her fan. "And then, in a few days I'll run to Papa in tears and confess my terrible sin."

"Your father will confront Mr. Thixton and he will have no choice—"

"But to marry me or never show his face in public again." Clarice took her friend's hand and squeezed it.

Myra turned slightly toward Sapphire and opened her eyes wide.

Sapphire clenched her jaw and took a sudden step in front of Myra. "May I take your glass, Miss Lawrence?" she asked, looking directly at the beautiful young woman as she thrust out the silver tray.

"Why, yes, I suppose." Clarice took a step back, obviously surprised by the servant's forwardness.

"Take mine, too," the friend said, dropping her glass carelessly onto the tray, nearly tipping it. "It really wasn't very good lemonade. Tell your cook," she ordered Sapphire without looking at her. Then she grabbed Clarice's wrist and they walked away. "The moment you're wed, some changes will obviously need to take place in this household. The insolence of the servants is simply unacceptable."

"What are you doing?" Myra whispered insistently

under her breath the moment the two guests were out of earshot.

"Collecting the glasses." Sapphire walked to the next guest, nearly snatching the glass from her hand. Then the next, then the next. All Myra could do was follow behind her.

"What was that about?" Myra gasped when they were in the servants' hall, bound for the kitchen.

Sapphire sighed. "We have to stop her."

Myra shook her head vehemently. "The house staff never interferes. We only listen."

Sapphire raised her eyebrows, feeling for the first time in days that she was taking control of her own life. "In this case, that's simply not acceptable."

Myra's eyes narrowed. "It simply ain't acceptable?" She perched one hand on her hip. "You know, I didn't ask about why you were on the street that Mr. Thixton needed to be rescuin' you, but tell Myra the truth—you weren't no servant before, were you?"

"I don't want to talk about my past, Myra." Balancing the silver tray with one hand, she reached out and caught her friend by the sleeve and led her down the hall. "What I do want is for you to help me with something. Something that will keep Miss Lawrence out of Mr. Thixton's bed."

Myra was shocked. "That's no concern of mine nor yours, missy. You want to be tossed out on your ear?"

Sapphire looked her in the eye. "Do you want Miss Lawrence to become your mistress? Because you know, the first thing a woman like her does when she marries is fire every pretty young parlor maid in the house."

"And bring in the ugly cows or girls so used or old they don't turn the master's head."

Sapphire nearly laughed. "Myra, do you like your job here?" She rested her arm on Myra's shoulder.

She nodded. "Easy work, long as you stay in Mrs. Dedrick's good graces."

"Then Miss Lawrence cannot come to the house tomorrow night."

"Molly, what are you going to do?" They both started down the hall again.

"I'm not exactly certain," Sapphire said, but she was already forming a strategy in her head. It was terribly mean, but it would serve to be effective if she could manage it. "Didn't you say your grandmother was a healer and that she taught you how to make all kinds of tonics?"

"That's right, but mostly for belly ailments—sour stomach, women's complaints, stuff like that."

Sapphire stopped at the kitchen door. "Yes, but did she teach you how to make up a…" She glanced around to be sure no one was behind them, and began to whisper into Myra's ear.

22

"What on earth are you going to do with it?" Myra asked as she held the kitchen door open for Sapphire, who was carrying a tray of soup bowls. One of the footmen led the way as he carried a monstrous porcelain soup tureen. Mrs. Dedrick had just announced that Mr. Thixton and his guests had adjourned in the dining room and the turtle soup must be served at once.

"I don't know," Sapphire whispered, hurrying behind Myra. "I'm half tempted to dump it in the soup and give it to them all."

"No, you mustn't," Myra gasped. "Then they would know soon enough it was us."

Sapphire chuckled under her breath. "I'm not going to give it to them all, although Mr. Thixton deserves it, being such a fool when it comes to Clarice."

"But she's his friend's daughter," Myra said in Blake's defense. "He's bein' such a gentleman."

Sapphire frowned. "Sounds like you're half in love with him yourself."

Myra giggled. "Ain't we all?" she called over her shoulder. Then she lifted her chin and entered the dining hall behind the footman, carrying the tray of silver soup spoons and serving ladle.

"Ah, ladies and gentlemen," Blake announced from the head of the fine mahogany dining table Sapphire had polished herself the day before. "Please have a seat. I believe dinner is served."

For the next half hour Sapphire remained occupied following Myra's explicit directions, serving as Mr. Thixton liked to have his guests served. Though she caught Blake glancing in her direction several times, she did not make eye contact with him. Instead, she concentrated on doing the best job she could, considering that she had never served anyone a meal in her life, never mind in a formal dining atmosphere. As she worked, she kept her eyes and ears open, waiting for an opportunity to dole out a little feminine justice.

Halfway through the meal, she found her chance.

"This truffle sauce is so divine." Clarice Lawrence poured the last of it from the serving dish onto her plate. "Isn't there more?" she whined, seated to Blake's right, in the chair that had originally been intended for her father, according to the place cards she had apparently switched before the guests took their seats.

Myra looked quickly at Sapphire. "Yes, mum," she announced softly, scooping up the empty tureen from the table. "She's already eaten half of what Mrs. Porter made, which was 'sposed to be enough for sixteen," she whispered to Sapphire when she faced the dinner buffet they served from, her back to the guests.

"Perhaps she needs her own portion."

Myra frowned in confusion as she began to refill the gravy tureen from the covered bowl one of the footmen had brought from the kitchen. "Little Miss Piggy does not get her own," Myra whispered under her breath. "She's already had quite enough. Have you any idea the cost of them dirty mushrooms?"

"Oh, I think she most definitely needs another helping," Sapphire whispered back as she snatched a small container from one of the shelves beneath the buffet table and slipped a bottle of specially-made tonic from inside her apron pocket. A quick turn of her wrist, a ladle of truffle sauce swimming with fat, and she slipped the small bowl on a porcelain dish and wiped the lip with her apron.

Without giving Myra time to protest, Sapphire hurried to Clarice's right side. "Your very own, mum," she whispered. And with a quick knee bend, she placed the small tureen beside her plate. At the same time, Myra placed the larger gravy tureen at the head of the table.

As Sapphire backed away, Blake caught her eye and, for a moment, she allowed her defiant gaze to meet his. He parted his sensual lips as if to speak to her, but then pressed them together again.

Now who's being stubborn? she asked herself.

Myra had insisted the tonic she had helped Sapphire concoct would work swiftly, and Sapphire was not disappointed. A fresh Maine blueberry cobbler with cream custard was just being served by Myra's capable hands while Sapphire reset the table with silver spoons for the last course when Clarice began to perspire and her face began to contort as if she were in great discomfort.

Out of the corner of her eye, Sapphire saw a guest seated beside Clarice clasp her arm and lean toward her to whisper in her ear. Clarice took a sip of water and then rested back in her chair, her forehead beading with sweat. At this point, the other guests knew something was wrong, but they continued their conversations politely, only glancing in Clarice's direction, then continuing with their exchanges.

From across the table, Myra caught Sapphire's eye and Sapphire couldn't tell if the young maid was about to burst into tears or laughter.

"Clarice, dear, are you quite all right?" Patricia Lawrence asked her daughter from across the table.

"I..." Clarice's face suddenly turned green and she shot up. As she stumbled from the table, nearly kicking over her chair, she reached out to Myra. "The closest necessary," she groaned, not seeming to care who else heard her.

Myra raced out the door to lead Blake's guest, and Clarice gathered the folds of her white silk gown in her fists in a most unladylike manner and trotted after Myra. Mrs. Lawrence muttered under her breath to her husband to call for their carriage.

Sapphire had to turn her face away so that no one would see her smirk. But when she turned back, Blake was looking directly at her.

"I should go to her," Mrs. Lawrence, a pleasant enough, plump woman said with concern in her voice as she rose from her English-made Sheraton dining chair.

"Yes, see to her," Mr. Lawrence agreed.

Suddenly everyone at the table was talking at once in discreet but excited tones. Apparently everyone had an embarrassing tale to tell concerning hasty retreats and it was all Sapphire could do not to laugh.

As time passed, Sapphire continued to serve the dessert, but not Clarice nor her mother nor Myra returned. Sapphire was just beginning to remove dishes from the table when Blake rose and announced the ladies would retire to the keeping room and the men would have a cigar in his office. She had almost gotten past him with a tray of dishes to be carried to the kitchen when he caught her sleeve and in plain sight of his guests leaned over and whispered in her ear.

"Tell me you are not part of my guest's illness."

Sapphire looked up at him innocently, batting her eyelashes the same way she had seen Clarice do it. "Why, Mr. Thixton," she said, "I am but a lowly servant. What could I possibly have to do with Miss Lawrence's illness?" She then met his gaze directly. "Perhaps it's just the ill-humors of her personality coming out."

For a moment Sapphire thought Blake was going to smile. Instead, he scowled. "I want to talk to you later," he grumbled under his breath.

"Certainly, Mr. Thixton." She bobbed a quick curtsy and then sidestepped him, hurrying out of the dining room with the tray before he could stop her again.

An hour later, Myra finally appeared in the kitchen.

"'Bout time you decided to do a little work," Mrs. Porter snapped as soon as she came through the swinging doors.

"One of Mr. Thixton's guests fell ill and Mrs. Dedrick told me to stay with her, case she needed something," Myra said without so much as a smile.

With a harrumph, Mrs. Porter turned away and Myra

darted toward Sapphire, grabbed her arm and rushed her out the back door and into the enclosed courtyard.

As they stepped outside, Sapphire took a deep breath of the summer air, cooler than that inside the house. Myra turned in a circle, burst into laughter and then covered her mouth with her hands.

"So it worked?" Sapphire asked with a chuckle.

"Worked? I spent the last hour standin' outside the outhouse." She burst into laughter. "She couldn't come out. Must have been filled right to her eyeballs with ill-humors."

Sapphire tried hard not to laugh. "No," she whispered.

Myra nodded rapidly. "Finally Mrs. Lawrence had the mister bring the carriage 'round back. I brought towels and a washbowl just like I was asked, but 'pparently Miss Lawrence's white gown wasn't so white no more."

Sapphire stared at Myra.

"Well, it's a long hike to the outdoor pot when you're runnin' for it."

Sapphire choked on her laughter. "And you didn't just take her upstairs to B—Mr. Thixton's bathing room?"

In her excitement, thankfully, Myra didn't catch Sapphire's slip of the tongue.

"Let her use Mr. Thixton's fancy flushin' necessary? Certainly not! Not when you and me the ones cleanin' that room."

Sapphire couldn't help herself. She burst into laughter, throwing her arms around Myra. "I don't believe Miss Lawrence will be seducing anyone for at least a few days."

Myra wrapped her arms around Sapphire and they did a little spinning dance. "I don't believe she will be," she laughed, imitating Sapphire perfectly.

*   *   *

Sapphire nearly made it safely to bed without encountering Blake. Almost. After the cook and other servants had turned in, leaving Myra and Sapphire to put away the last of the freshly washed china, Mrs. Dedrick appeared in the doorway removing her apron, which always remained white no matter how long a day she'd had. "You, new gihl, Molly. Mr. Thixton is not pleased with the state of his bedchambah and bathing room. He wants fresh linens at once."

"I'll do it," Myra said, squeezing Sapphire's hand. "He gets into these moods."

Sapphire wanted to tell her friend how well aware she was of Blake's moods, especially concerning her, but she didn't dare. "No, you go to bed. I'll take care of it."

"He can be darn stinkin' picky when he gets himself like this."

Sapphire handed Myra the last stack of lovely Irish porcelain dinner dishes. "No, you had outhouse duty. I'll see to this."

"Just see it's done right," Mrs. Dedrick ordered sourly. "I am retiring."

"To have a little nip of 'er gin bottle," Myra whispered, standing beside Sapphire, waiting at attention for the housekeeper to go.

Sapphire sank her elbow into Myra's side and both women were able to contain their laughter only until Mrs. Dedrick disappeared through the swinging kitchen door.

Sapphire stalled for half an hour, finishing up in the kitchen and sending a sleepy Myra up the back stairs to bed.

"I'll wait up for you," she mumbled.

"Don't," Sapphire said, having a feeling that she and Blake might come to an understanding. "You're exhausted. I'll see you in the morning."

Myra gave a little wave and started up the steps again.

"And thank you," Sapphire called after her.

"For what?" Myra turned on the stairs. "For settin' a lady straight who needed settin' straight?"

Sapphire smiled up at her. As awful as her situation here might seem to her at times, she would never have met Myra had Blake not kidnapped her. "For being my friend," she said softly.

Another smile and Myra was gone. Sapphire then scooped up the clean sheets and towels and headed through the dark house for Blake's bedchamber, and decided, at the last moment, to take the front grand staircase.

Sapphire tapped on Blake's door, and when she heard him call for her to enter, she walked in, arms piled high with sheets and towels.

"I thought maybe you wouldn't come," he said, closing the door behind him. He had removed his frock coat and silk cravat and rolled up his sleeves to his elbows. He had a glass of scotch in his hand.

"The master ordered that his sheets be changed. I'm told by the other maids that if I don't follow Mrs. Dedrick's orders, I'll be out on my ear."

Blake pushed the pile of linens to the floor and pulled her into his arms, covering her mouth with his. "I've missed you, little vixen." He pressed his hips to hers, setting his glass on a carved rosewood table beside the door. "Can you tell how much I've missed you?" he asked, his voice low.

She closed her eyes for a moment, resisting him and the little tremors he sent through her, refusing to allow her body's desires to overtake her mind. She opened her eyes. "I understand Miss Lawrence missed you a great deal."

He kissed her neck and dragged his mouth over her collarbone. "I told you. She's my friend's daughter. I can't very well be rude to her. And you can't poison her."

Sapphire raised her hands to Blake's shoulders, allowing herself a small giggle. "I didn't poison her. She had designs on you. Illicit ones."

"I have absolutely no intentions of bedding my friend's daughter. She's a child."

"How old is she?"

He lifted his head. "Hell, I don't know. Twenty, I guess."

"I'm twenty," she said softly, gazing into his eyes.

He was silent for a moment. "That's different."

"I don't see how."

"When do you and I ever see eye-to-eye?" He drew his thumb along her jawline in a tender caress. "Hmm?" he murmured. "I wonder, is this the way it will always be with us?"

She looked down. She had come to tell him in private that he must send her back to London, but she didn't want to quarrel with him, not yet. "I don't know." She caught his hand in hers and threaded her fingers through his. "There are some things we agree on."

He leaned over and kissed her cheek. "I'll say." Then

he reached down to remove her apron, but she pushed his hands aside.

"Don't. I'm hot and sticky. I look a sight."

"You don't." He kissed the top of her head and stepped back from her. "But why don't you take a bath?"

She looked in the direction of his bathing room longingly. "I shouldn't."

"Don't be ridiculous." He reached for his glass of scotch on the edge of the table.

"It's not fair. The other girls have gone to bed without a cool bath."

"You are not one of the other girls." He gave her an easy push in the direction of the bathing room.

The door stood ajar and she could see the big white tub that was so long that a person could sit in it with legs out in front. "You're just trying to get me to take my clothes off so you can take advantage of me."

He tilted his head back and laughed.

"Why are you laughing?" she asked indignantly.

He wiped his eyes, which had teared up from laughing so hard. He took a sip of the scotch. "Sapphire Fabergine, you have never done anything in your life that you did not want to do. I pity the man who would try to bend you to his will."

She stared up at him, exasperated by the fact that he had brought her across the Atlantic Ocean against her will, but that wasn't what he meant, and she knew it. "I'm going to take a bath," she said, "but if you come in there—"

"You'll what?" he challenged with that cocky grin of his. He took one look at her face and then laughed and looked away, waving her off with his hand. "Never mind. All I know is that I should probably take care in staying on your good side or else I may be seated in the latrine with Clarice."

Chuckling, Sapphire grabbed several towels off the floor where Blake had dropped them, entered the bathing room and closed the door soundly behind her.

In the next hour, Blake knocked on the door twice, but both times Sapphire sent him away, and he remained true to his word, staying out. She knew she couldn't stay submerged in the exquisitely cool water, hidden in his bathing room from the world forever, but each time she rose to step out of the tub, she would rinse her hair or scrub her entire body head to toe with perfumed bath salts one last time.

But finally, when her skin began to wrinkle, she got out of the tub and wrapped her hair in one of the smaller towels, using a larger towel around her body. She just couldn't bring herself to put on the scratchy black maid's uniform; even the old gray skirt and faded blouse Blake had given her were more comfortable than the heap of clothing on the floor.

She opened the bathing room door and walked into the bedchamber. Blake had turned off most of the oil lamps so that only one glowed softly beside the bed. She did not see him but she could smell the smoke from one of his cigars, and when she went out on the balcony, she saw the outline of his form. He stood leaning against the rail, peering out over the cliff onto the dark water far below.

Sapphire walked over to stand beside him, and though he rested one hand casually on her hip, they were both quiet for a long time. They just stood there, enjoying the cool breeze, being together without arguing. "I should go," she said softly at last.

He tightened his arm around her but did not look at her. "No. Stay with me. Stay the night."

"Blake, I can't. If someone wakes in the dormitory and realizes I'm missing, they might come looking for me."

"Sapphire, tell me what you want from me." He ground out his cigar on a glass plate that was balanced on the rail and he turned to her.

"What I want?" she said, taken aback by his sudden question.

"Yes, what you want, what will satisfy you. Do you want me to say I love you? Is that it?" He stared at her through the darkness. "Do you want me to declare my undying love for you?"

He said it as if *love* were a dirty word, and instead of being angry at him as she should have been, all she felt was sadness, and pity. Sapphire released the white towel and let it fall to the smooth stone floor of the balcony. She tipped her head back and removed the towel, letting her damp hair fall over her shoulders. Then she reached out to him. A part of her wanted to pull him into her arms, draw his head to her breast and smooth his hair, smooth away the lines on his face, smooth away all the pain she heard in his voice at this moment.

Instead, she rested a hand on each of his broad shoulders and she lifted up on her toes and kissed him on the mouth. His lips remained rigid for a moment, but then they softened and suddenly his arms shot out, pulling her against him. He thrust his tongue into her mouth, kissing her hard, turning her in his arms to push her roughly against the railing.

Sapphire felt her hair hang free over the open space; she felt as if she were falling, and yet as long as Blake held her in his arms like this, she knew she would never hit the rocks far below. They kissed again and again, Blake cupping her breasts with his hands, squeezing them, kneading them.

She pulled the tail of his shirt from his trousers, found the buttons with her fingers and pulled it over his head. She loved the feel of his hard, muscular chest beneath her fingertips, loved to take his nipple in her mouth, loved creating the same sensations in him that he created in her.

Blake drew his hands up and down her arms, over her rib cage, over her waist, in a frenzy of desire for her. He rested his face between her breasts and then began to kiss his way downward. Before she could stop him, he was on his knees pushing her legs apart. Sapphire grabbed the rail behind her as he thrust his fingers between the damp, aching folds of her womanhood. She cried out in pleasure, in agony. First his fingers, then his tongue. The stars overhead began to swirl, pulling her into their vortex.

She ran her fingers through his dark hair, arching her back, groaning as she found glorious release. Then Blake was on his feet, stepping out of his trousers, pushing her up against the rail again. He grasped his erection and entered her as she held on to the cool forged metal with one hand, lifting her hips to meet him…to take all of his length inside her. She rose and fell in a rhythm of ecstasy under a canopy of stars that seemed to be theirs and theirs alone. Soon she heard herself cry out again, felt him thrust one last time, and then he slid out of her, dropping his cheek to her shoulder.

For a moment they just stood there, clinging to each other. Sapphire was trembling all over. What had Blake meant when he asked her if she wanted him to tell her he loved her? Did he love her? Was that his way of saying he did but that he was afraid to admit it? They had never spoken of love and yet she knew she loved him, and she knew it at this moment as well as she knew herself. Was it possible that this man who seemed to have no emotions possessed feelings as deep and vast as her own…was it possible that he truly loved her…or was it only more deceit and lies?

"Let's go inside," he whispered in her ear when he could breathe evenly again. "Where are my manners."

She laughed and allowed him to lead her into his room. They lay down on his bed on the cool sheets and she rested her cheek on his shoulder, reveling in the feel of his arm around her. On the mantel across the room, she could hear the small case clock ticking.

"You asked me what I want," she said softly.

She knew he was awake, listening, even if he didn't answer. "I need for you to accept me for who I am." She paused. "Accept me for who I might be. Accept the possibility."

"Sapphire—"

She half sat up, pressing her finger to his lips, looking down at him in the shadows of the lamplight. "I never asked you to believe me when I told you that I was Lord Wessex's daughter. All I ever asked was that you give me the opportunity to prove it to you."

"You have no proof."

This time she was the one who was silent. Again the clock ticked hollowly in the large, airy bedchamber.

"Do you truly love me?" she asked quietly.

He turned his head, shifting his gaze. "I don't know," he said.

She was saddened at once by the thought that he didn't say he loved her, but she felt a flicker of hope. If he didn't *not* love her, did that mean that perhaps he did love her? Or was there something inside him that kept him from ever feeling love?

"So what are we going to do?" he asked after another long silence with nothing but the tick of the clock and the thumping of her heart making a sound.

"I don't know," she sighed, lying down with her head on his pillow, not yet ready to leave him. "Perhaps we both need some more time to think."

"Perhaps," he agreed. "In the meantime, will you join me here in my bedchamber?"

"I can't," she whispered. "I just can't, Blake." She swallowed. "And really, it's not so bad in the kitchen. I've made a good friend."

"Sapphire, I hate to think—"

"I think that's enough talk for one night, don't you?" she asked.

He rolled over to face her, playing with her hair. "I'm a Harvard graduate and you were schooled by the Good Sisters of the Sacred Heart," he said, sounding more like himself again. "And yet time and time again, I think to myself that you're the far brighter of the two of us."

She laughed, looking up at him, finding herself lost in his dark eyes. "Will you kiss me?" she whispered, her lower lip trembling with emotion. All she wanted to do at that moment was to tell him she loved him. She wanted to stand on the rail of the balcony and shout it to all of Boston. But Blake kissed her and her words were lost, lost to his touch and her own fears.

23

"Jessup?" Lucia sang, bustling down the corridor to his office, a letter clutched in her hands. By now, his clerk, Mr. Turnburry, knew better than to try to stop her from bursting into his office whenever she pleased. "Jessup, dearest."

Angelique followed behind her, removing her lace gloves one finger at a time. "Really, Aunt Lucia, have you any idea how unfashionable it is to be in love with the man keeping you?"

"Keeping me?" Lucia stopped in the middle of the hallway and turned to her young charge, one hand on her ample hip. "No man is keeping me, I will have you know, young lady! I keep myself. I may not be wealthy, but it has been many years since I have been forced to have a man to pay for the roof over my head. How dare you! How dare you," she accused, taking a step toward Angelique.

Angelique was genuinely surprised. "Aunt Lucia,

please. I'm sorry." She held up her hands. "I didn't mean to upset you. I see nothing wrong, obviously, with allowing a man to pay for my favors."

"I'm not upset! I'm insulted."

"I didn't mean to insult you." She gave a little laugh. "I am the last person to judge a woman for allowing a man to care for her. You know that. I was only saying that because…well, it's embarrassing the way the two of you carry on, not just in private, but in public, as well."

"*Mon dieu*, but I love you. I love our dear Sapphire, and I make no bones about that, in private or in public."

"I know."

Angelique looked at Lucia with those beautiful eyes of hers. Lucia still wondered sometimes, after all these years, if the girl was not Armand's child. She certainly had his passion. "But you're too old to be kissing in public." She chuckled. "And it is different."

Lucia adjusted her new straw bonnet with its wide grosgrain pink bow that tied beneath her chin. "It most certainly is *not* different."

"It's a different kind of love," Angelique insisted. "And you know it. My love for you and Sapphire, for Armand, will last a lifetime. Henry's so-called love for me will last only a few weeks, a few months, a few years, perhaps, but eventually he'll tire of me and he will no longer be in love with me."

"You are too cynical for a girl your age." Lucia played with the lace of the collar on Angelique's pretty blue walking dress. "Love is different between a mother and her daughter and a mother and her lover in many ways, *dulce,* but as you grow older, not as much." She sighed, wishing she knew how to better explain it. "Both kinds of love can be overwhelming, sometimes the passionate kind even more. I think perhaps that is why you are afraid to love your Henry."

"Afraid to love Henry? Where did that ridiculous notion come from? Has Henry called on you again? Because if he has—"

"Angel, calm yourself," Lucia said as she took Angelique's cheeks between her palms. "Young Henry has not been by to call alone since the last time you punished him for that full week. I only speak of what I see. What I see in your eyes when you're together."

"Really, Aunt Lucia, you're as daft as he is. Now, are we going to ask Mr. Stowe if he would like to join us for tea or are we going to stand here and talk about my lover?"

Lucia considered carrying the conversation concerning Henry a little further, but then decided that the subject of Angelique's true feelings for him needed to be dealt with a bit at a time. For Angelique, the thought of loving a man had to be difficult, especially because she had been determined never to love, only to be loved. Lucia knew the young woman needed time to get used to the idea. Why, it had taken a year for Angelique to actually sleep in a bed when she joined them at Orchid Manor. For the first year she was with them, she slept on a mat on Sapphire's bedchamber floor because, for all her appearance of being enlightened and impulsive, change did not come easily to her.

"Lucia, dear heart, there you are." Jessup came down the corridor toward them, his arms outstretched. "I thought I heard your lovely voice."

Angelique looked at Lucia and then rolled her eyes

as if to say, *This is what I'm talking about,* but Lucia only laughed and let Jessup kiss her on the cheek. Unlike the young Angelique, Lucia knew how infrequently true love came in a lifetime.

"I have some wonderful news," Lucia told Jessup. "We thought you might like to join us for tea, Angelique and I."

"I would love to join you for tea. And I have news, as well." He gestured toward his office. "Won't you both come in? You can tell me your news while I finish up this one task and then we can be on our way."

"We've a letter from Sapphire, at last," Angelique said, passing the two of them to enter Jessup's office first. Inside, she turned around, pulling her bonnet off and letting it dangle by the ribbon from her fingers as she studied his floor-to-ceiling bookshelves with interest. "For all our little Sapphire's priggishness, I think she's become Lord Wessex's mistress."

"We know nothing of the sort," Lucia contradicted, taking a seat in the red leather chair in front of Jessup's desk. "Her letter says nothing of the sort."

"Well, what does it say?" Jessup asked diplomatically as he returned to his chair behind his desk and reached for his spectacles.

"It's very brief." Lucia smoothed the paper she had already read at least ten times. "She says that she has gone to Boston with Mr. Thixton, but that we are not to worry. She says that she is having a grand adventure—" emotion rose in her voice but she swallowed it and continued "—and that she will return to London soon." She folded it, glancing up at Jessup. "She asks that I look after the casket she left behind, where she keeps her mother's keepsakes, and she asks that I please implore the good-hearted Mr. Stowe to continue his research into the legal marriage of her mother to Lord Edward Thixton."

"I see," Jessup said. "So she and Lord Wessex have not settled this matter between them?"

"I told you, Jessup—she wants proof of her mother's marriage. It would do my heart good before I leave this mortal coil to know that my beloved Sophie's wish was realized." She began to fold Sapphire's precious letter on its creases. "You said you had good news. I do hope it's in reference to my Sapphire's request."

"It is, indeed." He scrawled his name across a document and then removed his glasses to look at her across the desk.

"Well, do tell, Mr. Stowe," Angelique said, removing a book from one of his shelves and dusting its cover to read it.

Jessup drew himself up with pride. "I believe I have found Miss Sophie Barkley's residence in Sussex."

"Jessup, that's wonderful, *mon amour!*" Lucia turned in her chair. "Do you hear that, Angel darling. Mr. Stowe has found our Sophie's family."

"He didn't say he found her family, Auntie." Angelique returned the book to its place and chose another. "Mr. Stowe, have you any books on America? At dinner the other night one of Henry's friends was spinning an amazing tale about Indians. It's all Henry has talked about for days. I wonder if they have wild Indians in Lord Wessex's Boston."

Jessup chuckled, rising from his chair to walk to the bookshelves that lined one wall of his comfortable of-

fice. "I believe I might." As he began to run his fingers across the spines of a row of books, he glanced
at Lucia and then at the books again. "As Miss Fabergine said—"

"Oh, for sweet heaven's sake, would you please start
calling Angelique by her Christian name, at least when
we're alone?" Lucia rolled her eyes. "I cannot imagine
how many hours of life you Englishmen waste rattling
off titles and these formal names."

Angelique looked to Jessup, lifting her brows in
amusement.

He glanced at her for consent and she nodded. He
then cleared his throat and continued. "As Angelique
said, I have not located her family. I am sad to say that
they are gone, parents dead, some siblings dead, others
scattered to the winds."

"But you're closer than you were before?"

"I believe I am. I intend to go personally to the village in Sussex where Mr. Wiggins, the gentleman I hired
to research this, believes she may have resided." He offered Angelique a book. "Of course, you should not get
your hopes too high, yet. We don't know if this was your
Sophie or if anyone there will remember anything about
a young viscount romancing one of the village girls."

"Oh, they'll remember," Lucia said.

"You don't have to worry about my hope, Jessup. I
never understood why this quest was so important to
Sapphire to start with. I never knew my father, and that
fact certainly does not keep me tossing at night." Angelique opened the cover of the book Jessup had given her.

"You're of a different cloth than Sapphire." Lucia
folded her hands in her lap. "Thank you, Jessup."

"You are welcome, my love." He came to stand beside her in the chair and took her hand, lifting it to his lips.

"May I borrow this book, Jessup?" Angelique raised it in the air. "It's about the American West and some people called Lewis and Clark. Henry will adore it."

"You most certainly may," he answered as he stared adoringly at Lucia.

"Thank you. I'll be waiting in the carriage for you two love doves." She left the room. "Don't be long, and please do keep in mind your age and the fact that it is broad daylight."

Lucia laughed as Angelique sailed out of the office and Jessup leaned over to kiss her. "If I didn't know better, I would think that was a challenge," she said against his lips.

"A challenge? Whatever do you mean?"

Lucia rose out of the chair. "Does your door lock, Jessup, *mon amour?*"

"It does." He looked at her, his brows knitted quizzically. Then he realized why she had asked. "Oh my," he said. "Oh my."

"Please tell me that you and your wife did not only exercise your marital rights in that bed, Jessup?" She looked over her shoulder as she made her way to the door and turned the key to lock it. "No offense to the dearly departed, but how dull."

"Oh my," Jessup repeated, just standing there, his arms akimbo.

Lucia came back to him, and standing directly in front of him, she lifted on her toes, kissed him and took his hand. "Let us go visit this settee, shall we, Jessup dear?" She led him toward the piece of furniture in the corner of the room. "It doesn't look like it's been used in a decade." She smiled mischievously at him. "But we can resolve that, can't we?"

"Molly, wake up."

From a deep sleep, Sapphire heard a name being called, but she was in a far-off place and resisted the voice. Her head danced with thoughts of Blake, memories of his touch, of the taste of him and of the words they had exchanged the previous night, the most serious, probably most telling conversation they had ever shared.

She remembered the cool, refreshing water of the bath. Lying in that tub of sweet-scented water had reminded her of the pools in Martinique, of the laughter she and Angel had shared, swimming and diving. Then she thought of the crisp, smooth, linen sheets of Blake's bed, the softness of the down tick beneath them, the plumpness of the pillows and the comfort of his arm around her as they finally drifted off to sleep, exhausted but content. Nothing had been resolved, but there had been something different between them last night. She had been able to hear it in Blake's voice, almost feel it.

But this was not Blake's voice calling her, and she was no longer in his bed. As she slowly woke, she became aware of the sound of Myra's insistent voice and the feel of the lumpy pallet beneath her.

"I tried to let ya sleep," Myra said as she tugged on the sheet that was hot and sticky against Sapphire's skin. "You looked plain worn out this morning. I didn't have the heart to wake you, but Mrs. Dedrick is lookin' for you. Somethin' about you not bringin' down Mr. Thixton's sheets last night."

Sapphire opened her eyes and blinked. The windows under the eaves of the attic were small but a blinding light poured through them.

"Molly," Myra said again.

"All right. I'm awake, I'm awake." She threw off the sheet and sat up. "What time is it?"

"Nearly eight. Mr. Thixton's gone, but he asked that he have dinner tonight on his upstairs balcony. Apparently, he's expectin' someone." She rested both hands on her hips, looking down at Sapphire. "He wants you to serve. He gave Mrs. Dedrick 'plicit instructions."

Sapphire reached for her gray skirt and blouse. It was the same clothing she wore every day, but at least she'd been able to wash them out yesterday after she'd donned Felicity's black uniform. "Why are you looking at me like that?" Sapphire asked, stepping into her skirt.

"Where were you last night?"

"Where was I? Here." She turned her back to Myra as she donned the dingy blouse. She didn't want to lie to Myra but she certainly couldn't tell her the truth. She had no idea after her conversation with Blake last night where their relationship was going. Now that she had finally admitted to herself that she loved him, she didn't even know what to do about it. He hadn't said he loved her. He'd only asked if that was what *she* wanted.

Myra tapped her leather shoe on the rough, wide floorboards. "When I fell asleep, you weren't here."

"When you woke I was."

Myra just stood there, and when Sapphire turned back around, Myra's pretty mouth was frowning. "If you want my advice, you'll stay 'way from the master."

Sapphire stuffed her blouse into the waistband of the

hateful gray skirt and began to rake her fingers through her hair, tying it back as best she could without a mirror. "I don't know what you're talking about."

"I think you do. The two of you come over together on that ship. You was grateful for what he offered, a new life. Maybe escape from an old one, a bad papa, a bad marriage, debt. A girl does what she has to do sometimes to get along in this world," Myra said philosophically. "But you're here now and you got to guard your heart." She hesitated. "'Cause I've known men like Mr. Thixton before. You're not one of his kind, no matter what you think. No matter what sweet nuthin's he might be whisperin' in your ear. But in the end, you'll have nuthin' but a broken heart. He'll break your heart, Molly, and maybe leave you ruined with a little stranger to raise. No decent house would have you as a parlor maid, then. I can tell you that fer nothin'."

Sapphire grabbed her mobcap off the peg on the wall, stuffed her auburn hair beneath it and stepped into her shoes. "I don't mean to be unkind, but this is complicated, more complicated than I can possibly explain to you, which I cannot."

Myra just stood there and stared at her. "A broken heart ain't that complicated, no matter who you are." She turned for the door and walked out.

Blake left the house early for his offices, located in a brick building on the street facing the harbor. It was one of the oldest buildings in Boston, having been occupied for a hundred years by businessmen such as himself. Since the founding of the colonies and the arrival of his mother's people in the seventeenth century,

Boston Harbor had been an important one, first to the colonies and Mother England, now to the world.

Manford had been urging Blake for years to take office space in one of the newer Greek Revival-style buildings downtown, offices that offered less drafty winters and pubs and fine eating establishments close at hand. But Blake's father had purchased the building when he was a young man, and though he had never been fond of his father, there was something comforting to Blake about passing through the same redbrick doorway his father had once used, so that he could be reminded each day what a bastard the man had been. It helped Blake check his words more times than he cared to admit. Of course, no man wished to acknowledge he had more of his father in him than he led others to believe, especially when his father had been such a man.

Blake had a busy day planned, which was why he had left the house early, without breakfast or taking time to bathe. He also did not want to run into Sapphire.

He'd been surprised when, at close to three in the morning, she had climbed out of his bed, donned the ugly black maid's uniform and left him. It had angered him. What the hell did she want from him? He was offering her the world. He had the money, the capability to give her anything. Why was she so stubborn on this matter of who she was or was not? Didn't she understand that he didn't care?

Blake took a sip of his coffee and spat it back into the cup. "Givens!" he bellowed.

"Sir?" The paneled door opened and the tall, slender man stuck his head through the doorway.

"My coffee isn't hot. I ask little of you, Givens, considering the exorbitant salary I pay you. Can my coffee not be hot first thing in the morning?"

"Yes, sir. I'll get another cup, sir. Mr. Lawrence is here to see you."

"Send him in." Blake pushed back in his chair.

"Good morning," Manford said, walking in through the door, offering his hand.

Blake rose and shook it. "How is your daughter this morning?" He gestured to a leather chair much like the red leather chair in Mr. Stowe's office. He'd been thinking a lot about Mr. Stowe these past few days for some reason. Perhaps because he'd had to fire two barristers since he returned from London. Was there no barrister in Boston who was not a thief?

"Thank you." Manford sat, as did Blake. "Clarice is better, I think, though she was up most of the night. A most peculiar ailment." He shook his head, reflecting. "And no one else at the dinner party became ill last night?"

Blake shook his head, refusing to allow his thoughts to wander. Sapphire had not confessed to producing poor Clarice's symptoms, and how would she do such a thing, anyway? Perhaps she'd been right, that it was just the sour young woman's ill-humors coming out in her. "No one else was ill, as far as I know. I slept well last night." He almost smiled, thinking how nice it had been to fall asleep with Sapphire's warm, soft body against his. He'd missed sleeping with her since their arrival in Boston.

"Well, a few days and I'm certain my dear Clarice will be fine." Manford flashed a smile. "Though I imagine her social activities will be curbed for a few days as she is still unable to get more than a few feet from the necessary." He slapped his hand on the desk. "So tell me what I need to know before this Mr. Falkin arrives. I told Mrs. Lawrence this morning that we were meeting with a man from Philadelphia who thinks he can produce fuel to light lamps from rock and she wanted to call in her physician to see if I was ill, as well."

Blake chuckled. "I know the idea sounds far-fetched, but I imagine many things have seemed impossible throughout history. I traveled here by steam engine— we rarely needed the sails and crossed in record time. A hundred years ago such a feat was beyond our imaginations. Hell, in our fathers' time it was beyond our mind's eye."

"So this Mr. Falkin, he believes he can produce this miracle from rock?"

"He's a scientist, a geologist. He's been in close contact with an Englishman out of Nova Scotia whose work I've read. In England I met one of his colleagues. Mr. Falkin lives in Philadelphia but his research is known around the world."

"Yes, in the insane asylums worldwide," Manford joked.

Blake smiled. "I want you to listen to what Mr. Falkin has to say about this rock oil and the possibility it can be found in western Pennsylvania, but I don't want you to feel in any way obligated to invest in this venture."

"Well, it is a bit different from what we usually do. Transportation of goods I know, but this..." Manford shook his head.

"I understand, Manford. I also understand the importance of diversity, as do you. What if all of your assets had been tied up in whaling like the Crawford family's?"

"I hear what you're saying, friend. I'm willing to listen, but I'm not positive I'll be able to convince Mrs. Lawrence that this is a place she wishes to invest my hard-earned money."

Blake laughed. He had always admired Manford's marriage, one of the few good ones he knew of. Manford loved his wife and she him, that was obvious, and they were true partners. Manford never made any important decisions without consulting his wife first.

"According to geologists, there are rivers of rock oil flowing beneath the surface of the earth in Pennsylvania and many other places. The potential of such a new resource is unlimited. If rock oil can produce the power that ships need—that factories need—the possibilities are endless. Not to mention the profits those wise enough to invest early might realize."

Manford brushed at his graying sideburns with one hand. "And that brings us to another subject, one I'm not as comfortable speaking of."

Blake leaned back in his chair, linking his fingers. When he moved, he could have sworn he caught Sapphire's scent, but it had to be his imagination. "What is it, Manford?" He frowned. "When are you ever reluctant to discuss anything with me? I thought you and I were beyond that."

Manford smiled. "As did I. Let me say first that I expect your complete honesty."

"Which you always get, whether you expect it or not."

Manford nodded. "It's about Clarice…"

Blake waited.

"She...apparently fancies herself in love with you, according to my wife."

Blake looked down at his desk, piled with neat stacks of paper that needed to be attended to, as well as several books he'd acquired to read up on his geology before meeting with Mr. Falkin.

"Go on."

"Now, I know you've escorted her to quite a few events, events Mrs. Lawrence and I also attended. Really, I saw it more as a favor than anything else. I thought perhaps the two of you...I suppose a part of me hoped..." He looked up. "A finer man I would not choose for my daughter, but—"

"No, Manford," Blake said quietly. "I'm not in love with Clarice."

Manford looked down at his hands again. "I thought not, but I had to ask."

"She's a sweet girl, but—"

"No, she isn't," Manford interrupted, tenting his hands in his lap. "I love her. She's my flesh and blood, but she's spoiled and self-centered. She is her grandmother through and through, and honestly, I would not wish that hell upon anyone."

The two men shared a laugh. Blake had met Manford's mother-in-law on several occasions, so his friend had no need to elaborate.

"I'm sorry," Blake said.

"You shouldn't be." Manford looked up. "I worry about you, though."

"About me?" Blake arched a brow. "That's ridiculous."

"Is it? That beautiful mansion on that hill. Empty."

"I have my visitors." Blake cracked a smile.

Manford smiled with him. "But that's not what I mean. You deserve to be happy. You deserve to have someone love you and know what it is to love without condition."

"You sound like one of those romantic writers," Blake scoffed.

"Be that as it may. It's time you found a wife, started a family."

Blake was quiet for a moment. "Marriage is not what everyone strives to obtain," he said, trying not to think of Sapphire, or how empty his bed had seemed this morning without her.

"I just don't want you to go your entire life, pushing your way blindly, missing what is the sweetest, what offers the most reward."

Blake scowled teasingly. "I'm with Mrs. Lawrence on the matter of you taking ill. You should have her call that physician of hers." He rose, offering his hand.

Manford got out of the chair, accepting it. "I'll see you here at one, then?"

"I've already received a message from Mr. Falkin this morning. He will be here promptly at one."

"Excellent." Manford released Blake's hand, stepping away from the desk. "I'll see you this afternoon. Right now, I need to meet with a shipping agent and see if I can't rip out his heart and have it transported with my next load of goods bound for London."

Blake laughed and returned to his chair. He reached for one of the geology books on his desk, pushing aside his conversation with Manford and any thoughts of Sapphire still lingering in his mind. "Givens!" he called. "Where the hell is that coffee?"

* * *

"Mon chèr," Tarasai sang as she entered Armand's bedchamber. "Look what I have brought for you."

He had been reading one of his botany books but not with much interest. "What have you brought me, dear?" he asked sitting up farther in his bed and removing his reading spectacles.

She perched on the edge and reached behind his head to move a pillow. "Guess." She grinned, her tiny, beautiful face seeming to glow with her pregnancy.

He smiled and took her small hand in his, thinking it was probably just as well that he was dying. He was too old for young women like Tarasai, too old for such vibrant energy. "I cannot guess."

"Something you have wished for, *mon amour."* She leaned forward bringing her face very close to his. *"Une lettre."*

"A letter?"

She nodded, her smile ear-to-ear.

"From Sapphire?"

Again she nodded as she slipped her hand into the fold of her dress and drew out the paper addressed in handwriting he knew at once.

"What does it say?"

"Foolish old man," she teased. "I do not read your letter."

He took it from her hand and grabbed his spectacles off the book, then pushed them onto his nose. His hands trembled as he opened the letter and smoothed it out on the linen sheet that covered his thin legs.

"What does it say?" Tarasai asked. "She is well, yes?"

The letter was short, but Armand read it through

twice. "She has gone to America," he exclaimed, feeling better than he had in days, perhaps weeks. "With a man she says I would like."

"She has married. You see, I told you your Sapphire would be well."

He shook his head. "No, no, it does not exactly say she married him." He looked up, absently refolding the letter. "Actually, the note is quite odd. She usually rambles on. This was written quickly."

"But it says you are not to worry, yes?"

"Yes, but—" He looked at Tarasai. "Bring me my writing box. I must send a letter to Lucia at once. Sapphire says nothing of her godmother or Angelique. They must still be in London. I have to know if she's all right, if this man is a good man."

Tarasai reached out and covered his hand with hers. "*Mon chèr,* with the winter coming and the mail so unreliable, it could take many months for letters to cross the ocean."

He looked into her eyes, understanding what she said. He might not have months left. But he smiled and placed his hand on her expanding abdomen. "My letter box please, Tarasai."

"You look tired." She stroked his cheek. "You should rest first."

He closed his eyes for a moment and then opened them, rallying his strength. "First I will write Lucia a letter and you will take it down to the wharfs," he said firmly. "Then I will be able to rest."

She lowered her head to kiss his hand and then rose, walking away from his bed, wiping the tears from her eyes.

24

Sapphire knocked on Blake's door, truly feeling foolish about this entire farce they had created out of their own stubbornness. For three nights in a row, he had ordered that he be served dinner on the balcony off his bedchamber and that she serve him. No one, not even the staunch housekeeper, questioned the master's orders or his intentions with the new maid. Three nights in a row she had come to his private rooms, shared a meal with him, made love with him and then had redressed in the ridiculous maid's clothes and had taken the dishes back to the kitchen before retiring to the attic to sleep alone under the eaves.

When Blake didn't answer the door tonight, she knocked again, this time with the toe of her shoe as she shifted the weight of the tray in her arms. The smell of fresh bread wafted from beneath the domed silver lids and her stomach grumbled.

Myra had said nothing more to her about Blake or the

time she was missing between serving him dinner and midnight, but as Sapphire crawled into bed on her hard pallet each night, she could feel her friend's eyes on her through the darkness.

The door opened and Blake appeared barefoot, wearing only dark trousers and a white linen shirt half unbuttoned. He'd cut his hair shorter after their arrival in Boston, but tonight it looked pleasantly unkempt. He must have been reading on the windy balcony before she arrived.

It was all he seemed to do these days whenever he had a free moment. Books on geology were stacked everywhere in his bedchamber, as well as in his office. Last night, the entire household had searched for half an hour for a particular book on mechanical pumps he was certain someone had moved while cleaning, only to find it in the carriage.

"I carried this all the way up the stairs," she told him. "Then I had to knock twice." She was perturbed with him tonight and she didn't know why.

Perhaps she was annoyed with herself for allowing this stalemate to continue. As it was now, Blake was getting much of what he wanted. He had dinner companionship and a good roll each night. She was even supplying first-rate maid service. Why would he ever want to change anything between them now?

"I'm sorry," he said, taking the tray from her. "I must not have heard you. It's windy on the balcony tonight."

"Reading?" she asked, softening her tone, not meaning to be such a shrew. She hadn't seen him all day and she missed him.

"Yes, and there's something I want you to hear. I

think we should go to Pennsylvania to see this. I'll read it to you over dinner."

He carried the tray out onto the balcony, and she halted in the doorway, pulling her mobcap off her head and letting the breeze ripple through her hair. She breathed deeply, filling her lungs with the tangy, evening air that blew off the bay. "What a relief. It's cooler tonight than it's been."

"Weather's finally turned." He set down the serving tray and began to lift the silver covers off the dishes. "A few weeks of nice weather and then the chill will set in. Wait until you see how much snow falls."

"I've never seen snow," she said wistfully. "Not a lot of it in Martinique."

"No, I don't suppose there is, but then we have no coconuts." He looked up at her, seeming more relaxed than usual. "Nothing like a snowy day to stay wrapped up in bed with a good book and a better woman."

When she looked over to him, there was a hint of devilry in his eyes and she couldn't help but smile. But all he referred to was his desire for her and that wasn't enough. She'd decided sometime over the past few days that for some, for people like Angelique, perhaps, it was enough, but not for her.

"Let's eat," she said, walking toward the chair he had pulled out for her. "I'm famished. You can read to me about your rock oil while I dine on these oysters. Wait until you taste them. Mrs. Porter has—"

An insistent banging on the bedchamber door startled Sapphire and she looked through the doorway into the room, then back at Blake. No one had disturbed them on previous nights. If anyone knew she was here alone with him, the household certainly pretended otherwise. It was as if when she passed over a threshold, she and Blake existed in their own world.

"Sir…Mr. Thixton," Mrs. Dedrick called from the other side of the door, her voice higher in pitch than usual.

Sapphire leaped out of the chair, pulling on her mobcap.

"Sapphire," Blake intoned.

She ran for the door. "Mrs. Dedrick," she said, pulling it open, dipping a quick curtsy. "I was just—"

"Mr. Thixton. You have a guest, sir." Mrs. Dedrick said. "Mrs. Sheraton—"

"Step aside," ordered Mrs. Sheraton from the corridor.

Sapphire recognized her from the dinner party.

The forty-year-old woman walked into the bedchamber in a swish of blue organdy. "Send them away, please, Blake," she cried, red-eyed, a lace handkerchief knotted in her small hands.

Sapphire turned to Blake. He stood in the doorway to the balcony and she realized that they had reached a defining moment in their relationship, if a relationship was what they had.

"Come at once," Mrs. Dedrick hissed at Sapphire, snapping her fingers as if calling a child or a pet. "Come."

"Oh, Blake, you cannot believe what Rufus has done," Mrs. Sheraton moaned, putting out her hand to him.

"What's wrong, Grace?" Sapphire heard him say as she followed Mrs. Dedrick out of the bedchamber.

"The tray and covers from the meal," Sapphire mumbled.

"Leave 'em." Mrs. Dedrick snapped, her keys jingling at her waist. "The mastah's bechambah is not the place for you."

"Oh, Blake," Grace Sheraton sobbed, putting her arms over his shoulders.

He stood stiffly in the center of his bedchamber, unsure of what had just silently taken place between him and Sapphire. The ticking of the case clock on the mantel and Grace's sniffles filled his head.

What had Sapphire expected him to do, turn Grace away? "What's the matter?" he asked. "Has Rufus fallen ill?"

"Fallen ill?" Tears ran down a face that was still pretty for a woman almost ten years older than he. "If only I could be so fortunate."

"Do you want to sit down?" He was more than a little uncomfortable with her body draped over his.

They had carried on their affair for more than five years. Her husband cheated on her with society women and maids alike and generally ignored her. It had seemed harmless enough, Blake's liaisons with his neighbor. Grace was discreet, emotionally undemanding, and he enjoyed her company in bed. But since his return to Boston, he had avoided her invitations. He felt as if their time together was done and he had hoped it would just fade rather than having to come to a tearful, ugly ending, the way it was sometimes did with women. He had hoped to avoid a scene such as the one that appeared to be unfolding. Blake didn't deal with crying women very well, certainly not crying women who were other men's wives. He was never sure when the distress was genuine or when he was being manipulated.

"No, I don't want to sit," Grace cried, pulling herself closer to him, pressing herself against his chest. "I want you to hold me. Hold me, Blake."

Reluctantly, he wrapped one arm around her waist, but as he caught a whiff of the perfume that had once tantalized his senses, all he could think of was Sapphire and how differently she smelled than other women. Even back in London, she had rarely worn perfume. It was her hair that he smelled when he drew her close, her soft skin, her *essence* that beguiled him.

"What has Rufus done now?"

"He wants an annulment," she murmured, pressing her face to his chest.

"An annulment?" Blake laughed. "You've been married twenty-five years. You've given him three children—"

"Then a divorce. He doesn't care, he only wants to be rid of me now that I'm of no use or interest to him." She began to cry in earnest, her tears dampening his shirt. "He says he's fallen in love with another and that he's leaving me to marry her."

"Perhaps he doesn't mean it." Blake patted her shoulder. "You know how Rufus can be, especially when he's been drinking."

"He hasn't been drinking," she sobbed. "It's...it's some whore. A child from the pub where he takes his midday meal. I should have known there was something wrong when he stopped returning home for his nap."

"I don't know what to say," Blake muttered.

"I don't want you to say anything." Grace looked up at him, her face sad and wet with tears.

Though he knew she cheated on her husband, he

also knew that she loved her husband and that she was truly devastated.

"Just hold me," she whispered. "Make me feel something good, just for a little while."

She kissed him on the mouth and, at first, he resisted. In the back of his mind, he thought of Sapphire and of the word they had talked about the other night. The word that scared him more than he could admit to her or himself. He had asked her if she wanted him to say it, to say that he loved her. She hadn't answered him and he didn't know what that meant. Did she think she loved him, or was this part of her game to get what she could from him?

Blake didn't know how he felt about Sapphire. But even if he did love her, if he gave in to her and said so, where would it lead him? How long would it last before she left him? Or saw him for the man he really was, leave taking what she could and then move on to the next man?

Grace's insistent mouth slowly pushed aside his thoughts. She was a beautiful woman whom he had made love to many times. What reason did he have not to make love to her again?

"Blake," she whispered, grasping his shirt, looking up at him with teary eyes. "Love me," she begged.

He kissed her back and closed his eyes.

Downstairs in the kitchen, Sapphire busied herself cleaning up after the evening meal. Next, she began to clean off the old wooden table Mrs. Porter used to make bread each day. As she scrubbed viciously with a rag, she fought her tears.

In time, Myra appeared and moved to stand beside

her, scraping damp flour off the table with a flat-edged blade. More than an hour had passed since Mrs. Sheraton arrived, and she'd still not left by the front door.

"I heard Mrs. Sheraton pushed her way into the master's bedchamber," Myra whispered.

"How do you know that?" Sapphire glanced at her friend. Unlike the others on the household staff, Mrs. Dedrick was not a gossip. She took her post as head housekeeper too seriously for that.

"Felicity saw her go bargin' up the stairs." She looked sideways at Sapphire. "Said you were still inside with the master."

"Myra, I knew Blake from London." Sapphire's voice was thick with emotion.

"Thought as much," Myra said. "So you come already in love with him?"

Sapphire nodded, afraid to speak for fear she would start to cry.

"Poor thing." Myra put out one arm and gave her a quick hug. "And now he's upstairs dallyin' with Mrs. Sheraton."

Sapphire threw down the washrag. Myra was only voicing what Sapphire had already feared. She had seen the look on Mrs. Sheraton's face when Mrs. Dedrick closed the bedchamber door. She knew what the older woman wanted from Blake.

"You think so?"

Myra looked up as if she could see through the timber and plaster walls to the upstairs rooms. "It's t' be expected. You know, she's been comin' to his bedchamber for years. Everyone in the house knows it."

"I didn't know—" Sapphire's throat caught. All her

silly hopes seemed to disappear in an instant. Blake didn't love her. If he did, he wouldn't have allowed Mrs. Sheraton to stay. He wouldn't have allowed Mrs. Dedrick to lead Sapphire downstairs so he could be alone with his guest.

"Even when I still worked for her, we all knew. Some of us even said 'good fer her.' You know, what being good for the gander."

Sapphire wiped her nose, trying to form a plan in her head. "I need you to help me."

"Of course." Myra clasped her arm. "You want to find a job elsewhere, I can see what I can do. More than likely Mrs. Dedrick would even help you, considerin' the circumstances. She's mostly bark, you know. Underneath, she's got a good heart."

Sapphire shook her head. "No, you don't understand. I'm not a lady's maid." She lifted her lashes to look into Myra's eyes. "I'm a lady," she whispered. "And I need to return to London to my family."

Myra stared but didn't question her. Somehow she seemed to know that Sapphire was telling the truth. "I haven't much money—most I give to my mama for the babies—but you can have what I got."

"I wouldn't take your money, Myra. I just need some clothes, a few other necessities."

"I don't understand. How will you get on a ship to get back to London without coin? Maybe you could ask Mr. Thixton—"

"No," she insisted. "I won't ask him." She looked into Myra's pretty face. "I don't want a thing that belongs to him, not a stitch of clothing, not so much as an apple, do you understand me?"

"The others'll help out. When you goin'?"

Sapphire pressed her lips together, refusing to cry. "The sooner the better," she said stoically. "Tonight. I cannot abide to remain in his house another minute."

It was well after dark, close to ten thirty, when Sapphire stood in the kitchen courtyard and accepted the canvas bag that Myra offered.

"You look good," Myra said, tears causing her cheeks to glisten in the rising moonlight.

Sapphire looked down at the canvas trousers and rough, darned cotton shirt she wore. When Myra had agreed to find her clothes, Sapphire had insisted it would be safer for her to travel as a young boy rather than as an unescorted woman. There were enough dangers on the road for a young man, but those for a woman were even greater.

"You think so?" Sapphire asked. "Do I look like a boy?"

"Like a handsome stable boy." Myra reached out and pinched her cheek.

Sapphire laughed, feeling her own tears begin to well. "I can't thank you enough for what you've done for me."

"Don't be silly."

"I mean it." Sapphire squeezed her hand. "You've been as good a friend to me these past weeks as I've ever had."

"Haven't done nothin' you wouldn't 've done for me," Myra said almost shyly.

"True enough. Now I have to go and I want you to go inside and get to bed so no one is suspicious."

"But where will you go? The coins I collected are barely enough to buy a few loaves of bread."

"It's better if I don't tell you where I'm going—that way you won't know if you're questioned."

"You're prob'bly right. Better I don't know a thing to tell Mr. Thixton when he starts his bellowin'." Myra rolled her eyes. "He scares me a little when he starts hollerin' the way he does sometimes."

Sapphire smiled. "He may not holler at all. He might not even ask for me."

"Oh, he'll ask. Mr. Thixton's like that, like any man. He wants to be in charge, not just of himself, but everyone else, too."

Sapphire hugged Myra one last time, adjusted her cap and walked through the gate. "Bye, Myra."

"Bye, Molly. I hope you find your way home," the maid called after her, tearfully. "I hope you find happiness."

Happiness? Sapphire was beginning to think happiness was beyond her reach, but she was determined to go home.

"Gone? What do you mean, gone?" Blake demanded, setting down his newspaper. "Gone to the market? Gone to the dairy? What?"

"No, sih," the housekeeper said, keeping her gaze fixed on the carpet in the small dining room.

Blake had chosen to have breakfast this morning in the dining room, rather than his bedchamber, so that when he spoke with Sapphire, she would remain calm.

"Where has she gone, Mrs. Dedrick?"

"I don't know. Quit."

"Quit?" He hit the table with his fist. "She can't quit. Where did she go? This is preposterous! Ask the servants—the dark-haired one—they seemed to be friendly."

"I've already asked them. All the house gihls—boys in the stable, too. No one's seen heh. Not since last night, Mr. Thixton."

He snatched his coat off the back of the chair. "Call the carriage."

Mrs. Dedrick stepped back out of his way. "Yes, sih."

"She couldn't have gotten far in this city alone with no money, knowing no one," he said under his breath as he strode out of the room. "She couldn't have."

25

Sapphire didn't want to remain in Boston and run the risk of Blake finding her. She cut through the elegant properties on Beacon Hill and headed south. She didn't know how long it would take her to find a job and save the money she would need to book passage to London, but with the coming of winter, she surmised, a girl who had grown up in Martinique would survive better in less frigid temperatures. Especially a girl who, presently, didn't even have a place to live.

So, dressed like a young man, canvas satchel thrown over her shoulder, she followed the coastline south and tried not to think about Blake or her broken heart. Instead she entertained herself with memories of growing up in Martinique and of the love and laughter she had shared there with her family.

She followed main roads all night, keeping the water on her left shoulder, but when dawn came, she decided that she had better stay out of sight, just in case

Blake was angry enough to send someone, perhaps an officer of the law, looking for her. There was no telling what the man might do; perhaps he would accuse her of theft or of committing some other crime just to get her back under his control. A few miles out of the city, she came upon an abandoned stone building on a stream, a structure that appeared to have once been a mill. After eating some apples she'd found along the road, she curled up in a ball on a pile of tattered feed bags, wrapped herself in a wool blanket Myra had found for her and drifted off into an exhausted, dreamless sleep.

Sapphire must have been more tired than she realized because by the time she woke, stiff but refreshed, the shadows inside the old mill were already beginning to lengthen. After eating another apple and half a slice of Mrs. Porter's bread, she packed up her meager possessions and prepared to set off again. She was just slipping her arms into the woolen barn coat one of the boys in the Thixton stables had given her when she heard something move outside.

Sapphire froze. She wasn't easily frightened. On the island, she had grown up hearing natives' tales of spooks and haunts, none of which she feared—but what she did fear was man. It was dangerous for a woman to travel alone and she knew it. She was just hoping her own sense of self-preservation and a little luck would keep her safe.

She heard the sound again: weeds snapping, something brushing against the partially closed door that hung crooked off its old iron hinges. Sapphire held her breath. There was someone out there, but who? Maybe just another traveler looking for a safe place to take shelter.

It was quiet outside again and she slowly exhaled, her heart racing. She heard the snapping noise again. Then a strange sound, almost like a whine.

As a wet, black nose appeared through the crack in the door, Sapphire burst out in relieved laughter. The dog poked its head through the door to look at her almost quizzically.

She laughed again and crouched down. "Hey there, boy," she said, putting out her hand.

The small, round-barreled, brown and white spotted hound squeezed through the opening in the door, wiggling its stumpy tail. Halfway to Sapphire, it stopped and regarded her cautiously. The dog was thin and homeless...like she was.

Smiling, Sapphire reached into her canvas bag and drew out the other half of a slice of bread she'd been saving for the next day. The dog came at once, tail wagging excitedly, and she laughed as he took the bread from her hand and wolfed it down. After licking every last crumb from her hand, the dog looked up expectedly.

"I'm sorry," she said, patting his head. "That's all I have." She showed him both of her hands. "See, all gone. Now, go on, shoo." She made a motion with her hands to chase him out the door, but he only wagged his tail more and danced around her.

She slipped through the narrow opening in the doorway, out into the cool early-evening air. The dog followed, but she noticed that it was limping. "What's wrong?" She crouched down, wondering if the animal would let her look at his sore leg or take a bite out of her. It didn't seem vicious, so she carefully lifted the injured paw. "You poor thing. You've got a thorn in there."

A black thorn protruded from the dog's pad. "No wonder you're limping." Carefully, Sapphire extracted the long thorn. "That should make you feel better."

The dog licked the paw and then her hand.

"Good boy," she said, walking away.

The dog followed.

"No, you can't go with me," she told him, and she went a long way before she looked back to find the dog still trotting after her. "No. Absolutely not. Go home. Go anywhere."

She turned, walking backward to watch him, unable to stop smiling. He was so ugly he was cute.

"Dog, you can't go with me. The last thing I need is you trailing after me. I don't even know where I'm going," she explained. "I don't have enough food for us both and I don't have much money."

The hound whined in response and continued up the road.

Sapphire turned, walking forward again, and glanced over her shoulder every once in a while at the hound who seemed to be walking a little better on the injured paw. "So you're loyal, are you?" she asked him after a mile or two. "Better than someone else I can think of."

Again, she got a whine and a tail wag.

"Utterly devoted, just like Aunt Lucia's Mr. Stowe." She stopped on the hard-beaten dirt road and crouched down again. The hound came to her at once, and this time he licked her hands and tried to lick her face when she got too close.

"All right, all right. So you love me, do you?" She frowned. "At least someone does." She scratched him behind a ragged ear that had been torn at some point. The wound had healed ages ago but had left him with a broad scar. "So you love me for who I am, do you, Stowe?"

The dog wagged its tail faster, seeming to like his new name.

"All right," she said, standing up. "But we're headed south and I don't know for where, and I don't know how long I'll be able to feed you because I'm guessing you don't eat apples."

The dog stared up at her with big, dark eyes, not unlike the English barrister's.

"Does that mean you're in?" she asked him.

Sapphire knew full well that dogs didn't smile, but he appeared to be smiling.

"All right, come on." She waved her arm. "Let's go. I was thinking New York City. I've read about it but never seen it."

The dog caught up to her and fell into step beside her, his little legs pumping rhythmically, his tongue lolling.

"I'm not even certain how far it is—are you? I only know what Blake told me. We were supposed to go so that I could see the art museum and some of the buildings. Blake, you see, he was—"

Sapphire's voice suddenly broke off and she halted for a moment, letting her head drop, refusing to let the tears flow. After a minute she opened her eyes to see Stowe sitting on the ground, staring up at her. "He was this man," she said softly. "I loved him, but he didn't love me back."

She began to walk again, somehow feeling better now that she had actually said it out loud. "So maybe we'll go see New York together. What do you think, Stowe?"

The dog bounded up beside her again, wagging his tail.

"Fine. You can go, too, but you have to keep up, do you understand me?" she warned. "Those little stumpy legs of yours will have to carry you all the way to New York City."

"This is ridiculous," Blake declared angrily, pacing the floor of the keeping room. "How can a penniless, twenty-year-old girl just disappear in a strange city where she knows no one?"

Mrs. Dedrick and Mr. Givens stood in front of him, both of them with their hand clasped, their gazes fixed on the exquisite Persian rug on the floor.

"No one has seen her," Givens said. "No one in the shops, at the wharf—"

"Which is equally ridiculous!" Blake reached the edge of the carpet, turned on his heels and started back in the opposite direction. "She's a redhead, for Christ's sake. A redhead with one green eye and one blue eye. How could no one have seen her anywhere?"

"Pehaps she has gone to anothuh city," Mrs. Dedrick offered, her eyes remaining downcast.

"Is that what the other servants say? Is that what—" he snapped his fingers "—what is her name? Myra? Did Myra say she went elsewhere?"

"She didn't know whehe the miss went, sih."

"I want to speak to her."

"Mr. Thixton," the housekeeper began.

"Now, Mrs. Dedrick," he insisted, changing directions again. "And you, Givens, cancel my appoint-

ments. I'll go down to the docks and have a look myself. I'm not sure either of the two of you could find a
pig in a pantry."

The two made a hasty retreat and Blake continued to
pace, trying to figure out how he could find Sapphire
rather than why she was gone. To go over again in his
head what he had said, what he had done, what she'd
said and done, was pointless. First he would find her
and bring her back to Thixton House, and not as a maid,
either. Then they would work this out. He would make
her understand.

The little dark-haired housemaid rushed to the keeping room and dropped a curtsy. She then stood in front
of Blake, hands held at her sides.

He tried to forcibly calm the tone of his voice. He
knew he could sometimes appear intimidating and he
didn't want to scare the girl; he just wanted to see what
she knew. "I understand you were friends with S—
Molly," he corrected himself.

She nodded.

"And when she left, she didn't say anything about
where she was going?"

The girl, who could not have been more than seventeen or eighteen, slowly lifted her head, meeting Blake's
gaze. "She said it would be better if she didn't tell me
where she was goin' so when you ask, I wouldn't be
able to say."

He noticed the hostility in her voice and wondered
what Sapphire had told her. Lies? The truth about them?
Half-truths? What *was* the truth? he wondered.

Blake turned away, wiping his mouth with the back
of his hand as if he could wipe away the taste of the red-

haired beauty, the memory of her. "Did she try to find a ship to take her back to London? Did she obtain money from somewhere in the house?"

"Said she didn't want nuthin' of yours, Mr. Thixton." Again the hostility.

This maid had worked at the house for at least a year. He had accepted her as a favor to Grace, something about the chit seducing her sixteen-year-old son. But Blake had never found her to be anything but polite, if not a little fearful of him. She didn't seem terribly afraid of him, and now he thought if Sapphire may have had something to do with her new attitude. Had Sapphire remained any longer on his staff, he could have had a maids' mutiny on his hands.

"She said she didn't want anything of mine?" Blake asked Myra.

She tucked her hands behind her back defiantly. "Said not so much as an apple she would take."

He laughed, startling Myra, then shook his head, beginning to pace again. That sounded so like Sapphire that he knew it had to be the truth. So she was clever and it would take some time to find her. Maybe time was what they both needed. Maybe in time, he'd know what to say to her when he found her. Because he *would* find her.

He had to.

Sapphire and Stowe walked for hours along the road, and all the way she talked to the dog, rambling. She told him about her godmother, Lucia, and her days as a high-priced courtesan in New Orleans, and about Angelique and the village she had been born in. Walking in the dark with nothing but moonlight to guide her, Sapphire found herself telling him all about her mother and her father and how she had gotten into the mess she was in now.

Stowe was the perfect listener, the perfect companion, and when the dog began to tire and slow his pace, she scooped him up and dropped him into the canvas bag she carried, allowing his head to peek out of the top.

"Now, I'm not carrying you all the way to New York City, you understand me?" she told the dog. "This is just to let you rest those short legs of yours."

The dog closed his eyes and Sapphire walked for the next hour in silence, not feeling quite so alone or quite so forlorn. Sometime after midnight, the dark sky began to cloud up, and fearing it might rain, Sapphire began to look for shelter. With no abandoned buildings in sight, she ended up taking refuge under a bridge. And when the raindrops began to fall on the floorboards over her head, she and the little dog were wrapped up in a wool blanket, safe and dry.

The next morning, she decided they were far enough from Boston to risk walking during the day. She met an old woman on the road who said she was headed to the market to sell her biscuits and cheese, and she sold Sapphire six biscuits and a piece of cheese the size of her fist. She even gave Stowe a crumbled biscuit, saying she wouldn't be able to sell it anyway and it would only go to waste. She pointed Sapphire in the direction of her house on the hill overlooking the road and offered to let her draw water from her well, calling her "young man." She also told Sapphire where she was—a place called Connecticut. Sapphire asked if she was headed the right way to go to New York City—to see her aunt, she explained in as deep a voice as she could muster—and the gray-haired woman confirmed that she was going the right way. "Just follow this big road south," she said in her funny accent.

So, after a breakfast of cheese, biscuits and all the fresh water Sapphire and Stowe could drink, the two set out again. Sapphire walked with a stick she had found along the road, her shoes slung over her shoulder, as Stowe took his place beside her. Walking barefoot was easier once the soles of her feet got used to the road. She knew she'd have to buy a pair of shoes that fit. Again, she talked to the dog; she told him about things she had seen, things she hoped to see, and she promised to take him to London with her, if he wanted to go. The little spotted dog's presence was a great comfort to her and she found herself smiling as the sun came out and shone warm on her face.

Sapphire knew she had done the right thing in leaving Blake; she would not dwell on regrets. She was certain there was a future out there waiting for her. There would be another great adventure, just as she'd had with Blake. She had no time for tears. She would go back to London to be with Aunt Lucia and Angelique and she would find the proof she needed to petition the courts to have her recognized as her father's child. Then, and only then, would she contact Blake. She would send him a letter in Boston and tell him who she was and then she would be free of him.

"It's a good plan, don't you think?" she asked the dog.

Stowe wagged his tail.

A wagon approached and Sapphire and Stowe

stepped off the road to let it pass. But the old man driving the wagon slowed down and glanced in Sapphire's direction, squinting beneath the broad brim of homemade straw hat.

"Afternoon, son," he said gruffly. He had worker's hands, wrinkled, rough and nicked with cuts, that he wrapped the wide leather reins around.

"Afternoon, sir," Sapphire said, self-consciously tugging on the brim of the cap she wore, taking care to keep the pitch of her voice low.

"I'm headed to New York City with this load of ladders to sell," the old man said, hooking a thumb in the direction of the bed of the wagon. "Get a good price there. Lotta building goes on. Them New Yorkers need good ladders."

Sapphire looked into the back and could discern the outline of several ladders under an oiled tarp. She caught the scent of freshly cut wood on the light breeze. "Me, too," she said, trying to imitate the speech of the young boys in Blake's stable. Some spoke like Mrs. Dedrick, without any *r*'s, but others were easier to understand. She walked a little farther and the old man continued to ride beside her. He kept squinting, his eyesight apparently poor.

"You a carpenter?" she asked him.

"Been a lot of things in my lifetime—fisherman, cook, an iceman when I was younger." He gave a nod. "But mostly I was just a mess." He grinned.

The wisps of hair that poked out from beneath his straw hat were salt and peppered, as was his short-clipped beard, but she couldn't tell by his face how old he was. Maybe as young as forty-five, as old as sixty.

"Is that right?" Sapphire asked, beginning to relax a little. Either the man's eyesight was so bad that he couldn't tell she was female, or her disguise was working, at least so long as she kept her hair pushed up under the cap.

"Why you headed to New York City for, boy?" the old man asked.

"Going to see my mother's sister," she answered, thinking it was easiest to use the same story over again.

The old man nodded. "Long walk."

Sapphire shrugged. "Weather's good."

He cackled. "It is, but it won't be long before the cold winds blow through here."

Sapphire fell silent and all was quiet except for the creak of the wagon's wheels and the flapping of the oilcloth that hung over the side.

"You want a ride?" the old man asked as they passed a walnut tree that dropped nuts to the ground with every slight gust of wind.

Sapphire picked some nuts off the road and dropped them into her bag as she contemplated what her response should be. She didn't know the man. How did she know she would be safe with him? But he did think she was a boy, and it was an open wagon. She could jump out of it if she had to. And though she could probably walk all the way to New York City, it was a long way, especially for Stowe and his short legs.

"I'd be much obliged," she said.

He pulled back on the reins, speaking beneath his breath to the two dapple mares.

"Do you mind my dog?" she asked, scooping Stowe up into her arms.

"Nope. I like dogs. Got me two when my wife left me. Good riddance, I say." He laughed at his own joke. "Dogs don't put up a fuss when a man smokes a pipe in his own kitchen."

Sapphire put Stowe on the buckboard seat and pulled herself up to sit beside him. "Do you want him in the back?" she asked.

The man looked at the dog and the dog stared back.

"His name is Stowe," she explained.

"Nice to meet you, Stowe." He took one hand off the reins to lift the dog's paw. "Name's Petrosky."

"Nice to meet you, sir." Sapphire gripped the rough side of the wagon as it jerked forward. "I'm…"

It wasn't until that moment that she realized she needed to have a boy's name. "Sam," she said quickly.

"Nice to make your acquaintance, Sam." He offered his hand.

She shook it. "And yours, Mr. Petrosky."

His forehead wrinkled beneath the straw hat. "Nope. Not mister, just Petrosky."

She nodded. "Petrosky." She opened her bag. "Biscuit?" She held out one of the fresh ones she'd bought that morning. "I've got cheese, too, and apples and nuts."

"Don't mind if I do. And I know the perfect place to stop tonight. Best fishin' around these parts." He glanced at Sapphire. "You know how to fry a fish on an open fire, boy?"

"I can learn."

Sapphire and Stowe traveled with Petrosky for the next day and a half. True to his word, they stayed the night in a secluded cove where the old man, who she

learned was close to seventy, caught two fat fish, and
she fried them in a pan he'd brought along. The next
day, the countryside began to change, getting rockier,
hillier, and she became more and more thankful that
Petrosky had come along.

The old man was good company. He didn't ask a lot
of questions and seemed content to rattle on about people he knew, things he'd done in his lifetime, things he
wished he'd done. The best thing about Petrosky was
that he liked Stowe and the little hound liked him.

"I'll almost be sorry to see you go when we reach the
city," Petrosky told Sapphire. The sun was beginning to
set and the air had grown cooler. They were riding along
a beautiful river he said was called the Hudson. "You
sure the two you don't want to go into the ladder-
makin' business with me?"

Sapphire laughed. "Thank you, but no. We got our
hearts set on New York City."

"And seein' this aunt of yours," Petrosky offered.

"Yes." She smiled.

He was quiet for a minute, then looked at Sapphire
from beneath the brim of his hat. "You got no aunt,
do you?"

She didn't answer.

"Run away from home, haven't you?"

She wrapped an arm around Stowe, but still she said
nothing.

"Eyesight's bad, but it ain't so bad that I can't see you
got rough hands. Your mama make you work hard?
Woman's work? Cleanin', scrubbin'?" He cackled. "Was
the same way with me, only I was younger than you
first time I took off. It's what young boys do."

"No, I don't have an aunt," she said quietly.

"So you got no job and no place to stay once you get to the city?"

She hugged Stowe close to her side, trying not to be afraid. "No," she answered.

"You know," Petrosky said after a while, "I was thinkin' I'd stay with a cousin just outside the city tonight. Mama's brother's youngest. First groom, he is, in the Carrington stables. You heard of the Carringtons?" he asked.

She shook her head.

"Rich people. Family been here a hundred years, at least. They're rich people who like horses and horse racin', which is big in these parts. Got them a big stable. Always lookin' for a strong, healthy lad to shovel stalls." He moved the reins back and forth in his hands, then leaned back. "Yer a bit on the skinny side but ya look like ya could muck a stable or two. Ya afraid of hard work, boy?"

At the mention of stables, Sapphire was immediately captivated. It was something she'd missed tremendously since she'd come to Boston. Mrs. Dedrick had kept her so busy with household chores that she'd barely even had time to steal a moment to walk through Blake's stables.

Petrosky eyed her. "You want me to ask my cousin Red if he could use another lad for the winter?"

The opportunity would give her a place to stay for the winter while she saved money for passage back to London. The only problem Sapphire could immediately foresee was that she would have to continue to be Sam; no one would hire a woman to work in a stable, and certainly not a rich man's racing stable. She had apparently been convincing enough as a young man with Petrosky, but, as he'd admitted, his eyesight was poor. Could she fool this head groom, and what of the other stable boys?

Without thinking, her hand went to her cap. Her hair was too long; she would never be able to keep it all hidden beneath the hat while mucking stalls all day. But she'd already made her decision.

The hair would have to go.

26

*"M*on *chèr,"* Tarasai said, gently shaking Armand's shoulder.

He startled awake in his chair on the veranda, knocking his book to the ground. "Yes? Yes, what is it?"

"A letter," she said as she offered it to him. "George said it was from London."

"From Lucia, I hope. My glasses—" He reached to his head, and when he discovered they weren't there, he began to glance around him, still befuddled with sleep. "Where have my glasses gotten to, Tarasai? I had them here just a moment ago, I know I did."

She made a shushing sound as she searched the table, then the area around the chair for his reading glasses.

"I had them just a moment ago. I was reading," he said tersely.

When she couldn't find them on the stone patio, she began to look through the folds of the blanket on his lap.

"Don't fuss," he said. "Please don't fuss." With his last words he began to cough.

Tarasai stopped what she was doing and looked up at him, her usually sweet face turning stern. She waited until his coughing fit had ceased and he had wiped his bloody lips with a clean handkerchief. "I am not fussing," she said quietly. "I am looking for your glasses." She hesitated. "Do you want your glasses, monsieur?"

He sighed and looked away. "You're right. I'm sorry, Tarasai. It's just that I am distraught. I cannot read my letter without my glasses. I cannot protect my Sapphire and I do not—"

"Here they are, *mon chèr*," she said, rising from the stone pavers, the wire frame reading glasses in her hand. "Now calm yourself or you will be too ill to read your letter."

Armand put on his glasses, tore open the letter and quickly scanned it. "It is from Lucia. She says I am not to worry about Sapphire."

"You should know that by now."

"She says she has not heard from her again, but letters have probably crossed in the mail." He looked over his glasses at Tarasai. "She doesn't say why this man has not married my daughter." He threw the letter down in his lap. "It is so frustrating being here when they are so far away! I don't know what to do. I must write to Sapphire in Boston. No! I should write to Lord Wessex and tell him he must marry my daughter at once."

Tarasai picked up the book that had fallen, closed it and placed it on the table. "Perhaps she does not wish to marry this man."

"That's ridiculous. If she went to America with him, surely she must want to."

She shrugged her delicate shoulders. "Some men are meant to wed, others only to be lovers."

"Bring me my writing box, Tarasai."

"I will not," she said. "You will come inside, take your medicine and read me the letter Lucia has sent." She leaned over him, taking the letter from his hand and removing the blanket from his lap. "Come."

"Who are you to tell me what to do?" he asked.

"I am someone who cares for you, and I will not let you meddle where you should not meddle—now come." She offered her hand to him, and after a moment, he took it.

That night, Petrosky took Sapphire to the Carrington Farms stables and introduced her to his cousin Red. The jolly, red-haired man took an instant liking to Stowe and hired "Sam" immediately. Later, alone in a tack room where she'd been given a pallet to sleep on, Sapphire stood in front of a tiny piece of cracked mirror with a pair of scissors in her hand. Taking a deep breath, she began to cut her hair, and she didn't stop until it fell just above her shoulders, the length two other teenaged boys around the barn had worn their hair.

She laughed at herself, turning this way and that in the mirror with only the light of a kerosene lamp to see by. Between the linen strips Myra had given her to bind her breasts—which fortunately were not large to begin with—and her short hair and stable boy's clothing, Sapphire really did look like a young boy.

The next morning, with her newly shorn locks and

the cap pulled down over her head, she met Petrosky, who was headed into the city, to say goodbye. "I don't know how to thank you," she told him as she stood beside his wagon, knowing she mustn't cry. Stable boys didn't cry over old men who were kind to them.

"No need for thanks." Petrosky settled his straw hat on his head. "An old man did the same for me some fifty years ago, first time I ever took off." He looked up from under his hat and winked. "Just returnin' the favor." He picked up the reins. "You take care of that dog."

She nodded. "Yes, sir. I'll do that."

Petrosky tipped his hat to his cousin and the wagon rolled down the drive.

"You be knowin' what you doin', Sam?" Red asked, handing Sapphire a pitchfork as they entered the barn's center hall.

His Irish brogue was thick and Sapphire had to listen well to follow his orders. It wasn't so much the dialect that was difficult to understand as the musical lilt with which he spoke.

Sapphire took in her surroundings as Red gave her instructions; the stable was the largest she'd ever seen. There were fourteen stalls on each side of the aisle and behind the barn was another identical to it. She wondered how many horses these people owned.

Sapphire grinned, taking the pitchfork from him. Stowe ran behind her. "Well enough."

"Good. You'll be startin' on the far end, eh?" He pointed. "Most the horses are out on pasture. Any in their stalls, you just move to a clean stall while you fork the dirty one, then put 'em back in the right stall, eh? Mr. Carrington is funny 'bout his horses bein' in their own stalls, he is. Says they run better, and who am I to say diff'rent?"

"I'll get started right away, sir."

"'Round here, we're pretty relaxed. Take a break to piss when you need it. Grab eats same place we had them biscuits and ham this morning," he said, referring to the main room in the building where the jockeys, trainers and horse handlers and Red slept. The lowly stable boys put down a pallet wherever they could. "Take time noonday to have a smoke, wink at the dairy lasses, whatever your pleasure." Red winked himself. "Just don't let me see you bein' lazy," he warned. "And them stalls better be whisper-clean, eh?"

She nodded. "Will do."

He made to go, but turned back. "One other thing, me boyo. I said you could move horses. All but one. Hisself you daresn't lay a hand to. Prince Caribbean be his name." He pointed. "Last stall on the end, eh? Black as the devil's heart, that stallion. Mean bastard, eh?" He shook his head. "Runs like that Caribbean wind he's named after, but as foul-tempered as they come is Prince Caribbean. You mind now, boyo. Stay clear of that'n, eh?"

Sapphire nodded. She liked horses, but she was no fool; some were just of bad disposition and a person had to respect that, considering their size and strength. "So I don't clean his stall?"

"Wait until the trainer takes him out. Cosco's the only man that'll get near him. Once hisself goes out into the paddock, then you can go to it, eh?"

"Sure."

"Now, don't get cocky with me, Sam," Red warned, pointing his finger at her. "You new lads always want to show the boss how good you be with horseflesh, eh? Well, I'm tellin' you that son of Satan horse has broke two legs, three arms and a jaw, not to mention our best jockey's ribs and knee. You follow?"

"The stallion breaks people's arms and legs?"

"Sure's the sun comes up in the east, me boyo. Like's to dance on 'em once they go down." Red shrugged his massive shoulders. "Don't say that I blame 'im. The man Mr. Carrington bought him from, a man down south, is known for havin' a stable that beats his horses."

Sapphire cringed. "That's terrible."

Red turned away again. "I'll look in on you later, eh? And don't forget my words or you'll come to regret it. You stay clear from that black devil of a horse."

"You hear that?" Sapphire said to Stowe as the dog walked through the barn beside her. "You stay away from that killer horse, otherwise he'll trample you, eh?"

Stowe wagged his tail.

"What a good boy," she said, reaching the last stall and flinging the door open. The smell made her draw back for an instant, but she swallowed against her revulsion and walked in wearing the rubber galoshes Red had dug up for her. Mucking stalls for Red would certainly be better than serving Blake his dinner on silver platters.

Morning came and went and Sapphire continued to fork manure into a wheelbarrow, roll it out to the compost heap along the woods line and then return to the barn to fill it again. Each time she rolled the wheelbarrow out of one of the stalls, she took a different path to the manure pile.

The Carrington farm was nestled along the Hudson River and was breathtaking with its rolling hills and open pastures dotted with fine horses grazing, its red barns and outbuildings, and the white and gray limestone and granite mansion perched on a hill overlooking the river. The landscape was beautiful. The leaves had turned all colors of red and yellow before drifting to form bright carpets beneath the trees and the vast sloping fields were broken up by random jagged outcrops.

Setting her pitchfork against a wall, Sapphire leaned over to scratch Stowe behind the ears. "So, boy, are you hungry?"

Stowe whined and panted.

"Me, too," she said as she grabbed her canvas bag and tugged at the brim of her hat. "And I know the perfect place to picnic. Did you see that rock off in the pasture to the south? It must be as big as a carriage and I bet it's as warm as a winter hearth out there in the sun like that."

Stowe danced around her as they made their way out of the barnyard through two gates and into the pasture. The rock was farther than she had guessed, and by the time she reached it, she was famished.

Lifting Stowe onto the rock, she crawled up after him. They ate the last biscuit she had bought from the old lady, three pieces of bacon she had brought with her from this morning's meal and her last apple from the ones she had picked up along the road after leaving Boston. Stowe enjoyed his piece of biscuit and his share of the bacon, but scoffed at her offer to take a bite of her apple. He whined for more bacon.

"All gone," she laughed, holding her hand out to let

him lick it. "You see?" She took a bite of the crisp, cool apple and lay back on the warm rock. Every muscle in her body ached but she felt good—surprisingly good. She'd been so busy today that she'd barely thought about Blake, and she knew that with time, she'd forget him…no, not forget him, but at least her chest wouldn't ache when she thought of him.

Sapphire closed her eyes and, tossing the apple core over her head, wrapped her arm around Stowe who had settled down for a nap beside her. She was just drifting off, thinking she needed to get back to the stalls, when she heard men shouting and cursing in the distance.

When she looked in the direction of the stables, she saw Red waving his arms and another man running. Ahead of them was a black horse that galloped over a paddock gate, his lead rope flying behind him.

Sapphire scrambled off the rock and set Stowe in the grass, then brought her hand to shade her eyes from the bright sun. The horse had cleared another paddock gate, rounded a clump of elm trees in a hollow to the west and slowed to a trot, headed in her direction. In the far distance, she could see Red and the other man walking back toward the barn. She could still hear their voices on the wind. She looked back at the horse coming right for her, then Stowe, and stopped where she was.

Stowe dropped his bottom to the grass at once and the two waited until the stallion slowed his pace to a walk. Spotting Sapphire and the dog, the horse snorted, halted, pawed the ground and snorted again, blowing through its nose.

"What's the matter boy?" Sapphire asked softly. "A little spooked?" She took a step toward him, concerned about the rope still dangling from his halter. A horse could step on a lead rope and seriously injure himself. This was such a beautiful creature; she hated the thought that he might get hurt.

"What is it, boy?" she murmured. "Did those big men scare you? Well, let me tell you, they don't mean anything by it, those men with their big voices all stomping all over the place." She took another step.

The horse watched her cautiously. "I know one of the biggest stompers and shouters in all the land, and I'm not a bit scared of him, and you know why? He's a good person. He's got a good heart." She slowly extended her hand to the horse that was still two arms' lengths from her. From here, she couldn't possibly reach the rope. She had to move closer.

"That's right," she said. "So I just don't pay any attention to him when he gets loud." She inched forward and the horse tossed his head, backing away from her.

She stopped again. "Whoa, there, whoa, boy." She slowly lowered her hands to her sides and contemplated her options. She could hear the men in the distance again. They were still shouting, but their voices were getting closer.

The horse turned his head in the direction of the barn, whinnied and snorted.

"I know," Sapphire murmured. "They are frightfully loud."

She glanced down at the dog. "So what do you think, Mr. Stowe?" she asked. "How are we going to convince him to let us catch him?"

Then Sapphire remembered the apple core she had tossed earlier when she finished her meal. Slowly, she

slid one foot behind her and then the other, backing up toward the rock. Stowe remained with the horse. When she was far enough away to think she wouldn't spook the stallion, she rushed around the other side of the rock in the direction she had thrown the apple core. Luckily, she found it in the browning grass and was back beside the spotted hound in a minute.

"Look what I have," she cajoled, holding her hand out to the runaway, balancing the apple core on her palm.

The horse caught the scent of the sweet apple, lifted his head and snorted.

"Nope," she told him. "I'm not bringing it to you." She looked down at the dog. "Just like a man," she said. She looked up again. "If you want this apple, you'll have to come get it." She recalled that Armand had had a gelding that was afraid of shadows, so she would edge around him until she was standing where her shadow wouldn't frighten the stallion.

The black horse took one step toward her, then another and tossed his head and snorted as if fighting himself. At last, he reached out and took the core gently from her hand while Sapphire very slowly raised her other hand and caught the lead rope.

The horse started to back up, but Sapphire continued to talk quietly to him and he calmed again. As he munched on the core, she walked him around the rock. She couldn't see Red and the other man now, but she guessed they had disappeared into the grove of elms, probably thinking the horse was still there.

Done with his apple, the horse began to snatch at little sprouts of still-green grass near the rock.

Sapphire looked back to the barns and then at the

horse. She was probably half a mile away and she had already lingered here too long. "What do you think?" she asked the horse. She laid her hand on the horse's neck and he nickered, still a little spooked but much calmer than before.

"I think he likes us," she told Stowe, who was busy scratching his pink belly. Then she turned back to the horse. "Will you let me ride you back? I promise to be nice and I won't holler."

Sapphire could have sworn the horse understood what she said.

Moving cautiously, she led him closer to the rock, then climbed up it. "Here goes," she said.

She landed as carefully but as quickly as she could. As expected, the horse took off like a shot and she had to grab his mane to keep from flying off his broad back. "Easy there," she called, patting his neck when she caught her balance.

She looked behind her to see Stowe coming after them at a dead run. Still holding tightly, the black mane wrapped around her fingers, Sapphire faced forward again and gently used pressure with her legs to try to ease him back. "We have to slow down, boy, else poor Stowe will run his little legs off."

To her surprise, the horse slowed to an easy canter. She was halfway back to the barn when she heard Red calling from behind. Using one leg, she guided the black horse back around and trotted up to Red. "I'm sorry," she said, breathing hard. "I didn't ask permission to ride. It was just that I saw him running loose and—"

At that moment she realized that Red and his companion had come to a halt in the field and they were just standing there, staring at her. She couldn't tell if they were angry or shocked or both, but she knew she was not supposed to be on this horse. "Are you Caribbean Prince?" she whispered to the horse. "Something tells me you are, and I am in big trouble."

"How the hell you get on him?" the other man asked.

"His name's Cosco. Head trainer for Mr. Carrington," Red explained, still staring at her.

Sapphire nodded. "Sir."

"You didn't answer the question." Cosco was a man of average height, in his midthirties, his face lined by wind and sun, with sandy hair and a broad nose.

Sapphire patted the horse's neck, and when he began to dance nervously and both men stepped back, she urged him around in a circle to give everyone a little space. "I'm sorry," she said. "I saw he was loose and when I caught him, I thought I might as well ride him as walk him back."

"New shit shoveler," Red explained, beginning to grin. "Name's Sam."

"Do you know who this horse is?" Cosco scrunched up his wind-burned face. "This horse doesn't let anyone just jump up and ride him, boy."

She looked down at the man sheepishly. "You…want me to get down, sir?"

"Hell and shitfire, yes, I want you to get down. Do you know how much this horse is worth? A sight more than you are to your papa, that's for sure."

When Sapphire began to dismount, Red put up one hand. "Now wait a minute, Cosco. Use your head, here, eh?"

Sapphire stayed put.

"You were just sayin' the other day," the red-haired man continued, "that you didn't know who was going to ride Mr. Prince here all winter, what with Jimmy laid up with those broken ribs and his hand."

"This boy doesn't know anything about riding this kind of horse," Cosco argued, the nostrils of his huge nose flaring.

The black horse had stopped to nibble a patch of the last clover of the season with the new stable boy seated comfortably on his back.

"Don't look to me like Mr. Prince knows that, eh?"

Blake stood in front of the fireplace in Manford's study, listening to the crackle of the fire. He swirled his scotch around in a crystal glass, sipping it and savoring its peaty taste. It was only the second week of October but today Boston had seen its first flurries. Soon the snow would begin to fall in earnest and the long New England winter would begin.

Blake had been cold all day. Since he rose in the morning and saw the snow on the rail of his bedroom balcony, all he'd been able to think about was the fact that Sapphire might be out in this weather, cold, alone.

He told himself it wasn't his fault. He'd offered her everything he had to give and she was the one who had walked away without even bothering to say goodbye.

"Blake?"

He glanced up and saw Manford standing there looking at him. "Where are you today?" his friend asked. "You haven't heard a word I've said."

"I'm sorry." Blake turned away from the fireplace

and its warmth. He didn't deserve to be warm. "What were you saying?"

"I was saying that I've looked over everything you've given me. I've talked to your man in Pennsylvania and I think I'm in."

"In?"

"The rock oil. I think I'm ready to invest."

Blake perched on the arm of an upholstered chair. "Maybe you should think about this. There won't be any drilling until spring."

Manford took the chair across from Blake, drew close to the fire and scrutinized his friend. "You still believe this?"

"Of course I do. I wouldn't ask you to risk money if I didn't think it would be profitable down the road. Why?"

"I don't know." Manford sipped his scotch. "You just don't seem as enthusiastic about this as you were a few months ago."

Blake shrugged and looked down at his glass. "I still believe in it. I've just been preoccupied."

Manford shifted forward in his chair. "Do you want to talk about it?"

Blake sighed, pushing back in his chair, staring out into the room at nothing in particular. "No."

"Please tell me this is not about Clarice. She swore to me that there would be no more private calls and I truly believe she understands—"

"It's not Clarice." Blake looked at the amber liquid in his glass, then up again, but he did not meet Manford's gaze. "It's—" He stopped and then started again. "It's just that I think I might have made a mistake."

27

"Hey, Sam, wanna go sleddin'?" Paulie called from the stable door.

Sapphire was just finishing watering down the last of the horses and she looked up as she transferred water from one bucket to another, trying not to slosh water onto her overalls. "When you goin'?"

The small freckle-faced boy shrugged. "Dunno. After evenin' chores. 'Fore supper."

"Up on Big Hill?" It was one of the favorite sledding hills for everyone in the valley and Sapphire had been there several times with the five other stable hands. She didn't do a lot with them, like play cards and sit around and talk at night when they built a bonfire in the paddock, but being from Martinique, snow still fascinated her. Surprisingly enough, she didn't mind the cold too much, although the other stable boys did tease her about always wearing one extra layer more than they wore. Even though it was still early December, there had already been several snowfalls. Sledding was the one activity that allowed Sapphire to be one of the boys.

"I reckon that's where we'll go, least if Adam gets his way." Paulie grinned.

Adam was the oldest and the largest of the stable boys and generally what Adam said went. Sapphire didn't mind. He seemed nice enough. Not terribly bright, but he was a hard worker and he didn't press her about joining the group most of the time. He seemed to understand that "Sam" was a loner, which made it easier for her to hide her identity. He'd even taken up for her when Red had offered to allow her to continue sleeping in the tack room alone rather than joining the other boys who slept dormitory style over the grain shed when several of them had protested.

In the tack room, she could be closer to Caribbean Prince, Sapphire had proposed to Red—and he had agreed. The horse had obviously taken to her and it wasn't unusual for someone, either a groom or a jockey, to sleep near an expensive horse, especially one of the skittish ones.

"I'll see you shortly," Sapphire told Paulie as he heaved the last two buckets of water onto her shoulders, balanced on a pole.

"Want help?" Paulie asked, pulling on the hand-knit mittens his grandmother had just sent him from Pennsylvania.

"Nope. Got it." Sapphire headed for the farthest stall.

Alone with the horses again, she wiped out the last buckets, filled them with water and then moved from stall to stall saying good-night. She offered a scratch behind the ears to this one, a pat to that one. And to Caribbean Prince, she offered a wrinkled apple from the pocket of her overalls, beneath her canvas coat. Then, with a strong sense of satisfaction at having put in a good day's work, she retired to her tiny room at the end of the barn to write a letter to Lucia and Angelique and one to Armand. Tomorrow, which was Saturday, she would ride Prince all morning and get the afternoon off, then she'd catch a ride into town on one of the household wagons going that direction and post the letters.

Inside her cozy little room with its cot covered with a plaid wool blanket, wooden crate turned on its side that served as a nightstand and a chest of drawers for her meager possessions, Sapphire lit a kerosene lantern and settled down with paper, pen and ink. She knew her family was worried about her and she knew she had to write, but the question was, what would she tell them?

She sat back on the cot and called to Stowe, who was asleep in a box of straw on the floor near the door. She was happy to see him because he often wandered off to follow Red, whom Sapphire suspected lured the dog away with food.

Stowe leaped onto the cot and curled up beside her. "What do you think, old boy?" she murmured, scratching the dog behind his ears. "What do I tell them about this place? About our life?"

Stowe yawned and rested his head on her knee, closing his eyes.

After several false starts, she began her letter to Lucia and Angelique by telling them again that she was safe and begging them, once more, not to contact Blake Thixton. That was her biggest fear at the moment, even more than being discovered for a girl at Carrington Farm.

The first week she arrived at the stables she sent Lucia a letter explaining that she had left Boston alone, without giving many details, including where she was. All she had said was that she and Blake had parted ways and that if he contacted Lucia, she was to say she hadn't heard from her niece. Sapphire still felt guilty about not telling her godmother specifically where she was, but she couldn't risk Lucia sending Blake word of her whereabouts. Lucia would have to trust her until she could return to London, at which point she would tell all, she had explained. If her godmother was angry with her, she would just have to be angry.

Sapphire kept her letter to Lucia and Angelique short. She told them that despite her separation from Blake Thixton, she was still enjoying her adventure in America, which was entirely true. She told them about how much she loved the snow, about how she didn't mind the cold, but that she wore something called a union suit. She told them about sledding on Big Hill and she even mentioned Caribbean Prince, though not by name. She did not mention her broken heart or the fact that though the wound seemed to be healing over, there were days when it was still quite raw. Of course she didn't tell them that she was pretending she was boy.

Sapphire ended the letter by saying she didn't know how often she would have time to write. In truth, she found the letters difficult to compose. But she promised to see them by summer's end, and sent all her love.

While her salary as a stable hand came only to a few dollars a month, Red had promised her that if she and Prince won the races he was betting she would win, Sapphire would take home a small portion of the winnings each week. Surely by summer's end, she thought, she would have the one hundred and ten dollars required to book passage back to London.

Sapphire's letter to Armand was more difficult to write. She had put off contacting him long enough. She knew that if he didn't hear from her soon, he would be worried. Fortunately, she had not given him Blake's address in Boston when she had written him on arriving in America. Her letter to Armand was even shorter than her letter to Lucia and Angelique. She told him she was well, that she was spending the winter in New York City and that she would be returning to London in the summer. She told him not to worry about her and that she was enjoying her time in America. She sent all of her love, and with dry eyes, sealed the letter and dressed to go sledding.

"Oh heavens!"

"Jessup? Are you all right?" Lucia called through the open door down the hallway.

They had made love and then Jessup had excused himself to use the necessary. He was a dear man. He refused to use a chamber pot in her presence and always bundled up and traipsed outside, no matter how cold it was or how hard it was snowing. Lucia was far more practical. She just went out into the hall and squatted over the chamber pot there.

"Jessup?" she called.

"Oh dear. Oh my," he repeated.

"Jessup, what is it?" She slid out of bed, pushed her feet into her boiled-wool slippers and walked to the doorway.

Jessup stood halfway down the hall bundled in his nightshirt, stockings, night robe and a striped green and white stocking cap, his hands clasped as if in fright.

"What's wrong?" Lucia asked. "Are you ill? Are you injured?"

"I…I'm terribly embarrassed."

She looked him up and down, wondering if he had had some sort of accident. It happened at their age if something didn't sit right on their stomachs—a sour bit of cabbage, a bad piece of pork. "Have you need of the washbowl, love? Some clean undergarments?" she asked, not in the least bit offended.

He looked up at her, horrified. "Certainly not!"

"Then come to bed, Jessup! A man could freeze to death out here," she snapped, watching her breath as it rose in white puffs in the hallway.

"I…I cannot."

"What do you mean you cannot?" she demanded, lowering her hands to her hips as she stood in the doorway of his bedchamber. She'd just gotten toasty warm in the bed and now her feet were cold again. "Jessup, I'm losing my patience with you. I can very well go home, you know, and sleep in my own bed."

He still hadn't moved an inch in the hallway. "I'm very sorry, love."

"Jessup, what's wrong?" She took a step toward him.

"Don't!" he cried, throwing up one hand. The point on his knit cap swayed wildly.

"What's wrong?" She could see nothing. No hole in the floor. No nail sticking up. She could smell no smoke. "Jessup, you have to tell me," she implored. "Why is the menace here, my love?"

He glanced away. "I'm mortified."

"Tell me," she insisted.

He closed his eyes. "You'll laugh."

"I won't."

"Emma always laughed."

"Jessup Stowe, are you comparing me to your dead wife?" She shook her finger at him. "Because if you are, I can tell you right now I'm going to pack up my clothes and my personals and be out of your way for good within the hour."

"You're right. I'm sorry." He opened his eyes, putting out both hands apologetically. "I'm sorry, Lucia."

"Now stop being ridiculous and tell me what's wrong."

He was quiet for a moment and then he pointed to his right. "A mouse."

She looked and, sure enough, there in the shadows, along the floorboards, was a tiny gray mouse huddling against the molding.

Lucia had to cover her mouth with her hands to keep from laughing. "You're afraid of *mice*, Jessup?"

"Since childhood when I was bitten on the toe while in my cradle."

Lucia walked toward him, putting out her hand. The mouse startled and scampered away. "There, there," she soothed. "You see, the poor wee thing is more frightened of you than you are of it." She put her arm around him and ushered him toward the bedchamber.

"I'm sorry, Lucia. It's no wonder you don't want to marry me. Who would want to marry a man afraid of mice?"

She smiled in the darkness as she led him to his side

of the bed and helped him out of his robe. She lifted the heavy goose-down comforters, eased him onto the bed, and pulled off his slippers and his cap as he lay back. She walked around to her side, kicked off her slippers and climbed in, crawling under the blankets until she was beside him, facing him nose to nose.

"What am I going to do with you, Jessup Stowe?"

"I don't know?" he whispered.

"A man afraid of mice."

"I know, I know. An Englishman afraid of mice, no less."

She slid her arm around him, nuzzling his neck. "You know, there really is only one thing to be done with such a man."

"And what would that be?"

"Marry him, of course. After all, there's got to be someone in the household who can chase away the mice!"

Jessup laughed and rolled over, pinning her to the mattress. "I love you, Lucia," he whispered in her ear.

"I love you, too, you old goat. Now roll over and get some sleep. Only one go-round per night for us old folks, you know." She kissed him and they rolled over onto their sides, snuggling against each other, warding off the winter chill.

Blake stood at the rail of the balcony in his overcoat and let the snow hit him directly in the face. At least the cold, wet sting made him feel like he as alive.

He stared down into the darkness and at the twinkle of the occasion light in the harbor. There wasn't much moving on the water tonight. Any sensible sailor was snug in his house or beneath battened-down hatches. It was nearly Christmas and Father Winter was bearing down on Boston.

He thrust his gloved hands into the pockets of his black wool overcoat. He'd received reports tonight from two separate agents he'd hired to search for Sapphire, and neither had been good. That was six in the past two weeks. Six reports and more than two hundred dollars, a fortune by some standards. Not that he cared about the money—hell, he had more money than he knew what to do with.

No one had seen Sapphire. She had just disappeared from Boston. From his life. She was gone. Vanished into thin air, as hard as that was for the private agents he hired to believe.

And yet, in a way, it wasn't hard for Blake to believe. They didn't understand her the way he did. Sapphire was so determined. It didn't surprise him that once she decided to rid herself of him, she'd just done it. Didn't surprise him a bit.

Blake heard a knock at the door, a knock that became a pound when he didn't respond. "Mr. Thixton?" a voice called from the bedroom door.

"What is it?" he barked, having to almost shout for the maid to hear him above the howling wind. "I told you I didn't want any supper."

"Mr. Lawrence is here to see you, sir." Molly dropped a curtsy and hurried out of the room as Manford walked in, still in his overcoat.

"I didn't know you were coming," Blake said, leaning back against the rail.

"Didn't think I needed an invitation." He walked to the open doorway, buttoning up his coat. "What the hell are you doing? It's freezing out here."

Blake turned to stare into the darkness. "It doesn't feel that cold."

Manford was quiet for a minute. "Listen, Blake. I know this isn't any of my business, but this girl you told me about—"

"You're right. It isn't."

"This is getting a little silly, don't you think? I mean, honestly, she was just a serving girl. She—"

"Don't you say that! You understand me?" Blake spun around, raising his fist. "Don't you ever say that again or I swear by all that's holy, I'll—" He stopped himself before he drew his fist under Manford's chin and let it fall to his side. He looked down and scuffed his boot in the snow. "God, I don't know what's wrong with me, Manford. I'm sorry."

Manford clamped his hand on Blake's shoulder. "How about a scotch? One *inside*, out of this snow. Maybe a little something to eat? You're wasting away, old friend."

"Maybe a drink," Blake agreed.

The two men stepped into the bedchamber and into the light. Manford closed the door behind them, shrugged off his coat and walked to the table to pour them both a drink. "So she's not just a servant. Tell me about her, then. You never even told me her name."

Blake stood by the glass doors, still in his coat, feeling out of place, even in his own bedchamber. He had felt out of sorts ever since Sapphire had gone missing— out of place in his own house, in his own office, even in his own skin.

"It's complicated."

"It always is." Manford crossed the bedchamber and

pushed a crystal tumbler half full of scotch into his hand. As he did so, their fingers brushed. "You're ice-cold," he remarked. "How long have you been standing out there?"

"Not long." Blake lifted the glass to his lips and drank deeply.

"So tell me about her." Manford walked toward the bedchamber door. "I'm going to order us both some supper because I, for one, am famished. Then I want you to tell me everything."

Blake stared into his glass, swirling the amber liquid. "I don't know that I can."

28

Lucia entered her apartments to find Angelique sitting on a chair in the parlor and staring out the window to the busy street below. "This is a surprise," Lucia said with a smile, placing several brown-paper-wrapped parcels on the floor beside the door. "Is Avena here?" She didn't hear the maid's footsteps, even as she closed the door. Usually Avena was more than efficient when it came to her duties.

"I told her she could take the afternoon off. Wedding preparations." Angelique rolled her eyes.

Lucia plucked off her yellow gloves and removed her bonnet. "I'm happy for her. She and her tailor make a handsome couple. I knew he was worth hanging on to when he told her he wasn't interested in her past." She walked to the window and leaned over to place a kiss on Angelique's cheek. "So to what honor do I owe this occasion? It's been ages since you've come to visit. It seems that Jessup and I only see you at social events."

Sapphire 423

Angelique turned to look out the window again, propping her chin on the heel of her hand as she leaned on the broad windowsill. "I can't believe we've been in London almost a whole year. It seems as if we only left Martinique a few weeks ago." Her tone was uncharacteristically pensive.

"You sound like an old woman." Lucia chuckled. "Usually girls of your age think a year is a lifetime." Lucia glanced out the window to see carriages passing, venders selling fresh eggs and gingerbread, men and women hurrying up and down the street, carrying their wares; it was the first warm day of spring and it seemed as if all of London was coming out to greet her. She looked back to Angelique and smoothed her dark hair, which was looped with ribbons in tiny, whimsical braids. "You're in a particularly contemplative mood today, *ma fille.* Is there anything wrong?"

Angelique sighed, still staring out the window through the diamond-cut panes. "Do you really think Sapphire is all right? I've been worried about her since her last letter. I really thought she would stay with that American, marry him and have babies."

Lucia took the chair across from Angelique. "I think she's fine."

"She's being very secretive. All we know is that she's somewhere in New York and that she's no longer with Blake. It's just not like her to be so reticent. She must know we would worry, and it isn't in her nature to prolong it."

Lucia shrugged. "Obviously things didn't work out between her and Lord Wessex the way she had hoped. I suspect she simply needed the winter to be alone, to lick her wounds and get back on her feet."

"But it's April! It's no longer winter."

Angelique turned to look at her, and Lucia realized that her charge was beyond simple worry—she was truly concerned, which again was uncharacteristic of Lucia's little carefree vagabond.

"What if she's penniless and has no way to return to London?" Angelique continued. "What will become of her? Will she be forced to turn to her mother's trade simply to buy bread? I think we should write to Mr. Thixton and find out where she's gone in New York."

"You can't do that," Lucia said sharply.

"And why can't I? Someone's got to do something." Angelique rested her hands on her hips. "You're so busy acting ridiculous with Mr. Stowe that you've completely abandoned your responsibilities as Sapphire's guardian!" Angelique gasped as the last words slipped out and covered her mouth in horror at having said such a thing. She looked away, tears welling in her eyes.

Lucia took Angelique's hands in hers. "Look at me," she said softly, not a fleck of anger in her voice.

Angelique slowly turned from the window to meet Lucia's gaze. "I'm sorry," she whispered. "I shouldn't have said such a terrible thing. I didn't mean it. I truly didn't."

"I know you didn't. You're afraid for Sapphire, and that's all right because I'm afraid for her, too."

"You are?" Angelique sniffed.

"Of course I am." Lucia patted Angelique's hand. "But if a parent, a guardian, a godmother, reacted every time he or she was fearful for a child, well…well, we wouldn't get much accomplished in this world because we'd all be running about fretting, twisting our hands and pulling at our hair, wouldn't we." She paused, giving Angelique a moment. "Now listen to me. You cannot write to Lord Wessex in Boston and you know it. When Sapphire wrote to us, she passed on her trust and we cannot betray that trust. Now, she said in her letters that she's fine and that we'll see her by summer's end. She said we have to have faith in her—and we have to do just that."

Angelique glanced down at the floor and then up at Lucia again. "Henry and I, we're thinking of going to America."

"How exciting!"

"To look for her."

Lucia frowned. "That's very noble, but you must go for your own reasons. America is a very big place to look for a person who doesn't wish to be found."

"Oh, Aunt Lucia, won't you go with us?" Angelique slid to the edge of the chair to be closer to her aunt. "Jessup said Blake Thixton is a very important man in America. I imagine all I have to do is step off the boat and ask someone, and I'll be told where I can find him."

Lucia frowned. "And Henry is willing to do this for you, to cross the ocean and look for someone important to you? Why, she could already be on her way home and you could pass each other, one on a ship sailing east, the other on one going west." She released Angelique's hand to demonstrate with her hands.

"This isn't just about Sapphire, Aunt Lucia. Henry says he will go to New York and look for Sapphire if I'll go west and see his Indians."

"And you want to do this with him?"

Angelique nodded.

"You should marry him, then."

Angelique rose with a contemplative smile on her face. "That's what he says. Henry claims there's nothing to stop us from marrying. His parents have all but disowned him. The only monies he has now are those left to him by his grandfather."

"And yet he remains true to you."

She rested her hand on the windowsill. "Yes."

"Do you want to marry him?" Lucia looked up at her niece, thinking how truly beautiful she was. And more mature than when they arrived a year ago. Love did that to a person.

"I don't know," Angelique answered quietly. "Aunt Lucia, I don't know what to do. I wish Sapphire were here," she said almost desperately, drawing her fingers down the drapes. "I wish that I could ask her what I should do. She would know—I know she would. She knows me better than I know myself." Her lower lip quivered. "She has always been there for me, you see? I have always had her good sense to rely on."

Lucia fell quiet, allowing the young woman she loved as if she were her own a chance to think.

"I never saw myself marrying anyone, and certainly not a proper Englishman like Henry. I didn't think I wanted to spend my whole life with one man. It...it sounded so dull."

"You live with Henry now. Is life dull?"

Angelique laughed. "It's many things, but dull is not a word I would use to describe it."

"Then perhaps you have answered your own question."

"You think I should marry him?"

"I think you should follow your heart. I also think you should take into consideration the fact that Henry is willing to give up everything, his family, his inheritance, his title, to have a life with you."

"I at least owe him this?" Angelique looked out the window again, pressing her palm to the cool glass.

"No one ever owes another their life."

Angelique smiled. "And what of you, Aunt Lucia? Will you be happy marrying your Mr. Stowe?"

"I think I will be," she said honestly. "I never expected it. Never expected to love again, certainly not this way, so late in life. But Jessup is a good man. I cannot tell you how many times this winter he has gone to one shire or another in the hopes of finding the church where Sophie and Edward might have been wed."

"He wants to make you happy."

"True." Lucia rose from the chair. "But I also sense this has become an obsession with him, his holy grail of sorts. He is determined to get to the truth, no matter what."

Angelique stepped forward, smiling. "I think you will be a happy couple."

"And I think you should go to the kitchen and see if Avena has left us some biscuits and coffee, because I'm famished!"

"Are you ready, Sam?"

Sapphire gripped the reins tightly in her hand, staring straight ahead between Prince's ears. "I can't do this, Red," she said under her breath.

"Of course you can." He patted her calf. "Don't matter anyway, boyo, because you're doing it."

Sapphire gazed overhead at the puffy white clouds

drifting in the clear blue sky. When Red had convinced Cosco last fall to allow "Sam" to ride Prince through the winter while his jockey's broken bones mended, Sapphire had never imagined she would actually be racing the steed. But as the winter passed it became more and more apparent to everyone that the horse adored the new stable boy called Sam Water, and it was Mr. Carrington himself who made the decision.

A month ago when the snows were still swirling around them, he had watched Sapphire race Prince out through one of the fields, and he had decided by the time Sapphire dismounted, breathless. "Sam" was no longer the lowliest stable boy, but now held the coveted position of one of Carrington Farm's jockeys. And Sapphire would be Prince's jockey. She had felt guilty about taking another man's position, but Red had insisted she shouldn't because Prince had never liked Jimmy to begin with. Jimmy hadn't the hands for it. Besides, the pay as a jockey was a far sight better than the pay as a stable boy. A stable boy, besides room and board, only made a couple of dollars a month. But a jockey, if he was good, could earn a small percentage of his race wins.

"Are we ready?"

Sapphire looked up to see Mr. Carrington approaching her. He was a pleasant older man with a shock of white hair and a smile that never left his craggy face. He walked with a cane because of a bad leg break he acquired years ago after a fall from horseback. He no longer raced his own horses, but he had become one of the best breeders on the Hudson and was known for his ability to produce fast horses.

"Ready as we're gonna be, Mr. Carrington." Red

swiped his cap off his head while still holding tightly to the lead rope attached to Prince's halter.

The black steed pranced in place. Sapphire could see the other horses beginning to line up for the race a hundred feet ahead. She fingered the reins nervously, thankful for the tan kidskin gloves she wore. Her hands were so sweaty inside them that if she were barehanded, she feared she couldn't have held on to the reins.

"No need to be nervous, kid," Mr. Carrington said, reaching out to pat Prince's neck.

The horse pawed at the ground, snorted, seeming anxious to join the other horses.

"Just along the bank and back, that's all it is. Just you and Prince going for a ride along the riverbank," Mr. Carrington assured her.

Sapphire realized this race was of little importance. It was the beginning of the race season and owners just wanted to let their horses stretch, wanted to see how their jockeys would fare, new and seasoned. But Sapphire also knew Prince was already entered in other races; in a few weeks they would be in a place called Long Island where there would be hundreds of spectators, unlike here where mostly horse breeders and racers and their families had gathered to welcome spring.

"You're not nervous, are you, Sam?" Mr. Carrington asked, looking up at her perched on Prince's back.

Feeling tense, she shook her head. It had all sounded like a good idea in the beginning, when it was cold outside and she was lonely and missing Blake and spent most of her day grooming Prince. Even when the train-

ing had begun and Cosco had taught her how to race,
it still hadn't seemed real. Now, as the other horses and
riders lined up and the spectators placed their final bets,
there was no denying what she was about to do. She just
hoped it didn't involve breaking her neck....

"I'm not nervous, Mr. Carrington," Sapphire said.

"That's my boy." The older man stepped back. "You
win today, Sam, I'm telling you now. It's dinner at my
place tonight and you will have the seat of honor. That
and a couple more dollars jingling in your pocket." He
winked.

"Thank you, sir." Sapphire tipped her hat the way
she saw other jockeys do it.

Red looked up. "Ready, me boyo?"

Sapphire pressed her lips together and nodded.

Red led her to the starting line, marked in the new
grass with ground limestone poured from a bucket.
Around her, Sapphire could hear the other jockeys and
trainers whispering, staring at her, talking of the new-
comer who had tamed the wild Prince Caribbean and
taken Jimmy's seat in the Carrington barns. She ignored
their stares and whispers and concentrated on the patch
of white between Prince's ears.

"All right, boy," Sapphire whispered to the horse as
Red unhooked the lead rope and stepped quickly out
of the way of her mount's powerful hooves. "Just a ride
along the river," she told him softly. "A quick ride
around the track and you'll be back in your stall with a
bag of molasses oats, all right, old boy?"

The horse nickered.

One of the men, an owner of a farm down in the valley, stepped up to the line of racehorses. There were nine

in all. Ordinarily, Prince Caribbean would have been the favorite, but he was unpredictable and word had it in the horse-racing community along the Hudson that no one knew if the kid Carrington had hired had it in him to make the mile race and stay on the horse's back.

The distinguished gentleman in the bowler hat produced a white handkerchief from inside his frock coat and Prince put his head down, snorting.

Sapphire tensed on the horse's back. Out of the corner of her eye, she saw the handkerchief fall and she loosened the reins and sank the heels of her new boots into Prince's flanks. Prince shot over the white line and suddenly the countryside was a blur. Sapphire ignored the horses beside her, and the shouts of the riders as they tried to urge their mounts faster, as Prince pulled away. She used no riding crop. She didn't even carry one because the horse never seemed to run as good a race when she tried one, perhaps because of his experiences with his previous owner. Instead, she sat high on his back, crouched forward on his withers and let him take the lead.

In no time, they were rounding the elm tree with its budding green leaves and the bank of Hudson was now on her left shoulder. She had only been two lengths ahead of the closest horse before they rounded the halfway mark, and now they were four or five ahead.

As the wind whistled in Sapphire's ears and the faces of the onlookers flew by in a blur, she found herself thinking of Blake. What would he think of his maid now? Would he laugh? Scowl?

The wind brought tears to her eyes.

As the pounding of Prince's hooves echoed in her head, she wondered if Clarice had wheedled her way into Blake's bed, into the house. Was he still seeing Mrs. Sheraton? She didn't know why she cared. He'd made it obvious to her what she meant to him—what she did not mean to him. He'd told her from the beginning the purpose women served in his life; she'd been foolish to think he had not been entirely truthful. If there was one thing Blake was, it was honest.

Ahead, Sapphire heard the calls of the spectators waiting at the finish line, Red the loudest.

"There ya go, me bully lad!" he called in his Irish brogue. "You got it! Come on!"

Sapphire flew over the finish line on Prince's back and slowly pulled back on the reins, circling him around the group of people all waiting to be the first to run their hand over Prince's glossy neck and offer Mr. Carrington their congratulations.

Red appeared at her side and clipped the lead rope onto Prince's halter. "Good job, lad! Told you you'd keep your seat."

She smiled, thankful for Red's friendship. She'd kept to herself all winter, avoiding the other stable boys and grooms, mostly because she was worried someone would realize she wasn't one of them. But Red had been kind to her, keeping his distance but supporting her, boosting her confidence.

"Well, son," Mr. Carrington said, limping toward her, a wide grin on his weathered face. "Looks like you have the seat of honor at my dining table tonight."

Two months later

"Come with us," Manford said, standing at Blake's hotel room door, his hand resting on the door frame. "It will be fun."

Blake stared at him. "It won't be fun. And just the other day, wasn't it you who told me I was never fun anymore? That all I did was work?"

"Come on." Manford laid his hand on Blake's shoulder. "I was just trying to make you see what you're doing to yourself. You're getting as bad as your father."

Blake scowled. "Well, Manford, old friend, that certainly makes me want to dress and attend this dull dinner party with you."

"I didn't mean it that way. I apologize." Manford ran his fingers through his hair, seeming frustrated. "I just don't know what to do for you, Blake. I'm serious."

Blake stared at the hand-painted wallpaper in the corridor of the Martin-James hotel in New York City where he and Manford had come to meet with some gentlemen concerning the shipping of cloth. The trip coincided with a well-publicized horse race that took place on Long Island each year and Blake had been able to avoid attending with Manford. He had no interest in gambling on horse racing; he never gambled, not on cards or dice or the number of rats a crew would find in a particular crate when it was pried open on the dock. He wasn't a man of odds. He liked a sure thing.

"Come on," Manford prodded. "The gentleman hosting the supper party is quite a businessman. I think you would like him."

"He raises horses for a living, races horses for a living. I know nothing of horses beyond which side to mount," Blake said drolly. But he was beginning to waver. Manford was right. He was working too hard, spending too many long hours alone with his thoughts, haunted by regrets over Sapphire.

He'd spent the entire winter looking for her, but to no avail. It was as if the night she had left his house, she had simply been swallowed up. Several times in the past few months Blake had considered writing a letter to Mr. Stowe inquiring as to whether she had returned to London; once he'd even drafted one. But he never sent it. Perhaps he feared the answer. If something terrible had befallen her, he didn't know what he would do, if she had come to harm through his selfish desires. No, he had a feeling none of those possibilities had come to pass or he would have heard from Stowe or her godmother. Sapphire was out there somewhere. He could almost feel her. She was the ache in his chest that kept him awake at night. She was the tremble in his hand that made him unsteady when he reached for a glass or a book. She was what made his mind wander when he tried to concentrate on business matters or a conversation at the dinner table.

"Did you hear me, Blake? The reception is right here in the hotel, downstairs in one of the parlors. If the conversation is dull, you can climb back into your cave." Manford poked his head through the doorway. "Though quite a cave you have here, I must say. A suite." He stepped back into the hallway. "Please don't let Patricia know you're staying in such magnificent rooms or she'll wonder why I didn't spend the money to get a suite for us, as well." He looked back at Blake. "Tell me you'll join us."

"I'm not hungry. I have those new reports on—"

"Just a drink, that's all I'm asking. Just join us downstairs for a drink."

Blake drew his pocket watch from his waistcoat. "What time?"

"Eight. Excellent." Manford began to walk away. "I'll tell Patricia. She'll be pleased. She's been worried about you, as well. Now that she's accepted the fact that you are not marrying Clarice, she continually wants to introduce you to young women. You know what a matchmaker she is, and she has always been fond of you."

Blake ignored Manford's reference to his recent social habits. It had been months since he attended an affair with a woman on his arm; in fact, he'd not done so since his return from England, but the subject was not up for discussion.

"Perhaps you'll see me at eight," he said as he walked into his room.

"I had better."

Sapphire fumbled with the knot of her white silk cravat, groaned, pulled it loose and began to tie it again. It was the third time she had attempted to tie the ridiculous contraption, and there was no way she could ask anyone to help her. Who would she ask?

She had come in one of Mr. Carrington's carriages all alone and had been shown to this room to change into the trousers, frock coat and linen shorts he had purchased for her to wear to affairs such as this. And there had many recently. It didn't make a great deal of sense to

Sapphire—after all, Prince was the one running the race, all she had to do was simply try to hang on—but she was somehow being toasted as the jockey of New York.

All winter Sapphire had enjoyed her time with the horses, time spent mostly alone with her thoughts in the warm, quiet barn where the only sounds she heard were that of horses munching on their oats, the occasional squeak of a mouse and the beating of her own heart. It had even been fun pretending to be a young man, not caring what she looked like or how dirty she got. She enjoyed the freedom the clothes provided as well as the freedom to come and go where she wanted without an escort as she had needed in London, but all of that grew dreary more quickly than she had thought it would. Then spring had come and the racing had started. It had been so exhilarating at first. She and Caribbean Prince had begun winning races and suddenly they had been the talk of the stable, then the talk of the town. Mr. Carrington had even invited her and Red to dinner in the big house and then their neighbors had begun to invite them to dinners and parties. Mr. Carrington had bought her a man's suit. Fortunately, he'd allowed her into the city alone to purchase it in a store where a person could buy clothes already made rather than tailored.

The weeks had flown by, one race running into another. Mr. Carrington had been true to his word and she had been given a few dollars with each purse the black horse had taken with their win, allowing her to add slowly to her savings. But as the months passed, so did the excitement. Lately, everytime she stepped into a room to hear the applause of her admirers in the horse-racing circuit all she could think of was how desperately she wanted to wear a lace ball gown and how much she hated cutting her hair each month.

But by the first week of June, she realized that with just a few more weeks of riding, just a few more dollars, she would have enough money to buy some decent women's attire and her passage back to London. As much as she had enjoyed her time with Prince and all of the nice people she had met at Carrington Farms, she yearned to see Lucia and Angelique, and to touch the precious letters and the sapphire her mother had left for her.

There was a knock at the door and Sapphire quickly pulled the ends of the cravat. "Coming," she called in the voice that she was now accustomed to using.

"Mr. Carrington awaits you downstairs, sir," said a young man through the door.

"Thank you." She reached for her frock coat, slipped her arms into it and, opening the door, entered the hotel corridor. She followed the wide hallway with its wainscoting and stylish floral wallpaper to the curving grand staircase, and as she took the steps, she couldn't help but imagine what it would be like to walk them in an elegant satin ball gown on the arm of a handsome gentleman.

Of course, there was only one handsome gentleman she could imagine walking down the stairs with, and just the thought of him made her stomach knot. After all this time, she was amazed he could still do that to her. She wondered if he ever thought of her. She doubted it.

Reaching the bottom of the stairs, Sapphire crossed the pink marble floor, trying to remember to strut like a boy rather than take dainty steps, and not to gaze up at the blazing chandeliers overhead because the beauty of crystal wasn't something Sam Water, a simple stable-boy-turned-jockey, would have appreciated. The Martin-James Hotel was one of the most beautiful pieces of architecture, inside or out, she had ever seen and she longed to explore it. However, she would not be staying the night; Mr. Carrington had already ordered the carriage to take her home at ten. His best jockeys always attended the parties and balls, but never stayed long.

"Mr. Water," one of Mr. Carrington's rivals' wives called to him, fluttering her fan in Sapphire's direction. "Do come and let me introduce you to a dear friend."

"Mr. Water," someone else called.

"Sam!" cried another voice.

Sapphire could feel her life spinning out of control. She didn't know what she wanted beyond her father's name, but she knew she could not live this way much longer.

"Very nice to meet you, ma'am," Sapphire said, taking a middle-aged woman's hand and kissing the back of it.

The woman giggled.

"Sam rides for Carrington," the younger woman explained to the older. "But my Jonathan has made Sam an offer I cannot imagine he could refuse."

Sam smiled absently, much the same way she had seen Blake smile at this kind of affair.

"Would you care for a drink, Sam?" someone behind her offered.

"No, thank you," she said, turning around. As she faced the next well-wisher, just out of the corner of her eye, she thought she saw something.

Someone.

He was standing under a monstrous chandelier just outside the double glass French doors with their frosted design, his hands stuffed into his trouser pockets. He appeared to be debating whether to enter the reception parlor.

Sapphire's breath caught in her throat and for a second she was paralyzed with fear. She didn't know which way to escape, and at the moment when she started to turn away, Blake's gaze met hers.

He was not fooled by the short hair or the men's clothing.

"Thank you so much," Sapphire said, blindly shaking hands, taking the glass someone handed her. "Thank you." She nearly stumbled in her effort to get away.

He was walking straight toward her.

"If you'll excuse me," she heard herself say, making a beeline for a door at the rear of the salon. She had no idea where it led, but hoped that it would take her from this nightmare.

29

"You, wait a minute. Sir!" came Blake's uncertain voice behind Sapphire.

She left the glass someone had pushed into her hand on a table as she hurried through the door. It led into a narrow, dimly lit corridor—used by staff to move about the hotel without disturbing guests, she recalled. She closed the door behind her and leaned against it, her pulse pounding in her ears.

"Sir?" Blake said again.

Sapphire looked up and down the hall, not knowing which way to go. There had to be a way out of here, perhaps a way onto the street. Then she could just disappear in New York City the same way she had disappeared in Boston.

But Blake was right behind her, no more than three or four steps away when she closed the door. She held her hands to her racing heart, feeling light-headed. He spoke again from the other side of the door.

"Excuse me, but did you see that young man go through here?"

Sapphire heard another voice responding, but she couldn't make out what the woman was saying.

"Who?" Blake asked.

"The jockey," the woman said, her voice loud enough for Sapphire to hear this time. "You must meet him. A young boy Carrington found in his own stables. Sam Water is his name. He rides that wild steed of Carrington's, you know, the black one, Prince Caribbean."

"Does he?" Blake intoned, as if he knew what she spoke of.

The doorknob rattled.

Sapphire darted to her right but she wasn't fast enough. The one second she had hesitated had been too long.

She heard the door open behind her.

"Sam?" Blake called.

She ignored him, walking faster, hoping he thought he had made a mistake. After all, hadn't the helpful woman said she was Sam Water?

"Sapphire...please."

Something in his voice made her halt. Was that *emotion? Longing? Regret?* Blake Thixton, the arrogant, self-righteous, never-feels-a-thing Blake Thixton, Earl of Wessex? Surely she was mistaken.

"Is it really you?" he breathed, grasping her forearm and forcing her to face him. She felt as if she were falling. Being so close to him frightened her more than she had ever been in her life, and yet at the same time, a sense of overwhelming relief washed over her. All these weeks, months, she had wanted him, needed him so desperately, and now here he was. So suddenly. So unexpectedly.

Sapphire lifted her lashes, tears stinging the backs of her eyelids. "Sam Water, stable hand, sometimes jockey," she said softly, her voice trembling. "Pleased to make your acquaintance, Mr. Thixton."

"I knew it was you!" He grabbed her and pulled her into his arms, covering her mouth with his. "God, I was afraid I would never—"

Sapphire couldn't breathe, her chest felt so tight. She was bombarded by a mixture of anger, relief and resentment, by the sight of him and the feel of his mouth, his touch. She had thought she would never see him again.

And he was so happy. There was no denying it.

Of course he was pleased to see her. She had abandoned him, left without his permission. No one left Blake Thixton without his blessing.

She tore her mouth from his, panting hard. "Let me go!"

"Where the hell have you been?" He still clasped one of her arms, holding tightly even when she tried to pull away. "What are you doing in men's clothing?" He looked her up and down in disdain. "What is this nonsense about you being a horse jockey?"

"Let me go," she repeated from between clenched teeth.

"What? And then chase you through the streets of New York? I don't think so."

"Blake, please. I have to get back inside. People will begin to notice I'm missing. My employer, Mr. Carrington—"

"A jockey?" he asked. "You told these people you were a man and a damn jockey?"

She looked up at him through a veil of wet lashes, anger beginning to fill the pit in her stomach. "I *am* a jockey! This party is in honor of me, of the horse I ride and the man who owns him."

"You have got to be kidding me," he murmured.

She looked him in the eye, defiance plain in her voice. "You know I'm not."

He glanced away, then back at her. "Do you have any idea how much time, how much money I have spent looking for you?"

"Well, you shouldn't have." She tugged hard on her arm, trying to escape as she fought her emotions. "You had Mrs. Sheraton. You didn't need me."

He pulled back even harder. "Sapphire—"

"I have to go back inside," she insisted, not wanting to hear whatever he had to say about Mrs. Sheraton. It didn't matter. All that mattered was that Sapphire would never be more to him than a mistress.

"You're not going back in there. You're going with me."

"What are you going to do? How are you going to stop me?" she demanded. "Kidnap me again?"

"No, I'm not going to kidnap you." He released her so suddenly that she nearly fell. "But you go in there and I'll tell them all who you are...or rather *what* you are." He looked down at her. "What have you done, bound your breasts?" He reached out with his free hand to brush her hair with his fingertips. "And you've cut your hair, your beautiful hair? Sapphire, have you lost your mind?"

She looked down at the floor, at the tips of her polished black boots. Mr. Carrington had to have them made just for her because they were so small for a man.

"Sapphire," he said quietly. "Think. Use that brain of

yours that I know you have. We don't need this kind of scandal. Nor does the gentleman who hired you when you falsely represented yourself."

We? What did he mean by *we?* She bit down on her lip. And she hadn't thought about the others at Carrington Farms. She and Prince had been winning every race; her competitors would jump at the chance to discredit her, the horse, Carrington. Even in America, women were not allowed to race. They would all be disgraced, and not just Mr. Carrington. Red had hired her. Cosco had reluctantly allowed her to ride Prince. She owed it to these men not to make them pay for her falsehoods.

"All right," she said softly, wrapping her arms around her waist, hating him for doing this to her, hating herself for getting into a position that could allow him to do this to her again. Worst of all, she hated herself for wanting him the way she did right now.

"You'll go with me?"

He held out his arms and she couldn't stop herself; she stepped into them and closed her eyes, burying her face in his shirt, in the scent of him.

"I'll go with you," she said, and then whispered, "at least for tonight."

As Blake promised, he discreetly escorted Sapphire down the corridor, through the kitchens, and up a rear staircase. No one saw them and they were soon in his hotel room. "Let me get you something to drink," he said as he locked the door behind them.

She just stood there in the middle of his lavish hotel suite, not sure if she wanted to laugh or cry.

"Champagne?" he asked.

She shrugged. "That would be fine."

"I'll order something for us to eat later."

"Later," she repeated.

He popped the cork on the champagne bottle and poured her a glass. As he pushed a fluted crystal glass into her hand, she lifted her gaze. "Did you intend to have a private celebration with someone?"

He scowled. "It was a gift from a colleague. I was here on business and Manford—he's downstairs—he was the one who convinced me to come down. If I hadn't given in, I might not have—" He fell silent.

Sapphire wished she knew what he was thinking. He had seemed happy to see her downstairs, but now…now she couldn't be sure.

"Drink up," he said. "And come sit down. I want you to tell me where you've been all these months." He led her to two chairs beside each other in front of a fireplace glowing with burning coals. Though it was June, it was still cool at night, and Sapphire sat on the edge of the upholstered wingback chair, appreciating the heat coming from the marble hearth.

"There's not that much to tell." She sipped the champagne, looking at him over the rim of the glass. He was thinner than he had been when she last saw him. He didn't look as if he had been taking very good care of himself. Had it been because of her? Had he been worrying over her? "I left Boston that night, and a day later I met a nice man and I ended up at the Carrington stables, riding as a jockey."

He shook his head. "I want the whole story, Sapphire. Every step you took on that road. Every person you spoke to. I can't tell you how distraught I've been."

She studied the lines across his forehead, still wishing she knew what he was really thinking. No, what he was *feeling*. Then she began to tell him what had happened in the months since they had last sat beside each other—the people who had helped her, the boys in the stable, the horses she had groomed. She told him about Petrosky and Red and the kittens in the barn. She told him all about Stowe back at Carrington Farm who seemed to be more Red's dog as of late than hers. She talked about her riding lessons and cutting her hair and how she'd nearly been caught once bathing in the tack room.

Before she knew it, the case clock on the mantel was chiming midnight and she had been in the chair beside Blake so long that her legs were stiff when she stood to stretch them.

"I should go," she said.

He stood in front of her and drew his finger along the collar of her starched white shirt, nearly identical to his. "I still can't believe you've been masquerading as a stable boy, a groom, a jockey, whatever the hell they think you are, all these months." He shook his head. "I can't believe you got away with it."

She smiled. She didn't know what had happened to her anger in the past four hours, but it was gone. Now, all she felt was a strange sense of peace.

"I don't understand why you would be surprised that I could get away with pretending I am a young man." She reached up and stroked his neck just above his collar, mimicking his gesture. "I got away with pretending I was a maid, remember? Molly the maid."

He smiled, tipped his head back and chuckled. "That

was wrong of me." He pulled her into his arms and she gazed into his eyes, lifting her brows.

"Was that an apology?"

He kissed her lightly on the lips and for a moment she held herself stiff in his arms. A thousand thoughts flew through her head. What she wished he would say. What she wished could be…

Then she felt herself relax and sensed that peace again. She parted her lips, allowing her eyes to drift shut.

"Sapphire, Sapphire," Blake whispered, holding her so tightly that she could barely breathe. "God, I've missed you."

She clung to him, kissing him until she had to tear her mouth from his to get a breath of air. He slid her coat off and let it fall to the floor, and his followed. Desperate to touch him, to feel him, she pulled his shirt from the waistband of his trousers and slid her hands under the hem, running her fingers over his flat stomach, over his chest. Their mouths twisting, she kicked off her polished boots and he slid her black trousers over her hips. She trembled at his touch. It had been so long, too long.

With Blake's aid, she stepped out of her trousers revealing a hint of the red triangle of hair between her thighs as the shirt rode up and then fell. He reached beneath the shirt.

"Take this off," he murmured in her ear, tugging on the cotton fabric she used to bind her breasts. Gazing into his eyes, she found the end of the fabric, untucked it and began to unwrap it, letting the material trail to the floor. At last her breasts were free of the confining material and she threw her head back, sucking in her breath as his hands found her breasts, his thumb brushing her swollen nipples.

When Blake lifted her into his arms and carried her to the huge bed in the center of the room, she put up no resistance. She wanted to make love with him one last time, to feel his mouth on hers, to feel him deep inside her.

When he lowered her to the bed, her legs dangled over the side, and when he leaned forward, he pushed her shirt up, and she caught the hem of his, pulled it over his head and flung it.

With a growl of lust deep in his throat, Blake lowered his head over her breast and flicked his tongue around her areole, drawing groans of pleasure from her. When he caught her nipple between his lips and sucked gently, she arched her back, grasping a handful of silk sheets in one hand.

"Blake," she whispered, wrapping her arms around his shoulders, trying to bring him closer. "Please," she said, wrapping her legs around his hips, lifting her groin to his. She could already feel the evidence of his arousal and she was desperate for him. All these months she had remembered, dreamed, and now he was here with her once more.

"You're always in too big a hurry," he teased huskily, kissing a hot, wet path from the tip of her breast over her belly.

"Blake, please," she cried desperately, half sitting up to tug at the waistband of his trousers. "Quick first, then slow?" When she looked into his eyes, she again thought she recognized something new in them.

"All right, all right," Blake said, laughing as he unbuttoned his trousers and stepped out of them. "But only for you would I comply."

Still standing on the floor, he offered both hands and she threaded her fingers through his. Eyes locked with hers, Blake thrust his hips forward and she moved toward him, taking him deeply. One stroke and she was halfway gone to him. She let her eyes drift shut as she lifted her hips off the bed again and again, meeting his lust.

It was over all too quickly. Sapphire cried out, arching her back, tightening her grip on his hands. A heartbeat later, Blake groaned and fell forward, burying his face in the crook of her neck.

Both lay there panting for a moment, and then he withdrew from her and she slid up into the bed to make room for him.

"I'm hungry," he said as he climbed into the bed and dropped down beside her, flat on his back.

She laughed and turned her head to face him. "Me, too."

"Fortunately, that is one problem, Master Water—or is it Molly?—that I can solve." He sat up and kissed her and then strode naked across the room to pull a long rope with a tassel that hung from the ceiling.

Somewhere in the walls, Sapphire heard tiny bells ring.

Momentarily, a butler arrived, and Blake poked his head out the door long enough to order a meal. Half an hour later they were seated in the middle of the bed, eating cold roasted partridge with mint jelly, soft, warm bread fresh from the oven and the first strawberries of spring with mounds of fresh whipped cream.

They finished the bottle of champagne and Blake

placed the empty bottle into the wine cooler. "Shall I order more?" he asked her.

She laughed, dropping a strawberry into her glass and then fishing it out with her finger. "I think I've already had quite enough, sir."

"Not even in celebration?"

She popped the strawberry into her mouth and looked at him across the bed. "In celebration of what, Lord Wessex? Or is it Blake Thixton?"

He scowled and scooped a bit of cream from a bowl onto his plate of strawberries. "Your return to me, of course."

She only smiled and reached for another berry. And when they were fully satiated, Blake cleared the bowls and plates from the bed and set them on a silver tray near the door—except for what was left of the sweetened cream. That he placed on the table beside the bed.

"What's that for?" she asked, tipping her champagne glass to get the last drop.

"I suppose I'll have to show you." He took the empty glass from her hand and set it on the table behind him. "But the shirt will have to go."

"Oh, it will, will it?" She laughed, but lifted her arms to allow him to pull the shirt off. She watched through her lashes, her eyes already heavy with passion as he removed his own shirt. Then, seated on the bed, utterly naked, Blake began to run his hands over her body, over her shoulders, down her arms, over her back, her thighs, his hands ever moving. He touched every inch of her skin with slow, caressing movements, and when he was done, he began at the top again, massaging her neck, her shoulders, her breasts… Sapphire lay out on the bed, her head cradled in his lap, him looking down on her, her looking up. She felt as if she were drifting on a cloud, her body filled to overflowing with a calm she had never possessed before.

Something cold touched her nipple and her eyelids flew open. She looked down to see a perfect white dot of cream on her breast. "What—"

Blake leaned over and covered her nipple with his warm mouth, licking until every bit of cream was gone. Sapphire moaned, writhing under him as he did the same to the other nipple. There was something incredibly erotic about the coolness of the cream and the heat of his mouth that sent her body and her mind spiraling.

But this time, he showed no mercy. No matter how much she begged, Blake took his time, touching, caressing, licking. Sapphire lost all control as again and again he brought her to the edge of the threshold of pleasure and then eased her back again. When at last they coupled, Sapphire found herself laughing and crying at the same time as she found fulfillment. Then, when both were satisfied, she curled up in the crook of Blake's arm and allowed him to cover them with a blanket—and she slept.

It was nearly five in the morning when Sapphire woke and slipped out of Blake's bed. She did not wake him because there was no need for confrontation. All the same, she couldn't stay. Nothing had been resolved between them. She would not stay with a man who did not love her.

Refusing to allow herself even a single tear, she pulled on her trousers and shirt, slipped into her boots and grabbed her coat on the way out the door. As she eased into the dark hallway, she allowed herself only one glance back.

Blake lay asleep on his back, his arms flung to his sides, his hair dark against the white pillowcase, his sensual lips slightly parted as he inhaled and exhaled.

Smiling, fighting tears, she drew her fingers to her lips. "I love you," she whispered, and then she was gone.

Sapphire walked the New York City streets until the hour was decent and then she entered a pawnshop where a narrow-faced man with bad teeth asked no questions when she offered her fine coat and trousers in return for a simple pair of boys' tweeded knee pants, a burlap jacket, a dirty cap and a few dollars. He allowed her to change behind a curtain in his back room. Again on the street, she headed in the direction the shopkeeper had pointed her—the wharves. She was going home.

Tears filled her eyes as she stuffed her hands into her pockets, lowering her head against the wind whipping between the tall buildings. Without the money she had hidden in the tack room under a floorboard back at the farm, it was not going to be easy, but she was determined. Nearly penniless except for the money she had earned from the race and money from the pawnshop, she was going home to Lucia and Angelique if she had to swim to cross the ocean.

Down at the docks, Sapphire moved from ship to ship making inquiries as to anyone headed for England who might be in need of a cabin boy. When a man with a patch over his eye and fish breath told her the *Sally*

Mae was looking for kitchen help because their boy had fallen overboard the night before and drowned, she thanked him. Tugging on her felt cap, she headed for the *Sally Mae,* a schooner out of Bristol.

Sapphire found the ship's cook on the deck of the small transport vessel overseeing the loading of crates of chickens and geese. He took one look at her, inquired as to her health and then gave a nod. "A might skinny, but I guess you'll do," he grumbled. "'Least you won't eat much." He pointed to the crates of chickens still on the dock. "Whattaya standin' there for? Get the blessed chickens on board, boy." He hooked his thumb behind him and spat a long stream of tobacco over the side of the rail. "We sail on the afternoon tide."

Hours later, Sapphire was standing on the deck beside the cook, trying to stay out of the way of the lines as they were thrown from the dock onto the ship. She saw Blake an instant before he saw her, and she seriously considered diving off the ship and swimming toward England.

"Wait! Wait!" Blake shouted, running down the dock. "You! On the ship! *Sally Mae,* wait!"

One of the sailors just beginning to pull up the gangplank peered over the side to the dock. "Cap'n," he called. "We got a gen'leman sayin' to wait 'ere."

Sapphire glanced around her but there was nowhere to go, no place to run, and to dive into the water would have been pure stupidity. Anger flared in her as she knotted her hands into fists and turned away so as not to have to see the exchange about to take place between the captain of the ship she had nearly escaped on and Blake Thixton.

"Sir, are you the captain?" Blake called up, shading his eyes against the afternoon sun.

The captain nodded, pulling off his hat, recognizing in an instant that the fellow in the black frock coat and top hat was an important man. "Yes, sir, how might I help you, sir?"

Sapphire couldn't resist turning her head, curious as to exactly how he would explain himself.

"Sir, my son. You have my son on board. A red-haired young fellow." He touched his neck. "Hair to here. A slight boy."

Had she not been so angry that he had found her, Sapphire might have laughed. Blake Thixton was a man who could think quickly on his feet, she would give him that.

The captain turned to face the cook still standing beside Sapphire. The cook raised his dirty hands. "The lad was lookin' fer work, Cap'n. I didn't know he was a rich boy run away."

"Please. No harm has been done," Blake hollered up, sounding every bit the concerned father. "Just send him down. If I don't return him to his mother by sunset, I'll not be able to return at all."

The captain chuckled as he signaled for the deck hand to lower the gangplank again.

"Go ahead, lad," the captain said good-naturedly.

Sapphire stood her ground for a moment, her jaw set. Surely there had to be some way to avoid this. She didn't want to argue with Blake on a dock, she didn't want to embarrass him by telling him she couldn't be with him because he didn't think she was an honest woman. Because he would never love her.

"Go on, do's the cap'n says." The cook gave her a push.

Sapphire walked slowly across the deck. When she reached the gangplank, Blake was standing on the dock, as handsome as she had ever seen him, looking tall and regal in his proper coat and top hat.

"Come along, Sam," he called, offering a hand.

Sapphire slowly walked down the gangplank. At the bottom, Blake grabbed her arm and began to walk her away briskly. "Thank you," he called. "Safe sailing!"

She walked beside him in silence until they were far enough away that those on the *Sally Mae* could no longer see them.

"My carriage is this way," Blake said gruffly. "Come on."

"No." Sapphire stopped on the street that abutted the dock. There were men everywhere—sailors, merchants, venders selling and buying wares. She ignored the confusion that swirled around them, focusing on Blake's face.

"No? What do you mean, no?" he demanded. "What the hell did you think you were doing on that ship?"

"I was going home!" she shouted at him.

"Home? Home is with me."

"No, home is not with you, Blake. When will you get it through your thick American head that I will not be your mistress? I am the daughter of Lord Edward Wessex and I will be no man's mistress! No man's, not even yours."

"Let's get into the carriage." He glanced around, not appearing to have heard a word she said. "People are beginning to stare."

When he tried to rest his hand on her shoulder to

move her along, she flung it off. "I will not get in your carriage and I don't care if people stare. I'm going back to England, away from this place. Away from you!"

His face, which had been lined with anger a moment before, changed expression. "You're serious, aren't you?"

"Of course I'm serious!" She flung herself at him, beating him with her fists. "Bastard. I wouldn't stay here with you, not if you—"

"Not even if I would marry you?"

"What?" She drew back, looking up at him. "What did you say?" she whispered. She could have sworn she saw moisture in his dark, stormy eyes.

"I said," he told her so softly she could barely hear him, "would you stay if I married you?"

"You would marry me?" Her head was spinning again. Suddenly her life was full of possibilities. "But why? Why would you marry me? What about Mrs. Sheraton? I know what went on that night so there's no sense in you denying it."

"I won't deny it because I won't lie to you. But that was a mistake with Grace, Sapphire. It was wrong. I don't know what I was thinking. I cared so much about you, I...I was afraid."

She shook her head, trying to understand, needing to understand. This was a part of Blake she had never seen before. He was actually admitting he had been wrong. "You were afraid? Afraid of what?"

"Sapphire, sometimes you are a woman far beyond your years and other times, you—" He pulled off her hat and smoothed her hair with his hand. "I was afraid, my dear, my beloved, because I loved you and I have never loved anyone in my life—" His voice cracked. "I didn't know what to do. I didn't know how—"

"You love me?" she breathed, not allowing him to finish. "You love me and that's why you kidnapped me? That's why you forced me to be a maid in your house, because you *loved* me?"

He gave a wry grin. "Obviously I wasn't thinking in quite that manner, but yes. I suppose that is why I did those things. You were just being so obstinate about being Wessex's daughter and—"

Sapphire's stomach suddenly tumbled. "Wait," she said, feeling so light-headed that she could barely think. "Are you saying you still don't believe me when I say I am Edward Thixton's daughter?"

"That's not what I'm saying." He caught her hand and drew it to his heart.

If Blake thought people on the docks and on the street were staring at him a moment ago, they were really staring now. A gentleman in a top coat, holding a young boy's hand to his heart? They would be lucky if they weren't rushed by an angry mob for indecency.

"Then what are you saying, Blake?" she repeated desperately.

"You left Boston. You lived as a boy—"

"Yes, to earn money for my passage back to England."

"Exactly. And then when I foiled that, you apparently decided to sell yourself into some sort of child labor to get back."

"To prove to you." She lowered her lashes as she rested both hands on his chest. "No. To prove to myself."

"Which is exactly what I guess I'm trying to say." He held her hand, kissing her palm. "I cannot be honest with you, Sapphire, and tell you that I believe you were Edward's daughter, but I can say that I believe you believe it and…"

"And what?" she whispered, praying he understood that everything rested on his next words.

"And so, I'm willing to return to London with you and find out if Edward did indeed marry your mother." He looked into her eyes, lowering his head over hers. "If you will marry me in exchange."

"Because you love me," she whispered, tears filling her eyes.

"Because I have loved you, whoever you are, from the day you stood in that parlor waiting to set my arrogant self straight." He smiled roguishly. "So will you? Will you marry me so that I do not have to continue searching the streets of Boston and New York and heaven knows where else?"

"Yes," she cried, throwing her arms around him.

Blake wrapped his arms around her waist and lifted her into the air. "Yes?"

"Yes!" She held him tightly, lifting her face to his. "Yes, I will marry you, Blake Thixton, Earl of Wessex, and, yes, I love you. I just wanted to hear you say it. It's all I wanted. I've loved you from the very first day you walked your arrogant self into my father's parlor."

30

Three weeks later, Sapphire and Blake arrived in London and parted at the docks where they disembarked. Blake took a hired carriage to his town house in Mayfair while Sapphire took another to Lucia's apartment in Charing Cross. As she alighted from the carriage, tipping the driver well, she adjusted her bonnet. Even after three weeks, she was still happy to be back in women's clothing again. She didn't even mind the corset she had once complained about.

After Blake's epiphany on the docks in New York, they had remained there in the city, booking passage on the next passenger steamer leaving for London. In the week's time they had to wait, they spent many hours shopping, and the hours they weren't shopping, they spent in the huge four-poster bed at the Madison-James hotel. They made love more than a dozen times, and ate more than one bowl of strawberries and cream.

Blake had offered numerous times to make her his

wife in one of the lovely churches in New York or Boston if she preferred, before they set sail. It seemed important to him that he make up for what he had seen as infidelity to her, but she had assured him that the subject of Grace was forgiven and forgotten, so long as he never walked into a room alone with her again.

It was important to Sapphire that Aunt Lucia and Angelique be present at their wedding, so London it would be. Her only regret was that Armand would not be there to celebrate her day, but that was of course impossible. She wasn't even certain he was still alive.

At the door of Aunt Lucia's apartments, Sapphire took a moment to smooth her blue and green floral barege gown with its full Marie sleeves tied at intervals with ribbon and a fashionable full *pelèrine*. She wore gloves dyed to match the blue in the dress and her wide-brimmed high-crowned bonnet was decorated with blue and green flowers. The flowers matched her eyes perfectly, Blake had pointed out as he kissed her goodbye on the docks and readjusted her bonnet for her.

Sapphire smiled to herself as she knocked on the door. Blake told her every day, practically every hour, that he loved her, and still she couldn't get enough of those words. She couldn't wait to hear what Angelique would have to say about that.

The door opened and Avena appeared in the doorway. She took one look at Sapphire and squealed in delight, grasped the hem of her white apron and raised it up over her face. "A ghost, God save me," she swore. "I've seen a ghost!"

Sapphire laughed and walked in, removing her gloves. "Not a ghost, Avena—it's me. See, me in the flesh." She tapped her chest with her gloves and then hugged the maid.

"Is that Jessup, Avena?" Aunt Lucia called from down the hall. "Tell him I'm coming. We mustn't be late. They'll not hold the ship!"

Avena slowly drew the apron off her face, her eyes widening. "Not Mr. Stowe, madame," she said in excellent English.

"Not Mr. Stowe?" Lucia's voice grew louder as she came down the hall. "Then who—"

Sapphire turned to the hallway just as her godmother entered the parlor, slipping an earring onto her ear.

"Sapphire!" Aunt Lucia cried.

Sapphire ran into her aunt's arms. "I'm so glad to see you," she laughed, hugging the plump woman, resting her cheek on her shoulder to smell her French perfume. "I've missed you so much and I have so much to tell you!"

"It's you! It's really you!" Aunt Lucia leaned back and pressed her hands to Sapphire's cheeks, looking up into her face. "I told Angelique you would be fine. That you were safe and that you would come home to—" Her hands flew suddenly to her mouth. "Oh, no. Angelique and Henry! Avena!" Aunt Lucia cried, hurrying toward her, flapping her arms. "Mr. Stowe, you must meet him on the street downstairs. He must get to the ship."

"What ship?" Sapphire asked in confusion.

"The ship bound for Boston, of course," Lucia said, as if Sapphire was a foolish child.

Avena ran out of the apartments, leaving Lucia to close the door behind her. "The one with Angelique and

Henry on it. They married last week, packed their bags and booked passage to America. They were coming to look for you!"

Sapphire laughed, her eyes brimming with tears as she walked into Lucia's arms again. "We can't have that, Aunt Lucia. She has to be here for *my* wedding!"

Less than a month later, Sapphire stood in the vestibule of the Collegiate Church of St. Peter, Westminster, trembling inside her new pale blue silk slippers. Because of the title Blake held as the Earl of Wessex, he had been given permission to be married at Westminster Abbey and everyone who was anyone in London society had been invited, despite her protest that nothing more than a small, private ceremony was necessary.

Now, as Sapphire stood waiting for the trumpets to sound that would signal her entrance into the chapel, she found herself shaking all over. Nothing in the past six weeks seemed real to her, but suddenly, standing there, seeing Blake at the altar, it was all too real.

Her hand shaking, Sapphire brought a gloved finger to the jewel at the base of her throat. Blake had insisted he have the sapphire left to her by her mother set in a wedding necklace for her, and as beautiful as the jewel had been lying in the velvet bag in her mother's keepsake casket, it was even more beautiful framed in diamonds, set in gold.

"Are you ready?" Angelique whispered in her ear.

Sapphire glanced down at the pale blue gown she wore. Avena's fiancé's mother had sewn it for her, finishing it just in time for the wedding. Made of satin and lace, it was of the most elegant French fashion with a neckline that bared her shoulders and demi-gigot sleeves that made her feel as if she were a princess.

Trumpets blasted, startling Sapphire out of her reverie, and she stared up at the marble columns that stretched high into the ceiling above her. She looked to Angelique, who smiled.

"This is it, what you've always wanted, what you've waited for your whole life. True love," Angelique murmured. "Now, stop looking so frightened. It's Blake." She swept her hand in his direction. "He's waiting for you."

Sapphire looked down the aisle she would soon walk, and at the very end, standing beside the rector, she saw Blake. He was dressed exquisitely in black and he was waiting for her.

Angelique gave Sapphire a little nudge, and closing her eyes, sending a silent prayer heavenward, Sapphire began the long walk down the aisle of Westminster Abbey.

The next hour was a blur of faces, voices, music, the low rumble of the rector's voice, and the warmth and comfort of Blake's hand. All of London truly had come out to see Lord Wessex wed a girl who a year ago had been scandalized by rumor. The Dowager Lady Wessex was there with her pinch-faced daughters, Lord and Lady Morrow and the Baron and Baroness Wells and even Lord and Lady Carlisle who, a year before, had put Sapphire out of their house. Somehow, the past was all forgotten and the well-wishers who gathered were all smiling, whispering to one another how beautiful the bride was and what a gentleman the American had turned out to be.

Sapphire felt as if she were floating on a cloud of blue silk when, at last, the rector pronounced them wed and

Blake lowered his head over hers to kiss her. Their lips met and he whispered to her, "With this kiss, I thee wed."

She wrapped her arms around his neck and he drew her closer, deepening the kiss.

The trumpets sounded again, echoing off the flying buttresses high overhead.

At last, breathless, Blake lifted his head and offered her his arm. Side by side, they walked back down the aisle of Westminster Abbey, now scattered with white rose petals, their gazes for no one but each other. The wedding party and guests followed behind them and back in the vestibule, everyone gathered around to wish them well.

"Countess Wessex, my love, congratulations," Aunt Lucia cried, pushing her way through the crowd to throw her arms first around Sapphire, then Blake. "My Jessup has a gift for you."

"Perhaps once we arrive at Lord Morrow's," Blake suggested, putting his arm around Sapphire in an attempt to protect her from everyone crowding around.

"No," Aunt Lucia insisted. "Here. Now." She looped her arm through Sapphire's and dragged her toward a small alcove near a life-size statue of St. Francis.

Blake had no choice but to follow.

I'm sorry, Sapphire mouthed over her shoulder to Blake. Blake only laughed.

"Our bride, the new Countess Wessex, will meet you at Lord and Lady Morrow's," Aunt Lucia called to the guests, waving a handkerchief over her shoulder. "Jessup, love, come at once," she called.

In the alcove, Sapphire turned to Aunt Lucia. "Please, our guests. The coach waits for us."

"A coach and eight," Blake teased, adjusting his silk top hat. "I'm not certain I can afford to pay them to wait much longer."

"Please, Aunt Lucia."

"This will take only a moment," Aunt Lucia insisted. "Here he comes now."

Sapphire looked up to see Mr. Stowe, hustling toward them, an elderly frail man in tow. "Congratulations," he declared, red faced and laughing as he kissed Sapphire on both cheeks and pumped Blake's hand. "My lord."

"Jessup, please, do get on with it," Aunt Lucia sang. "They have a coach and eight waiting to take them to the reception."

"Yes, yes of course." Jessup grinned. "Well, I would like to introduce you to Father Paul Seton."

Sapphire dipped a quick curtsy and Blake offered his hand. "Father."

"Tell them, Jessup," Aunt Lucia urged, sounding as if she were about to burst with excitement.

"Father Paul was the rector in a small church in Shemingsbury Cross for many years and there he married many couples. Mostly poor couples, but not all."

The elderly man in a collar bobbed his head, grinning, as pleased with himself as Lucia seemed to be with him.

"Father Paul remembers one marriage in particular, though, more than twenty years ago, a wedding he performed between a distinguished gentleman and a village girl."

Sapphire gasped and she reached for Blake's hand.

"The church burned to the ground many years

ago," the old man said, his voice reedy. "Records all burned. Gone."

"But tell them what a sly fellow you were, Father Paul," Aunt Lucia urged. "Tell them."

"I kept copies of all church records," Father Paul explained. "It's a practice I've followed from my first parish in Whitford Downs. Not so difficult. Shemingsbury Cross was a small shire." He reached inside his black frock and produced a faded, torn piece of paper. "I have here a letter of marriage signed in April of the year of our Lord eighteen hundred and ten by a Miss Sophie Barkley, yeoman's daughter, and a Lord Edward Thixton, Viscount of Hastings."

The old man offered the piece of paper, but Sapphire's hands were trembling so hard that she couldn't take it from him. Blake took the paper and studied it for a moment, then he turned to Sapphire, looking down at her as if no one else were there. He took her gloved hand in his and went down on one knee.

Sapphire fought tears of happiness.

"Will you forgive me, Lady Wessex, for ever doubting you for a moment?" he asked.

Sapphire threw her arms around Blake, suffocating him in a cloud of blue wedding silk. "Come, Lord Wessex, we have three hundred guests and a coach and eight that we mustn't keep waiting."

31

"Armand, are you awake, *mon chèr?*" Tarasai asked, sitting down on the edge of his bed. When he didn't answer, she took her son, sleeping in the crook of her arm, and laid him on the bed beside his father. Then she slowly leaned over to turn up the oil lamp beside the bed.

It was the middle of the night and Tarasai had risen to feed the baby. As always, she came to check on Armand before going back to sleep. He had had a day full of excitement between the arrival of the letter announcing Sapphire's marriage to the American, telling of the church records that had been found verifying his stepdaughter's legitimacy, and the subsequent arrival of Armand's barrister, whom he'd demanded be brought to his bedside at once. Tarasai had tried to argue that whatever business he had with the barrister could wait until the following day when he had rested, but Armand would not hear of it. The barrister had remained locked up in the bedchamber with Armand for hours and later Armand had seemed more tired than usual when she had said good-night.

"*Mon amour?*"

The baby made little sucking sounds in his sleep.

"Armand?" Tarasai's heart fluttered inside her chest as she leaned over him, drawing the lamp closer with her hand.

He lay flat on his back, the sheet pulled neatly to his chest, his black hair now peppered with white. His eyes were closed, his lips parted slightly, and even before Tarasai checked for his breath on her cheek, she knew she would not feel it.

"*Non,*" she whispered, tears welling in her eyes as she took his cool hand in hers and brought it to her lips. "*Non,* Armand. Not yet."

Tears ran down her cheeks as she rested her head on his chest. Tonight, when she had been helping him prepare for bed, he had seemed so happy. The relief that his Sapphire was safe and loved was plain on his face. He had held their son in his arms and kissed his little fingers, making a fuss about what a strong man he would grow to be and what an excellent planter he would make.

Tarasai had paid little attention to his nonsensical talk, shushing him and insisting he hand over the baby and get into bed. He had seemed so much stronger than in the weeks past. How could he have just lain down and died?

The baby began to fuss and Tarasai sat up, reaching for her son and bringing him to her breast. She pushed aside the thin fabric of her nightgown and the baby nuzzled and latched.

"My Armand," she murmured, gazing down on his handsome face. "I did not even tell you that I loved you."

But Tarasai knew he knew. *"Au revoir, mon amour,"* she whispered, smiling down at him through her tears. *"Au revoir* and thank you, my Armand. Thank you for my son."

Epilogue

Sapphire sat on the edge of the bed rereading the letter Aunt Lucia had sent her from London. There was also one for Sapphire to forward to Angelique as soon as she learned where out West she and Henry were.

Armand was dead. Her beloved Armand. And because Sapphire was now wealthier than he was, as the wife of American millionaire Blake Thixton, he had left his plantations to his son. Armand had a son!

"I'm very sorry," Blake said, rising from the chair at his desk in the corner of their bedchamber. "Is there anything I can do for you?"

She shook her head, wiping her tears as she rose from the bed. "No, but thank you. We knew this was coming. It was why he sent us away in the first place, you know. I'm just sad that I didn't have a chance to see him one last time." She folded the letter and placed it on the desk, taking care not to bump into the basket where her new puppy—a wedding gift from Blake—lay sleeping.

After they returned from London, Blake had offered to return to Carrington Farms and retrieve Stowe, but she had declined, knowing after all this time that he was now more Red's dog than hers. And now she had a new pup to love.

Blake pulled Sapphire into his arms, kissing the top of her head. She hadn't cut her hair in months and it had grown quite a bit, and tonight she wore it long, down her back the way he liked it. "I don't like to see you sad."

She looked up at him and smiled. "I still have my memories and I still have him here." She rested her hand on her left breast.

"Here?" he asked, leaning over to kiss her breast through the thin fabric of her sleeping gown.

"Yes." She giggled, threading her fingers through his hair.

"And here, as well?"

He kissed her other breast and she laughed, lifting his head so that he could meet her lips. "Yes, my Lord Wessex. Or is it, yes, sir, Mr. Thixton?" she teased.

"Well, I don't know. Who are you tonight?" He held her around her waist, pinning her arms behind her and leaning over her so that she arched her back. "Are you the Countess, Lady Wessex, the Earl of Wessex's wife?"

"Hmm." She sighed, tapping her chin, pretending to think on it.

"Or are you Sapphire Thixton, wife of Mr. Blake Thixton, shipping magnate?"

"I don't know," she said, wiggling out of his arms. "Perhaps I'm Molly the maid." She picked up a pile of clean towels left for them on the chair near the door.

Myra now served as a lady's maid, with her own

bedchamber next to Mrs. Dedrick's on the third floor and a new dress for each day of the week. Myra always made sure her mistress had clean towels in case she wanted to share a bath with the master.

"Clean towel, Mr. Thixton?" she asked, batting her eyelashes.

"Give me those!" he growled, thrusting out his hand to catch her.

But Sapphire was too quick and she darted away from him. "What of your bedsheets, sir? Should I change those, as well?"

"Get over here!" He cornered her against the bed, and she squealed with laughter as she tried to scramble up onto it and escape off the other side.

But Blake grabbed her ankle and Sapphire fell on the bed, the clean towels flying from her arms. "Blake, stop," she laughed, trying to free her ankle from his grip. "That tickles!"

"And this, does this tickle, as well, Molly?" He ran his hand up her calf and higher to her inner thigh.

"Mr. Thixton, really. I thought you had vowed to Mrs. Thixton that you would never again take a lover."

He climbed onto the bed, lowering himself over her, gazing into her eyes. "Do you think Mrs. Thixton meant Molly, as well?" he whispered.

She smiled, so happy she wondered if she was dreaming. But if she was, it was the longest, best dream she had ever experienced. "Perhaps we should ask Mrs. Thixton," she whispered back, looking up at him as she ran her hands up the smooth plane of his chest and over his shoulders.

Blake stroked the hair at her temple. "One blue eye,

one green. Who would have thought these eyes could hold such magic for a curmudgeon like me?"

She raised her head to kiss him. "Say it," she whispered.

"I love you."

"Again."

"I love you. I love you, Sapphire Fabergine, Sapphire Thixton, Lady Wessex, I would love you no matter who you were."

"And Molly," she said, drawing his head closer to hers. "Don't forget Molly."

"How could a man forget Molly?" He deepened their kiss, making it impossible for Sapphire to answer. At least for the moment…